This book is dedicated to the wives and families of men who have chosen espionage and, in particular, operational work as a way of life.

My personal thoughts are for the one woman I knew who suffered because of her husband's profession and who finally chose to change her life rather than have it become a tragedy.

Author's Note

In Egyptian mythology the tears of the goddess Isis faithfully replenished the waters of the Nile once every year, and thus she came to be called "the woman who weeps." Her role in ancient myth was to preside over the destinies of both men and gods. Always the controlling influence, she was alternatively benevolent or sinister and malicious.

For these characteristics and in memory of a certain woman who too has wept, I have chosen ISIS as the fictitious name for an existing semiprivate espionage organization whose name is also derived from mythology. Like its namesake, ISIS presides over destinies, those of private individuals and sometimes of entire governments. It too can be benevolent or evil.

The Secret Vatican Archives are real. The term "Secret Archives" is used by the Church as a general reference to *all* manuscripts, records and papers resting in the Court of the Belvedere. My story deals with one very small fraction of this collection—documents that are less than fifty years old and that relate to living people, to existing political, social and economic circumstances.

These extremely sensitive papers lie at the end of the Court of the Belvedere, in a black, guarded vault. They were never meant to see the light of day.

PHILIPPE VAN RJNDT

The Tetramachus Collection

THE THEFT

CHAPTER ONE

Vatican City covers an area of seventeen square miles in the form of a trapezoid within Rome, bounded on the east by St. Peter's Square, on the west and north by the Vatican Walls and on the south by the Congregation for the Doctrine of the Faith.

Aside from St. Peter's, approached through the Via della Conciliazione, only two of the city's six entrances are open to the public—the Arco delle Compare and the gates on the Viale Vaticano.

At seven o'clock on the damp gray morning of Monday, September 16, Father Martin Belobraditz, secretary to Rozdentsy Cardinal Meyerczuk, made his way from the Via di Porta Angelica across the great square of St. Peter's, empty and silent at this hour save for the sweepers who were cleaning the fountains and pavement after Sunday's papal audience.

He passed the Leonine Walls, built as a final defense against the Saracens, and went through the Gate of St. Anne. There he took the curved road going past the *Osservatore Romano* to the Court of the Belvedere, next to the Vatican Library.

The Court of the Belvedere is one of the proudest monuments of Vatican City, second in size only to St. Peter's itself, in architecture more impressive than either the Court of St. Damaso or the splendid Government Palace. Built from drawings generally attributed to Raphael, the court is dominated by a series of granite steps, two feet wide, forty feet long, divided into three tiers of twenty steps each. In climbing these, a man of reasonable condition might have lost some wind, but the Polish priest was a cripple, obliged to wear a heavy orthopedic boot on his right foot. When he had struggled to the top of the stairs, Father Martin leaned against a pillar, the earth swimming before his eyes. The labored breath he drew brought no relief, only a sharp, stabbing pain to the chest.

"Good morning, Father."

The Swiss guardsman, complete in blue, red and yellow uniform, looked down at the pale, worn figure in black. Himself a man of robust health and appetites, he felt uneasy in the presence of one whose devotion had earned him only wretchedness. The guardsman had seen Father Martin pass up these stairs many times, and he had never been able to turn his eyes away from that pitiful figure. The priest shamed him and made him afraid of his own good fortune.

"It is a good morning, yes," Father Martin murmured. He rarely noticed the state of the weather.

"Father, your pass please."

The guardsman smiled uneasily, embarrassed by his duty. Father Martin noticed his discomfort and, putting his briefcase down, drew out a plastic card from his habit.

For the guardsman, the review of the pass was a formality. During his eight months of duty he had never had any difficulties, not even with academic visitors. Still, he looked at the date, and it was valid.

"You might make an application for a new one," the guardsman suggested, trying to be helpful. "This permit expires in a few days."

"I suppose I should."

Father Martin replaced the card and, twisting his withered leg, knelt down to retrieve his briefcase.

The security of the Vatican was a subject Father Martin had come to know intimately over these last several months. Until 1970 the Holy See had four groups responsible for order within its walls. The protection of the Pope's person was entrusted to the Guardia Nobile and the Guardia Svizzera, the Swiss corps. There were also an honor guard, the Guardia Palatina d'Onore, and a special detachment of police, the Gendarmeria Pontifica, responsible for order within the city and its palaces.

Paul VI had decided to simplify matters and disbanded two of the four corps, regrouping the Swiss Guards and adding a new civilian security branch. Three of its principal members had served in Italian counterintelligence and were responsible for the sophisticated alarm system installed throughout the city in spring of 1971. Built to Vatican specifications and installed by Chubb of London, the electronic warning devices guarded not only the priceless Vatican treasures but also the most secret part of the archives.

Although there is no security system in the world that is absolutely foolproof, that of the Vatican comes close. A successful robbery would require a strictly frontal assault, and even then the odds would be heavily in favor of the machine-gun corps who discreetly patrol the holy grounds from dusk till daybreak.

Father Martin's plan required neither armaments nor accomplices. He had the only weapon he needed, his pass, and this morning would be the last time he would ever use it.

The guardsman unslung his walkie-talkie and spoke briefly to the men inside.

"You may go in," he said. "The prefect is waiting."

At the top of the stairway leading into the inner sanctum of the Court of the Belvedere, the Polish priest was greeted by the statue of the third-century antipope, Hippolytus. He crossed himself, then made his way down the Borgo Passageway to the court's central corridors, whose bookshelves, if put end to end, would run for more than seven miles. At the end of the corridor he entered the Hall of Parchments, a grand oval room with a ceiling frescoed by Rossetti. The hall contained the thousands of documents relating to the temporal rights of the papacy. In the next room, housing the court's inventories and indices, he was met by a final guard and Monsignor da Silva, prefect of the archives.

Antonia Cardinal da Silva was a tall, rigid man who, over the years, had cultivated a serene detachment toward all earthly matters, excluding only those relating to his work. Formerly a leading financial adviser to the papacy, the prelate had been appointed prefect by Pius XII. He was sole curator of the monumental archives and held the power to grant or deny permission to any member of the Church or laity to examine its contents. To help him run this complex institution, Da Silva had a vice-prefect, three archivists and three *scrittori*—seven people to do work which a hundred would have found overwhelming. This is one reason why not even the Vatican knows all that the archives contain. Examination and tabulation of the papers proceed at the pace of a few hundred volumes a year.

Cardinal da Silva, dressed in a simple black cassock with a small silver crucifix around his neck, greeted the priest with a nod that recognized neither friendship nor familiarity. He held out a soft, creased hand, and Father Martin bowed to kiss the ring in an expression of fealty.

There was no reason for the cardinal to speak to the cleric. Da Silva knew Father Martin had been sent here by His Eminence Mayerczuk to bring some documents back to the monsignor's study. He had been waiting for the Polish priest since half past six.

The two men proceeded down the stairwell to the basement of the court. On this level are found the records of the Consistory, the senate of cardinals that once advised popes on state issues; the indulgence files, holding papal dispensations to such men as Louis XIV of France, the Duke of Avignon, Petrarch and Boccaccio. Farther on are the catalogues of the Rota, the ecclesiastical court whose records contain more information on their supplicants and petitioners than a modern procurator could ever hope to obtain on his suspects.

The stone halls were completely deserted, and the footsteps of the two men echoed softly in all directions. Every thirty paces the prefect reached for a light switch on the wall. The pale yellow bulbs illuminated just the distance to the next switch and shut off automatically. Father Martin shivered in the dry cold. Whenever he walked here, he felt as though he were moving on islands of light with only darkness behind and before him.

At the end of the corridor, at the far end of the court's basement, is a large black door that was originally solid ebony but has since been reinforced with steel sheets. The key that opens the plate over the dial is always on the person of the prefect. When the key is inserted, the plate springs back. After the correct numbers are spun, the door, a solid three tons, will roll forward. A second combination must be used before the door slides to the side on well-greased rollers.

The room behind the ebony door, equipped with an

electronic beam alarm plus a sophisticated humidifier and dry-powder sprinkler system, contains Vatican records less than fifty years old. These are the documents which constitute the heart of what are called the Secret Archives.

The scope of this information cannot be overestimated. It covers everything from dietary peculiarities of certain Vatican officials to political details gleaned by the ranks of the "black pope," Cesare Cardinal Guarducci, head of the Society of Jesus. The economic sector covers not only the immense worldwide holdings of the Church but also voluminous material on those with whom the Holy See deals. The political collection is even more detailed with excellent analyses on heads of state, principal advisers and fulcrum influences. In short, the ears of the Church are to be found everywhere, and information given in confidence and regarded as privileged may easily find its way to Rome if such information is thought to be of value.

Only the Pope and five of the most trusted and senior members of the Curia are allowed to examine the contents of this room, and even though many Vatican decisions are based on these papers, they are never permitted to go beyond the reach of the six men.

The black vault was Father Martin's ultimate destination, for among other secrets it contained the Tetramachus Collection.

"The collection concerning Poland during the war is now found in the fifth row, on the left," the prefect said dryly, leaving the door open. "Pass Monsignor Meyerczuk my greetings when you return."

A faint musty odor greeted the priest as he stepped into the most secret room in the whole of the Vatican. He looked back once but saw nothing except an empty black hallway.

Father Martin followed the numbers on the shelves until he came to the correct row. He turned right and disappeared among the stacks, following the numbered code to the volume on Church history in Poland. He passed it by.

At the end of the row he saw seven thick volumes, the title on each spine reading: *The Activities of the Holy See in the Second World War.* The fifth volumes of these was the Tetramachus Collection.

Father Martin removed it from the shelf and began to leaf through its twelve hundred pages of small print. Although he had held the Collection in his hands before, never had he felt its value as acutely as now. For this visit was different from his others. The Collection would go out with him, secure as before in his dilapidated briefcase. The guardsmen would not stop to question him on the way because they knew no one could leave the Secret Archives without the prefect's knowledge or consent since the prefect himself had to escort the guest to the final security post. To those inside the court, Father Martin was only a faithful messenger, privileged to enter this most rarefied of places because of a stroke of his superior's pen.

The Polish priest smiled at this image of himself. It was a true one, and so the truth would hide his falsehood.

There was no one waiting for Father Martin when he finally buckled his case and emerged from the vault. He began making his way slowly down the corridor, his trembling fingers running against the stone walls to catch the light switches. As he reached the end of the hall, he heard the closing of a door somewhere behind him. He uttered a few short words of prayer, then hurried on. No one shouted after him. He heard no alarms.

In ten minutes Father Martin was standing before the first Swiss guardsman. The prefect was already there, waiting for him. For the second time, Father Martin knelt and kissed the seal on the cardinal's long, elegant finger. A few minutes later he was on the outside steps of the Court of the Belvedere, feeling the cold bite of the wind on his face. For the first time he was conscious of a dull ache from his foot, but he could not rest now.

The young guardsman who had examined his pass saluted Father Martin in a gesture of respect. He watched as the priest carefully made his way to the bottom of the steps and turned around to face the court, gazing first across its breadth, then beyond, in the direction of the apartments where princes of the Church were waking to another day. The last thing the guardsman remembered about Father Martin was the crippled figure disappearing into the Via della Conciliazione, slowly moving in the direction of a taxi rank.

It was now seven forty-five in the morning of September 16.

And so it had been done. That crime without precedent in history for which he had betrayed his Church and calling would rock the Holy See to its very foundations. Then the terrible secrets of those who wore the red caps, their lies and cheating, the blood that had dried on their palms and the cold cruelty in their hearts—all would rise from the well and overwhelm them. So he prayed it would be.

But it had not always been like this. There had been no vengeance in his heart when he had left his native Warsaw shortly after the death of Stalin, in 1953, and traveled to Rome, an exile from a bleeding passive nation whose heritage was devoutly Catholic, yet whose postwar masters had no use for priests. He had come because Rome was the last shelter left to him in this world, and there he wished to give himself to the Church, to offer his love and devotion to the one thing which had sustained its meaning in an age gone mad.

For his faith had not crumbled when his father and his mother had been dragged from their house in the spring of 1940 and shot. It had not died when his two elder brothers, fourteen and seventeen, were rounded up with Communist partisans one year later, to be executed within the week before the eyes of the townspeople who knew them so well, yet whose faces remained impassive all the while. It had not dissolved before the terror and pain he had felt when at the age of twelve he had been tortured because the Gestapo believed he was a runner for the underground. His faith had stood like the Rock upon which the Church had been founded. But when the nightmare was over, he realized he was also a man who could be afraid of darkness and loneliness, who needed to belong to that which he believed in.

So he had made his way to Rome, completed his studies and was ordained by the hand of an émigré bishop who looked with pity on his deformity and took him into his heart. From that humble man he learned the quiet dignity and gentle words which served him well in the tiny groups of Polish immigrants. They sought him out and made him one of them, and he was proud to serve these who became his second family.

For ten years the eye that had looked into the past grew dimmer and dimmer as his joy in the present expanded and sometimes overwhelmed him. To have survived at all he once considered a miracle in itself. But to have survived and been reborn, that was surely the benevolence of God. Father Martin desired nothing more than to preserve these days of faith and holy labor and prayed that they be his until the end of his sojourn on earth.

Yet his wish, so small and unselfish, was not to be granted. Father Martin's stature in the community grew. His reputation for faith and scholarship spread by word of mouth even unto the Vatican City. It surprised no one but Father Martin himself that one day Rozdentsy Cardinal Meyerczuk came to his parish and after a brief conversation with the priest asked Father Martin to serve him.

When he remembered the prelate, Father Martin bowed his head, his eyes closed so tightly that his head ached. Cardinal Meyerczuk was a living symbol of Catholic Poland, a legendary hero who had fought to preserve the Church while his country was occupied alternately by the Germans and Soviets. His temper was that of a medieval ecclesiastical autocrat who saw no place for the state within the workings of the Church. His reverence of dogma and mystery made him contemptuous of lay constitutions and governments which believed that ideology alone held the key to the character of a nation. He demanded respect for his church and obedience to its canons and laws. For him, there was only one faith, the faith that had survived almost two thousand years of barbarism and dark superstition, which refused to be destroyed by ignorance and fear and which lived on, a beacon of hope and direction in a world of vain and proud men bent on each other's annihilation.

The first ten years Father Martin passed in Rome had been filled with happiness. In the next decade his love rotted away to hate as the Church he so desperately embraced was slowly stripped of its divinity and simple charity.

Rozdentsy Cardinal Meyerczuk was held to be a great

man, second in reputation and status only to the Pontiff himself. He belonged to the highest circle of papal advisers. The documents coming to his desk for signature referred to the highest matters of the Vatican state—agreements on how much the Church would invest in a given country, the terms and benefits of those investments, notes from certain Catholic countries warning the Holy See not to make an issue of a political law about to be passed, letters expressing support and satisfaction when the Vatican moved to condemn Italians who wished to vote Communist in local and national elections. Because he was the cardinal's secretary, entrusted to keep the office functioning smoothly, Father Martin saw a great many papers classified as secret, whose subjects were far removed from questions of faith and spiritual guidance. He was drawn inexorably into recognizing that there existed another Catholic world, standing apart from the one of faith and good works, where the Church marched step by step toward a *modus vivendi* with the strong so that they might negotiate their differences and prosper. He read agreements printed on fine parchment that were no less politics of convenience than the infamous Molotov-Ribbentrop pact that had helped destroy his country. He heard holy men speak out for justice before their flocks, yet in secret meetings condone the workings of tyrants. He listened to cardinals proclaim that the Church was the foremost protector of the poor and helpless, and then he watched as these same prelates turned a deaf ear on the cries of the oppressed. Yes, the Church was their protector, but millions must wait until she could help them without injuring her own interests. The Catholic multitudes were important, for they were the body from which the voice of the Church issued forth. But they were also mortal, whereas the Church had to remain forever. If the time was not at hand to help them, the Church did not hesitate to beg them suffer a little longer, a little while longer. . . .

Such were the actions, decisions and considerations Rozdentsy Cardinal Meyerczuk exposed his secretary to. He believed the logic of the Church's actions was clear to any Catholic and needed neither explanation nor apology. He thought a man such as Father Martin, who owed the arts of survival and faith his very life, would understand how strong and necessary the instinct to preserve was. Cardinal Meyerczuk did not consider that men who endure and survive do not necessarily emerge only to understand how important power is. They might be frightened and eschew power since they themselves have suffered under it. But Father Martin never gave the Polish prelate reason to consider this. For ten years he kept silent watch as the hand of power silently and quickly guided the actions of the Church. He listened as the voices of moderation, which spoke of greater concern for the common man, were lost in the depths of the Vatican chambers. Prelates far more influential than himself, more experienced and ready to challenge the Church's direction, were tolerated, but in the end their opinions were passed over and their warnings ignored.

Six weeks ago, during the first hot days in August, Father Martin decided to take his own life. Although he knew suicide was a sin in the eyes of the Church, he felt he could no longer withstand the weight of his doubts. He therefore resolved to make his private peace with the Lord, to leave to Him rather than to His vicar on earth the final judgment on his death. Would that God showed him even the smallest mercy, it would be enough.

On the appointed afternoon, after he had completed his duties in the prelate's office, Father Martin returned to his room and knelt before the crucifix for his last earthly prayer. A few feet away, under the pillow on his bed lay the knife with which he would cut open his throat.

As he remembered now, Father Martin thought it ironic that the cardinal should have appeared behind him when he had completed his prayers. Earlier in the day the prelate had noticed his secretary's feverish complexion and had come to ask him to dinner. Father Martin felt the weight of Meyerczuk's hand on his shoulder, and he trembled. Raising his head, the priest squeezed back hot tears, the fingers of his clasped hands digging into his palms. Why did he not face his tormentor and cry out his accusations? What was the force that held his tongue, imprisoning him in his own torment, a coward unable to break the bonds of suffering? The hand dropped, a signal. Father Martin crossed himself and, leaning forward on the bed, struggled to his feet. The Lord would not release him yet, not yet.

Dinner was a simple affair: boiled beef with horseradish, cabbage and potatoes. The Polish prelate, sensing his secretary was troubled but unwilling to speak his mind, offered only anecdotes and gossip, reflections on the psychological subtleties of politics and sarcastic opinions about the state of the current Italian government. Raising a glass of wine to the light, he examined it critically and said, in no apparent context, "I have learned that if a man desires a thing to be done, then he must do it himself from a position of power or not consider it at all."

Father Martin gazed up at the prelate, who was refilling his glass. The words stirred him. They were like a slow rise of the morning sun over the horizon. He sensed a clue in them, a veiled hint of a direction to follow, possibly an answer. He turned to the prelate and asked, "Please, could you explain this?"

Cardinal Meyerczuk could not have foreseen the terrible implications his words carried. He did not know that in them his secretary was to find the strength to endure once more and that in the long days to come, he would carry these words close to his heart.

On Monday, September 16, a kind of power had come into Father Martin's hands. At first he was afraid of it, in the same way an inexperienced man's hand would tremble when it reached for an unfamiliar but deadly weapon. But in the end Father Martin had seized that weapon, he had stolen it, and now he was running. He knew that if he had waited any longer, he would have waited too long. Now he, a humble priest from Poland, whom all considered kind and just, would hold this power before the Church and watch as the Holy See trembled. Father Martin had endured, but the price of that survival had robbed him of any mercy he might have felt for that which he would destroy. There was nothing but a cold, aching loneliness within him.

"Father, we've arrived."

The driver pushed back his cap and turned around to the silent deathly white priest.

"Father?"

"Forgive me," he murmured, and reached inside his habit for some crumpled lire.

He got out and made his way down the Via Venitri into the doorway of a noisy, decrepit house. With his useless foot dragging behind him, it took Father Martin ten minutes to climb to the seventh floor, where he had rented a garret room one month previous.

Inside the miserable little room with its one window grimy with pigeon droppings, Father Martin deposited his briefcase on a desk that had once belonged to a schoolchild and collapsed on the mattress that was supposed to serve as his bed. He closed his eyes in an attempt to blot out the pain throbbing through his foot, but the darkness exploded into whirling lights. Like a wounded animal dying in its lair, he groaned and trembled, curling his knees up tightly against his chest. The sweat was pouring from him, and his body was convulsed in terrible shudders that picked him up again and again, tossing him against the wall like a broken puppet.

"*Miserere mei Deus . . . miserere. . . !*"

Through the heat that blinded his vision and parched his throat, Father Martin Belobraditz cried out to the God who had led him to this life of suffering, who had always rescued him from ultimate destruction, yet who forever denied him peace. He cried out for his own misery and self-pity, but no angel came to bear him away toward the kingdom of heaven. As he howled his outrage at the Creator who had abandoned him and at the mortal who had destroyed his last faith in this world, Father Martin felt his consciousness fade, and he thought he saw himself spinning dizzily away from earth, far, far away into the blackness and toward the dull, glowing pillars of hell.

The rain began falling shortly after eight o'clock, coming down in fat, lazy drops that spattered over the pavement, making it greasy and treacherous to walk on. Clerics on their way to devotion or duty glanced up at the impassive gray sky and hurried as carefully as possible across St. Peter's Square. They knew, as Romans do, that this was only the prelude to a thunderstorm.

The raindrops gathered force from the wind which drove even the Swiss Guards to seek shelter, and suddenly the storm unleashed itself. The servant of Cardinal Meyerczuk hurried to the rattling windows, bolting them and drawing the curtains.

"Let them remain open!"

The dry imperious tone stopped the servant's hands at once.

"We need this rain. It is clean and fresh. There has been enough heat."

The servant bowed and withdrew with the breakfast tray, leaving the prelate to contemplate the rain in silence.

Although he had spent almost twenty years in Rome, Rozdentsy Cardinal Meyerczuk had never reconciled himself to the city's climate. A Nordic by temperament, he felt deprived of the biting cold he had lived with for almost a half century before. Meyerczuk loved the glacial winds and blue ice of a Polish winter, the crackling of frost and firm, crunching footsteps on packed snow. Winter hid the wood for a man's fire and froze the water for his tea. It chilled him to the bone when he hunted and made game scarce as though to mock his efforts. But it also stripped the laziness from the man, challenging him to survive.

In Rome there was no winter like this, nor anywhere in Italy. A thunderstorm was the best to be had, and the more powerful these were, the more satisfied was the cardinal.

But he was not at all pleased at the way the morning was unfolding. He had wanted to start work early today, and the Tetramachus Collection, which Belobraditz had been sent for, should have been in his office before eight o'clock. It was all the more irritating since there remained only two sections of the collection he wished to study, and this had to be done before he would be able to proceed with the day's work.

The Polish prelate listened to the clock chime the quarter hour and dialed the number of the prefect of the Secret Archives. Cardinal da Silva answered after six rings.

"Good morning, Antonio," Meyerczuk said.

"Rozdentsy?" The prefect was honestly surprised to hear from him.

"Yes, Antonio," Meyerczuk said dryly. "Hasn't Belobraditz come yet?"

"Of course he has come. He was here at seven o'clock. He hasn't returned?"

"I am afraid not."

"I met him shortly after seven." Da Silva began speaking rapidly. "We went to the vault, and I told him, out of habit, I suppose, where to find the collection. I met him again at the first security post on his way out, then returned to check that only the collection had gone, and it had. There was nothing else missing from the shelves. I do not understand, Rozdentsy. Was he not told what to do?"

"He knew perfectly well what to do," Meyerczuk said, forcing himself to keep his voice level. "But it would appear he has not done it. You didn't see him outside, did you?"

"No."

"Ask one of the guards on duty whether he saw Belobraditz leave. Phrase the question carefully, for there must be no hint of anything wrong. I will be waiting."

Rozdentsy Cardinal Meyerczuk folded his large scarred

fingers together and stared intently into the rain. One minute passed, then another, the telephone was silent, and panic began to twist slowly inside the prelate's chest. He told himself there was a rational explanation for this. On his way over to the cardinal's apartments Belobraditz had remembered something left behind in his room and had gone to fetch it. He would be here directly. In fact, Meyerczuk could hear someone approaching his door now. He turned in expectation, but it was only the servant.

"What is it?" Meyerczuk asked mildly.

"Cardinal di Porto and Mocata have called just now. Will Your Eminence meet with them at the appointed hour?"

"I shall. Go around to Father Martin's room and see what is keeping him. And bring me the day calendar with my appointments. It is in the office, on his desk."

The servant bowed and closed the door as the telephone rang. There was no mistaking the panic in Da Silva's voice now.

"The guard remembers him going toward the gates on the Via della Conciliazione."

"Is he certain?"

"He is. Rozdentsy, what is happening?"

"There is no need to shout," Meyerczuk said crisply. "I have just asked someone to go down to Belobraditz's room. If he is not there, one may assume, I think, that the good father had his own plans for the collection."

"Are you saying he has stolen it?"

"Choose your words carefully, Antonio," Meyerczuk warned him. "There may, after all, be a very satisfactory explanation for this."

"But what is one to do in the meantime?"

"First, do not ask any more questions of the guard or anyone else. I will search for Father Martin within the Vatican and call you when I have done so."

"What if he is not found?"

"Then it would appear we have a problem to deal with, Antonio."

Meyerczuk replaced the receiver without another word. The priest's absence was already a problem, compounded by the possibility of the prefect's panicking. There was so little to Da Silva, Meyerczuk thought, beyond that calm, frigid exterior—a man of straw, useless in action.

The servant came in to inform him that Father Martin was not in his room, although the bed had been slept in. He placed the day calendar before the prelate.

"Yes, I have just received word about Father Martin," Meyerczuk said, with concern in his voice. "He is in the infirmary. His lungs are very weak, and this weather does them no good."

He rejected the servant's offer to replace Father Martin for the day and dismissed him. Cardinal Meyerczuk wanted no one else involved in what he would be doing.

Turning the pages of the calendar, he saw that while the morning was completely filled with appointments, the afternoon was free. After lunch he decided to pay visits across the Vatican. He knew that he would not even be obliged to ask if anyone had seen his secretary in the papal suites or the secretary of state's room. He would be told at once, for a priest did not enter such places unless he was coming on specific business. But Cardinal Meyerczuk had, in fact, no idea where to look for Belobraditz. He did not know why the priest had not brought him the collection or where else he might have gone with it. The cardinal understood only one matter: that the contents of the Tetramachus Collection, if revealed to the Sacred College of Cardinals, would cost him the papacy he had coveted for so long and to which he was, at the moment, the acknowledged successor.

CHAPTER TWO

The thunderstorm raged over the city until the early afternoon, reducing Rome to a gray cacophonous nightmare. Minor accidents had traffic piled up along the main arteries. Side streets were clogged with hastily parked cars as motorists gave up trying to drive through the deluge and chose to wait it out in the more convivial atmosphere of cafés. For a city whose population was forever moving, always in a hurry to get to one place or another, Rome was strangely silent.

Father Martin slept through it all. When he awoke, his fever had disappeared, leaving only a sour odor on his clothes to testify to his illness. It was now half past one.

Father Martin raised himself on one elbow and stared around the little room. The rain had washed the pigeon droppings across the window so that almost no light found its way inside. His fingers searched for the switch on the wall, and he sheltered his eyes against the glare of the naked bulb. Still half asleep, the Polish priest stumbled over to the cold water basin. He was no longer ill, he could feel that, tired, yes, very tired, but awake and conscious. When he emerged from behind the partition, Father Martin was naked and wet, his skin crawling from the scrubbing he had given it.

From a small footlocker in the corner of the room he brought out fresh underwear and a gray worn suit bought at a secondhand store. His deformity would always be noticed, but it was better to appear a civilian than a cleric.

He would attract less attention that way. When he had dressed, he went over to the little desk and opened his briefcase.

Running his hands over the red leather binder, he thought it strange he should now feel no fear and so little sense of wrongdoing. The sleep had calmed him, allowing his mind to observe his action clearly, without panic. He thought of reading the Collection again, if only a few pages, but he smiled, knowing there was no need to go over it this one final time. The Collection had not been magically transformed into a fairy tale. It still told the truth, a harsh, ugly truth which time could never change. He had read it all very carefully. Now he hoped the world might do the same.

On an ancient typewriter bought for the occasion Father Martin slowly wrote out his letter to His Holiness Urban XI. He stopped several times, awed that it should ever have come about that a simple priest would be setting down his thoughts and beliefs before the Vicar of Christ. But every word was born of his agony and the pain that had nourished it, and he chose to let that speak for him. The truth could be simply stated—always.

Father Martin reread the two-page letter, corrected the erratic typing and from the desk drawer brought out a long thin blue envelope emblazoned with the personal crest of Cardinal Meyerczuk. After he had affixed sufficient postage to the envelope, Father Martin pressed both sides with the cardinal's seal, stolen last night. Ordinary mail was always opened before it reached the Pontiff, while sealed matters bearing the mark of the sender arrived intact.

He wrapped the Collection in waterproof oilskin, which he covered in brown paper and placed in his briefcase. Everything he had planned to do was done. He only wished he had had a radio. Doubtless the theft had been discovered, and he wondered if the police were looking for him. As long as he had a chance to mail the letter and deliver the Collection, it mattered very little what fate had waiting for him.

Father Martin made his way down the greasy staircase and out into the courtyard of the apartment block. The storm had spent itself, but rain continued to fall. He moved carefully under naked wash lines and past overflowing garbage bins that ringed the courtyard and poked out into the street. On the corner of Via Venitri, beside a battened-down café, he posted his letter and waited for the Number Fourteen bus, which, when it came, took Father Martin into the center of Rome.

Alfredo Sabatini was more than just a publisher. A millionaire Marxist, he was master of Italy's most prestigious publishing enterprise, Unita, and a living legend in literary circles.

Born in the village of Ales in poverty-ridden Sardinia, Sabatini had begun working at the age of eleven at the local registry office.

"I was earning nine lire a month," he once told a *New York Times Magazine* editor. "That meant one kilo of bread for ten hours' work a day, including Sundays. I shifted registers weighing more than half myself and many nights cried myself to sleep because of the intolerable pain in my body."

In spite of this, Sabatini distinguished himself as a student in the Santa Lussurgia *ginnasio* and later at the University of Turin, where he studied philosophy and history under Benedetto Croce.

During his final year in Turin, Sabatini was introduced

to socialism by Palmiro Togliatti, founder of the Italian Communist Party. From that time on Sabatini never strayed from his idealist philosophy, which tended to infuriate orthodox Communists as much as it did the growing right wing. His humanitarian revolt against the wretched conditions existing in Italy during Mussolini's rise found its expression in his first newspaper, the *Ordine Nuovo.* Anticlerical and antifascist, the *Ordine Nuovo* was responsible for both Sabatini's growing fame as a left-wing intellectual and his internment during Mussolini's rule. For five years, beginning in 1939, the young editor-writer occupied a solitary cell in Santas Prison, twelve kilometers outside Rome.

"Every word written about men, men living and working in societies, hoping and struggling for a better world, pleases me more than anything else in the world," he wrote in his prison notebooks.

In early 1944, when Santas Prison had been reduced to rubble by Allied bombardments, Sabatini learned what price had been extracted for that better world. During his stay in a U.S. Army hospital, he was told that in April, 1943, three-quarters of the Italian socialist movement had been destroyed by the Gestapo in a mass slaughter outside the town of Ceccano. The few who remained were scattered in camps throughout Europe waiting for disease, hunger and cold to do what the Germans had failed to finish. The more fortunate had fled to Britain; the luckiest made it to America.

Like Springer in Germany, Sabatini was given a printing contract by the Allies to produce ration coupons and propaganda tracts. Within two years there was enough money to buy new presses for his paper. Ten months later, with Togliatti acting as midwife, the small publishing house of Unita was born.

Unita survived the publishing jungle through Sabatini's brilliant editorial talents. He afforded a voice for promising writers and nutured them with a singular care. Their manuscripts were read by him and him alone. Some of these authors went on to establish solid reputations: Bossé, the existential philosopher; Carmelitas, novelist and bitter opponent of Franco's regime; Paul Hitchfield, whose studies on revolt and revolution made him a leading thinker in America of the sixties; and the famous Italian playwright Luigi Farrelli. In spite of his avowed anticlericalism which, like Dante's, grew out of a moral disapproval of Church wealth and political policy, Sabatini also published Catholic writers such as the novelists Mauriac and Evelyn Waugh.

At the end of the fifties Sabatini had the Italian rights to every major writer on the Continent. His friends included such diverse personalities as Castro and De Gaulle, Che Guevara and John F. Kennedy. In 1961 Sabatini achieved world-wide recognition by capturing the international copyright to Andrei Antonov's *Life's Journey,* written in the exile of the Siberian wastes.

By the middle of the decade Sabatini's literary voice was second to none in Europe. His fortune helped reestablish the Italian socialist movement, and his powerful name provided a drawing card for one of Europe's foremost left-wing parties, the Partito Socialista Italiano, the PSI.

The rain had all but subsided, and Sabatini stared out the window, slowly drawing on his favorite cigar, the same marque that Castro preferred—Angelica—then turned to his desk. For all the incompetence of the Italian postal service, the mail had piled up during his two-day retreat to his country lodge on Lake Como. But today was not the day to bother with it. On his tooled leather blotter there lay only one piece of paper which required his attention, a memorandum concerning the upcoming PSI broadcast, a major policy address.

Four months before, the PSI had expanded its so-called Red Belt up to the French border, winning control of the Liguria region. The party gained three and a half million popular votes, enough to oust the regional government of the Christian Democrats and, with the help of the Communists, to extend that victory into the municipal elections of Genoa, Milan, Bologna and Ferrara. Two months later Giannino Fransci, the PSI leader, brought forward a non-confidence motion which delivered the coup de grâce to the shaky coalition of Christian Democrats and Republicans. The subsequent national election brought Fransci's PSI into power with the largest majority gained by any party since the war.

Staying close to his promise, Fransci swept the government of aging ornamental senators, pruned the bureaucracy and began to lay the foundations for a referendum which would allow the people of Italy, rather than the Catholic Church, to decide whether an abortion law should be passed that would guarantee every woman the right to a safe, clean operation. Sabatini thought it a fair gamble. Fransci was riding a high tide of personal and party popularity. If he challenged the conservative elements, headed by the Church, while fortune was favoring him and won on the issue of abortion, the power of the right, which was still omnipresent and strong, might be broken once and for all. The right feared nothing so much as people who thought for themselves. The ranks of

Jacopo Lorenzo Borghese, the so-called Black Prince of Italian fascism, would wither away if the Church failed to discourage Italians from participating in the socialist experiment.

Alfredo Sabatini walked around his nine-foot draftsman's desk, occasionally running his fingers through silver brown hair. Once as a joke he had attached an odometer to his belt to see exactly how much he walked in a day. The figure had been four and one-half miles, and Sabatini understood why he had kept his lean, paunchless figure.

Having focused his attention on the matter of the broadcast, Sabatini sat down and began drafting a few notes for his speech that evening. Although he helped support the PSI financially and allowed his name to be used for the fund gatherings, he preferred to stay in the shadows. He did not like publicity in an age where idiots targeted victims for assassination by watching prominent people on the evening news. Only on important occasions, when he felt a moral obligation to state his position, would he agree to appear on the PSI's behalf.

The red light on the intercom unit came on, breaking into his thoughts. Sabatini glanced at it irritably, wondering what it was the cat had dragged out of the rain. His secretary used the red light when she wanted to speak to Sabatini before admitting the visitor. Usually this meant she had reservations about the caller or his business.

Pia Monti came in, her ash blond hair billowing over her shoulders and onto her breasts, a fresh cup of tea in her hand. Sabatini relieved her of the tea, his thick mustache brushing her cheek.

"I'm busy," he said gruffly. But his manner did not draw the usual laugh from her.

"There is a priest to see you," Pia said in a low voice. "It seems very important, Alfredo."

Sabatini rose from his desk, his chest swelling as he flexed his hands. Pia was a level-headed girl who wasn't afraid of shadows, yet now her fingers were ice cold.

"What's wrong?" he asked softly.

Pia handed him a plastic identification card. The photograph was clear if not very complimentary. It showed a man of forty or forty-five, with black, oily hair, one lock tumbling across his forehead, and a slightly quizzical expression in the eyes. The whole face had a terrible, worn look to it, as though it had aged suddenly and prematurely.

"What does he want?"

"He says he has Vatican papers which will be of great interest to you. I think you should see him, Alfredo. There is something desperate about him, something I'm afraid of."

"Ask Giuseppe to come up here at once, then cut off all calls and send him in. Leave your intercom on."

Giuseppe Urbanetti was the publisher's bodyguard, recruited after the Squadra Azione Mussolini, a terrorist group of right-wingers, had sent a letter bomb to the Unita offices. The letter was not addressed to any specific recipient so it was opened in the mailroom. Two seconds after he had torn the envelope open, Benito Urbanetti lay dead on the floor, his face and chest torn away by the blast. It had taken Giuseppe one month to track down his brother's killers. After the last man responsible had been found floating gently in the Tiber, Giuseppe presented himself at Sabatini's office, ready to protect the man his brother had died serving.

Sabatini remembered this incident when he saw Father Martin Belobraditz coming through the door with his package. The fact that a priest was not wearing a habit set Sabatini in motion.

"Giuseppe, get in here!"

The priest stopped moving as soon as the words left Sabatini's lips. The door crashed behind him as the bodyguard kicked it back, training a long black revolver barrel on Father Martin's neck.

"You may put your bag there, on the coffee table."

Sabatini indicated a low table at the far end of the room.

Father Martin obeyed instantly.

"Now open it, and please, be very gentle."

Father Martin fumbled with the latches of the briefcase and brought out his package, removing first the brown paper, then carefully unwrapping the oilskin. He held up the red leather folio for Sabatini to see clearly.

"Open it," the publisher said. Father Martin did as he was told and opened the volume to the first pages, then flipped through the rest. Only then did Sabatini come over to him, at the same time dismissing Giuseppe with a nod.

"You must forgive me, Father," he said, offering his hand. "A member of my company was killed by a bomb hidden in a letter. One death is already too many."

He took the priest by the arm and walked slowly with him to a chair.

"Father Martin Belobraditz?"

"Yes," the priest answered, the word catching in his throat. He reached forward and placed the volume on Sabatini's desk. The publisher's unexpected behavior had unnerved him, and all that he had carefully prepared to say was lost, leaving only panic in its place.

Sabatini was about to open the volume when Father Martin finally spoke.

"Signor Sabatini, the papers you have before you, the

Tetramachus Collection as it is called, was stolen this morning from the Secret Archives of the Vatican,'' he blurted out. ''I am the thief.''

Sabatini looked up at him curiously, taken aback by the sudden confession.

''And why did you do this?'' he asked.

''The papers will speak for me,'' Father Martin said. ''I brought them to you because you are a reputable man who would know what can be done with them.''

''You bring me stolen papers because I am a reputable man?'' Sabatini asked gently.

''That is not what I meant,'' Father Martin whispered, summing the last reserves of his courage to cover his embarrassment. ''I do not know who else to trust.''

''I assume you want me to read this material.''

''I would be grateful. . . .''

''And publish it, even though both actions on my part constitute my being an accomplice in your felony.''

''I understand the risks I am asking you to take,'' Father Martin said weakly.

''Then don't you think you should explain exactly who you are and what these papers are all about?'' Sabatini asked him.

''I can tell you only that I am—I was—secretary to Rozdentsy Cardinal Meyerczuk,'' Father Martin said. ''After you have read the Collection, I think you will understand why my personal motivations are unimportant and why I acted as I have.''

Father Martin stood up and looked directly at the black, glittering eyes that were carefully searching his face for the truth behind his words.

''Please understand, signor, that I know only too well what I have done and do not think I have not suffered for my actions. I beg of you, do not judge me or throw me over until you have read the papers. I will call you tomorrow, and if you do not want them, then I shall take them back. I will return for the Collection even though you may have set a trap for me by informing either the Vatican or the police of what I have done."

"You trust me a great deal," Sabatini murmured.

"I have done as much as is possible for one man to do," Father Martin said dully. "Now I must trust someone."

Father Martin turned and walked slowly to the door, his foot dragging along the carpet. Sabatini was still looking after him when Pia came in.

"What did you do to him?" she exclaimed. "He appeared as though he had met the devil himself."

Sabatini did not answer her at once. His eyes had settled on the red leather binder, his fingers running along the edge of the gold pages.

"Can you stay tonight?" he asked abruptly.

"Of course."

"Good. Ask Giuseppe if he would as well. Should the police come around have them wait outside and call me first."

"Is it that serious?" she asked, glancing down at the volume.

"I don't know yet," Sabatini replied thoughtfully. "And if anyone from the Vatican calls, tell them nothing—about the priest, this book or the fact that I am in!"

When Pia withdrew, Sabatini lit a fresh Angelica, turned on his reading lamp and opened the volume to the first page.

THE TETRAMACHUS COLLECTION
VOLUME FIVE

THE ACTIVITIES OF THE HOLY SEE DURING THE SECOND WORLD WAR
REFERENCE FLX/40-48
KEEP FOREVER WITHIN THE SECRET ARCHIVES

Above these words was set the personal seal of Pope Pius XII.

For the next two hours Alfredo Sabatini did not move from his chair. As the Unita staff began to pack up and go home, they noticed the red light burning over the publisher's door. It meant Sabatini was not to be disturbed by either calls or visitors, regardless of who they were or what they wanted. In his office, Sabatini kept on reading, oblivious to the existence of everything but the Collection, mesmerized by the cruel words which would not let him go.

CABLEGRAM

WARSAW POLAND
MAY 15 1940

MONSIGNOR ROZDENTSY MEYERCZUK TO PIUS XII

AN ACCORD WITH THE GERMAN HIGH COMMAND HAS BEEN ARRIVED AT. LETTER STATING CONDITIONS AND TERMS WILL FOLLOW. GENERAL BRONITZ DEMANDS STRICT SECRECY IN THE MATTER OF OCCUPATION FORCES COOPERATION WITH THE CHURCH AND HAS RECEIVED MY ASSURANCES ON THIS.

THE ROMAN CATHOLIC CHURCH IN POLAND SHALL SUFFER LITTLE FROM THE GERMANS.

No papal reply on record

CABLEGRAM

BUDAPEST HUNGARY
FEBRUARY 3 1941

MONSIGNOR GABOR SULOK TO HIS HOLINESS PIUS XII

OUR BROTHER IN CHRIST PETRO NAGY OF THE HOLY SEE IN HUNGARY DIED PEACEFULLY IN HIS SLEEP LAST NIGHT. AS YOUR HOLINESS REQUESTED I SHALL CONTINUE MSGR'S WORK IN BUDAPEST UNDER CONDITIONS WHICH I MUST SAY ARE ENOUGH TO DRIVE ONE TO DESPAIR.

APPALLING RUMORS ABOUT THE FATE OF JEWS AND CHRISTIANS ALIKE REACH THE CITY DAILY. IT IS SAID THAT IN NORTHERN GERMANY AND POLAND MONSTROUS CAMPS HAVE BEEN BUILT WHICH USE SLAVE LABOR TO FUEL THE GERMAN WAR MACHINE. AT THE SAME TIME SOME OF THESE CAMPS SERVE AS EXTERMINATION CENTERS FOR PEOPLES WHOM THE THIRD REICH REGARDS AS UNWORTHY OF LIFE. THIS APPLIES MAINLY TO JEWS ALTHOUGH THERE ARE THOUSANDS OF POLES RUSSIANS AND SLAVS INTERRED AS WELL.

THE TRUTH OF THIS RUMOR MAY BE SEEN IN THE FEAR WHICH HAS GRIPPED BUDAPEST. WHAT JEWS REMAIN KNOW THE FATE IN STORE FOR THEM WHEN THE GESTAPO ARRIVES. THE HUNGARIANS TRY TO LOOK AWAY HOPING THAT IF THEY SEE NOTHING THE ANGELS OF DEATH WILL PASS THEM BY. IT IS A CONDITION WHICH TURNS MEN INTO BEASTS AND BRINGS FORTH ALL THE PREJUDICE HATRED AND TREACHERY WHICH LIE AROUND THE HUMAN HEART.

I BEG HIS HOLINESS TO USE THE POWERS AT HIS DISPOSAL TO DETERMINE WHAT IT IS THE THIRD REICH IS DOING WITH PRISONERS OF WAR NOT SOLDIERS BUT ORDINARY SIMPLE HUMAN BEINGS WHO ARE VICTIMS OF INSANE CIRCUMSTANCES.

IF THE CHURCH DOES NOT ACT TO PROTECT HER CHILDREN AND SPEAK FOR THOSE WHO ARE SUFFERING NOW THEN SHE WILL REAP THE SCORN AND VENGEANCE OF POSTERITY.

I SHALL CONTINUE TO WORK AS BEST AS POSSIBLE UNDER THESE CIRCUMSTANCES AND AT THE SAME TIME KEEP HIS HOLINESS INFORMED ON MATTERS IN THIS WRETCHED CORNER OF EUROPE.

No papal reply on record

CABLEGRAM

BERLIN GERMANY
SEPTEMBER 4 1941

MONSIGNOR CESARE ORSENGIO TO MONSIGNOR GIOVANNI BATTISTA PAPAL NUNCIO

REGARDING THE URGENT MATTER OF THE DEPORTATION OF JEWS WHICH IS TAKING PLACE DAILY I REPORT THAT GERMAN AUTHORITIES HAVE OFFERED NO NEW INFORMATION SINCE MY LAST MEETING WITH THEM.

THIS SUPPRESSION OF NEWS ALLOWS FOR THE MOST MACABRE POSSIBILITIES SURROUNDING THE FATE OF NONARYANS.

EVERY INTERVENTION IN FAVOR OF JEWISH CONVERTS TO CATHOLICISM HAS BEEN MET WITH THE REPLY THAT BAPTISMAL WATER DOES NOT CHANGE JEWISH BLOOD AND THAT THE THIRD REICH IS PROTECTING ITSELF FROM NONARYAN RACES NOT FROM THE RELIGIOUS BELIEFS OF BAPTIZED JEWS.

I HUMBLY REQUEST THE INTERVENTION OF HIS HOLINESS PIUS XII IN THIS MATTER.

No papal reply on record

CABLEGRAM

BRATISLAVA SLOVAKIA
MARCH 9 1942

MONSIGNOR JAN SLIMA TO HIS HOLINESS PIUS XII

THE DEPORTATION OF 80,000 PEOPLE TO POLAND AT THE MERCY OF THE GERMANS IS EQUIVALENT TO CONDEMNING A LARGE NUMBER OF THEM TO DEATH.

ALL MEANS MUST BE USED TO PERSUADE THE GERMAN REICH TO DISCLOSE THE REASONS FOR THIS MASS SHIFTING OF HELPLESS PEOPLE. RUMORS WHICH TRAVEL BACK FROM POLAND SPEAK OF THE MOST HIDEOUS ATROCITIES INCLUDING A MASTER PLAN FOR THE EXTERMINATION OF THE JEWISH RACE.

THE INTERVENTION OF HIS HOLINESS IS PARAMOUNT TO THE SAVING OF COUNTLESS THOUSANDS OF LIVES.

No papal reply on record

CABLEGRAM

PARIS FRANCE
DECEMBER 21 1942

MONSIGNOR ANTONIO D'ANDREA TO HIS HOLINESS PIUS XII

I HAVE SPOKEN WITH HITLER PERSONALLY. HE ASSURES ME THAT THE DEPORTATIONS WHICH ARE TAKING PLACE THOUGHOUT FRANCE ARE ONLY A PROPHYLACTIC MEASURE TO ENSURE THAT THE HOMELESS MASSES DO NOT SUFFER NEEDLESSLY FROM HUNGER AND DISEASE. THEY ARE BEING SENT TO RELOCATION CENTERS IN GERMANY WHERE FOOD AND MEDICINES ARE AVAILABLE THROUGH THE INTERNATIONAL RED CROSS AND GERMAN BENEVOLENT SOCIETIES.

I HAVE PERSONALLY INSPECTED THE TRANSPORT FACILITIES AND MAY ADD THAT THEY ARE THE BEST AVAILABLE UNDER THE CIRCUMSTANCES.

THERE IS NO NEED TO VOICE CONCERN OVER THE FATES OF THESE PEOPLES ESPECIALLY NOT THE JEWS.

No papal reply on record

MEMORANDUM COPY

ROME ITALY
JANUARY 7 1946

ISTITUTO SANTA MARIA DELL'ANIMA

VATICAN PASSPORT RECEIVED FOR MARTIN BORMANN IN THE NAME OF JUAN HERNANDEZ JESUIT MISSIONARY TO ARGENTINA.

MARIO HULAIS
RECTOR

During the 1941-42 period alone more than six hundred cablegrams and letters of this nature were sent back to the Vatican from its representatives in occupied Europe. Together with such postwar documents as Bishop Hulais' memorandum, this correspondence was sorted, sealed and filed away in the Secret Vatican Archives under the official papal code name of the Tetramachus Collection. The most incriminating material was placed in Volume Five.

After the discovery of the extermination camps and the wave of human outrage which swept the world, the Vatican must have been tempted to destroy any evidence which would tarnish its carefully prepared war record. Certainly, why the Church never rid itself of the Tetramachus Collection is an unanswered question.

The most plausible explanation would rest in the respect the Church has for its own history, an esteem which would not permit the destruction of even such criminal evidence. Veiled in holy secrecy, the details concerning Church activities during the 1938-48 period were intended to lie in Vatican vaults as quietly as the inquisition manuals of four hundred years ago do to this day. It was, considering the security of the Vatican, a fair gamble.

"But it did not pay off!" Sabatini whispered hoarsely. "It did not pay off!"

Sabatini marked his place in the folio and ran his hand over the dull red leather binding. He had no doubt that what he had just read was a genuine papal document, the existence of which had only been rumored but never substantiated. Its theft, therefore, was nothing less than the crime of the century. No art robbery, no jewel heist or bank holdup could even begin to approach such magnitude. If Volume Five of the Tetramachus Collection were made public, it would destroy the Vatican's sovereignty and cripple an already-atrophying faith. What politicians of the left wing had been unable to do since the unification of Italy, bring the Vatican to the bar of lay justice and accounting, could now be accomplished. On the basis of these pages alone it would be possible once and for all to break the wall of secrecy surrounding the Vatican's temporal affairs.

"And what irony!" Sabatini thought to himself. "That this should happen on the eve of a Holy Year!"

In a few months, hundreds of thousands of pilgrims,

most using their last savings, would descend on Rome from the four corners of the earth to answer Urban XI's call for "reconciliation and renewal." They would come seeking a scrap of faith, perhaps the last thing they had to look up to in these lean and uncertain times. They would come wanting to believe, and the Church would gaze down on them and bless them so that their toil did not go unrewarded and the mystery would be preserved.

The Tetramachus Collection jumped as two closed fists slammed down upon it. Even though he hadn't seen the inside of a church for thirty years, Sabatini considered himself no less religious than the most pious pilgrim. But he had no need of any confessor or of any dogma. He had always despised the superior attitude of his village priest, who lived off the offerings of the poor, which, added to his holy stipend, had made him better off than anyone else there. In the pages of his first newspaper he had constantly argued for the need of a supervisory body to oversee the financial and political affairs of the Church where these went beyond strictly ecclesiastical matters. Most of all, he bitterly resented the paltry offerings the Vatican bestowed so sanctimoniously on the poor while its own wealth compounded itself year after year.

While professing to be the custodian of all that was good in the human spirit, the Church systematically betrayed that spirit. And like any political power, it had its secrets, although these had always been carefully hidden by the mantles of the popes.

"The Church shall suffer from your overconfidence if you repent too late for having neglected the people. If you postpone it longer, the harm will be incurable. Do you think the people will suffer forever? Who do you think can endure your abuses and for how long?"

More than four hundred years ago these words had thundered forth from the mouth of Martin Luther, the signal for the greatest schism in Christendom. Now, in the last quarter of the twentieth century, in a Holy Year, they might perhaps be uttered once more.

Sabatini sat back in his chair and leafed through the remainder of the volume, the pages sliding in a blur before his eyes. There was no question but that he wanted the Tetramachus Collection. Stolen or not, he would publish it and fight the Vatican in the civil courts if the Holy See tried to bring an injunction against him.

But the first order of business was to make a copy. Sabatini turned to the end of the collection and removed a manila dossier that seemed to have been appended to the main body of the text. He set this aside and called for Pia.

Even though she had promised herself it would not happen, Pia Monti, after three months as Sabatini's personal secretary, had fallen deeply in love with him. That had been four years ago. There had always been a great deal of passion in their relationship, and although he never told Pia he would marry her, Sabatini was more faithful to her than most husbands were to their wives. Still Pia had just turned twenty-nine. The longings for a family and home were growing stronger. Sometime she shuddered when she looked at herself and saw that in spite of her intentions, her love was lavished on a man who could never be satisfied with the life of a simple husband and father.

As she came toward him, Sabatini recognized the smile that was meant to hide her worry, and he reached out for her hand, catching her fingers and squeezing them hard.

"What is it, Alfredo?" Pia asked softly.

Sabatini looked up at her with a slight smile and shook his head.

"We have been handed a piece of history," he murmured. "A piece of history that will tear the Church apart! . . . I suppose someone else besides yourself saw Father Martin when he arrived?" he asked.

"Maria at the reception desk. She was the one to bring him to me."

"There's no one out there now?"

"No."

"Then take this and begin photostating—every page. It will take about two hours. And don't stop to read it. There will time for that later."

"What is it?" Pia asked, drawing deeply on a cigarette. "Besides a piece of history, I mean."

"What is it?" Sabatini wondered aloud. "Where is one to begin? The papers of the Tetramachus Collection—that is the proper name for the volume—are an indictment against the Church. They are evidence that the Vatican knew of the atrocities being committed across Europe between 1939 and 1945, that it knew the location and function of death camps, that Pius the Twelfth refused to intervene on behalf of humanity in order to spare the Church, especially the German and Italian churches, retaliation. . . . And that is only the beginning, Pia, only the beginning."

"How did Father Martin obtain this document?"

"He stole it." Sabatini answered with a ghost of a smile, as though silently saluting the action. "He stole it from the Court of the Belvedere, from under the nose of the prefect of the Secret Archives and an elite security corps. Quite a coup, don't you think?"

"But there has been no news of any theft," Pia objected.

"I would have been surprised if there had been," Sabatini said dryly. "The Church will not run to the police, not when it is information as valuable as this that's got out. Perhaps they aren't even aware of the theft yet."

"And you intend to publish stolen material which you haven't yet verified as being accurate?" Pia asked incredulously.

"You know I am not a sensationalist," Sabatini said. "I will publish this because the world must know about the other side of the papacy, the dark side which hides under golden vestments and splendid ritual. I want to pull the mask of sanctity off the Church!"

"But how can you be certain the material is genuine?" Pia persisted.

"The Collection bears the personal seal of Pius the Twelfth, the signature of the prefect of the Secret Archives, as well as the seal of the Court of the Belvedere," Sabatini replied. "Latin, the language of the cablegrams, is not unfamiliar to me. God knows I had enough of it at the university. But you are right: I should eliminate that tenth of a percent of doubt—for your sake. So a check is in order. In fact, I know exactly the man to do it. Tomorrow evening, after I have spoken with Father Martin, you will take a flight to Paris."

"Paris!"

"Where you will give the original to Dr. Aaron Vogel, professor of history at the Sorbonne, specialist in twentieth-century history, particularly where the Holocaust is concerned," Sabatini finished.

Pia stared at him in disbelief.

"What kind of man would want to betray his Church?" she said at last. "And who are *you* that you should be so willing to help him?"

Sabatini stood up and walked over to the window.

"Father Martin asked me not to judge him when I raised the same question," Sabatini said slowly. "Having read the papers, I know better than to do that now.

"Pia, understand me. I am a Catholic if for no other reason than I was baptized one. But I do have a belief in the existence of some kind of deity or force which is far greater than anything man is able to comprehend. I would not think to deny another man his belief or form of worship any more than I would permit him to deny me mine.

"What I am speaking of here is the *individual* relationship between man and his God, which transcends the trappings of ritual and dogma. Obviously this kind of personal association is not popularly held, or else there would be no need for organized religion. But that does not mean that a cult of priests should set itself between man and God and lay claim to possessing an infallible interpretation of God's will. History has revealed, through the Inquisition and the religious wars, that the Church has as mortal a face as any of us, that popes, curias and Vaticans are subject to prejudice, malice and the pursuit of self-interest. Thus, this cult of priests has moved from interpretation of God's will to the enforcement of that interpretation and punishment for those who may not agree with the canons of the cult.

"I do not believe such coercion is just. It makes a mockery of that communion a man might seek with his Creator. God has never punished a man for questioning His existence; why should the Church condemn the same man if he questions its practices or dogmas? Why should it be that only the flock is required to confess its wrongdoings and not the cult as well? Has the Church grown so proud and jealous of its authority and so contemptuous of man that it feels *no need* to expiate its sins? The contents of the Tetramachus Collection suggest it has.

"No," Sabatini said with conviction, "I am beginning to understand a little more about the man who stole these documents. You too will understand when you read about the fine 'concordat' His Eminence Meyerczuk made with the Germans. And when you read, bear in mind Father Martin was, until he stole the papers, the secretary to this cardinal."

"So it is revenge he wants," Pia said quietly.

"Vengeance sometimes goes hand in hand with a desire for justice. But more than that, I think Father Martin wants to prevent Cardinal Meyerczuk from ascending to the papacy, an act which, in the light of the collection, would be a terrible mistake. Our present Vicar is very ill, perhaps critically so, and Meyerczuk is considered the heir apparent to the throne of Peter."

"From what you have read, would it be such a dreadful mistake?"

"Cardinal Meyerczuk is unfit to consider himself even a man of the cloth," Sabatini retorted. "All the ablutions in the world would not remove the blood on his hands."

Pia let this remark go. It was useless to talk to Sabatini when his passions were this strong. Passion was what made him tireless and brave, willing to gamble and, more often than not, win. But there was folly in such emotion as well, and it had shown itself two years ago when Benito had been killed. At the time Unita had published a highly unflattering biography on the Black Prince, which Sabatini was to use to undermine Borghese's political campaign. Sabatini had wanted to destroy the fascist, yet Borghese was reelected to his seat in Parliament and Benito Urbanetti had been the one to pay for Sabatini's actions.

"What if the Vatican were to come to you about the Collection?" Pia asked.

"Assuming first that they *find* Father Martin, and secondly, that he tells them where it is, I will not give it back to them."

"You still believe they will not go to the police?"

"Let them go."

"There are other ways to get it, Alfredo. If the papers are as damaging as you say, our friends in the SAM will kill you to get them back."

"That is why you are leaving the country tomorrow night," Sabatini answered, narrowing his eyes. "And why I want that copy. Time is pressing—you should get started."

When Pia had gone, Sabatini scribbled down several points on his note pad. The more he thought of the Collection, the faster various questions associated with it came to his mind.

The lines to Paris were clear, and the operator was able to put him through without delay. But the publisher was not able to speak with Vogel. The professor's housekeeper announced that he was dining out tonight and would be delivering a special lecture later in the evening. She could not say when he would be home. Sabatini left his name and number and told the housekeeper that a representative from Unita would be in Paris early the day after tomorrow to discuss a very urgent matter with Professor Vogel, a matter pertaining to his special area of study. The housekeeper, an elderly Jewish woman who had survived

Bergen-Belsen, asked no further questions. She had heard Aaron Vogel speak well of Sabatini, and that was all that mattered. She assured the publisher Vogel would receive the message.

Next Sabatini compiled a list of libraries, public and private, newspaper offices and national war victims' associations. Some names came to him from memory, others he had to look up. Tomorrow morning he would send out three research teams to each address to sniff for anything remotely connected with Vatican policy, planning and execution throughout the course of the war. He might, on the off chance, be able to cross-check the names and dates on some of the cablegrams with other sources. Although he was willing to rely solely on the Tetramachus Collection to testify to the statements he would at one point deliver before the public, any additional information would not go to waste.

As for the question of going to the public, if the Vatican accused him of being an accessory to a robbery, so be it. Let the Curia take him to court. They might win on that charge, but not before the whole world knew of their secret shame. More likely, Sabatini thought, they would either deny such papers existed or remain silent. The idea of exposing the papers now, while no alarm had been raised, appealed to Sabatini. It would put the Vatican on the defensive, catching it unawares. He could begin to put that plan into action, but if the story of the Collection were made public, Father Martin would need protection, not so much from the Church as from those Pia had mentioned.

Finally, he needed a secure hiding place for the copy. His office was out of the question. A bank vault was better, but still too accessible by both force and influence. Too many conservatives sat on the boards of too many banks. For Pia to hide it was no good. Someone could get to her or her apartment as easily as he could to Sabatini's. In any case, it was public knowledge Pia was his mistress.

Sabatini pondered over this last problem while he called Alitalia and reserved a seat for Paris on the evening of Tuesday, September 17. When it was confirmed, he rang up PSI headquarters. The secretary offered to put him through to the chairman, but Sabatini declined, asking her to inform him that the publisher would not be able to appear at tonight's meeting. Something Sabatini had eaten during the day violently disagreed with him. He rang off before the secretary had a chance to ask any questions.

Sabatini knew the PSI would not be pleased about the last-minute cancellation. But neither Fransci, the prime minister, nor his government could now be touched by the publisher's decision to act. The PSI was waging its own war against the Church on the question of abortion. When the time came for Sabatini to launch his attack, newspapers and political commentators would strongly suggest that Fransci had been privy to both the contents of the Collection and Sabatini's statement. Let them think what they will. Sabatini laughed silently. Everything would remain conjecture as it should, and he himself would have committed no indiscretion.

Satisfied, he turned his attention to the manila folder.

The cablegrams in the folder were in German and Italian. They were all addressed to one man, Antonio Cardinal da Silva, in his capacity as senior adviser to the Vatican Bank. Each cablegram bore the following heading: STATEMENT OF DISPOSAL

ROME ITALY
JUNE 17 1946

ANTWERP ESTIMATE FIRM SEVENTY-FIVE THOUSAND US DOLLARS FOR DIAMONDS. INSTRUCT HULAIS TO MEET WITH ME ONE WEEK FROM TODAY IN ROME. HAVE SECURED SWISS INVESTMENT FOR SAID FUNDS.

LONDON ENGLAND
JANUARY 2 1947

RECEIVED FROM HULAIS GOLD COINS ESTIMATED VALUE SIXTY-TWO THOUSAND ENGLISH POUNDS.

BEIRUT LEBANON
DECEMBER 17 1947

REQUEST TRANSFER OF ALL AMERICAN MONIES HELD BY HULAIS AT ONCE. ACCOUNT *RUDOLF* COMMERCIAL BANK OF LEBANON.

ZURICH SWITZERLAND
MARCH 22 1948

HONIKER ET FILS ELECTRONIC CONCERN ACQUIRED. REQUEST IMMEDIATE TRANSFER OF 400,000 SWISS FRANCS FROM HULAIS.

Throughout the course of the war papal silence on the atrocities committed by the Third Reich in both Germany and occupied Europe had allowed the Nazi regime to operate without moral censure from the Church. After 1945, however, for a reason the Vatican explained as having to do with Christian charity, the Holy See became actively involved in aiding the escape of known and wanted war criminals. Among these were: Adolf Otto Eichmann, head of Section Four B IV, the executive arm of the "Final Solution"; Heinrich Müller, the Gestapo Chief; Martin Bormann, Hitler's *éminence grise* and heir to the Third Reich; SS Hauptsturmführer Rajakowitsch, Eichmann's representative in Holland, responsible for the execution of more than one hundred thousand Dutch Jews.

The clerical organization that contributed most to the flight to these and lesser Nazi fugitives was the Istituto Santa Maria dell'Anima. The Vatican Refugee Bureau under the direction of then Giovanni Cardinal Battista, now Urban XI, and Caritas Internationalis, an organ of the Curia supervised by the Secretariat of State, reinforced the Istituto's efforts.

At first, Bishop Hulais, an Austrian rector of pronounced fascist sympathies and director of the Istituto, used it as a clearinghouse for escapees. However, he soon found that his facilities could not accommodate the large demands for sanctuary, food, new identification certificates and traveling papers. He thus asked for and received the cooperation of both the Refugee Bureau and Caritas Internationalis in procuring the documents. Nonetheless, there remained the problem of feeding, housing and giving the Nazi escapees some means with which to continue their flight.

Vatican officials in the postwar era have emphatically denied that their benevolent institutions in any way gave money to fugitives. Shelter, yes, false papers, yes, help in evading justice, yes, but not money. Yet why should have the Holy See touched its own exchequer? The majority of high-ranking Nazis had planned their flight well in advance. They did not begin the long run to Syria or Argentina penniless. The valuables that had poured into Auschwitz, Lubin and other "resettlement" areas were returned to the Main Security Office of the Reich once the legal owners had been liquidated, minus whatever the SS guards kept for themselves. In Berlin this loot was placed at the disposal of the senior hierarchy to be used for, among other things, the time when common sense dictated the war was lost and flight inevitable.

Some "refugees," like Müller, who arrived at a Dominican monastery with a suitcase of American thousand-dollar bills, would have spared a little from their stash, leaving a contribution with the fathers to help their comrades. No, the Vatican did not have to finance the clandestine movement of war criminals to safe havens. The Nazis paid their own way, leaving whatever contribution they wanted or could afford for the continued good work of the Church on their behalf. This money in its raw form of diamonds, gold and other valuables was then processed through the office of the Vatican treasury. According to the cablegrams, Antonio Cardinal da Silva, then head of the exchequer, was the man responsible for the booty's ultimate disposal by Cavaliere Massimo Siboda, former Mussolinite, bankroller of the Black Prince and one of Italy's shrewdest investment bankers. It was Siboda's signature that appeared at the bottom of every cablegram in the manila dossier.

The silence of the office was broken only by the monotonous ticking of the copying machine. In that silence, Sabatini turned over page after page until he came to the end of the dossier. When he was finished, he rose and went over to the sideboard. The heavy decanter tapped nervously against the glass. So the Vatican had dealt with Nazi blood money, that was clear. But to what extent? Did the war criminals leave some of their booty behind to be sold by the Church, for how else would the Church, *immediately after the war,* obtain such amounts of raw currency? And if the Vatican had served as a kind of exchange control, had it then forwarded the newly converted funds to Nazi havens, as any agreements with the fugitives must have read? Or had the Church invested that money within Europe, as the cablegrams suggested?

There was one more possibility. Had the Vatican kept for itself that which the Nazis had dropped off on the way and invested it under its own name?

Sabatini put his drink down so quickly that half of it spilled onto his hand. He half ran, half staggered to the bathroom, where he was violently sick.

CHAPTER THREE

Within the confines of the holy Vatican walls, Urban XI, aged seventy-eight, was dying. A small, frail man with a thin, twisted mouth and sharp, sunken eyes, he was succumbing to a disease that knew neither mercy nor cure. Over the last months, his skin had deepened into a sickly yellowish color, contracting around the sharp bones of his face. His public appearances had been reduced to the most important one, the blessing of the Sunday crowds in St. Peter's Square. Private audiences had stopped altogether. Those who still had access to him, the camerlengo, papal chamberlain, and senior members of the Curia, were not fooled by his alertness or quick turn of phrase in discussion. They knew they were speaking to a wasted man, soon to be delivered up to his Maker.

Yet in the whole of the Vatican there was only one person who knew exactly how much time was left to Urban XI. The Pontiff had instructed this man, his personal physician, Dottore Emilio Frenza, to turn a deaf ear on all inquiries, no matter how subtle, on the subject of His Holiness' health. When the moment was at hand, the Pontiff himself would reveal the details to the Curia. But this would not come about until Urban had played his role in arranging a successor of his own choice to the throne, the man who would become the next Vicar of Christ of the Roman Catholic world.

At one thirty in the afternoon of Tuesday, September 17, a thin blue envelope was taken from the morning post and left along with the other unopened letters on the papal writing table. Father Martin Belobraditz thought it would take at least four days for his letter to reach the Pontiff, counting on both the inefficiency of the Italian post office and the huge volume of mail the Pope received daily. However, the intervention of chance did not work in Father Martin's favor. A half hour after he had finished eating a meager lunch, His Holiness was reading the following words.

> I speak with all respect before the Holy Office. When Your Holiness receives this letter, the documents I speak of, the Tetramachus Collection, will have been in my possession for three days. As proof that the Collection has been removed from the Secret Vatican Archives I offer the page containing some of the cablegrams addressed to Monsignor Battista. Your Holiness will doubtless recognize these as being genuine.
>
> The Tetramachus Collection records a shameful period in the history of the Church. It casts a terrible shadow over certain members of the Curia who to this day have neither acknowledged nor repented their crimes. These men still enjoy the privileges bestowed on them by the Holy See. They continue to speak for a faith they themselves have betrayed. They make certain that the chronicles of their past sins remain hidden within holy walls, unknown to the world.
>
> I have watched these men work for the Holy See. I have witnessed their calm manner and the dispatch with which they see to Your Holiness' commands. For a long time I had only the greatest love and

admiration for the devotion of these men. Now I feel nothing but pity for them.

The sins of those spoken of in the Tetramachus Collection, the errors they knowingly committed during the horrors of war, cannot go unpunished. But the Church has been more than reluctant to examine the conduct of these men. Perhaps the Church believes that they in some way helped prevent the destruction of the Faith by their acts and so obeyed the holy directives which said that, above all else, the Church must remain protected and eternal. But at what cost?

I beg to submit that the Rock upon which the Faith is built is not one of falsehood, lies or secrecy but honesty, forthrightness and the dignity of the conscience. Yet the Church has not seen fit to face those who have acted ignominiously in her name, and I have no hope left that she will every carry out such a task. The power of secrecy and silence has proved itself over the ages while confession and repentance, however desirable, have been neglected because, it has been said, such a trial would only strengthen the enemies of the Holy See.

Yet I humbly suggest that the Church, as keeper and protector of the Faith, cannot ignore her duty. The sins brought upon her must be cleansed from her soul and the purveyors of those sins called forth to repent. The passage of time alone will never exculpate them since there are thousands who suffered and died because of their actions. The victims can never be asked to forget the trespasses made against them.

But there is no tribunal within the Church that will dare to summon forth the men of the Tetramachus

Collection. Nor is there any court of law that will try them, for they are protected by the scarlet cap. Therefore, only the conscience of the world, both Catholic and non-Catholic is left to sit in judgment.

When the Tetramachus Collection is revealed to the peoples of all nations, the true verdict will at last be delivered, a verdict not even the sanctity of the Holy See will be able to ignore or move against. On that day of judgment, the faces of those men who directed the activities of the Church in the last war will be shown, and they will be filled with a bitter shame. But what is the shame of a man when put beside justice? And what is justice if not a fundamental pillar of faith?

I understand that my placing the Tetramachus Collection before the eyes of humanity is an irrevocable action. I understand I shall no longer be considered a servant of the Church, or a member of the Faith, or even a human being. But to desist from this act would be cowardice and a betrayal of my conscience. I pray that God have mercy on me in this hour of my choice. I deliver myself into His hands and into the mystery of His love for all men.

The letter was signed in the stiff, nervous hand of Father Martin Belobraditz.

Urban XI read the letter through twice. It was not the first such threat he had received during his years as Pontiff, and normally he would have dismissed it without a thought. But the enclosed page, torn from a folio volume, was one he recognized immediately. He should have since most of the cablegrams sent during spring, 1942, had been addressed to him, Giovanni Cardinal Battista, in his capacity as adviser to Pius XII.

A sharp exclamation mixing surprise, anger and memory passed through the Pontiff's bloodless lips. The sound would be the only show of emotion he would permit himself.

Urban XI had learned his lessons under the tutorship of Pius XII. He was an administrator, not a prophet, martyr or saint. Practical and cosmopolitan, he strove only for the success and development of the Church through the pursuit of its self-interest. Experience had taught him that compromise, cunning and an ability to serve a number of masters, the first of whom was not necessarily God, formed the path on which the Church prospered and remained independent.

"You are the heir of Peter, custodian of the annals of Saint Lawrence, bearer of all that is mysterious and sublime, the hand of God and servant of His will. You are the continuation of two thousand years of a true faith and in your voice shall be found the resonance, the clarity, the honesty and strength of the Truth. . . ."

Thus had written a monk of the eighteenth century on the subject of the papacy. Remembering these lines, Urban XI at once realized that history had sought him out. For the first time since he had boldly and surely taken the power of the Church into his hands he felt them tremble and grow weak.

Amid the ancient tapestries and aging wood frescoes, Urban XI felt the weight of the Church sink slowly on his soul. As a ruthless and capable administrator he wielded absolute authority over every detail of Vatican life. He could break the very men who had elected him; he had the voice to summon national and world leaders before him, and the leaders would listen to him. A conservative who respected dogma and demanded obedience, he watched with complete dispassion as the younger cardinals elected to the Sacred College under the reforms of John died, while men who had brought him to Peter's chair lived on, crusty octogenarians too busy to be bothered by death.

Yet all the authority he possessed was worth nothing because one priest had had the audacity to move against him. Urban XI did not learn, until he once more picked up the blue letter, the meaning of that terrifying loneliness which stands beside those on the pinnacle. He had been challenged and his Church threatened.

Besides himself, the prefect of the Secret Archives and Meyerczuk, there were three other men who knew of the existence of the Tetramachus Collection. Only one of them was in Rome now, the historian Claudio Cardinal Marrenzo. Foucault was in Paris investigating the scandalous demise of a French bishop found dead in a Paris brothel, and Settembrini, the aging doctrinist, was still in the Alta spa. Urban XI saw no need to call these two prelates as yet. Reaching for his ornate telephone, he dialed the number of the prefect of the Court of the Belvedere.

Antonio Cardinal da Silva was taken aback by the papal request. The Pontiff asked him no questions but said only that the prefect should descend into the vault and see if the Tetramachus Collection still lay there. If it was, the prefect should bring it to His Holiness' quarters immediately.

Da Silva hesitated, then answered that the Collection was absent from the shelves since Cardinal Meyerczuk's secretary had called for it yesterday morning and it had not yet been returned. Urban XI ordered the prefect to the papal suites at once.

While Da Silva was hurrying from the Court of the Belvedere to the Vatican Palace, the Pontiff telephoned Rozdentsy Cardinal Meyerczuk. The Polish prelate's apartments were only a few minutes from the papal quarters, and Meyerczuk arrived well before Da Silva.

"Your Holiness," Meyerczuk murmured, stooping to kiss the great seal.

The Pontiff waved him to a chair and passed him Father Martin's letter.

"This arrived in today's mail," he said tonelessly. "Da Silva will be here shortly."

Meyerczuk glanced at the Pope but said nothing. As the cardinal began reading the letter, Urban XI reached for a tiny silver pillbox and discreetly swallowed one tablet. He had already taken three today, and Dottore Frenza had cautioned him on their use. But his chest was aching intolerably, rushing blood to his head. There was little choice.

"Has His Holiness verified the alleged theft?" Meyerczuk asked softly.

"I have. Volume Five is missing from the archives. Da Silva tells me your secretary came to fetch it yesterday morning."

Meyerczuk put the letter back and closed his eyes.

"He may have fetched it, but I did not send him for it," he whispered. "May God help Father Martin!"

"Not only him."

The words came from the doorway where the prefect was standing. Da Silva's eyes caught Meyerczuk's and held them for an instant, and the Polish prelate knew Da Silva was afraid.

''Please show him Belobraditz's letter,'' Urban said, dismissing the traditional bow with a wave of his hand.

The Pontiff would have preferred not to have Da Silva involved in the council, for he thought the prefect a loquacious man who did not understand the full meaning of discretion. But at least now Urban could keep him under the directive of silence.

''The envelope is from my office,'' Meyerczuk said heavily, watching Da Silva read. ''The seals belong to me as well.''

''Have you seen this priest since yesterday?''

''No, Your Holiness. Father Martin has not been in my office since Sunday.''

''Did you not notice his absence?'' Urban asked frostily.

''I did, Your Holiness,'' Meyerczuk answered. ''When Father Martin did not arrive on Monday morning, I sent a servant to his quarters. Father Martin's bed had been slept in, but he was not there. Since my schedule was a heavy one that morning, I dismissed the matter, thinking Father Martin had gone on some errand—although not to notify me was contrary to his practice.

''Yesterday afternoon, when he had not even telephoned me, I made queries within the Vatican. No one had seen him. I waited through the evening and this morning called the infirmary and several hospitals in Rome. No one had taken him in. I was about to discuss the matter with the chief of the civilian security corps when Your Holiness called me.''

''Prefect, how could Father Martin have gained access to the vault of the Court of the Belvedere without some form of introduction?'' Urban demanded at once. ''How was this possible?''

Summoning up the last reserves of calmness, Antonio Cardinal da Silva replied. "It was all too possible, Your Holiness," he said in a dry, distant voice. "Over the past years His Eminence Meyerczuk has been conducting studies into the Catholic Church in Poland since the time of the Russian Revolution. His Eminence has made frequent use of the archives and of the material in the vault. On almost all occasions, Father Martin, as his secretary, was sent to me for particular papers.

"Habit makes one careless, Your Holiness. I was accustomed to seeing Father Martin. I knew him well from what His Eminence told me of him. But I never neglected to make certain Father Martin had come on specific business. Either I telephoned the cardinal or else Father Martin carried a note stating which text was desired. Yet in the last months I grew careless, overlooking the question of confirmation, and Father Martin did not betray this trust, for the books were always returned.

"He never betrayed me," Da Silva finished wearily, "until now."

"And on this occasion you did not ask Father Martin to go to the archives, Rozdentsy?"

"No, Your Holiness, I did not," Meyerczuk repeated. "I had intended to resume my work later in the week."

The Prefect da Silva stared at Meyerczuk in horror. He had never witnessed a cardinal lie so blatantly, or with such eloquence, as Meyerczuk had just now. But Urban XI was concentrating his attention on the Polish prelate and missed the prefect's expression completely.

"Have you any idea why your secretary should have done such a thing?" the Pontiff asked.

Cardinal Meyerczuk folded his large scarred hands before him and looked up.

"Your Holiness, Father Martin, a fellow countryman, came to my office more than ten years ago. His reputation for discipline and faith is well known. As men of God we were bound by a common suffering and the common dream of a liberated homeland. He was a man who had retained his spirit while the flesh had been brutalized and I saw in him a strength tested and true.

"I can only say that during the time he has spent in my service, Father Martin had proved himself a diligent, honest and sensitive man. I have never had cause to suspect him of anything, and so I am at a loss to understand this subversion. It comes as a great and sorrowful revelation."

"Do you know where he would go to hide or to whom he might pass such papers?"

"To the best of my knowledge, Father Martin has not been outside Rome for the last three years," Meyerczuk answered, his great head bowed. "No, Your Holiness, I do not know where he could have gone or whose influence he might seek."

"If we are to believe Father Martin's words, he has nourished the idea of vengeance for quite some time," the Pontiff said. "He also appears a man totally naïve in politics and unacquainted with the position of the Church during the war. On the face of it, his misinterpretation of history is alone what led him to steal the Tetramachus Collection. But what I do not understand is how a man could *hide* such an overwhelming passion from us."

"May God help me, but I cannot answer that," Meyerczuk replied in a hoarse whisper. "I have trusted a man who has worn but a mask of honesty while all the time he was nothing more than a Judas!"

Urban XI rose and, with the aid of his cane, walked

slowly over to the bay windows. His gardens had been stripped of their leaves by the storm, the gravel walks strewn with twigs and debris. He closed his eyes, trying desperately to ignore the fierce pounding around his temples. A few unintelligible words passed through his lips, followed by a thin train of spittle, absently wiped with a lace handkerchief. But beneath the illness and fatigue a mind honed to precision by experience and cunning was quickly putting together the pieces of an intricate plan. Urban XI knew he had to form a defense which would either destroy, discredit or retrieve the papers. Any one of the three solutions was acceptable to him regardless of what the two prelates might think.

He turned back to them.

"Somewhere in the city of Rome is a man who wills grievous injury to this Church, who can destroy its independence and make it a ward of the state. We must find this man before his threat becomes the death knell of the Vatican.

"We must do this to protect not only the Catholic faith but also the names and reputations of those mentioned in the Collection. I am especially concerned for Pius the Twelfth, whose beatification in the Holy Year would never be allowed to proceed should this volume become public knowledge. A man's whole life, his goodness and sanctity, would be reduced to nothing, and he would be denied the glory which is his by right. I, who have dedicated the remaining years of my life to this task, would be deeply grieved if it should not be completed.

"But my concern extends to the living also, including those in this room. The good names of a hundred clerics would be destroyed and hundreds others shamed. And why? Because in the postwar years the Church dedicated herself to aiding helpless refugees of all nations? Was it a crime to extend our hands to those professing the National Socialist creed, beaten men who had been accused of crimes against humanity *with no evidence for such charges?* No, I will not stand by and watch our charity be spat upon. For if charity is an evil, then surely the world is lost!"

Urban XI's hands shook from the passion of his words, the eyes raging and bloodshot as he said, "I seek your advice on a course of action!"

Meyerczuk had listened carefully to Urban's exclamations, relieved that the Pope had not suggested bringing up the theft before the Sacred College of Cardinals. Now he rose to remove this possibility himself.

"I am of the opinion, Your Holiness, that under no circumstances should we publicize either the theft or Father Martin's letter," Meyerczuk said coldly.

"We are agreed on that," Urban replied. "And I have no intention of sharing the secrets of this room with anyone else, not Sandri, the editor of the *Osservatore Romano,* not Volpe, the state secretary, although he will be very indignant, and certainly not with the leader of the Jesuits, Guarducci."

Da Silva expressed no surprise at these words. He knew that when it came to the mechanics of politics, Urban XI and Meyerczuk were cut from the same cloth.

"The reason for this," the Pontiff continued, "is based on the principle of discretion. The potential ramifications of this affair are tremendous. The fewer who know about it, the safer the secret and the easier it will be to deal with matters expediently. If the documents should come to public attention, as Father Martin obviously intends, any inquiries instituted either by the Sacred College, the press or the Italian government will be met with the full authority of the Holy Office. I will personally instruct Volpe and Sandri on a policy of silence at that time."

The Prefect da Silva rose to object.

"But if Your Holiness elects a policy of silence and by doing so makes it impossible to seek the help of the other members of the Curia and civil organizations close to the Holy See, then our options, in terms of action, are limited."

"One should first ask of what help any other advisers would be," Urban rebuked him. "Who among them regarded Father Martin as any more than a simple secretary? Who could say he knows the habits and character of this priest better than Rozdentsy Meyerczuk? Finally, who, in the whole of the Church has had any experience with the kind of problem facing us? I will answer for you, Prefect. None!

"Only if the Church should come under direct attack from the lay authority will I seek the council of the Curia, and I shall *not* seek advice as to how to bring Father Martin and the papers back, but on what the Curia regards to be the political ramifications of a civil investigation.

"Tell me, Prefect, when did Father Martin come for the Tetramachus Collection?"

"Early yesterday morning, shortly after seven o'clock."

"When he left, where did he go?"

"I do not know, Your Holiness. I did not follow him out."

"Does Father Martin have any family in the city?" Urban asked Meyerczuk.

"His family was destroyed in the war, Your Holiness.

Under what circumstances I do not know, for he never mentioned them."

"Do you know of any correspondnece from abroad he might have had?"

"Only that which related to his duties to my office. But Father Martin is loved by Rome's Polish community, Your Holiness. That would appear the logical place to seek refuge."

"No, Father Martin is not the sort of person, from what you have said of him, who would implicate anyone else in his crimes," the Pontiff said grimly. "Nor do I believe he would go where he is well known. Father Martin will pass the Collection to whomever he intends and then go into hiding. He realizes that he himself cannot bring the papers to the attention of the world so he shall choose a powerful intermediary, sympathetic to his views, and watch our misery from his lair!"

"It would seem, then, that our task is twofold," Meyerczuk observed. "Not only are we to retrieve the Collection, but Father Martin must also be brought back."

"That is so," Urban said. "Politically, the Collection is the more important of the two. Words cannot be silenced. But if we recover *only* the Collection, Father Martin remains to speak against us. His accusations would be so detailed that the state would not hesitate to order an immediate inquiry. We have already seen how far the prime minister is prepared to challenge us on the issue of abortion. Father Martin's voice could cause us a great deal of embarrassment at this rather tender time."

Urban XI returned to his chair and stared at his cardinals with pain-filled eyes.

"Neither of you has spoken out against my policy of silence. I will take that to mean you agree—at least until such time as silence obviously no longer suits our design.

"You have also raised no objections to excluding the Curia and the Sacred College from our deliberations as to how best to find both the collection and Father Martin. I am certain you realize the magnitude of your decision to let me proceed as I see fit. In a single stroke you have committed the fate of the Church into my hands alone."

Urban XI paused and ran his tongue over his parched, splintered lips.

"I now ask you to extend this trust even farther. Although I have not held the Tetramachus Collection in my hands for many years, I have not forgotten its contents. They are open to vicious interpretation by men who seek only to further their own careers without consideration for the circumstances under which hard and sometimes terrible decisions were made. But I do not wish to cause senseless anxiety within the Holy See, and so we are compelled to move quickly and with discretion. We must find the perfect method by which the Collection is to be restored to us. We are looking for an agent, someone trusted who is able to enter the right places, whose identity is secure from prying eyes and whose faith binds him to his task."

"Your Holiness, I wish to propose the name of one who I believe has the very qualities Your Holiness seeks."

The speaker was Rozdentsy Meyerczuk, and his voice had a ring of certainty to it. Urban looked in his direction, his lips creasing into a dry smile as he immediately divined the name.

"Say it."

"I am thinking of Father Domingo Martínez," Meyerczuk said.

The Pontiff silently nodded his assent.

"Forgive me, Your Holiness, but I am not familiar with this man." Da Silva spoke up quickly.

Again, the Pope gave Meyerczuk permission to speak.

"Until three years ago, Father Domingo headed the European bureau of the Agenzia Informativa Cattolica," Meyerczuk said. "The agenzia's responsibility is to keep abreast of political and social developments throughout the world and to keep the Holy See informed as to the potential effects of these developments on the Church. Although the agenzia is an open organization, its existence is not generally known or alluded to by those who are aware of it. It carries no official status, nor is it associated with the Secretariat of State.

"Father Domingo retired from the agenzia after twelve years of service. If my memory serves me correctly, he has returned to his native Mexico. This man is one of the few who I believe could bring Father Martin back to us. His face is not known in Rome, yet he is no stranger to the city. Father Domingo has always worked by himself, and perhaps, most important, in the end he has never failed to attain results. The agenzia's link with the Holy See is also tenuous enough to prevent people from making a direct association between the Vatican's interest in Father Martin and Father Domingo's.

"I would agree with His Holiness," Myerczuk finished, "that Father Domingo is the best-qualified person for the task before us."

"He will have to be told most of the details," Da Silva said.

"To a man who has been dealing with sensitive information for so long, one more confidence means nothing," Urban replied. "He will be under the oath of silence and for this matter, it is better to trust one agent of the Holy See than a thousand Jesuits who know nothing of such work.

"So we are agreed on the employment of Father Domingo," the Pontiff said with finality. "In which case I ask you both to leave me now. I will contact this man within the hour. We shall speak again when he arrives. In the meantime, watch for any developments which might arise from the theft. Know that my door is open to you at any hour. If, by the grace of God, there is any word of the Tetramachus Collection or Father Martin, I am to be informed immediately."

The Holy Father held forth his hand, and the two princes of the Church stooped to press their lips to the Ring of the Fisherman. The first council had ended.

Rozdentsy Cardinal Meyerczuk did not speak as he and Da Silva walked outside in the cold windy emptiness of St. Peter's Square. It was only five o'clock, but he noticed that already the buildings were stretching their shadows over the piazza and the stark grayness which had settled over the Vatican would become night. Throwing forward his powerful shoulders, Meyerczuk pushed on into the wind, toward the Court of the Belvedere where he would at last be rid of the prefect.

The Polish prelate did not once look at his companion, but he could feel the questions hanging on Da Silva's lips. Da Silva was badly frightened. He had listened to Meyerczuk lie to the Pontiff about not having sent Father Martin to the archives, and the prefect did not understand why Meyerczuk had done this. The cardinal doubted if Da Silva would ever understand.

"Will this Martínez find him?"

"If he has a little time, yes," Meyerczuk answered.

"What will then become of Father Martin?"

"I cannot say." Meyerczuk shrugged. "Perhaps nothing."

"But if Belobraditz comes before Urban, he will say you had sent him for the Collection and that I knew he was coming."

"Of course, he will say that. And whose words do you think Urban will believe—ours or those of a thief? You worry too much, Antonio. Return to your papers, and all will be well. I shall call you as soon as I hear of Martínez's arrival. Good night."

As he walked toward the direction of his apartments, Rozdentsy Cardinal Meyerczuk realized he had lied once more, for he too was afraid. In the course of his seventy years on this earth the Polish prelate had bled and suffered for his church. Throughout the Roman Catholic world and beyond, his name was synonymous with physical courage and moral fortitude. Yet now, in his hour of need, Meyerczuk found no solace in any of this. Having risen so high he, like the Pontiff, stood naked and alone on the summit.

In 1939, immediately after Hitler's invasion of Poland, Meyerczuk, then Bishop of Warsaw, set about to work out a coexistence plan with the Nazis which would permit the Church to retain at least some of its independence. Berlin reacted quickly and set only one price on continued Church liberty: that Polish clergy, regardless of rank, keep silent on German activities in Poland, a price Meyerczuk was willing to accept. By 1941 the negotiations had produced an agreement, and one year later Meyerczuk was capped with the red hat.

After the "liberation" of Poland by Soviet troops and the fall of Berlin, Cardinal Meyerczuk engaged the Gomulka regime in a bitter struggle which was to last more than ten years and make him a *cause célèbre* in international politics.

During the years 1946-48 nationalist sentiment in Poland was still smoldering, and Meyerczuk became the leader of that large minority which dreamed of a return to a democratic, Catholic Poland. In spring of 1948 the Soviet Security Service, acting under the orders of a nervous Kremlin, tried to silence this voice. At seven o'clock on the evening of June 4, Meyerczuk's house alongside St. Matthew's Cathedral was sprayed by machine-gun fire. The barrage lasted three full minutes, the house absorbing some fifteen hundred rounds of ammunition. Five Catholics visiting the prelate were killed, but Meyerczuk himself was only slightly wounded.

Having failed in its first attempt, the Gomulka government then set an armed cordon around the church for the prelate's "protection." This was the beginning of a siege which was to last two years, during which time Meyerczuk was effectively isolated from all contact with the outside world. The only human beings he saw from June 9, 1948, until the fall of 1950 were his interrogators, who came once a day, every day.

It was a very clever move on the part of the Security Service's psychiatrists to move the psychological battle into Meyerczuk's territory rather than have him build up his strength and reserves in a prison cell. Offering him the temptation of martyrdom had to be avoided at all costs. So at six o'clock each morning the prelate would be awakened by sound trucks parked outside his tiny house, their message uniformly loud and boring. It proclaimed that Meyerczuk's intransigence was causing a deep rift between the Church and Polish people, that the toiling masses of Poland would never tolerate the interference of this priest in their building of a socialist homeland, that Cardinal Meyerczuk had been a traitor and collaborated with the German Gestapo in the extermination of Communist resistance units. Within a few months, Meyerczuk had come to know every accusation by heart. There were seldom any new ones.

To this was added a weekly parade before the closed doors of the cathedral. Trade unionist and factory workers marshaled for the occasion demanded that the cardinal throw his support behind the new regime and end his shameful behavior while schoolchildren chanted, "Down with revisionist clergy!"

Inside his house the Iron Cardinal, as the Western press had named him, suffered in cold and silence. His hope and strength clung to a single rock, that beyond the Warsaw walls the vast machinery of the Roman Catholic Church was working for both his freedom and that of his people, that he was not alone and eventually, like Jonah, he would be delivered from the belly of the Leviathan through God's mercy.

In mid-October of 1950, after the Fast of the Hundred Days, which Meyerczuk had called his refusal to accept food from his torturers, the skeletal figure of a once-proud man was rushed by ambulance to the British embassy. In the end it was not the Church that had come to Meyerczuk's side, but another government. Only at Christmas, when he had regained some of his strength, did the Polish martyr learn that he too could be and had been the object of Church silence.

The Holy See had in no way been responsible for the release of Cardinal Meyerczuk. Beyond two carefully worded notes, Pius XII had not taken any other steps to free his servant, for fear of Kremlin reprisals against the

Church in other parts of Eastern Europe. The Archbishop of Westminister, Dr. Samuel Sutherland, had had no such qualms, and he convinced the British government it would be in their interest to free Meyerczuk by accepting him into the embassy compound.

However, neither Sutherland nor His Majesty's government had counted on the refugee's reaction. On February 17, 1951, on the eve of the anniversary of the Russian Revolution, Rozdentsy Cardinal Meyerczuk held a conference for the Western press in his two-bedroom suite on the third floor of the British embassy, overlooking the Czerniki Gardens.

"I wish to thank, with every ounce of my being, the Holy Roman Church, the Archbishop of Westminster and the British government, for having secured my release. Without their kindness and humanity, I would have surely perished.

"Through the offices of Dr. Samuel Sutherland, I have received word that the Holy Father, Pius XII, has requested my presence in Rome so that I might be better able to pursue my work. I have been assured of safe conduct across Poland by His Majesty's government.

"I have deliberated at great length upon this matter and on what I am about to say now. I beg that my words be shown the same understanding that has heretofore been granted me.

"Because of my position as prelate of Poland, because of the misery, injustice and suffering I have witnessed and experienced in my native land, because of my belief that the true Faith has been stolen from the people of Poland, for these reasons I feel I cannot leave. It is my intention to struggle for the Faith and the freedom to practice that Faith. It is my intention to offer whatever help I can to those who believe in and practice the Roman Catholic rites. If I were to desert those whose prayers supported me in my darkest hours, I would bring shame upon this office and sorrow upon my conscience.

"Here I stand, and I can do no other."

Within twenty-four hours the text of this message was on the front page of every major newspaper in the world. In one blow Cardinal Meyerczuk had done what the mighty Vatican had never been able to achieve: He had placed the eyes and conscience of the world upon this battle between one man and communism, the largest ideological empire in existence. In so doing, the Iron Cardinal neatly undercut everyone around him as well.

The British government was angered and annoyed at what seemed to it a blatant misuse of the sanctuary they had offered. Yet with tremendous support flowing in daily for Meyerczuk, the British ambassador, Sir Frederick Walpole, could hardly have been expected to return the prelate to his tormentors. The Foreign Office told him to wait and see, which he did—for ten years.

Communist reaction was predictable. Gomulka considered Meyerczuk's words an interference in Polish domestic affairs and a clear call for treason. But in Moscow, Stalin was dying, and a power struggle was being waged for the succession within Kremlin walls. Gomulka's threats of reprisals had no teeth to them, and the British, supported by the Americans, blithely ignored them.

But it was the Vatican that suffered most from Meyerczuk's action. Pius XII did not miss the prelate's reference to another great Church rebel, Martin Luther, and His Holiness took this as it had been meant: a personal insult. But the Vatican could not discount that Meyerczuk had made himself an international figure, his prominence in the Catholic world being second only to that of the Pontiff himself. There was no way to move against him.

After the announcement Rozdentsy Cardinal Meyerczuk retreated to his two rooms, removing himself as much as possible from the workings of the embassy. Those who came to visit him out of personal interest were greeted warmly; others, such as the papal nuncio, Monsignor Giovanni Meliore, the prelate treated with deference and icy politeness. He listened to the nuncio's argument in which Pius XII strongly questioned the worth of Meyerczuk's opposition to the Polish regime, but never did he permit it to permeate his resolution. There was no one in the world to change Meyerczuk's decision because no one could soften the great and unyielding bitterness upon which it was founded.

But as the cold war died, the British had finally been able to make him feel uncomfortable. The East German uprising and the short-lived Hungarian revolt had taught Meyerczuk that all politics is convenience since the West, tired of bloodshed, would never intervene to support the dream of democracy in Eastern Europe. His work in Poland was becoming more and more circumscribed as, on the one hand, the British sought to make amends with Khrushchev and Gomulka, and on the other, Pius XII further angered the Communist bloc by issuing a decree threatening excommunication for those Italians who dared vote for the party in national elections.

In April, 1961, the Iron Cardinal's vigil was over. On a gentle but firm directive from John XXIII, he left Poland, knowing he had failed to bring liberty to his country, realizing he would never be buried in his native soil. Many years had passed since he had come to the Vatican.

Rozdentsy Cardinal Meyerczuk entered his apartment

and, moving through the darkness, went out onto the balcony. The lamps along the pathways below had been lit and by the side of St. Peter's great floodlamps shone on the basilica, wrapping it in a cold yellow radiance. Over these last few months, Rozdentsy Meyerczuk had found himself thinking more and more about his long and tortuous road he had traveled, suffering in memory those moments he had suffered in life. None of this agony was recorded in the Tetramachus Collection. The letters and cablegrams he had sent in the course of the war never spoke of his own bravery and sacrifice. They had not concerned him then. Only the arrangements made with the German Kommandantur had been important in 1940 and 1941.

Cardinal Meyerczuk pressed his forehead against his two tightly closed fists and squeezed his eyes shut. He could see himself standing before the short, hollow-cheeked Bronitz, presenting him with a list of names that meant the Church's protection. The list had been obtained by the Polish nationalist underground. The names on it belonged to members of the rival Communist partisan groups. The price of Church liberty had been the condemnation to death of Polish Communists, fellow countrymen, fellow human beings.

Bronitz had examined the piece of paper and, when he was satisfied with the information, signed a statement to the effect that all Roman Catholic property in Poland was to be respected by German soldiers. He had even thanked the prelate for his cooperation since it saved the overburdened Gestapo a good deal of time and trouble.

Decades had passed since those few moments in Bronitz's office. Had history deemed otherwise, perhaps they would have remained buried forever. But when it became known that Urban XI was dying, Rome had quietly begun to search for his successor. It surprised no one that the name of Rozdentsy Meyerczuk was heard again and again in the conversation of the Curia.

The Polish prelate had done nothing to dissuade supporters of his candidacy. He felt both able and deserving of Peter's chair, for he had served it faithfully and understood the responsibilities it carried. But he also knew that if he achieved the vote of the Sacred College, he would move from the shadows of Church acitivity into the brilliant light of the papacy. He would be able to hide nothing.

That is why in the course of the summer, Meyerczuk had read all seven volumes of the Activities of the Holy See in the Second World War, and Volume Five, the Tetramachus Collection, three times over. In the Collection he had found his own words, the words that had contributed to the survival of the Roman Church in Poland, condemning him. The first time he had looked at the cablegrams he could scarcely believe they had been born of his hand. Yet as he reread them, he could not sustain even the slightest doubt. He had spoken, and so it had been recorded for all eternity.

In the days that followed he had sent his crippled secretary, Father Martin Belobraditz, to the archives at least once a week. At the end of his search, the Iron Cardinal knew more than perhaps any other cleric of the shame and ignominy that rested on the Church for its actions between 1934 and 1950. He could have destroyed three-quarters of the Curia with the information that was held within the black vault, but he could not find even a few lines from all the thousands of pages which might save him. On the contrary, if those words were ever discovered, he himself would perish.

So the Tetramachus Collection stayed on his desk for many nights. He would return it to the prefect only to send Father Martin for it a day or two later.

Father Martin . . . whom he had trusted so blindly because he could think of little else but the cablegrams. Whom he used as a messenger never thinking that the messenger might become curious, that he might chance to glance at the Collection, even to read it.

And he had read it. All of it. Perhaps as many times as Meyerczuk himself. That was the only way in which Father Martin could have known that the cardinal was stained by a shameful secret and, if revealed, would cast him from the proud tower he dwelled in.

But why reveal it now? What had he done to this priest that he merited such hatred? They were countrymen, common survivors, dedicated to the glory and eternal life of the Church. They were the same, the same, the same!

"But somewhere," he thought, "somewhere, we are *different!* I saw in him a kindred spirit, and I was deceived, perhaps the day I took him in or maybe even yesterday. And his hatred for me must be great, for he did not choose to make me suffer first by coming for money or demanding my resignation. No, he wants only to destroy me, to purge all those who worked to save the Church from the abyss of destruction!

"And I will discover his reasons. I will search out his history until I know him better than he does himself. Then I will at least understand!

"May God have mercy on my pitiful soul!" Meyerczuk

whispered. "I have sinned, but I will not be destroyed!"

Out of shame and anger the cold gray eyes of the Iron Cardinal let loose their tears, and along the empty galleries there echoed the wretched sobbing of a man who knew he had fallen beyond the light of his Lord.

CHAPTER FOUR

On Tuesday, September 17, Alfredo Sabatini worked only a half day.

After he had dispatched three of his senior assistants on the various research projects, the publisher closeted himself in his office, seeing no one but Pia and leaving only one line open, that for the priest. For two hours he devoted himself to the text of his press conference, arranged by Pia for five o'clock the same afternoon.

Punctually at noon, Sabatini left the office, carrying a fat package under his arm. His car was waiting for him in front of the Unita building, the engine running. In forty minutes the publisher had arrived at his flat on the Via Tasso, just as his housekeeper had put soup on the table for Sabatini's chauffeur.

The housekeeper had not expected Sabatini. Because of the irregular hours he kept, she almost never saw him. Sabatini pleaded lack of appetite to her insistence that he too eat, but asked her to have something ready for him this evening.

Sabatini left the housekeeper and chauffeur to each other and quietly withdrew from the apartment, taking an elevator to the underground garage.

Last night he had brought the Tetramachus Collection and the copy Pia had made of it home with him. Giuseppe, his bodyguard, had slept on the couch. Now the original was back in the safe with Giuseppe sitting in Sabatini's chair, his hand never too far from his revolver.

Sabatini walked quickly among the concrete pillars, looking carefully for anyone else who might be about. But the garage was deserted. He stopped behind his Bentley and opened the trunk, removing the tool kit from behind the spare tire. He climbed into the backseat and set to work.

Sabatini had thought long and hard about where to put the photostat of the Collection and had settled on his car. The Bentley was a machine that attracted attention wherever it stood. It was well enough known in the area of his offices and was so prominent that no one would think twice it might be used as a cache—which was why Sabatini had chosen it for that very purpose.

Kneeling on the cold cement floor, the rear left door open, Sabatini unscrewed the three pins which held the bottom of the seat to the back. Then he did the same on the right side. Stepping inside the car, he took hold of the seat by the bottom, dead center, and pulled. The dry metal runner held the bearings for an instant and reluctantly gave way. There was nothing under the seat save dust and two English pennies.

Sabatini reached over into the front seat and brought out the copy, neatly divided into three sections, each one carefully wrapped in heavy plastic. He placed them down lengthwise, making certain that the seat could slide over them without difficulty. He pushed the seat in, brushing out the dirt that had fallen onto the carpet and reset the screws on both sides. Finally, he replaced the tool box exactly where he had found it so that nothing would be out of place and locked up the car. When he returned to the apartment, Alberto was finishing a sardine sandwich under the watchful eye of the *matrona.*

"Ah, signor!"

Alberto bolted to his feet, leaving half a sandwich uneaten.

"I was to remind you before. The car is to be taken to the garage on Thursday, late in the morning. It needs an oil change and new spark plugs. The work will only take about an hour. Is that all right?"

"Thursday . . ." Sabatini murmured. Inwardly he was cursing himself. Alberto had mentioned the garage appointment last week. Now that the copy was inside the Bentley Sabatini had no wish for the car to be examined by anyone, not even during a tune-up. Chances of the mechanic's finding the Tetramachus Collection were infinitesimal, but there was no reason to ask for trouble. Then he remembered that on Thursday he was to see his banker, Saghi. The luncheon was their informal biannual meeting during which Sabatini was given a brief résumé of additions to his portfolio and some off-the-record advice concerning new investments. Sabatini thought it would be a very good idea to go over his holdings and set aside those that were readily convertible into cash. Money might be needed quickly, for publicity or legal counsel, if the Vatican demanded the Collection's return. As for the car, he could have done without it save for one consideration: Oftentimes his talks with Saghi demanded the utmost privacy. The Bentley served as a mobile conference room.

"No, Thursday is no good," Sabatini said at last. "I have to meet Saghi for lunch. It is traditional for us to take drinks at the Trattoria Romana, punctually at noon. Have the garage make another arrangement."

"Very well, signor."

"Now you will finish your sandwich." The *matrona* glowered. "We do not waste food in this house!"

When Sabatini arrived back at the office, Pia told him

that Father Martin hadn't called. As for the press meeting, technicians were already in the conference room, arranging the light and power lines for the cameras. Also the prime minister had phoned and requested that Sabatini get back to him as soon as possible.

"There is still no word from the Vatican?" Sabatini asked.

"Nothing," Pia replied. "And your research teams are coming back empty-handed. It seems there isn't very much in Rome on the subject of the Church during the war."

"It was worth the try." Sabatini shrugged. "Have you confirmed the airlines reservations?"

"I leave about two hours after your conference."

"Then we have only to wait."

"What if you don't hear from Father Martin?" Pia asked. "Would you still go ahead with the conference?"

"Because the Vatican has said nothing does not necessarily mean it has remained idle," Sabatini said shortly. "I do not know where Father Martin is or even if he is still alive. Should I not hear from him, it would be fair to assume he might have met with, ah, some sort of accident."

"Are you suggesting the Church would deliberately hurt him?" Pia cried.

"Is that such a shocking idea to entertain?" Sabatini demanded. "You might remember that in the mid-thirteenth century Innocent the Third made torture an integral part of the legal machinery to be used in cases of suspected heresy."

"What about Fransci?" Pia asked quickly. "Will you at least tell *him* what is going to happen?"

"My friend the prime minister will learn of the Tetramachus Collection at the same time as everyone else," Sabatini said. "When I say that neither he nor his government was in any way involved with me as far as the procuring of the collection is concerned, I want to say this with a clear conscience. Speaking of this, how *did* Fransci get word of the conference?"

"I suppose one of the editors I called later telephoned him, on the chance of picking up more details. Fransci's speech last night was beautifully delivered. I think he stands a good chance of getting that referendum."

"Perhaps he will even be guaranteed the results," Sabatini remarked thoughtfully.

Pia turned to leave but stopped at once.

"What have you done with the copy?" she asked.

He looked at her sharply. "Don't ever mention a copy!" he warned her. "The walls will be growing ears soon. It's in my car, under the rear seat. I hope there will never be a cause for you to go looking for it."

Sabatini returned to his office to catch up on work that was most pressing. As the afternoon wore on, his assistants filtered in from the field, their notebooks empty of the references he had asked them to unearth. If there were documents in Rome which could shed light on the Tetramachus Collection, it would require more than a day's work to ferret them out.

At four o'clock, the same time as Urban XI ended his council with the cardinals da Silva and Meyerczuk, the call from Father Martin came. The publisher picked up the receiver at once.

"Yes?"

"Signor Sabatini?"

"This is Sabatini." He recognized the voice as that of Father Martin and switched on the tape deck whose microphone was taped to the side of the receiver listening unit.

"This is Father Martin," the voice said softly. "Is there anyone listening to our conversation?"

"No one. But I am recording it."

"I have no objection."

"Father Martin, can you tell me why page 622 was missing from the original manuscript?" Sabatini asked at once. He had to be absolutely certain of the caller's identity.

"I appreciate your discretion, signor," the disembodied voice said. "It is not page 622 but 498 that is missing from the Tetramachus Collection."

"I am sorry, Father, but we cannot take chances."

"I understand. Have you decided to accept the manuscript for publication?"

"I have. I am holding a press conference this afternoon on the subject of the Tetramachus Collection."

"I leave the Collection in your hands, signor. My part has been done. I ask you only not to publicize my name."

"You have my word," Sabatini said tightly. "But is there anything else I may do for you? Do you need a place to stay or money?"

"I am quite comfortable where I am at present," the voice said. "I wish to be left in peace."

"Do you want to tell me where you are, should it be necessary for us to meet once more?"

"If I tell you, signor, then one day you might be obliged by law to reveal my whereabouts. I do not wish to lie to you, so no, I will not tell you where I can be found."

"There are also other factors to consider," Sabatini countered, "such as any monies accruing from publication and—"

"Signor Sabatini," the voice broke in, tired, yet patient. "You said you will publish this volume of cablegrams and letters. That is all I desired. I do not wish to profit from past sins of the Church. I have given thought to the money you mention, but I think you understand why the institutions I would want to give it to—the Catholic institutions in Poland—would never accept it. So I leave it for you to deal with. I ask only that, if accepted or given anonymously, it go toward helping the poor in some way, hospitals or various clinics. You understand what I am saying?"

"I do," Sabatini murmured.

"Then I leave you for the time being," the voice said gently. "I shall pray for you, signor, because yours is the difficult task now, far more difficult than mine ever was. The absence of the Tetramachus Collection from the archives is too important a matter for the Church to ignore. Doubtless you will be hearing from the Holy See shortly. I will call again. Good night."

Sabatini punched a button on the tape deck and stared at the silent receiver. He would still protect Father Martin, if only a little. This press conference would deflect the Vatican's attention from the thief of the Collection onto the current holder. In this way, Father Martin might at least gain a little time for the peace he sought for himself.

They all were waiting for him in the conference room, forty journalists who constituted the elite of both the Italian and foreign press. Sabatini greeted most of them as he made his way through cable wires and recording equipment to the small podium at the end of the room. Surveying his audience, he made a mental note to compliment Pia on having produced such excellent arrangements on short notice. The men before him had both the experience to recognize an important story and the influence to give it the widest possible coverage.

Sabatini straightened his papers before him, and the conversation drifted away, the camera lights coming on.

"Gentlemen! Today I wish to speak to you on a subject we are all familiar with, which is written about daily and which we contemplate either with passion or stoicism. I am talking about social justice.

"It is an unwieldy subject, uncomfortable for some, a major concern for others, but it is one none of us can turn away from. Within our society there are millions of people who are nothing less than victims—of poverty, ignorance, greed and malice. We who find this abhorrent have gone forward and presented laws to protect those who cannot protect themselves. We have exposed those whose actions make them enemies not only of individuals they have wronged but of mankind. Yet as much as has been done, so much more remains. However, I believe we are on the threshhold of taking a great step forward in the establishment of a new humanity, a new social contract within our society that will have ramifications not only for Italy but for the entire world.

"I have in my possession a set of papers that are at best ignoble and shameful. These documents speak of treason against the human spirit, and they are evidence of treasonable activity toward the state.

"Had this material been born of a government alone, its value, though still great, would have been diminished. Had these records been the property of an industrial concern, then public opinion would forget them in two days. Our cynicism in such matters is a lazy one, for there is no lack of scandals.

"But these documents belong to both a corporation *and*

a government. Their contents speak of slyness, cowardice, corruption and contempt. For more than thirty years they have been hidden from us, mocking our ignorance from their sanctuary. But no longer! Soon the whole world will know of this shame, and then by the strength of our outrage we shall remedy that shame and be done with it.

"From this podium I accuse the Vatican authority, its officers and the Pontiff himself of hypocrisy which has cheated the faith and efforts of toiling millions, those simple people on whom the Church has feasted and grown fat.

"I accuse the Vatican government of having entered into ignominious treaties with the Nazi regime in 1938 which guaranteed that the Church would refrain from speaking out against the growth of the Hitlerian cancer and through which the Church's survival was assured.

"I accuse the Vatican of perfidy, of systematically betraying helpless people caught in that insane nightmare of occupied Europe, where the Church, with few notable exceptions, stood by and watched the slaughter. Its only concern was that the Holy See should remain untouched, and for that it was willing to pay the price of a shameful silence!

"I accuse Vatican institutions—monasteries, nunneries, religious orders—of shielding known criminals, offering sanctuary to butchers fleeing from justice, providing them with new identities and opening Church channels through which these monsters, for they were little else, might escape.

"I accuse the Roman Catholic Church, in the postwar years, of profiteering in the grossest manner, by engaging speculators and financiers of dubious reputation to invest money whose origins the Church was not interested to know about. In the almost thirty years between the end of the war and the present day, the Church has gleaned some seven hundred billion lire for itself. Yet in 1945 it was supposedly as poor as the state in which it lived.

"Before this year is out, on the eve of the Holy Year, I shall publish evidence, written in the Church's own hand, concerning its wartime activity and postwar financial dealings, the latter including the *sources* of the funds invested by the Holy See. The evidence was brought to me by a man of God, a priest whose conscience refused to bend any further. Having read these papers, he realized that if he spoke out, he would be silenced, for where silence is a policy by necessity, all things may be done to preserve it. So this man chose the only way left. He brought the documents outside the Church, where the people might judge them.

"If the Roman Catholic Church has any answer, let it speak. But be warned! Do not lie, for your lies will in the end only bury you more deeply. And do not threaten, for your threats are hollow. The words in Volume Five of the Activities of the Holy See During the Second World War, the so-called Tetramachus Collection, speak for themselves!

"Justice will be done!"

Sabatini gazed fiercely into the glare of the lights and stepped back from the podium as bedlam exploded in the room.

"Signor Sabatini, *when* did you receive these papers?" *Espresso*

"I'm sorry, I cannot tell you that."

"Signor Sabatini, was the Vatican at all aware that you had these papers?" Reuters

"If so, the Holy See has not made any comment."

"Are you in effect challenging the Vatican to open its account books to a governmental inquiry?" United Press International

"That is part of it, yes. But what interests me most is for the Vatican to explain how certain funds entered its treasury through the organization called Caritas."

"Signor Sabatini, who is the man responsible—" *Corriere*

"That is strictly confidential!"

"Has the Socialist Party been privy to these documents?" Reuters

"I wish to state categorically that *no one* outside this office, no political figure from any party, knew either that the papers were in my possession or that they would be the subject of tonight's press meeting."

"Signor Sabatini, what effect do you think this will have on the entente cordiale between the Vatican and Signor Fransci's government?" *Espresso*

"You had better ask the prime minister that question. And please remember that it *was not* the present government that established this entente."

"Will this material have any effect on the Church's Holy Year program?" *Corriere*

"That you had better ask His Holiness!"

"Signor Sabatini, might any of this material be relevant to the establishment of a new war crimes tribunal either here in Italy or in Bonn?" Tass

"I doubt this very much. As I stated, the Church was never *directly* involved in criminal offenses committed between 1939 and 1945. It was a silent onlooker. However, an inquiry commission might be established if the Italian procurator-general feels there is sufficient cause to warrant an investigation into the actions of individual clergy both in Italy and in Occupied Europe."

"Signor Sabatini, why do you bear such malice toward the Holy Roman Church? What has she done that has been so terrible as to make you want to malign her?"

The speaker was the diminutive gray-haired Emilio Sandri, editor of the Vatican newspaper, the *Osservatore Romano.* His words were softly spoken, for he was sitting in the front row, but they brought a hush over the heated, noisy room.

Sabatini leaned over the edge of the podium and stared directly at him, his black eyes glittering.

"You are wrong, Signor Sandri," he said quietly, the tone honed to a precise edge. "I do not bear a personal grudge toward the Church. But I do believe that if the Church can choose to interfere in the workings of a state—it did this, did it not, in 1949—when Pius the Twelfth excommunicated communist voters, then it is not above scrutiny from the public.

"I do not believe that I or anyone else can destroy a faith, and certainly that is not my intention. But we can bring light on actions that were committed on behalf of that faith and ask ourselves whether such deeds were in keeping with the teachings and practices of that faith.

"While the Church has not refrained from interfering in other people's affairs, it has jealously guarded its own business. No one is supposed to ask the Vatican to explain anything, for it is a sovereign state. Ah, signor, such a conception of the Holy See is, I think, well out of date. If the Church has in fact nothing to hide, then this conference will show me to be nothing more than a sensationalist-hungry fool. The Vatican can take me to court for statements I have uttered. But will it? That is the question, Signor Sandri. If by tomorrow morning I do not receive word that libel action has been instituted against myself and my firm, we shall all know that what I have said here tonight has been the truth!''

Pia was waiting for him when Sabatini came into his office, tugging at his necktie.

''I thought you were supposed to be doling out the press releases,'' he said.

''I gave them to the receptionist.'' She rose and came over to him, helping him with his jacket.

''You're soaking wet,'' she murmured, feeling the back of his shirt.

''Nerves!'' Sabatini laughed shortly. ''Well, what do you think—did we light a fire under them?''

''Without a doubt,'' Pia said quietly. ''I listened in on the intercom. By tomorrow every newspaper in Europe will be preparing for the coming bloodbath.''

''You don't approve of the way I handled it?'' Sabatini asked coolly.

''I think I prefer it when you use the lancet,'' Pia said. ''This time you went in swinging a double-edged ax.''

''I'm sorry you thought my methods excessive,'' Sabatini replied with calculated politeness. ''However, it is done, and now we shall continue.''

Pia looked up at his hard, distant gaze and felt a sheet of ice descend between them. He was so very good at this, closing himself off from everyone and everything by a curtain of cold formality.

''No one else saw it, Alfredo,'' she murmured. ''As far as they were concerned, it was Sabatini, passionate, yet precise, champion of justice and freedom, pointing his sword at yet another dragon. Everyone loved it because you have never disappointed them. No, no one except Sandri saw your cruelty, your desire for some sort of vengeance."

"I'm too tired for riddles, Pia!" Sabatini snapped impatiently. "What is it you want from me?"

"I want you to understand what you are doing." Pia's lips trembled. She blinked her eyes rapidly to hold back the tears.

"I'm all right, really . . . I'm sorry," she whispered.

Sabatini cursed softly and went over to the liquor cabinet.

"When I was listening to your speech, I felt I was hearing a total stranger—one who had no love, no feeling, nothing left inside him except a desire to break open something millions consider sacred. Have you ever considered what you will be doing to those who believe, who need to believe? You shall destroy the one thing they can still look up to. Is your justice worth that much to you that you are ready to trample over something as meaningful and sacred as a man's faith?

"When these papers first arrived, I never realized they would lead to this," Pia continued, shaking her head slowly. "But now, Alfredo, I see you are only out for blood. You want the Vatican to squirm a little before you finally release the collection. Why do you insist on being so cruel?"

Alfredo Sabatini stirred his whiskey with his finger and sat down, letting his body sink into the soft leather piles of the chair. He closed his eyes to stave off an onrushing headache. She was right. He knew and was willing to admit it. But that changed nothing. The first attack had to be strong, going to the heart, so that whoever answered would be afraid, nervous or overly cautious. The Vatican had been caught off-balance, and the longer the Holy See took over its decision on how to answer him, the more time Sabatini would have to prepare the manuscript for the presses.

"What are you afraid of, Pia?" Sabatini asked softly, his eyes still closed. "Did you think I would walk in with clasped hands and bowed head and apologize for the fact that some priest, obviously deranged, had passed me these scandalous papers? You knew I would not mince words, not when I have the Collection which proves everything I say. So what is it you're afraid of, *really*?" he repeated.

"You—and what you're doing to yourself."

"Have you packed a bag?"

"Yes, I brought it with me."

"So you are still willing to go to Paris?"

"Of course."

"In spite of what you've said?"

"In spite of that."

"That makes you a hypocrite, doesn't it?" Sabatini said tenderly, feeling her wince.

"There are things I must do and can do no other way," Pia said dully. "At least I know what I am doing them for."

Sabatini raised his hand in a gesture of "touché" and pressed a button on the intercom.

"Have Giuseppe come in," he asked the receptionist. "And call for a taxi.

"Giuseppe will take you out to the airport," Sabatini said, turning to Pia. "Someone from the press might be tempted to follow us if we use my car."

"What about you?" Pia asked.

Sabatini rose and went over to a landscape painting,

which he removed from the wall. He opened the false panel, revealing a small stainless steel circular door. When he opened it, Pia saw a tape recording spool, a slim bundle of banknotes and something wrapped in a velvet cloth, all lying on the red leather cover of the Tetramachus Collection. Sabatini removed the collection and the object in velvet.

"Arrange the volume nicely in your bag—preferably under some of that scanty underwear you favor. Customs don't have any reason to present you with problems. One look at your lingerie, and they will have even less. But should you have any difficulties, call me here at once."

"You plan to spend the night in the office?"

Sabatini nodded and threw off the velvet cover revealing a Magnum revolver.

"And this is for any unexpected visitors."

The camerlengo, the papal chamberlain, entered the massive bedroom of Urban XI at eight o'clock, September 17, and in hushed tones informed His Holiness of Alfredo Sabatini's statement to the press. The Pontiff, who was awake but resting in his bed, listened to him and asked that a transcript of the speech be brought to him. He further instructed the camerlengo not to take any calls for the rest of the evening or to permit anxious clerics to intrude on the Pontiff's privacy at this time. This last order held even for senior members of the Curia. The one man Urban XI did want to see was Claudio Cardinal Marrenzo, and he was to be sent for at once.

Claudio Cardinal Marrenzo was one of the few princes of the Church who had no reputation to speak of. For thirty years he had served the Church in the Dolomite Mountains, overlooking schools, orphanages and monasteries while he continued to write his monumental histories. In 1962 his scholastic work came to the attention of John XXIII, who called Marrenzo to the Vatican. Bestowing on him the red cap, the former Pontiff gave Marrenzo access to all documents within the Court of the Belvedere so that Marrenzo might complete a definitive history of the Church in the age of the Renaissance. Thus, Marrenzo became a leading authority on Vatican papers and through his work built up a network of contacts with libraries and publishers around the world.

When Cardinal Marrenzo was shown into the papal chambers, Urban XI was sitting in his ancient velvet-lined chair, a soft blanket over his knees. The historian came up, bowed and pressed his lips to the great seal.

"You have heard the accusation leveled at the Holy See by the publisher Sabatini," Urban XI said without preamble.

"I have, Your Holiness," Marrenzo answered, his voice low and gentle. "I was dining with colleagues when a servant ran in with the news."

"What was the reaction of those at the table?" Urban inquired.

"Surprise and outrage," Marrenzo said. "A little fear, too, I thought."

"I would have been amazed had fear been absent," Urban remarked dryly. "There is good reason for it."

Urban cast a shrewd glance at Marrenzo. He had done right to keep the historian from the council held with Da Silva and Meyerczuk, for Marrenzo, unlike others, did not use politics to veil his words. He was an honest man.

"Before we proceed with our discussion," the Pontiff said, "let me tell you that Sabatini was speaking the truth. Volume Five, the Tetramachus Collection, is missing from the Secret Archives and the man responsible for the theft is a priest, Father Martin Belobraditz, secretary to Meyerczuk."

"Oh, my dear God!" Marrenzo cried out softly. "Forgive me, Your Holiness, but I believe there still existed hope, at least among those at the table tonight, that Sabatini was engaging in some horrible fraud. After all, there is nothing on record that he presented the Collection at the conference."

"From your own experience, Claudio, would you consider Sabatini the kind of man to court libel and censure?"

"Sabatini is very prudent, Your Holiness. It would be completely out of character for him to speak without foundation to his words."

"And he has not spoken rashly," Urban said. "Father Martin is nowhere to be found. He sent this letter to me."

The Pontiff passed Marrenzo the Polish priest's letter and the page that had been torn away from the Tetramachus Collection. The historian read it through slowly, his face draining of color.

"I think you understand our predicament," Urban said. "The priest has made good his threat. He could not have used a better instrument to carry out his revenge than this Church-hating publisher."

"Your Holiness has honored me by sharing his thoughts with me," Marrenzo murmured. "But I do not understand why this should be."

The Pontiff held up his hand to silence the prelate's protest.

"My reasons are simple," Urban said. "I seek your advice as to how Holy See shall reply to this infamy.

"You understand, Claudio," the Pontiff continued, "you are untainted by the Collection of any other documents held by the Church. I know this, for I have intimate knowledge of the Holy See's activities during and after the war. But Cardinal Meyerczuk will not survive the contents of the Tetramachus Collection, nor will some of my other advisers. Therefore, I seek counsel from you, a man who stands apart from the Curia, who will advise me without fear for his own position or future.

"I also tell you that I do not consider the men spoken of in the Tetramachus Collection evil. They acted with charity and compassion, yet our enemies will use our benevolence against us and attempt to turn our deeds into sins. But I will not abandon these princes of the Church. Always remember this!"

"I understand, Your Holiness," Marrenzo said.

"Very well," Urban said. "This afternoon, after receipt of this letter, I summoned cardinals da Silva and Meyerczuk to my offices. The theft was verified, and at that time we assumed Father Martin to be in possession of the Collection. I instructed both prelates to remain silent in the hope that the secretary might be found before he passed on the papers. It was agreed we would use the services of Father Domingo Martínez, formerly of the Agenzia Informativa Cattolica. Are you familiar with this organization?"

"I am, Your Holiness."

"This evening a communiqué was to be sent to Father Domingo in Mexico. I have already drafted it, but before it is issued, I ask for your opinion: Is Father Domingo the right man to bring both Father Martin and the Collection back to us?"

The historian considered the question carefully before offering his answer.

"Had Father Martin not given the documents to Sabatini, then I would have agreed to the summoning of Father Domingo. But as the matter stands now, I do not see what value a clerical investigator would be. Father Domingo could not influence Sabatini in any way. Furthermore, his association with the Church and indirectly with the Holy Office would show Sabatini how anxious we are to retrieve the Collection. If the Church remains silent but sends an envoy to Sabatini, he will not hesitate to use Father Domingo's investigation as proof that the Holy See intends to recover the papers, even by surreptitious means.

"Therefore, Your Holiness, I would advise against sending a cleric into Sabatini's territory," Claudio Marrenzo concluded.

"Your argument is well taken," Urban said. "It shows me I did not err in holding the communiqué. We are also in agreement on the potential danger of using someone such as Father Domingo. What, then, are the alternatives open to us?"

"A third party is needed," Marrenzo said softly. "An agency with no connection to the Church, one which has resources and experience in investigative matters. Not only would such a body be able to approach Sabatini to negotiate a possible release of the papers, but it would also find Father Martin, whose return, I venture to assume, His Holiness still desires."

"I do," Urban said. "But I thought Father Domingo would have been able to take charge of that."

"I respectfully suggest that if one is to employ an outside group, there is no need for Father Domingo," Marrenzo said.

"Then you must have in mind the name of such a group," Urban said.

"I do, Your Holiness. It is—"

"The particulars of it are of no interest to me," Urban interrupted him. "I need only to know if this organization is based in Rome and, if so, what its politics are."

"It is not located in Italy at all, Your Holiness, and to the best of my knowledge it has no politics save those based on money. I also know it has served several prominent Romans very well in areas where absolute secrecy was required."

"But will you yourself speak for the integrity of these people, who can be bought by the highest bidder?"

"I am aware that Your Holiness is reluctant to put faith in mercenaries," Marrenzo said. "But this group is more than a band of soldiers of fortune. It has, I have been told, contacts in the very highest levels of the Italian government and in other European parliaments. In Italy those who have employed it have always spoken highly of the organization, both of its methods and results. Needless to say, Your Holiness, men who employ such a group are liable to blackmail, but this has never, never come about."

"For one so apparently removed from such affairs you are very well informed," the Pontiff said mildly.

"I am confessor to Simone Cliotia, the car magnate. His son is my secretary. It was Signor Cliotia who was obliged to use the organization I speak of."

The Pontiff nodded and motioned for Marrenzo to rise.

"I hereby charge you with the duty of seeing that the Tetramachus Collection is returned to the Secret Archives. You have my permission to seek help from any quarter you think is effective and trustworthy. You may go to any person or organization so long as it is not associated with any political faction here in Italy. Furthermore, no link may be established between your instrument and the Holy See. The only other condition I place on your final choice is one of secrecy."

"Then Your Holiness is permitting me to break the silence imposed on cardinals da Silva and Meyerczuk and, I assume, the rest of the Church?"

"I am. Because if we wait, we will have waited too long."

"How much am I permitted to say about the Collection itself?"

"Sabatini has already said it for all of us. But be certain no copy is kept by those whom you employ."

"Sabatini has probably made a copy already," Marrenzo said.

"That may be. But it does not carry the authenticity of an original, and Sabatini's entire accusation rests on the fact that he has the *true* papers. But if another group should copy the Collection, then one day it may come to us threatening to disclose its association with us. We can, I think, refute one copy, but not two. Remember, those you go to may have proved themselves honest in the past, but there comes a time when one is tempted into betrayal."

"I understand, Your Holiness, and I shall make certain no photostat exists save the one Sabatini has, in all likelihood, made. Perhaps we might even obtain that."

"You understand, Claudio, that no one within the Curia or the Holy See is to know of our conversation tonight," Urban said. "This directive extends even unto Meyerczuk and Da Silva. You will not say anything to them and report the results of your investigation only to me."

"Very well, Your Holiness."

"Then go, and may God guide you!"

As he watched the historian take his leave, Urban XI

doubted if he would live to see the return of the Tetramachus Collection. He wished God had given him a little more time so that he might die with his work complete, the succession decided.

Before this day had dawned, Urban XI believed he would die as he had lived, a proud, powerful man who answered only to God and whose reputation would be preserved for all posterity. He wondered what God would say to him now or if He would even listen to him. Yet there was little choice. Even as he sent Marrenzo on his task, Urban knew that the time had come for him to test the mettle of his faith, and there was only God to help him, if He would, now.

Claudio Marrenzo left the papal suites, shaken by the authority that had been given him by the Holy Father. He eschewed glances cast in his direction from the prelates gathered in the antechamber of the Pope's quarters but caught a glimpse of the camerlengo patiently explaining that His Holiness would be seeing no one tonight. The papal chamberlain had his work set out for him. The telephone in his office would not stop ringing all night.

Marrenzo could not help wondering at the number of destinies he carried in his hands and how many of those in the antechamber had unwittingly had their careers and reputations placed into his trust. For to him and him alone had Urban XI admitted how dangerous the Church's position was. The Pontiff has also shown Marrenzo that there does come a time when even the infallible leader of the Roman Catholic Church appears as only another man, one who has come against a task too great to complete alone.

Kneeling in the corner of his bedroom beneath the figure of a broken Christ, Claudio Marrenzo prayed more for Urban's salvation than he did for himself or for the Lord's strength and wisdom.

At ten o'clock, after he was through, Marrenzo summoned his secretary, Pio Cliotia. Swearing him to secrecy, Marrenzo told the young Jesuit exactly what had overtaken the Vatican, then outlined the proposals he had submitted to the Pontiff.

"If there is no recourse, and certainly I cannot see any, then we must try them," Cliotia said.

"Will your father help in that respect?"

"There is no need to go to him," Cliotia said. "I know the name of the man we need, where he is to be found and how to reach him."

"Then go and do what you can," Marrenzo said quietly. "You shall report to me and me alone."

Father Cliotia bowed and returned to telephone the railway office, where a clerk reserved a compartment for him on the midnight express to Geneva.

CHAPTER FIVE

At nine o'clock on the evening of September 17 the servant to Rozdentsy Cardinal Meyerczuk brought Antonio da Silva a note from the Polish prelate. The message was very brief:

"He has made good his threat. Listen to any radio station on the hour if you haven't already heard. Doubtless you will be receiving calls shortly from the Curia, and I ask you to remember the directive of silence."

The custodian of the Secret Archives immediately called the vice-prefect and instructed him not to accept any telephone messages relating to the *alleged* theft. He was also to tell the three archivists and *scrittori* that under no circumstances were they to discuss the matter with either members of the Curia or the press. Da Silva then asked his servant to have a car brought around from the Vatican garage.

Antonio Cardinal da Silva had not found much solace in Urban XI's plan to use the services of Father Domenico of the Agenzia Informativa Cattolica. Although he himself could not think of a better proposal, the cardinal was wary of trusting a man of whom he knew nothing. But the prefect had been prepared to abide by Urban's decision so long as there were not any further developments. All that had changed now.

Antonio da Silva thought it ironic that he should be so personally concerned over the loss of the Tetramachus Collection. Since he had spent the war within Vatican walls, at the post which had few political overtones—adviser to the Holy See's bank—the worst that could be said of him was that he had in no way tried to influence Pius XII's wartime policies. Otherwise Da Silva had occupied himself by trying to balance the Vatican's budget at a time when revenue from European dioceses had been reduced to a trickle. Thus, where others such as Meyerczuk had everything to lose if the papers became public, Da Silva could only gain. Those whose ambitions would be destroyed by the Collection made room for others, untainted.

In theory at least, that is how the future should have presented itself—if only Da Silva hadn't placed that manila file at the back of the Collection for safekeeping.

At half past nine Cardinal da Silva arrived at the small, elegant Hotel Excelsior, fifteen minutes' drive from Rome, and was shown into one of the suites on the top floor.

The Excelsior apartment belonged to Cavaliere Massimo Siboda, a spritely gentleman of seventy-two with sparkling blue eyes, an electric temper and a shock of white hair that suited his aristocratic carriage. A prototype of that aristocracy nimble and flexible enough to move from tenant payments to corporate investments, Siboda lived in the hotel because its quiet charm and unobtrusive service suited him better than the ancestral seat in the Cataline Hills. The cavaliere was also a banking wizard who had read economics out of curiosity, never thinking his studies would end with his appointment as chief lay adviser to the Vatican purse.

Having listened to the eight o'clock newscast, Siboda was not particularly surprised to receive the cardinal at this unusually late hour.

"May I offer you some brandy, Antonio? I daresay you look as though you could do with one."

"Thank you, Cavaliere. It's been a trying day."

"To say the least," Siboda sympathized.

Crystal twinkled gaily under soft light as Da Silva, like all good men, threw back his cognac in one draft.

"More?"

Without bothering to wait for the polite refusal, Siboda refilled his guest's snifter, leaving the decanter on the sideboard.

"Fortunately I am something of a nighthawk," Siboda said. "All my life I have worked best at night, when it is dark and quiet and a man can hear himself think. So my wits are about me, curiosity quite keen—go ahead, my friend."

The prefect took a long reinforcing sip and, without wasting a word, related the details of the theft, the gist of Urban's policy of silence and the decision to bring in Father Domingo.

"Under different circumstances, Cavaliere, I would not have troubled you about this, but there is one complication of which I have not informed His Holiness—for the moment. Appended to the collection is a series of papers relating to the disposal of funds collected by Bishop Hulais and subsequently our dealings with Lambrett, the financier, and his Overseas Development Corporation."

"Lambrett!" Siboda started, his eyes flashing. "How on earth did they get mixed up in this?"

"Four years ago, when the Banca Esber collapsed, I removed all references of our dealings with it from the actuarial files," Da Silva said. "These dealings were based on monies given to Lambrett in 1948; the monies themselves came from investments gleaned through your offices on the sale of valuables accumulated by Hulais. Because of this link, I thought the safest place for the records was the Tetramachus Collection, whose security was absolute. If someone wanted to see the collection, he would have to notify me so there was always time to remove this particular portfolio. It seemed then like a wise move. But it never occurred to me until a little while ago. . . ."

"Well, thank the Lord it did!" Siboda murmured. "All our dealings with Lambrett were included, the fifty-six million as well?"

"Everything," Da Silva echoed.

"Then you realize what will happen if the Tetramachus Collection is not returned to you." Siboda laughed suddenly.

"I know," Da Silva said. "That is why I came to you."

From time immemorial Vatican finances have been the most closely guarded of Vatican secrets. A full budget has never been made public. The Pontiff has rights over all of the Vatican purse, and the Holy Father answers to no one but God and his conscience. Throughout the ages, popes had accumulated and lost fortunes with equal alacrity. Some, the politicians and kingmakers, had built vast storehouses of wealth from land, booty and tributes. Others were less scrupulous, spendthrifts who left a legacy of palaces and gardens and a treasury that was all but empty save for the pittance brought in by taxes, tithes, levies and the sale of indulgences.

The Church entered the twentieth century with more capital to invest in fledgling industry than any other single body in the world. With the help of men such as Siboda, who could deal with Arab and Jew, communist and fascist in the same breath, the Holy See's coffers were handsomely full. Only one element had changed in nineteen hundred years. This age was merciless in keeping records—in ledgers, recording tapes, computers. This bookkeeping was, aside from its sovereignty, the major reason why the Church survived all attempts to call it into account. There were simply too many documents pertaining to financial transactions which would have to be examined for irregularities. Financial dealings could also be hidden, disguised or destroyed outright. But if papers pertaining to an issue as controversial as Bishop Hulais' financing the Nazi escape routes arose, public outcry could well provide the government with an excuse to impound the Vatican ledgers for a complete investigation. Few feared such an accounting more than Cavaliere Siboda, who had made a substantial commission off the Hulais funds he had invested between 1946 and 1951.

"You did well by coming to me," the financier said. "Are you certain the Vatican plans to do nothing else but call this Father Domingo?"

"There is nothing more for Urban to do," Da Silva said grimly. "He will have trouble enough fending off the government."

"And you don't believe that Father Domingo will be effective in securing the papers?"

"If you were Sabatini and had made a virulent anticlerical speech whose words you could substantiate, would you turn your evidence over to the agent of the Pope?" Da Silva asked dryly.

"How important is the priest, Belobraditz, now that he's passed on the papers?"

"I would think he is familiar with the financial dossier, although there is nothing in his letter to Urban to indicate this," Da Silva said. "For our purposes, he is important enough. We must assume he has read the enclosed file."

"I think you may be right here," the cavaliere said slowly. "Lambrett has left a great many angry investors in Italy, especially after he bled the Banca Esber dry. There are still warrants out for his arrest, and the extradition papers are periodically renewed. If Lambrett is even so much as mentioned in regards to the Vatican, your precious account ledgers will be cracked open like a dry acorn. Fransci would like nothing more than to discredit those associated with Lambrett in Italy, and I can tell you there are a fair number of big financial investors who at one time were part of ODC's Italian operations—among them, the Vatican."

"How do you think Fransci will act?"

"With characteristic dispatch and efficiency." Siboda laughed. "I would not count on Urban's silence holding for too long. As soon as Fransci sees the connection between the Church and Lambrett, he will have all the authority he needs, since Lambrett is charged with criminal activities, to break out your financial statements. And what a sorry day that would be!

"That is why," the financier concluded, "we must get that Collection back at any cost. Since Urban has no intention of going beyond the Vatican walls, I will!"

The cavaliere looked thoughtfully at the glass figurine beside him and ran his fingers over its design. He wasn't particularly interested in Lambrett's predicament or the Vatican's. He worried only about his own tranquil lifestyle and impeccable reputation, as far as business astuteness was concerned, upon which his personal fortune rested. If there had been a way in which the cavaliere could have disassociated himself from the financial dossier, he would have expressed polite regret at Da Silva's position and shown him the door. But this he couldn't do. If all the Church was prepared to do was to use one man against Sabatini, it was sorely underestimating the publisher. Cavaliere Siboda had crossed swords with Sabatini before; he was a worthy opponent.

"What is it exactly you're thinking of?" Da Silva inquired cautiously. He had not liked the implication behind Siboda's last words.

"I am stating that Urban has no idea of what is required to retrieve the collection," Siboda said coldly. "His plan is foolish and completely ineffectual. Let us not mince words, Antonio: The documents have been stolen from you, and since Sabatini is obviously unwilling to give them back, then we shall have to take them away from him."

"The Holy See cannot be implicated in such an act," Da Silva said, shaking his head. "If its role should be discovered, then we will have delivered our fate into Sabatini's hands completely."

"I am not asking for your approval or participation," Siboda said, his tone slightly mocking. "Since Urban knows nothing of the dossier added to the Collection, he could not possibly understand the additional gravity of the theft. But we do, and so we shall act accordingly."

"And that is how?"

"Since neither your hand *nor* mine can be shown, for obvious reasons, it is left to Lambrett to take the collection away from Sabatini."

"When Lambrett is resting comfortably in Costa Blanca?" Da Silva asked dubiously. "Why should he help us now?"

"Because he is a man who understands such matters,"

Siboda said softly. "Any successful businessman would understand this."

Francis Lee Lambrett did in fact consider himself a highly successful businessman, although one obliged to defend his hard work and its just rewards from lesser and therefore envious talents. It did not matter that the latter included officers of five major governments, the United States Securities and Exchange Commission, twenty-two former associates, some behind bars now, and approximately one hundred thousand ruined investors. What did matter was that all these people harbored the unkind thought of Francis Lambrett's being a thief. And he was—one of the most successful and daring corporate plunderers in the long history of money.

Son of an Italian immigrant who worked on a Detroit assembly line, Francis Lee Lambrett, né Lambretta, decided at an early age to become very rich, very powerful and very influential.

In 1946, after a year's service as junior lieutenant in General Adamson's Rome Office of the Occupation, the twenty-three-year-old Lambrett got his start by selling shares of the respected Hirsh Fund of New York. In the first six months, Lambrett was able to report sales of more than seventy thousand dollars which Hirsh thought phenomenal. What the firm didn't discover until later was that Lambrett's clients were almost exclusively GIs, whom no one had ever considered a possible source of investment.

In a period of eighteen months Lambrett quadrupled his sales, increased his mini-fortune to just under one hundred thousand dollars, dropped Hirsh and began what he privately called the Fund to End All Funds, more conservatively known as the Overseas Development Corporation. The idea behind ODC was simple and in its own way ingenious. Lambrett knew there were millions of dollars to be found in Europe, not much in cash but a great deal in gold, silver, diamonds and jewlry, objects readily convertible into liquid funds. But European countries, especially France, Germany and Italy, had very tight revenue-reporting requirements. These rules meant that the owner of a diamond necklace, for example, if he wished to sell it, either did so to a reputable dealer, who dutifully reported the amount paid to the tax bureau, or went to the black market, where he wouldn't receive a third of the necklace's true value. ODC had been designed to give the owner of the jewelry a third option. Lambrett would go with him to have the piece appraised, and then, on behalf of ODC, registered in Zurich, Lambrett would sell the necklace. The original owner was not obliged to report anything since it had been ODC of Switzerland, a company untouchable by the tax laws of another country, that had consummated the deal. The seller received the best price possible for his item, and his only obligation to ODC, aside from Lambrett's negligible commission, was to invest at least fifty percent of the sales receipt in the corporation.

Within eight months, Lambrett had collected one and a half million dollars to invest from a supposedly penurious Europe. The normally cautious Continental investor, with the disaster of 1929 fresh in his mind, fairly leaped into the entrepreneur's arms since Lambrett, underwritten by the highly sophisticated Crédit Suisse bank, not only was bona fide, but was guaranteeing a phenomenal seven percent return over a minimum two-year plan. Investors were dazzled. They wanted dreams and promises, and Lambrett was the biggest dream peddler of the day.

In November, 1947, the two-room offices of the Overseas Development Corporation received a cablegram from one Charles Edward Bennett Ryan, scion of a wealthy Boston family who had also served in Adamson's Rome office at the same time as Lambrett. Ryan had invested a substantial amount of his trust benefits in his buddy's fund programs. Ryan's message was brief and tantalizing: There were two million dollars in Rome waiting to be invested. Hard cash, no strings, discretion required. Lambrett drove down to Rome in less than seven hours, ruining his Chrysler in the process.

In a meeting held in his Via Veneto flat, Ryan, a staunch Roman Catholic, introduced Lambrett to a diminutive, mild-mannered gentleman by the name of Cavaliere Massimo Siboda. For the first hour, Siboda interrogated Lambrett on everything from his religious beliefs (Lambrett was also a Catholic) to how the money would be used and what return could be expected. Employing the principle of charm he had learned in the General Staff Office, Lambrett held forth on his talents as a reputable dealer, relying on the glowing letters sent him by a grateful Hirsh vice-president to support his claims. The cavaliere was satisfied. He asked Lambrett to sign the transfer papers both as an individual and chief officer of ODC and these signatures were attested to by Ryan. Without a single question's being raised about its source, the money was duly handed over, with Lambrett promising to keep Siboda informed on a regular basis. For this purpose, the Italian had thoughtfully provided an anonymous post office box in Rome.

For the next six weeks Francis Lee Lambrett used every connection he had to try to track down the source of that two million. He knew if the origins of the money had been aboveboard, he wouldn't have seen it. Siboda might have taken a slight loss in interest and turned the whole sum over to a well-known brokerage house. Instead, he had chosen to go with Lambrett, whom he must have thoroughly investigated, before deciding that what ODC could do with small sums it could also do with a figure of two million—invest it without embarrassing questions.

In the first months of 1948 General Adamson had been elected to sit on the American advisory board of the Nuremberg trials, an appointment through which he became something of an authority on SS men and the Gestapo.

Adamson was amused when he received his former lieutenant's letter. He had always liked Lambrett, a hard worker who knew his place and scraped enough to flatter without offending sensibility. The only thing Adamson had never cared for was Lambrett's aggressiveness, which had made him stubborn and somewhat uncouth.

Lambrett wrote that he had come across a great deal of money from a rather mysterious source. Since he didn't wish to be involved in anything illegal, would General Adamson advise him if possible? With a patrician's bemusement at an opportunist, Adamson replied as follows:

My dear Francis,

May I take this opportunity to belatedly congratulate you on your success with Hirsh Securities and on the service which you performed for your fellow soldiers. It was indeed a very generous gesture.

At the same time, however, and this relates directly to your inquiry, I would warn you of straying from legitimate sources of funds. There is no need to worry about the quality of the American soldier's money; however, the same cannot be said for most German or Italian nationals. The reason is this: A great deal of money has and is being used by Nazis and their sympathizers in an effort to flee Europe. Even more capital is trying to associate itself with unimpeachable investments, the kind you are allied with. Therefore, it is my opinion you should scrutinize your contracting parties very carefully. As far as I know, only two concerns in Italy would have the quantity of money you are talking about: the Holy See and persons serving Nazi interests. As far as the latter is concerned, should you come across anything which might be of interest to American intelligence, I give you the name of John Berens, colonel in the Army Intelligence Corps, Rome.

The enclosed material may also be of some interest to you. Statements of financial booty sent to the Reichsbank from the Main Security Office of the SS indicate that there was the equivalent of four billion dollars held in the bank as late as September, 1944. An infinitesimal part of this loot was found in Berlin of 1945; another fraction was discovered in the salt mines of Thuringia. There are rumors, substantiated by high-ranking prisoners of war, that a sizable part of this booty has also found its way to Spain, Switzerland and Argentina. But as you see, more than half of the total sum held by the Reichsbank in Berlin, 1944, *has not been accounted for.* It is felt by the Nuremberg board that most of what is missing and was once thought lost is actually in the hands of Nazi fugitives still in Europe.

Wishing you all the best, I remain,

A. Adamson
Staff Commander
United States Advisory Board
Nuremberg, Germany

Lambrett looked at the figures Adamson had sent along and decided to gamble.

In February, 1948, C. E. B. Ryan received a note stating that Lambrett had to meet with Siboda at once, in Zurich. Failing a reply within seventy-two hours, the two million, along with other detailed but unspecified documents, would be turned over to Army intelligence in Rome. Upon receipt of this letter Ryan had just enough strength to get in touch with the cavaliere before signing himself into a military hospital for a complete rest.

On February 12 Lambrett ushered into his two-room suite the urbane Massimo Siboda, who appeared completely unconcerned by the financier's threats. The president of ODC showed the Italian copies of Adamson's documents and voiced his suspicions that the two million Siboda had presented him with was, in fact, a fraction of the "lost treasure" of the SS.

Cavaliere Siboda stood back and laughed, congratulating the American on his fine sense of imagination. Without a single reference to Lambrett's argument, the Italian explained that under no circumstances was he about to reveal the source of the money, a matter of confidence between himself and the party who had originally placed the money in his hands. If Signor Lambrett did not wish to handle the funds as per his agreement with Siboda, witnessed by Ryan, Lambrett was free to terminate his relationship with the cavaliere upon return of the two million.

Should Lambrett decide to tell Colonel Berens of his association with Siboda, the consequences would be unpleasant for everyone. Although there was nothing strictly illegal about ODC's operations in Italy, they were sufficiently bending the law as to warrant an investigation by the Italian government. Who, Siboda wondered aloud, would even listen, much less act on the word of a financial dealer himself under investigation?

On the other hand, Siboda was prepared to make another attractive agreement. The island of Costa Blanca in the Caribbean had a strong Catholic government. It was also a tax haven short on development capital. If Signor Lambrett had no objection, he would be given an additional one million dollars to be devoted exclusively to Costa Blanca's growth and a splendid opportunity to invest the remaining capital, the initial two million, as he saw fit.

There were, however, three conditions: Lambrett would sign for the one million in ODC's name; he would return the sum of two million plus ten percent in *five* years, not the original two, as had been agreed upon previously, to an organization as yet existing only on paper, Panitalia; he would also sign a paper pledging his secrecy on these transactions.

In short, Cavaliere Siboda had called Lambrett's bluff, sweetening the temptation to continue investing on behalf of Siboda by allowing Lambrett to keep the initial capital for five years. Lambrett and Siboda both knew that the two million could generate twenty to twenty-five percent interest within that time, if properly invested.

Lambrett gave the matter thirty seconds' consideration and shook on the deal.

All that had taken place well over a quarter of a century ago, years of intrigue, gambles, double-talk, lies and pressure, of which Lambrett had enjoyed every minute. He had seen his personal fortune swell from six figures to more than half a billion dollars. He had dined with two U.S. presidents and bought four others in the Caribbean islands. His friends included Arab oil ministers, German bankers, rotting European aristocrats and two shipping magnates. His enemies were of equal importance, the most powerful being the extradition officers of the United States, Canada, France, Switzerland and Italy. But Lambrett had eluded them all. In 1973, when ODC collapsed under its dead weight of a billion dollar in debts, he had simply packed up in Europe and moved in comfort to Costa Blanca, which had no treaties with anyone. Here Lambrett had peace, bought with the million dollars which he had handed over to President Juan Figueres, still one of his best friends, in mid-1948.

Francis Lee Lambrett had just settled himself before a dinner of steak and salad when his valet appeared with an extension phone.

"Long distance, sir, Rome."

"Who is it?" Lambrett demanded, irritated by the disturbance.

"The caller identifies himself as Cavaliere Massimo Siboda, sir," the ancient ebony black replied.

Dripping salad dressing on the white tablecloth, Lambrett gestured for the telephone to be set down beside him. It had been almost three years since he had heard from Siboda.

"Lambrett speaking."

"Signor Lambrett, how good it is to hear your voice after all this time."

"The pleasure is mine, Cavaliere. How have you been keeping?"

"On the whole, quite well, although I wish I were speaking to you under more pleasant circumstances."

"Well, things always look worse than they are. What can I do for you?"

"Signor Lambrett, our business relationship began many years ago, a January seventh. You remember?"

"How could I forget?"

"Then you will also remember that you signed, on behalf of the now defunct Overseas Development Corporation, a receipt for two million dollars which I entrusted to you."

"I certainly do," Lambrett answered, stretching back and scratching his paunch.

"Keeping that in mind, I go now to the year 1961. At that time ODC had acquired control of four medium-size banks, the Jefferson National in the United States, Bankhaus Wenzler in Germany, Wulfbank in Switzerland and the Banca Esber in Italy. In the case of Banca Esber, ODC received fifty-six million dollars from my offices to purchase the majority of the outstanding shares. I am certain you know where the money came from, although ODC never asked for specific information."

"The Vatican," Lambrett answered shortly.

"That is correct," Siboda said. "We offered fifty-six million in exchange for forty-two percent of all shares after you had completed the takeover. But we lost everything when ODC forced three of the four banks to suspend business."

"ODC didn't force anything on anybody," Lambrett

interrupted smoothly. ''The consortium was suffering heavily from foreign exchange operations which, if you remember, were being manipulated by the Japanese. At that time, nothing could stand up to the yen.''

He did not bother to add that ODC had been buying up Japanese notes itself and using them to bury struggling financial groups caught in the currency squeeze.

''I am not interested in ODC's maneuvers in the area of currency speculations,'' Siboda answered calmly. ''They are irrelevant at this point. The fact is that the Vatican had to cover this loss of fifty-six million which represented a little over ten percent of its total liquid assets.''

''I don't believe the last percentage figure is accurate,'' Lambrett said. ''At any given moment, the Vatican has one point two billion dollars in reserve—cash and investments readily convertible into cash.''

''I assure you your figure is incorrect,'' Siboda demurred. ''If you will permit to me finish. . . . The collapse of the Banca Esber was the principal reason in our government's decision to seek an extradition order for you from President Figueres. That move, as others before it or after, failed because of the intervention on your behalf by highly placed parties within the Church.

''Now, I return to our meeting in 1948,'' Siboda continued, ''and I would ask you to please consider my words very carefully. I have been informed by sources at the highest level of the Vatican that papers you signed on behalf of ODC and other documents relating to that transaction—the repayment of the two million and so on—have been stolen from the Vatican files. If they pass into the hands of the Italian government, at the moment a very likely possibility, then because of ODC's rather dubious reputation, the Parliament would immediately begin an investigation into the Vatican's connection with that company. I assure you it would not take the prime minister very long to discover the link between our initial dealings and the Banca Esber disaster, still a subject of debate within financial circles.

"The inquiry would show, Signor Lambrett, how you came to Costa Blanca and under whose auspices. While President Figueres can turn a deaf ear on institutions as powerful as the attorney general's office, he cannot dismiss a Vatican request to have your residence permit reviewed for certain, um, irregularities.

"To put it in very simple terms then, when the Church is forced to defend itself it will not be able to protect you any longer. On the contrary, you will be sacrificed first, and once you land on Italian soil, for I know the government of Costa Blanca will find you persona non grata, there will be several extradition orders awaiting you which the Italian government will honor—after it is through with you."

Lambrett leaned forward on his elbows, pushing his cold steak aside.

"Siboda," he said softly, "what in hell makes you think I believe all this?"

"You are familiar with the publisher Sabatini?"

"I've heard of him."

"This afternoon, at a press conference, he stated that he has the documents I am speaking of. If you doubt my word, please check any European paper issued this morning. You will find the story on page one."

Like most men of his kind, Lambrett had one particular phobia—his happened to be newspapers. They had hurt him badly in the past and were in large part responsible for the hasty liquidation of ODC by keeping Lambrett's name and string of finely engineered bankruptcies on their front pages. Lambrett believed what he read in newspapers.

"All right, Cavaliere, let's assume you're leveling with me. In that case, why are you going to all this trouble?"

"This is a time when I need your help," Siboda said quietly. "If those papers are not recovered, both you and I will have lost everything. But if you succeed in returning them to me, you are assured of further cooperation from President Figueres and his Catholic supporters."

"I thought you said the material stolen was Vatican property?" Lambrett countered.

"You know that my interests and those of the Holy See are closely related." Siboda said. "I am acting on behalf of the Church in this matter."

Lambrett sat back and considered the cavaliere's words, faintly conscious that his reflections were costing Siboda about thirteen dollars a minute. Lambrett was inclined to believe Siboda. Unlike other financiers who were long on wind and short on substance, the Italian had always acted with the right amount of dispatch and force in a given situation. He was not susceptible to overreaction or panic. So if Siboda was concerned, and he was, it was worth Lambrett's taking note.

"All right. Give me the details," Lambrett said harshly. "After that, leave everything in my hands."

That had been three hours ago. Since then Lambrett had seen a special edition of the *International Herald Tribune,* which, true to Siboda's word, carried the Sabatini story in headlines. He had telephoned a few friends in Europe and received more information. The pieces fitted.

Sitting in the warmth of the September sun, surrounded by his flow charts and figures, Francis Lambrett felt a cold trickle of sweat make its way down his back. He had no desire to follow Cornfeld into a damp Swiss jail, or worse, a U.S. federal penitentiary. The merchant who had made his fortune on the shattered hopes and broken dreams of others had only one great fear: the destruction of his own vision.

Francis Lambrett pulled a chain of keys from his trouser pocket, selected one and opened the top drawer of his fireproof wall cabinet. Tugging out a large sheaf of papers, he brought them over to his desk and laid them out in neat little piles. These charts, figures and commentaries were the beginning of a new world, waiting to be built with the help of a few politicians, global contacts and half a billion dollars. This venture was going to succeed where all others, including ODC, had failed, and its success would be based on the nature of the primary product, something men always needed and never had enough of—weapons.

Throughout ODC's long and illustrious career of acquisitions, Lambrett had kept one firm well away from the parent company: Eurotek, a small, efficiently run Zurich banking house located in Bahnhofstrasse, 61. Had Eurotek any traceable connection with ODC, the diligent Swiss authorities would have impounded its assets along with the rest of Lambrett's Continental holdings. But it didn't. Eurotek had been set aside, untainted and intact when all else had collapsed. With money channeled into the Continent through a half dozen banks, Eurotek was buying more and more shares in more and more death industries. According to Lambrett's connections, the modest Swiss bank should, within five years, have more than a third of all European weapons firms—manufacturing everything from field radios to teleguidance systems—under its control.

Provided that Lambrett himself could hold out that long. He thought he had covered himself in every way and from everyone—except the past. Now the past had returned.

Lambrett's blunt fingers punched the digits on the telephone, putting him through to an overseas operator. In twenty minutes he was speaking to Eberhardt Krieg, president of Eurotek and Lambrett's first lieutenant.

THE RECOVERY

CHAPTER SIX

"So in point of fact, Father Cliotia, you do *not* represent the Vatican, as you led me to believe, but only a single cardinal. Nor is His Holiness Urban XI fully cognizant of the measures Monsignor Marrenzo has taken."

The speaker was fifty-five-year-old Mitislav Vladimirovich Rokossovsky, former *éminence grise* of KGB chief Yuri Andropov, now director of a private European intelligence organization known as ISIS. He was looking at a man twenty years his junior, with brown tousled hair and dark-amber eyes resting quietly behind gold-framed spectacles.

At nine o'clock on the morning of September 18 Father Cliotia arrived in Geneva. After checking in at the modest Hôtel le Moulin, he had taken a light breakfast and waited for the car to fetch him, according to arrangements worked out between himself and Geneva the night before. The Vatican envoy was shown into the director's office by an imposing manservant. Within the hour Rokossovsky knew as much about the theft of the Tetramachus Collection as did the Vatican.

"You will forgive me if I misled you in any way," Cliotia replied with a thin smile. "But after all, monsieur, my business is on behalf of the Church, and I am empowered to use His Holiness' name as my authority."

"Are you now?" Rokossovsky said casually.

He cut a stout, although still-muscular figure in his impeccably tailored suit. Father Cliotia noted the swift, powerful movements of Rokossovsky's hands as he ground up fresh coffee beans and transferred the blend into an espresso machine. He was a very self-possessed man, a quality reflected in the light smile, in the hard, expressionless eyes in which Father Cliotia also saw undisguised and contemptuous cruelty.

Such a mark had been left on an entire generation of Russians who, like Rokossovsky, had killed their first German while still in their teens. Taught the meaning of death at the expense of youth, they had grown cold and cynical when the gray postwar light dawned. But in spite o. their ability to have survived, only a few did not disappear into Stalin's special camps, organized for Soviet soldiers who had fought their way across Eastern Europe so that they might not, upon their return from Germany, infect the homeland with Western ideas. Rokossovsky was one who had won the human lottery.

Unlike the ordinary soldier, disposed of as soon as victory was certain, Rokossovsky endured because in him the elements of strength, cunning and an ability to foresee events were all in the right proportion. Immediately after his arrival in Moscow, Rokossovsky sought out his former partisan comrade, Yuri Andropov. In 1944 Andropov had been appointed second secretary into the party machinery as special adviser on population resettlement and waited out Stalin's wrath on his army.

In the spring of 1951 Andropov headed for Moscow to take up the chairmanship of the Western political department in Moscow. Rokossovsky followed as intelligence adviser. That summer, after much stocktaking, he decided that Stalin's rule was coming to an end and allied himself with the upcoming Khrushchev faction. Two years later Stalin was dead, Andropov had been named ambassador to Hungary, and Rokossovsky emerged as Khrushchev's political adviser on security affairs.

Throughout the cold war, Rokossovsky worked at making himself indispensable to the leadership as an intelligence planner and analyst. He traveled to China to prepare a network which would provide raw data on Chinese defense groupings throughout and after the Sino-Soviet ideological split; to Yugoslovia, where he helped mend fences with Tito; and to Switzerland, from where he kept Andropov informed on the general condition of Western security alliances. From Zurich, Rokossovsky also set up liaisons with German intelligence, the Gehlen group, and, through it, the CIA.

In 1964, as the political wheel knocked Khrushchev out of the game and Brezhnev emerged as master, Andropov, who had silently switched his allegiance to Brezhnev some years back, nominated Rokossovsky for the directorship of ISIS. The Americans accepted him because Rokossovsky's brother, having fled Poland in the wake of the German invasion, was currently in California working on the Trident nuclear submarine missile system. Rokossovsky, who had proved his loyalty to Andropov by supplying damaging information on Suslov, Khrushchev's top security man, and was known to the Americans through the Gehlen group, was in an excellent position to play middleman.

Briefly stated, ISIS owed its existence to a concordat between the American Central Intelligence Agency and the Soviet Committee for State Security. Arrived at in Geneva in January, 1964, the concordat, labeled Memorandum One, was considered ultrasecret, and no minutes were at first transmitted to either Washington or Moscow. The reason for this was that neither the director of the CIA nor his counterpart in Dzerzhinsky Street informed either the President of the United States or the First Secretary of the Soviet Communist Party of these meetings. Both intelligence organs had stipulated beforehand that they would deal only with each other and no civil government was to be involved until such time as an agreement was reached on whether or not to establish an independent intelligence agency or scrap the scheme altogether.

By April, 1964, Memorandum One had grown from a single idea to more than seven hundred pages of details for a new espionage apparatus. The function of ISIS, as envisaged by the CIA and KGB, was twofold. First, it would carry out operational assignments, assassinations, destruction of military and civilian property and so on in areas where it was not prudent for the two giants to show their hands. For the CIA this meant primarily South America, Europe and the Middle East. For the Soviet Union the strategic points were Southeast Asia, where Moscow was at odds with Peking, Eastern Europe and also the Middle East. Second, ISIS was to gather its own intelligence, gleaned from operational work it rendered to private individuals, corporations or other secret services. By creating such a go-between, both the CIA and KGB hoped for an end to mistakes which had led to the U-2 affair, the Cuban missile crisis and other potential triggers of Armageddon. Certainly the private war between the two, with its electronic spying, disinformation and propaganda backed by billions of dollars and rubles, would continue unabated. But while such arm wrestling was necessary given national and global politics, there would be no victor if either the United States or the Soviet Union pushed the nuclear buttons. ISIS' job was to reduce that possiblity to zero.

As for restrictions, ISIS had none save one. While it could use its finances and manpower wherever and however it saw fit, while it could choose to accept or reject, on the basis of its own security, an assignment from either parent, while it answered to no civil government but lived in a comfortable neutral fashion benignly countenanced by the Swiss minister of the interior, it could never use its intelligence or agents against one parent on behalf of the other. That was the cardinal rule imposed on Mitislav Vladimirovich Rokossovsky. He in turn imposed it on the board, the ISIS executive body, and all those who worked for him.

While the director busied himself with the coffee, Father Cliotia glanced around the large, spacious office. The bay window immediately behind the desk looked out on landscaped grounds, an autumn blend of yellow, red and brown. Along the right-hand wall was a bookshelf, some thirty feet long, reaching from floor to ceiling. On the left, a marble fireplace waited patiently to be cleaned, while directly in front of it an ancient Persian prayer rug rested on polished hardwood boards. Along the window ledge were potted plants, only two of which Father Cliotia, an enthusiastic botanist, was able to identify.

The room was an excellent reflection of its occupant, comfortable, expensive and civilized. However, Father Cliotia's evaluation did not take into account the video camera half hidden by a thick *Larousse gastronomique* on the top right-hand corner of the bookcase. Had he seen this, Cardinal Marrenzo's aide might have had further thoughts.

"I trust this will be to your taste," Rokossovsky said, passing Cliotia his demitasse. "Chocolate coffee."

"The aroma is excellent," Father Cliotia replied politely.

The director returned to his desk, stroked the broad leaves of his favorite rubber plant and leaned back in his chair.

"Father Cliotia," he began in a deep fluid bass, "your story concerning these documents, the Tetramachus Collection, is intriguing. But it scarcely explains why you have come to see me."

"Do you remember, monsieur, the work your organization did for my father?"

"Antonio Cliotia, the Fiat executive? War records, wasn't it?"

"Yes, it was," Cliotia replied, sipping on his coffee.

"A delicate piece of work," Rokossovsky mused. "The Squadra Azione Mussolini was trying to blackmail him by using his early affiliation with Il Duce. I hope he hasn't had any reoccurrence of that particular problem."

"Not at all. Your intervention brought very effective results."

"Good, good." Rokossovsky nodded, lighting a thin Hagmar.

"It is because of my father that I am here today," Cliotia said. "If he is any example, then your discretion can be relied on—completely. From what I understand, your organization is equipped to deal with extraordinary circumstances."

"And just what do you understand about ISIS, Father Cliotia?" Rokossovsky asked mildly.

"To the best of my knowledge, ISIS is a mercenary group whose services are available to persons providing adequate remuneration. According to what I have learned from my father, you have had some dealings with the Italian government, but also with right-wing elements in Rome. There are rumors that your group has been active in Greece under the colonels. But that is not very much to know, is it?"

"And what are you asking of me?" Rokossovsky demanded suddenly.

"The return of the Tetramachus Collection, intact and uncopied. If you can do that, you will have rendered the Church an invaluable service. You will have saved her and Urban the Eleventh from destruction."

"Are you certain the Tetramachus Collection contains only war papers?"

"I am. As far as His Eminence knows, and given the urgency of the matter it would be pointless to hide anything, Volume Five contains only war records and cablegrams."

"As Alfredo Sabatini has suggested," Rokossovsky added unkindly.

"Yes."

"But Sabatini might have passed them on for a second opinion. He might have already made a copy," Rokossovsky suggested.

"I agree with you on the second part, that he probably has made a copy," Cliotia said. "However, it is the original which is important. That is the only true copy."

"I see," Rokossovsky said, forming a pyramid with his fingers. "Tell me, Father Cliotia, since this is not an official Vatican query, are you authorized to negotiate the financial aspect of your request?"

The question came so suddenly it caught the nuncio completely off guard.

''His Eminence *did* mention payment,'' he said icily. ''I may offer you as much as $250,000 for your services.''

''I imagine the Church will want to deal discreetly on the question of money. How will the money be channeled to us?''

''Through my personal estate. Even though I chose to devote my life to the Church, my father did not alter the terms of his will. A call to Banque Nationale Suisse will bear me out.''

''There is no need for that,'' Rokossovsky said crisply. ''There is very little your father did not divulge to us. You must realize, however, that should we accept this assignment, we would work in our own way. I am not suggesting our investigators would act as your Inquisition, but we tolerate no interference as far as our methods are concerned.''

''That is understood,'' Cliotia said. ''I have Father Martin's file with me, should it be of any value to you. I am also prepared to cooperate with you in any way possible.''

''Very good,'' Rokossovsky said, offering a completely insincere smile. ''Now, if you will excuse me for perhaps twenty minutes, there are some matters I must attend to. Your appointment was arranged rather hastily. I'm certain you understand. There is some literature you may peruse''—the director gestured at the bookcase—''but please bear in mind you are under constant video surveillance. My security people will be watching you now, and they are just outside the door.''

Rokossovsky pointed to the half-hidden video camera, took note of Cliotia's startled expression, then left through a side door which hid an automatic elevator.

The entire second floor of ISIS headquarters is taken up

by a single walnut-paneled room. At one end there is a large oval conference table with three telephones: one to the director's office at the CIA in Langley, Virginia; another to KGB headquarters on Dzerzhinsky Street, Moscow; a third to Klaus Jaunich, the Swiss minister of the interior. The long-distance lines are hooked into special circuits which provide instantaneous communications between Geneva and the East or West. The one to the minister's office is also connected to his personal line, which is checked for taps once a week.

Along one wall stand teleprinters linked to a UNIVAC 2000 computer that has more than three million pieces of information on its tapes. On the fall wall is a Mercator projection of the world, beside which stands a plotting board of various ISIS operations running at the moment. The long windows on the west wall are one-way and bulletproof.

As soon as Rokossovsky closed the door, the elevator carried him up to this nerve center. Waiting for him were the three men who made up the board.

''Well, gentlemen, where do we stand in the matter?'' Rokossovsky demanded briskly, taking his usual seat at the head of the table beside a video screen. The board had just watched the entire proceedings between the director and the Vatican envoy.

''This is all we have on the Secret Archives,'' a thin, long-faced Englishman, Stephen Waters, said. Seven years ago Waters' career as second-in-command of M15 came to an abrupt end when his son, age sixteen, was arrested in a male house of prostitution in London. As one of the chiefs of administration, Waters was responsible for all nonoperational business in ISIS. He passed a thin file to Rokossovsky.

" Precious little except the usual loose ends on SS men whose trails stop at the Italian border," Waters commented disinterestedly. "It's simply a matter of no one ever having been interested in the archives, possibly because no one could get at them."

"Well, someone has," Rokossovsky muttered, leafing through the onionskin pages. "Is this all?" he asked with annoyance.

"We've checked our sources on Church financial holdings," Joseph Passater said in his soft New England accent. Five years ago he had been director of the Plans Division for the CIA. Forced into early retirement by Helms' realignment of Plans policies in 1971, Passater was number two in administration.

Passater held up a six-foot sheet of pale-green teletype paper.

"However, this came in from our Rome bureau overnight."

Rokossovsky took the clipped sheet, noting the blue brackets around the bottom paragraphs. Because of Cliotia's arrival, he hadn't had a chance to go through the morning papers. The day sheet, containing a summary of international developments that had taken place within the last twelve hours, gave an accurate summary of the publisher's speech.

"You've all read this, I assume."

"Certainly adds weight to what Cliotia was saying," Passater remarked. "The Vatican is badly frightened."

Rokossovsky grunted and kept on reading.

"Sabatini landed one this time. Comments?" Waters said, gently tugging at his shirt cuffs. "He never speaks without sufficient evidence. My only objection is taking this thing on is that we might jeopardize our current operations in Italy, which, as the good father has pointed out, have already brought our name up in Italian domestic politics. The rumors as to which side we are taking are, of course, incorrect, still—"

"The usual reward for a job well done," Rokossovsky said sarcastically.

"It's curious that Cliotia should have chosen us," Waters added as an afterthought. "Surely he could have gone to the SID, the Italian Secret Service, replete as it is with old Jesuits."

"The Vatican is serious, and the SID leaks like a sieve," Rokossovsky said with a thin line of contempt under his words. "I'm certain Marrenzo thought of that and came to the same conclusion."

"I do not think our Italian commitments are reason enough to bypass such an opportunity," the third member said quietly. This was Philip Pelikan, former major in Czech intelligence, the STB, now chief of ISIS operations. "While the CIA has been too overt in its support of conservative factions within the Rome government—and without—and this has caused suspicion to be thrown on us in Italy, the situation is far from dangerous. Judging by what this priest has said, it appears to me we could easily run a class four operation, one man properly armed and documented. I would choose such a method partly because to mount a larger operation would take too long and partly for efficacy. If a single man finds the assignment impossible, then perhaps we can give thought to a full team. But one man is best to get the priest."

"Why should it be necessary to interfere with Belobraditz?" asked Rokossovsky. "He's not the one with the papers."

"Although my colleagues in administration might not

agree," Pelikan said coolly, "I believe there is a great deal more to the Tetramachus Collection than we are being told. Sabatini can be our starting point, but to find the truth of the matter, we have to find Belobraditz. He does not strike me as being an ignorant man and could be of value to us insofar as his position as secretary to Meyerczuk gave him an overview of Vatican politics. We might also consider that he might want protection from the Church itself."

"So we have two targets," Waters said thoughtfully.

"Very good," Rokossovsky said. He drew out his gold Karandash pencil and across the top of the manila envelope wrote: OPERATION IKONEN RATING RED

"The operation will be introduced into our terminals immediately," he said. "Our Rome bureau is to be alerted to pass on all relevant information, which, I imagine, will start coming in later today. I would like to get it as soon as it comes in, Stephen. The only thing left to decide is whom to use."

"Alexander Players," Pelikan said immediately. "He works best when he's alone. He also has papers for Opus Dei, the Catholic lay organization. It might be of some value in operating within a Catholic environment."

"I have no objection," Rokossovsky said, looking around at nods of approval. "We are all familiar with Players' work."

"Where is he now?" Waters asked.

"In Canada," Pelikan replied with a faint smile. "Where he succeeded in penetrating Canadian intelligence. We were to close that operation in a fortnight. It will be just as well to do so now."

* * *

Alexander Players, dressed in his habitual blue blazer, gray trousers, red, white and blue tie, entered the McGill University Faculty Club a few minutes before noon, Wednesday, September 18. He stopped briefly at the glass reception booth for a package of cigarettes, was handed his one telephone message by Mrs. Ryerson, then stepped into the lounge, choosing a small table away in a recess.

At thirty-five, Alexander Players was still at the peak of his physical condition. Medium height, with brown, neatly smooth hair and a face that retained a deep summer tan throughout the year, Players walked with a catlike grace that belied his strength. The athletic movements, honed to precision by constant exercise, were somehow out of keeping with the boyish face and mild eyes. But then nothing about Players was what it appeared to be.

Born in Kiev, son of a senior GRU officer, Players had been recruited into the KGB at the age of eighteen. By the time he was twenty-three he had taken on and shed three complete identities, traveled under a half dozen different passports and was the service's most effective assassin, responsible for the liquidation of two Ukrainian leaders in exile in West Germany and an Israeli bacteriologist.

In 1964 he faded from his Moscow circle of friends, who were only too glad to avoid him as word got around that he was slated for a senior position in Operations Department V of the KGB. It was not good politics to be seen in the company of one who dealt with "wet affairs," as assassinations were known.

Players did not consider himself an extraordinary man or one of particular appetites. Only different. He looked on the world with a mixture of cynicism and curiosity, ever aware of the weaknesses in men's natures that led to excess. He believed most of the world lived by violence and had trained himself to live within that violence. But he did not enjoy dealing with it. To kill a man gave him no pleasure or any release. He killed men as he did vermin. He was the instrument of other men's will, but he knew there was a scale within him that, if upset, would prevent him from pulling the trigger on a target. For the instrument was not without its own reason and conscience, and in the final result, it alone had the power to decide what it would do.

The chief of Department V, First Directorate, was very much aware of this flaw in Players' psychology, and while it fell to Players to carry out the most dangerous assignments, those done without embassy cover, the chief never pushed his man into that one-way street from which Players would never return. The strength and power of will Players expended on each mission could also turn him away from a job, regardless of consequences. Unlike other men, Players was not afraid of the power the directorate could use against him. He was one of the very few who knew the full extent of these powers and did not care.

In 1965, Players' name was quietly removed from the records of Department V. Equipped with a wholly new identity file, he traveled to Switzerland and in Geneva met his control for the next ten years—Rokossovsky. The transfer had been Rokossovsky's private joke, for he who had survived had, under Andropov, run Department V.

Settling back in his chair, Players slit open the thin envelope while looking around the room. The luncheon brigade was arriving for its daily doubles, tongue looseners that would reduce the chatter to the petty and personal. Normally Players would have come an hour earlier, but today the drivel would ensure that his own conversation was not overheard.

DR. SCHMIDT WISHES TO REMIND YOU OF YOUR APPOINTMENT AT THREE O'CLOCK SEPTEMBER 18.

As soon as Martin, the waiter, had brought the drinks, Players went into the washroom and flushed the message. When he returned, a trim-looking man of fifty occupied the chair opposite his, Peter Arthur Danby, head of PSPAG—Policy and Security, Planning and Analysis Group, or more simply, Canadian intelligence. Players smiled briefly and reached for the outstretched hand.

Pelikan had been entirely correct when he stated that Players had succeeded in penetrating the Canadian service. What the head of ISIS operations didn't know was that Players had also gone over.

"I came down as quickly as possible, Alex," Danby said. "What's happened?"

"ISIS made initial contact at six this morning by phone. I've been recalled. The confirmation was here at the club when I arrived. A jet will be waiting for me at Montreal International at three this afternoon."

"Why?"

"I don't know why. I thought you might be in a better position to tell me that."

"I haven't any idea," Danby said slowly, sipping his tomato juice. "There has been nothing of any importance over the last couple of weeks, nothing in which ISIS' hand has shown. Rokossovsky might have a long-range operation in mind. . . . Or have they found you out?"

"No," Players said bluntly. "Not unless there's a leak somewhere."

Danby set his drink down and squeezed more lemon into it. He had taken all possible care to keep Players clean. He was too valuable to lose, the sort of man Canadian intelligence would never get its hands on again.

In 1973 the CIA approached ISIS with a problem too delicate for its own Plans Division to handle. It required the placing of an agent inside the Canadian network to check out and evaluate PSPAG's internal security controls, information management and diffusion and personnel screening. Given the general state of Western security that year, it was not surprising the Americans were worried.

In December, a senior adviser to German Chancellor Willy Brandt, Günter Guillaume and his forty-seven-year-old wife, Christel, had been unmasked as Soviet spies. Brandt's resignation had been immediate, and it ground the West-East German reunification talks to a dead halt. Another security problem developed in Portugal after the military had established a frail left-wing democracy in that country. Henry Kissinger immediately ordered Portugal's exclusion from all top-secret NATO documents on the grounds that the Portuguese Cabinet could no longer be trusted. In Britain, Sir Peregrine Henniker-Heaton, a top Arab specialist in British intelligence, had been found dead in his home—three years after he had supposedly disappeared from his office in Whitehall.

Although it would appear that Canada was on the periphery of such covert activities, it figured greatly in U.S. intelligence schemes. Its long Arctic borders gave the Americans choice positions from which to monitor Soviet signal codes to bomber and naval fleets. Through its Commonwealth association, Canada had access to British, Australian, Indian and New Zealand intelligence, some of which never reached the CIA in spite of the multilateral information-sharing schemes. The United

States also used Canadian institutions such as the National Research Council for certain security operations. Therefore, while on the surface the most cordial behavior was displayed toward their northern neighbor, the Americans had no second thoughts about checking the care with which the Canadians handled both U.S. information and their own. All things considered, the CIA thought it was doing Canada a service.

It would have been a simple matter for Colburn of the CIA to get in touch with Danby and arrange for a liaison man to be put into the Canadian machinery. However, the American directorate felt that any honest advance would automatically be repulsed. Danby, as deputy minister of the Solicitor General's Office, would be obliged to take the matter to the Federal Cabinet, where unsympathetic ministers might be inclined to leak news of the American plan. The project would then be subject to a wearisome parliamentary debate and, in the end, be scrapped. It was not worth the CIA's time or effort to be honest. By contrast, a clandestine operation would be painless and discreet.

But one must tread a little more carefully with allies than enemies. On the outside chance that the covert operation was uncovered, the damage to U.S.-Canada relations would be irreparable. Therefore, a third party, with no visible connection to the CIA, was the obvious solution. That was ISIS.

"Have you any idea what this could be?" Danby repeated.

"ISIS won't say anything until I get back to Geneva. I don't know what will happen then. Perhaps nothing."

"Why not tell them now? You have all the protection you need."

"Do I!" Players laughed softly.

Yes, he could have the best protection Canada had to offer. It had succeeded in keeping Gouzenko alive and the Czech known as Sabotka. But he hadn't chosen to exit simply to be watched by the RCMP for the rest of his life.

On December 7 of last year, when he had been with PSPAG for only five months, Alexander Players broke the ISIS operation by walking into Danby's Slater Street office in Ottawa and handing him a typewritten note: "I WISH TO DISCUSS A MATTER OF THE GREATEST URGENCY. PLEASE DISCONNECT YOUR RECORDING DEVICES. WHAT I SAY MUST NOT BE MONITORED."

Danby had sat back stiffly and looked up at the operative. Players' hands were by his side, and he was staring at him intently. Danby took no chances. The emergency bell was three feet from his fingers. His hand might get halfway there before Players hit him the first time. Carefully, Danby stood up and pulled the plug to his desk lamp, lifting the shade to show the microphones studded on the inside.

"Cheaper than microbatteries," he said matter-of-factly. "Now, what can I do for you?"

"I am seeking your cooperation," Players said quietly. "In a certain way I am about to defect."

Danby hid his surprise well. He looked at the typewritten note once more, wondering how long Players had been preparing for this move, for nothing the agent had said or done would have indicated a defection.

"Yes, I have thought about it for a long time," Players said. "I have the entire plan worked out. Will you listen to me?"

"Yes." Danby brought out his cigarettes and offered one to Players.

"I am part of an operation mounted against you by ISIS at the request of the CIA," Players began. "You have been the target all along.

"Some thirteen months ago, Rokossovsky contacted you asking if you would put someone from his organization into yours so that this man might work under Canadian cover at the United Nations. As Rokossovsky explained it to you, the operation consisted of placing an agent close to the Arab delegation, primarily to keep watch on the Palestine Liberation Organization's influence over the Middle East circles. You agreed to this, at least in part because Rokossovsky was to pass certain information your way concerning the Caribbean islands, where, it seems, Canadian investments might be in jeopardy given the nationalist sentiments in places like Grand Cayman.

"Rokossovsky was afraid you might ask why ISIS was going to all this trouble of penetrating the UN through Canada instead of simply putting a man in New York. But when he explained to you how safe it was to use your ready-made apparatus—the good offices of Malcolm McQuinn, who teaches at the law school here and is consultant in air and space law to the UN—you saw the logic of his request. What you didn't think of was that the man from ISIS, who turned out to be myself, might be working *against* you.

"In keeping with the agreement between yourself and Rokossovsky, you arranged for me to work within McQuinn's bureau, gave me a top-security clearance since I was already vetted by the CIA and let me move around your headquarters with absolute freedom. It was too good to be true."

"You sound bitter about the whole matter," Danby

said. He was shaken, but nothing broke his calm exterior.

"I am. I wince when I see professionals like yourself get taken in so easily. But let me go on.

"My term here expires in September. I am to thank you very much for your cooperation, pack up and return to Geneva. However, I have made an alternate plan. I want out from intelligence. In exchange for bona fide Canadian citizenship, permission to settle here and destruction of my PSPAG record, I am prepared to give you one more piece of information, which has nothing to do with the ISIS penetration of PSPAG. But on this, as on what I have told you up to now, I must place one condition: that you do not use this information."

"I'm afraid I don't follow you," Danby said with a faint smile. "Your decision to, um, retire, is, of course, privileged information, but the rest—"

"If you tell the Americans, which, considering what they have done to you through ISIS, I would be surprised to see you do, or NATO, the value of what I know will be destroyed. But if you and you alone are privy to it, this information will give you an immense advantage."

"If this is as valuable as you say it is, then your life will be worth very little once word of the switch reaches Geneva."

"Not quite. ISIS doesn't know I have this information."

"What about other details you have stored away?"

"Most of it is out of date or will be shortly. There wouldn't be very much if you tried to squeeze me."

Here Players had been obliged to lie. There was something else which he knew would be of the greatest interest to PSPAG. Two years before, ISIS had placed an agent within the Canadian armed forces in Europe. He was still functioning, and the plan was to keep him active for another year at least. Rokossovsky was aware that Players knew the name and location of this man since he had been present at the board meeting which had dealt with that operation. When Players would tell Rokossovsky he was through and would be returning to Canada, the director would assume he had blown the ISIS agent to the Canadians in exchange for their sanctuary. He would assume this until he saw the plant was still functioning smoothly, without the slightest suspicion or loss in information value. The continued good work of the ISIS agent would speak for the fact that Players had not betrayed his organization.

Players knew that if he told Danby about the ISIS man, Danby would have to act. He might not go so far as to uncover the man, but he could effectively neutralize his value by introducing codes which the agent was not familiar with, or he could, more simply, stop feeding secret information into that base. Whichever method Danby chose, the end result for Players would be the same: He would be eliminated.

"Why didn't you go to the English?" Danby said. "For all their money problems they could still pay."

"I'm not asking for money!" Players snapped. "Yes, they would pay me and give me a house next to Thieu in London, and then they would strike up their own deal with ISIS because the English are a greedy lot. Somehow, I would rather trust you over everyone else in these circumstances."

"What is it you really want?" Danby said softly.

Players' features lost their sharpness, and his lips creased into a sad smile.

"A little kindness in an unkind world. A chance to live like a decent human being."

Neither man spoke for the next ten minutes. Players smoked his cigarette, looking alternately at the glowing end and the warm sunlight outside. His face was completely expressionless and serene. Danby walked around the office, trying to decide on a course of action. He felt Players was genuine, not only genuine but unique. If he had planned this move as intricately as Danby thought, the information he was willing to barter was high-grade. Yet Danby was aware of the enormous mistake he could be making if he took Players on his word. Although there was no love lost between them, the CIA was Canada's most reliable intelligence partner. Players could have been sent to change all that, just as he had admitted that ISIS had lied to Danby in the first place.

"Kindness in an unkind world."

No, men such as Players did not play on heartstrings because they themselves had been taught never to believe in them. They made simple and straightforward deals. Danby decided to gamble.

"All right. We do it your way," he said.

"You may use the information once, to test it if you like. After that, no one, not a minister, not Colburn of the CIA, no one to whom you might want to sell a favor, gets it."

"Very well."

Players looked into Danby's eyes. A man might control his features, the tone of his voice, even his minute nervous habits, but if he were lying, the eyes would give him away.

"You know the Americans have spent hundreds of millions of dollars trying to raise that sunken sub north of

Honolulu. Aside from the nuclear torpedoes, which will be valuable to them, the main target is the Russian code machine and deciphering unit.

"That wreck has been sitting on the ocean floor for almost three years. Admiral Bondarchenko had half his fleet looking for it, then gave up. As soon as he did, Moscow knew that one day the G-434 would be found and its naval code cracked. So in twenty-two months they developed a new one. When the submarine is raised, the hour it is dragged out of the water, the new system will go into operation and the Americans will have gained nothing.

"However, it so happens I know the new code and the time practice runs are made. There is one coming up tomorrow at four o'clock our time."

"Can we monitor that with our equipment?"

"Certainly. Just take everybody out of the room, I will go over it for little unwanted friends, and we shall listen in on the latest fleet gossip."

"If what you are saying is true," Danby said slowly, "we would know every move every ship makes at any minute of the day. This is something approaching ULTRA."

"It may be bigger than ULTRA should the same code patterns be adapted for the bomber and missile signals."

"I think I know why you wanted me to keep this to myself, but I would rather you told me."

"As with ULTRA, so here there is the temptation to get a little too cocky. If the CIA knew about this, or worse, NATO, word would get back to the Kremlin in less than six months. Somewhere along the line someone would become careless. It's happened before, and it will happen again. After that, in another twenty-two months or less, there would be a new code, and whatever advantage there was would be nullified.

"In normal circumstances the Americans can keep tabs on the Soviet fleet without your help. But if the nuclear countdown should ever begin, and you were to pass the code to the Joint Chiefs of Staff, Washington would need less than thirty minutes to have every submarine, surface vessel, *everything,* pinpointed and targeted. In the real game, Moscow might back down rather than risk the destruction of its precious flotilla."

Danby finally lit the cigarette he had been holding and took a deep reflective draw. Once, perhaps twice, in a lifetime did such a moment come in intelligence, where in one stroke you leapfrog over the opposition and plant yourself in his blind corner. In most cases it was a man you found in the right place, someone who was good for perhaps as long as a year, or even two. So long as you had him and they didn't know about it, you collected. But agents had short life spans. They were human. They made mistakes. Or mistakes were made for them by their controls.

Information, especially the kind Players had, didn't talk. It also had no time limit on its life. Only carelessness in handling would destroy it. That is why Players had insisted on secrecy, for there was no second chance with something as sensitive as this.

Danby reckoned that no more than six people in the whole of the Soviet Union knew the exact details of the new code: the cryptologist who had developed it, his superior, probably a GRU officer at the Frunze Higher Naval School, the three admirals of the Soviet fleet and the head of the KGB. Unless Players had come upon the code by chance, highly unlikely in Danby's opinion, then he had obtained it from one of the above.

Out of professional curiosity, the head of PSPAG wondered which one but knew better than to ask. The second great temptation would be to recruit the man.

Danby called up the military monitoring unit on the outskirts of Ottawa and asked that Room Fourteen, which was hooked into the Arctic lines, be vacated by two o'clock the following afternoon.

"Now what are we going to do about you?" he asked, turning back to Players.

"Nothing," Players answered. "My reports will be filed every fortnight. They will be a little more complex and detailed as befits an agent penetrating another service, and Geneva will be very happy."

"I would want to go over them with you."

Players shrugged. "You will find most of them highly commendable."

The telephone whirred softly. It was ten o'clock, the director was late for the day's briefing session.

"I'll get you some breakfast," Danby said, reaching for a portfolio. "Stay here until I get back. I'll cut this one short."

"We have an agreement, don't we?" Players asked, his fingers curling around Danby's forearm.

"Yes, Alex, we have," Danby said quietly. "And God help you if you've made a mistake with Geneva."

But Players saw to it that there was no mistake. Quietly, month by month, his reports were prepared and sent off. Judging from its replies, Geneva was more than pleased. Now, in September when the job was almost over, ISIS wanted him back, ahead of schedule.

"Have you spoken with Marianne?" Danby asked him as they sipped their drinks in the club lounge.

A faint grimace crossed Players' face, and he turned away.

"No, and I will not tell her."

"She knows you're a little more than a mere law professor," Danby observed dryly.

"Be that as it may, I will not have her involved in this."

But he caught the gentle sting behind Danby's words.

"Will you keep in touch with us?"

"I shall be in Geneva by eleven tonight. If you do not hear from me within six hours after that, they know of our arrangement and I am in difficulty."

"There's nothing you want me to do?"

"What is there? I am not one of yours, am I?"

"No, I suppose you're not," Danby said gently. "Let's get out of here."

"My pleasure."

They walked down the hill from the club, turned the corner at Sherbrooke Street and proceeded west to the Sutton Arms, where Players had his Montreal apartment. The hot autumn sun beat down upon them, and the winds swirled leaves at their feet. Neither man spoke until they were standing in the portico of the building.

"In case something happens to you, what shall I tell Marianne?"

Players fished out a long thin key from his blazer.

"To a safety-deposit box in the bank across the street. There is a letter for her along with a blank check. She can withdraw what is left and dispose of my personal effects as she sees fit. Give me three days to call you. If I don't, then pass it on to her."

"Anything else?"

"Just my thanks, Peter." He gripped Danby by the shoulders and smiled briefly. "I'll call you," he said, but the rest of his words were drowned out by a sudden surge of traffic.

When Players finally disappeared behind the glass doors, Danby was aware of a numbness in his stomach he hadn't felt in almost thirty years, a momentary paralysis that comes after one has given a command which could easily send another man to his death. Suddenly Danby wished Players had never become his friend.

He had to hurry now, for there was only an hour left before the plane came in.

"Marianne!"

He waited a few seconds. Sometimes she came home for lunch.

"Marianne!"

Not today.

Players telephoned the law faculty, pleading an urgent meeting in New York and asked them to cancel his classes for the rest of the week. After a five-minute cold shower he padded back into the bedroom and packed a few essentials in an overnight bag. From underneath the frame of the bed he brought out his revolver, a long-barrel Hanyatti 38 wrapped in oilcloth. A delicate piece of machinery, the gun had twice the stopping power of any similar caliber, yet was lightweight and much more accurate. He cleaned out the chamber, put in fresh bullets, then swung the straps over and around his shoulders until he and the gun became one.

He was ready in less than fifteen minutes. Placing the bag by the door, he returned to the bedroom and looked down at the rumpled bed. The faint but very particular odor of lovemaking hung over the sheets and scattered pillows. From one of the drawers, Marianne's sweaters and underwear peeked out; on the top of the chest was the stuffed cat he had presented her with last Easter at the Ritz. Here was the other half of his life for the past year. For an instant, Alexander Players felt himself slipping into that netherworld of memory and limbo, a defector's nightmare when one must return, so unwillingly, to reality, away from all one has loved and experienced. Such feelings were tinged with a desperation that made them dangerous.

"I will be back," he whispered. "I promise you I will be back!"

So his mind fastened on the one rock he knew would hold, the will that had made him break with intelligence in the first place and that would bring him back to start another life. When she learned he was gone, she would be hurt and afraid. Players hoped to God she knew how much he loved her and how unwilling he was to let her go.

Gently he closed the door to the bedroom and picked up his raincoat. He stopped to write her a few words about New York, then stepped out of the apartment, hearing the double lock slide into place.

Forty-five minutes later Players presented his Swiss diplomatic passport to Canadian customs, which made security checks unnecessary, and was escorted across the tarmac to a waiting airliner.

CHAPTER SEVEN

As Sabatini had expected, Pia Monti encountered no difficulties with French customs at Charles de Gaulle Airport in Paris. A dour-faced inspector asked her the perfunctory questions about liquor and cigarettes and scrawled an indecipherable chalk mark across her single valise. Shortly before eleven o'clock on the evening of September 17, Pia and the Tetramachus Collection were safely installed in the Hôtel Meurice, just off the Place Vendôme.

Breakfast was served in her room at eight thirty the next morning, the concierge remembering to include the day's edition of *Le Monde* with the order. The intellectual Parisian daily, which, as a matter of principle, never ran a photograph on the front page, had broken tradition by placing a large shot of Urban XI squarely on the cover. The caption read: "WHAT IS TRUTH?" PONTIUS PILATE.

The headline itself screamed out:

VATICAN SILENT ON SABATINI ACCUSATIONS

Pia read no further but telephoned Vogel at once.

On the morning of Wednesday, September 18, readers throughout Europe were confronted by similar front pages. The English and Continental dailies splashed the story on their covers in bold sensational type with pictures of Urban XI superimposed on those of death camps and the Nuremberg trials. The highbrow press was more restrained, although it too devoted entire pages to Sabatini's statements and an analysis of them.

In the United States the story had been immediately picked up by the major wire services and sent across the continent. In South America, newspapers were sold out in a matter of hours.

The morning talk in Rome consisted of nothing else but this scandal. A public which seldom bothered to read the *Osservatore Romano* now placed orders well in advance, with local vendors in some cases guaranteeing an issue with the aide of a bribe.

Jacopo Lorenzo Borghese, the Black Prince, read every paper available, slowly and carefully as was his habit. A thin, ascetic man who suffered from frequent bouts of asthma, Borghese had listened to Sabatini's speech twice last night. The Black Prince was a fervent supporter of the Roman Catholic Church. A royalist until the last war, he had found a new doctrine of autocracy in fascism and had kept this ideal alive through the creation and direction of the Squadra Azione Mussolini. It had been Borghese who had ordered the letter bomb sent to the Unita offices after Sabatini had publicly offered a reward for the arrest and conviction of those SAM members who had destroyed his presses two months previously.

When he had finished with the papers, Borghese told his secretary to telephone three of the central figures in the organization, asking them to come to his apartments for a council of war.

The air in Massimo Siboda's room was tinged with orange from the fruit bouquet the management sent up twice a week. The portly financier finished serving his guest a generous portion of soufflé, poured out a fruity sparkling rosé wine and fixed a starched napkin around his neck.

"A toast, my dear Krieg!" the cavaliere announced. "To the successful completion of our little enterprise."

Across the small cherry wood table a young German, his eyes slightly glazed by clear contacts, acknowledged the words with a deferential nod.

"To our success," he echoed in heavily accented Italian.

Krieg sampled the wine, commented on its lightness and set upon his food with the full concentration of a hungry man.

Dressed in a conservative dove-gray suit, Eberhardt Krieg was the typical product of and explanation for the continuation of the German economic miracle. Precise, efficient, with a flair for business management, Krieg was the driving force behind Eurotek, willing to gamble when necessary but a man who relied more on his intellect than instinct to mold the company's success. While he respected Lambrett and was afraid of him, Krieg nonetheless showed initiative when proposing a decision to the American. Eurotek, dealing as it did with primarily European firms, required a Continental mind to steer the company. Europeans did not hide their distaste of certain Yankee business practices which were too crude for their liking. They preferred to eat each other quietly, and thanks to Lambrett's unlimited financial backing, Eberhardt Krieg was equipped with some of the sharpest teeth of the lot.

Krieg had received the call from Costa Blanca in his flat in Rudolfstrasse, Zurich. Lambrett had been blunt and to the point.

Using every piece of information Siboda had or could

lay his hands on concerning Sabatini, Krieg was to find a way to take the Collection away from the publisher. Siboda would expect Krieg to hand the papers over to him, and Krieg was to agree to these terms. However, Lambrett instructed him first to go through the papers and destroy any evidence which would link Lambrett and the Overseas Development Corporation to the Church. After that, Siboda could have his collection.

A half hour later Krieg was in his office, looking down at two lists of names. The first was made up of prominent people who had once had a substantial interest in ODC and upon its demise had severed their connections with the company. Among them were a former British home secretary, a Roosevelt and the French minister of the interior, Sléton. Any one of these might be called upon if Krieg needed their help. The second list was much shorter, only four men and one woman. At one time or another these had served Eurotek in the field of industrial esponage. After speaking with Siboda, Krieg would have to decide which one of them to use. The criterion for selection was not a past record, for that was flawless for all of them. It was a question of who would be willing and able, if it became necessary, to kill a man as prominent as Sabatini.

"I assume Signor Lambrett has brought you up to date concerning this unfortunate situation," Siboda said.

"He has."

"And you have had a chance to look at the morning papers?"

Krieg nodded and helped himself to more wine. "A quagmire."

"The beginnings of one." Siboda nodded. "The question is what are we going to do about it?"

"Eurotek's facilities as well as those that remain of

ODC are at my disposal,'' Krieg answered. ''You have intimate knowledge of Italy's political and social fabric. Between the two of us, I am certain we can work this out.''

The smooth, unhurried tone irritated Siboda. He remembered such unfeeling precision during the war and wondered why a nation never changed its basic character from generation to generation.

''I shall be quite honest with you, Herr Krieg,'' Siboda began, dropping his pleasant, grandfatherly tone. ''Our situation is grave, and it is also delicate. Had it been possible for either myself or the Vatican to retrieve these documents, there wouldn't have been any need to involve Lambrett or you. This implies that normal channels, both legal and police, are not open to us. Lambrett and your company have experience in extralegal affairs. Therefore, I propose we work in tandem: you supply the appropriate individual, and I will gather any information necessary.''

''What is it you mean exactly by the term 'appropriate individual'?'' Krieg asked casually.

''Herr Krieg, I am too old a man to contemplate violence. But I am also a realist. We cannot preclude the possibility that Sabatini will *not* wish to give us the documents. Surely you have received advice concerning this.''

''I try to use legitimate means of persuasion wherever possible,'' Krieg answered coldly. ''However, I do understand you perfectly.''

''How long will it take you to find a suitable person?''

''I will have made my choice by tonight.''

''Tonight? That would be very quick work, Herr Krieg.''

''Will it be convenient for you to bring me plans of the Unita building and other relevant material at, say, four o'clock this afternoon?''

"I am at your disposal," Siboda said graciously. He rang his silver bell for the servant to come in and take away the remainder of the luncheon.

"May I ask what you have in mind, Herr Krieg?"

"Oh, something very simple to begin with," Krieg said, taking a proffered cigar. "I won't bother you with the details, merely the results."

And they both laughed.

Midafternoon, September 18, marked the beginning of a journalistic siege that was to last one full week. In addition to the accredited press corps of sixty-three, a slew of commentators and news analysts descended on the Holy See. The press smelled blood, and only out of respect for the religious surroundings did some semblance of order prevail within the holy walls.

Gioacchino Cardinal Volpe, secretary of state for the Holy See, returned to Rome at noon, summoned from his country residence by an urgent call from Cardinal Meyerczuk. Meyerczuk himself met the crusty seventy-two-year-old court officer at the private Vatican railroad station at the north end of the church's compound and escorted him immediately to the papal suites while outlining the general situation.

In the antechamber to the papal bedroom they found Dottore Emilio Frenza sitting with his shirt sleeves rolled up, a pile of bloodied towels at his feet.

"It looks worse than it really is," Frenza said, rising and coming before the prelates. He was completely drained, his fingers shaking ever so lightly from fatigue.

"What is it?" Volpe demanded.

"A classic case of abuse," Frenza replied in a tired, irritated tone. "I cautioned His Holiness on the use of the medicines prescribed for him. At approximately one thirty in the morning he began to vomit blood, then turned cold. A kind of delirium tremens followed. The symptoms are all normal given his extremely weakened condition. He is under sedation and will be confined to bed from now on."

"God is merciful," Volpe intoned, crossing himself.

"Sometimes that is very doubtful." Frenza shook his head. "His Holiness will never recover. And what is going on out there is *not* merciful. He should be allowed his peace now, like any other man."

"Do you think that was responsible—"

"In part, yes. To stave off the shock from Sabatini's attack and to gain strength to carry on, His Holiness relied too much on these pills. As a result, he overtaxed himself."

"Dottore Frenza," Volpe said heavily, "there are a hundred representatives from the press prowling around the Vatican. From what I am told we are being deluged by letters and calls from all over the world begging for some explanation to this affair. Since we have kept silent too long, it is imperative that I speak with His Holiness. He and he alone knows the full circumstances of what has happened."

"I am sorry." Frenza shook his head. "I understand your position, but you must also understand mine. His Holiness is my patient, and his welfare is my chief concern. To enable him to speak, I would be obliged to inject a mild amphetamine. He would be dead before he said two words. No, I cannot permit that."

"How much time has he left?" Meyerczuk asked thickly, realizing the full implication of Frenza's words.

"No more than a week. I will do what I can to ensure His Holiness does not suffer."

While the two clerics bowed their heads in silent prayer, Frenza gathered up the bloodied cloths.

"If I may have a few minutes to wash up, I shall speak to the press, unless of course you wish to speak to them yourself, Eminence."

"And what will you tell them?" Volpe asked him.

"The truth, Your Eminence," Frenza said simply. "That His Holiness is a very sick man of whom little can be expected. There will be no discussion of the nature of the illness, for that is a matter of privilege. But I will make it clear that his condition makes it impossible for him to answer the questions the press has undoubtedly put forward. The rest is not in my province to speak about."

"Given the extraordinary circumstances, surrounding us, your motives will be questioned," Meyerczuk said.

"That may be. But *my* reputation and honor are not subject to question," Frenza answered with dignity.

"Your answer to your responsibility speaks for itself," Volpe said. "I have no objections to your making a statement, Dottore, and I thank you for having come forward to help His Holiness at this time."

The surgeon bowed, kissed the ring on Volpe's hand and withdrew silently.

"This is what you brought me back to see," Volpe said to Meyerczuk, his tone carrying a mild reproof. "Why was I not immediately informed of this latest change in His Holiness' condition?"

"To have called you here in the middle of the night would have served no purpose," Meyerczuk said. "His condition remained constant. I know, for I kept vigil. I called you only when it was apparent Urban the Eleventh would never recover."

Volpe turned his gray inscrutable eyes on the weathered face of the Polish prelate and bade him sit down.

"I will call my office and have Umbretto bring us the details of the Curia's reaction. Meantime, I want to know what has been going on with Sabatini and these papers."

So Rozdentsy Cardinal Meyerczuk told Volpe of the theft and of the contents of Father Martin's letter. After he had spoken as much truth as he could, the Polish prelate began lying. He made no mention of Urban's council within him and Da Silva or of the papal decision to send for Father Domenico Martínez. All the time Meyerczuk was speaking, his calm, firm voice did not falter once. When Volpe asked him if Urban had sought the advice of any of the Curia, Meyerczuk answered in the negative. Urban, he said, had retired to consider the matter after having heard Sabatini's speech, but one might never know if His Holiness had ever arrived at a decision or what that might be.

"I am told," Volpe said, taking a note from his servant, "that as of this moment my office has received one thousand six hundred and twenty-three telephone calls and more than a thousand telegrams. These have come from both dioceses and laity all over the world. My secretary further informs me that fifty of the eighty-five cardinals of the Sacred College have sent in their queries. I expect to hear from the remainder by midnight. The Church, my dear friend, is being asked to act, yet she is little more than a rudderless ship!"

Rozdentsy Cardinal Meyerczuk smiled thinly at this last comment. For the second time in less than forty-eight hours the Holy See was trying to act. The cables to Father

Domingo in Mexico had never gone out. Meyerczuk knew this because he himself had called the priest in Mexico City. Father Domingo had received no directive from the Vatican. Now it was doubtful he ever would.

"Then it is imperative we call the Curia together to decide what is to be done," Meyerczuk said.

"There is no question of that," Volpe said. "But we also need a leader for the Curia. We need a man to direct us."

Meyerczuk did not miss the implication. According to two thousand years of tradition, the Church would be guided by the Pontiff until he gave up the ghost. No one, not Meyerczuk who was the Vatican's most prestigious international figure, not Volpe who controlled the internal politics of the Curia, not even the Curia itself, the papal court which advised the Pontiff, could wrest authority from a Holy Father not yet dead. The Curia could act only as a caretaker government, with no power to make pontifical decisions. Yet Urban XI *was* dying. He was incapacitated in a time of crisis. Could this then be the first time in Roman Catholic history that a pontiff would have his powers taken from him while still alive? Volpe was suggesting nothing less.

"Frenza has given us a reprieve to gather our forces," Volpe said. "He will feed the press vultures a few scraps of meat and buy us time to form a defense. We must use that time judiciously."

"Agreed." Meyerczuk nodded." I believe it should be the Curia as a whole which leads the Church against Sabatini."

But Volpe smiled and shook his head.

"What is the Curia if not the ecclesiastical equivalent of a political cabinet, with as many differences of opinion as there are men who constitute it? Without the leadership of a single man we will waste our time debating whether to wait to see if Urban recovers or to act at once, and, if so, how. . . . Ah, it would be all so complicated. We do not need questions at such a time, but answers!

"No," he repeated softly. "On the basis of Frenza's prognosis, I will reconvene the Sacred College of Cardinals, and they will come to Rome to elect a new pontiff. If, by the grace of God, Urban recovers, then I shall make apologies and send them all home again! I don't care at this point whom I inconvenience. The Church needs a spokesman, not an office, a man whom the clergy will rally round, one which the world will listen to and respect. That man, my friend, is you!"

"Your Eminence is asking me to usurp Peter's throne," Meyerczuk said softly.

"I am asking nothing of the sort!" Volpe retorted. "You understand that a leader is needed. You understand, or else I would not support you, that you are the man who can take command. And I respect your deference, Rozdentsy. Had you brought yourself forward, there would have been suspicion within the Church that you were trying to climb over Urban's grave into the throne. But no longer.

"I can tell you now that His Holiness explicitly stated your name when he spoke to me about the problem of succession only a month back. Now I will, in this hour of crisis, use all my influence to make certain that this choice meets with no dissent from the Curia. You have my resources behind you. I ask you to speak for all of us, for the whole Roman Catholic world, as you once spoke for it! We shall be mindful. We shall listen. The Holy Church has need of you, Rozdentsy. Take this responsibility into your hands immediately, and I promise you the chair of Peter when the Sacred College convenes!"

Rozdentsy Cardinal Meyerczuk opened his mouth to speak, but the words failed him. In the darkness of his soul the Polish prelate heard a dry, malicious chuckle. The goal he had desired for so long, which he had clung to with his life's breath, had been handed to him like the head of John. And Meyerczuk was afraid, revolted and afraid by what had been bequeathed to him.

The big jet climbed to twenty-nine thousand feet over Halifax, Nova Scotia, leveled off at longitude forty-five degrees north and picked up a brisk tail wind that increased its speed to just over seven hundred miles an hour.

From the outside, the aircraft looked no different from any other commercial liner. The change was completely on the inside.

Behind the pilot and copilot, to the left of the navigator, all employees of ISIS, sat the lone radio operator. The space normally reserved for first class belonged exclusively to him. Crammed with electronic receiving and jamming equipment, camera controls which operated the Zeiss Ikon lens on the belly of the plane and a communications apparatus which could link the speaker to any radio, telephone or shortwave unit in the world, the cabin was a miniature duplicate of the Geneva control center.

In the economy section, sixty seats had been ripped out to make room for working desks, sofas and video equipment, as well as an enlarged galley and sleeping quarters. This is where Players was now being briefed by Pelikan.

Ten minutes after he had walked onto the plane, Players knew Pelikan had nothing in mind but the current operation. The head of ISIS operations had given him the customary frigid smile, commented on the fact that Players was about three pounds overweight and settled down to business. The final proof came when Pelikan revealed Rome as the destination. For the sake of time they would be bypassing Geneva altogether.

Players read through the twenty pages of the IKONEN file, his memory retaining the pertinent names: Cardinal Marrenzo, who had called ISIS in; his secretary, Pio Cliotia, who would act as liaison between Geneva and the prelate; Giulio Musco, ISIS chief in Rome, who also doubled as lieutenant in the counterintelligence section of the SID, the Italian Secret Service.

"I don't really see the point," Players said. "You didn't have to pull me in for this job."

"You have been away too long," Pelikan said. "The condition in Italy has changed since your last visit. In spite of Fransci's majority or because of it, rumors have it that the right will make a big push in the next few months. Whoever has the papers will have quite a lever on the Church, which is certain to figure in any internal politics."

"How do you mean?"

"The Vatican has always been anticommunist. If friends of Borghese, the Black Prince and head of the SAM, obtain the collection, there will be nothing the Church can refuse them."

"And Fransci?"

"He is in a very tight spot. No one knows if Sabatini has yet shown him the papers and, if so, what Fransci will do. He has the majority now and may wait to see what the referendum yields on the question of abortion before making his move. Or he may just use the Collection to blow Italy apart by challenging the Vatican head-on."

"Then it's civil war," Players finished for him.

"A very likely possibility. So long as Italy's Parliament is filled with splinter parties that prevent ultimate cohesion, everybody is happy. But if Fransci's faction keeps gaining support, as it has been doing over the last year, the trouble and interference will begin."

"Where do the papers go when I get them?"

"Geneva. We would like to have a look at them first."

"Of course."

It made no difference to Players one way or another. The job appeared simple and straightforward, and that was all that concerned him.

"What about my cover?"

"The simpler, the better."

Pelikan spilled out the contents of an envelope on the desk. "There is a room reserved for you at the Intercontinental under the name of Rocchi. We've made you a Reuters correspondent for the sake of registration. With so many reporters in the city, nobody will notice one more. Car keys, Interpol card in the usual French name of De Bellefeuille, Canadian passport for normal traveling, license under the passport name and an Opus Dei card, also made out in your Canadian name."

"Opposition?"

"Only two possibilities at the moment. The SID and the Squadra Azione Mussolini. You have a free hand in dealing with both of them."

"The target?"

"The priest Belobraditz has not yet been located, but we continue to work on that. Your prime concern is Sabatini and whoever else may be involved in this."

Players opened the publisher's dossier and looked at the appended photograph of a volume similar to the Tetramachus Collection.

"He could have put the collection anywhere. What makes you think it's still with him?"

"We have looked in his safety-deposit box and other such places," Pelikan said indifferently. "He is keeping it with him."

"Why should he hand it over to me?"

"There is a girl," Pelikan said tonelessly. "These are her particulars. Use her, if you must, and you will get what you want from him, rest assured. Just be certain no one arrives before you."

Players looked down at the photograph of Pia Monti. She was the lever to be employed if he could not convince Sabatini that it would be in his best interests to part with the papers. Yes, it was a simple operation, straightforward and dirty. He did not even notice the slight turbulence as the aircraft banked sharply and sped toward eastern Canada.

Professor Aaron Vogel, Doctor of Philosophy and Professor Emeritus of Semitic Studies, was a tall, angular man with a hawklike nose and very large ears, which he invariably tugged while lecturing. An eminent scholar in a university saturated with eminent scholars, Vogel was something of a national treasure, lone survivor of that Jewish triad French academicians privately referred to as *nos trois bons juifs.* Stefan Strauss, the Viennese anthropologist, had been another. The third, who, like Vogel, had been admitted into the Academy well after his major work had been completed and overlooked, was the mathematician Schwartzkopf. He had died three years ago, a suicide by an open gas oven. Vogel had thought it ironic that a man who had cheated Bergen-Belsen should have chosen such a way out. But he understood why Schwartzkopf had done it.

A man who had reached the biblical age of eighty, Vogel had few things left to call his own except memory, and it was memory that had been slowly poisoning him.

Until July, 1942, the professor and his family had lived a quiet orderly life in the Paris suburb of Neuilly. At the outbreak of the war they had put their faith in the French ideals of tolerance and justice and in the strength of the French army. The army betrayed them in the early months of 1940. On July 16, 1942, after the French Pétainist government had so generously handed the Gestapo its master card files on Jewish citizens, it was the Republic's turn to sell them out.

At three o'clock in the morning Vogel's diabetic wife, Anna, was wrenched from her husband's arms at the same time as a truncheon smashed into the professor's kidneys. Esther, his daughter, submitted with graceful dignity. Mordecai, his son, had to be beaten senseless. Six French police had come for the family, and it was all over in less than fifteen minutes.

Not until Aaron Vogel arrived in Belsen did he learn that his wife had not survived the long journey to the same camp. Esther, removed from the internment center of the Vel d'Hiv outside Paris, was never heard of again. Mordecai was devoured in Treblinka.

Still, a few of the tears of God must have touched Aaron Vogel, for he managed to survive his hell. He lived and worked and suffered, partly because carpentry had been his hobby and the Germans needed skilled craftsmen and partly because he had fallen back on the one thing no one could take from him—his Jewishness. In the midst of genocide and horror, Vogel came of age as a Jew, and in the foulness of a world gone mad he began to dream of Zionism.

When he stumbled back to Paris from Germany, after a long treatment at a British hospital, the French intellectuals welcomed him with open arms. They clothed and fed him and left no doubt about his resuming his old job at the university. The government gave him a handsome pension and presented him with the Medallion of Freedom, which he always kept hidden away in a drawer. Even though he took their bread and salt and kind words, Vogel never forgave the French their sins. He hated them and in his heart renounced them forever. He stayed on only because there was nowhere else to go and because, by staying, he shamed them, serving as living memorial to their cowardice.

And all the time he worked for and dreamed of Israel.

Sabatini was one of the few men Vogel respected and admired. There was a streak in the Italian's character, a stupid, senseless, yet necessary preoccupation with justice that touched Vogel. Therefore, even though he had read the newspapers and realized he would be committing an illegal act, Vogel had returned Sabatini's call yesterday and had agreed to ascertain the authenticity of this volume called the Tetramachus Collection. He didn't care about consequences anymore.

Professor Vogel returned to his flat at six o'clock, Wednesday, September 18, carrying the collection in his ancient briefcase. The meal his housekeeper had prepared for him was warming in the oven. On the kitchen table was a half bottle of red wine, a bottle of mineral water and some stewed fruit for dessert. Vogel ate slowly and carefully, concentrating on every morsel. Not until an hour later did he lock himself away in his study with the package that that nice young girl had brought him in the morning.

Aaron Vogel had expected to find nothing of historical significance in these papers. The Church's role in the Second War was well known, if kept silent in scholarly quarters. Whatever papers would have been interesting from the point of view of possible criminal evidence had certainly been destroyed by that astute politico Pius XII. Still, the whole affair was intriguing, although Vogel was certain everyone would be disappointed in the end, especially after the clamor in the press.

He was wrong.

After the first four sections, which he was certain were authentic, Vogel began to take liberties. He skimmed Chapters Five and Six, which dealt with the stand of the French high clergy during the occupation, and proceeded directly to Chapter Seven. The heading for the chapter was titled "OPERATION SPRING WIND."

Aaron Vogel's shoulders sagged forward, his eyes widening as an ancient, yet all-too-familiar terror gripped him.

Operation Spring Wind. The name some Gestapo poet had given the roundup of French Jews on the nights of July 16 and 17. The Spring Wind was the death wind. Twelve thousand eight hundred and eighty-four Jews had been caught in *la grande rafle.* Betrayed by French citizens, rounded up by French police, placed in a French detention center, transported to Germany in French railroad stock cars, fewer than four hundred returned from the death camps. None of the four thousand and fifty-one children ever came back.

Three in almost thirteen thousand. Not so much. But they were mine. Oh, dear God, they were mine!

THE HOLY SEE
ROME JULY 15 1942

TO HIS EXCELLENCY PETAIN MARSHAL OF FRANCE

IN REPLY TO YOUR EXCELLENCY'S LETTER DATED AUGUST 8 I RESPECTFULLY AND WITH ALL CONFIDENCE STATE THE FOLLOWING: NEVER HAS ANYTHING BEEN SAID TO ME WHICH WOULD INDICATE EITHER CRITICISM OR DISAPPROVAL ON THE PART OF THE VATICAN OF THE LEGISLATION AND ORDINANCES THAT HAVE BEEN PASSED IN FRANCE.

JEWS ARE ALIENS IN FRANCE BOTH IN RELIGION AND RACE. THE PROPHYLACTIC MEASURES INSTITUTED BY THE GOVERNMENT REGARDING THE DEPORTATIONS OF PARIS JEWS ARE NOT ONLY NECESSARY THEY ARE RIGHT.

LEON BERARD
AMBASSADOR TO THE HOLY SEE

But they were Jews, and what was it to be a Jew in the history of Roman Catholic Christianity?

In the fifteenth century, during the august reign of Paul II, Jews were set at a table to eat for three hours without stopping or being able to relieve themselves, then made to run the streets during a festival while the populace jeered and goaded them on. In the sixteenth century, Paul IV cast the Jews into the ghetto. They could own no property, associate with no Christian, engage in no trade save that of collecting garbage. They could still pray, but their temples were afforded no protection. Pius V proclaimed Jews as servants of Satan, seducers, sorcerers, vagabonds and thieves. Innocent III forced on them the badge of shame, while John XXII laid the Talmud upon a pyre and burned it in the public square.

A newly crowned pontiff on the way to the Basilica of San Giovanni in Laterano would stop to receive the Pentateuch, the first five books of the Old Testament, attributed to Moses, from the chief rabbi of Rome. The Holy Father would hold the book, then turn it upside down, and the rabbi would bow and hold out his hand for the twenty gold pieces the papal chamberlain would place there, supposedly paying for the papal rebuke but, in fact, extending it by this gesture. This practice, institutionalized into one of the Church's most sacred pageants, endured until the late sixteenth century.

A Jew's place in Christian Rome was to serve as a *living* reminder of Christ's assassin. The Jew was a threat to the Christian spirit, and in defense of that spirit it was necessary to isolate him in the ghetto, ostracizing him from the rest of society so that Jewish teaching never infected the gentile.

Even though the state of Italy, since 1871, had shown itself the one of the least anti-Semitic countries in Europe, the Jew still provided the Church with an enemy to guard against. He was not subject to pogroms as in the Russian pale, for he was needed alive, to suffer humiliation and rebuke, a threat to be preserved so that Christian society might see him and so flock around its protector, the Church. So when the time for sacrifice came, as it did in the years 1939-1945, the Holy Father decided first to preserve the Church and later, if it was possible or advisable, to speak on behalf of the Jews.

Yet what was there left for Pius XII to say? While serving in Germany prior to the war, the man who would be Pope had concluded a number of agreements with the Reich that protected the Church. Yet these concordats also encouraged German Catholics to support Nazism without moral qualms. If Pius XII dared speak out for *anyone*—Jews or non-Jews—the German faithful would have to choose between the Church and Hitler.

What was there left to say when by his silence toward French Cardinal Tisserant, the Holy Father had said it all? One of the few clergy in France who did not enthusiastically endorse the Pétain regime, Tisserant advised His Holiness to issue an encyclical instructing Catholics, including German soldiers, to follow the dictates of their conscience rather than a superior's orders. His advice was rejected. Self-convenience was Pius's policy. He would not alter it.

What, in fact, could he do but watch as France handed over its Jews and as, a year later, Rome followed suit? There was everything to do, and the deeds of the clergy who helped were forever etched on the hearts of the survivors. But the hand which could have raised thousands more to work for the helpless and those about to be destroyed was never lifted, for it itself was already a dead hand.

Vogel flung his arm against the red leather volume, sending it, an ashtray and the mineral water flying across the floor. Then he threw his head back and wailed as he had that night when they had torn Anna from his arms, the wail of an animal in the agony of its death throes. He never heard the ringing of the telephone.

Whatever part of Aaron Vogel had died that night of July 16 was now reborn. After he had wept, the professor retrieved the book and carefully wiped the cover. Then he cleared up scattered bits of glass and ashes. When everything was again in order, he brought out his little telephone note pad and looked up the number of the Israeli embassy.

When the night operator, a young sabra girl, answered,

Vogel said in Hebrew, "*Shalom,* I have a message for Eli Mandel. It is urgent."

"Who is this?"

"A survivor."

The girl could not understand the weeping on the other end of the line, but she put him through at once to Mandel's private line.

"Survivor" was a term the Mossad, Israeli intelligence, had assigned to prominent Jews like Vogel whose travels and acquaintances might yield interesting information. They were to use it if they wished to contact the resident Mossad agent in any embassy around the world. Eli Mandel was the resident for France.

"He isn't answering at home either," Pia said.

"Have you tried the general department number?"

"That, and his own office. His secretary told me he had left at four o'clock. He had no lectures this evening."

"Did he say anything to you about how long it would take to verify the collection?" Sabatini took a last swallow of cold tea and grimaced.

"He said he would look it over at home," Pia explained patiently. "I asked him to phone you as soon as he got in."

"Well, he hasn't done that, has he!"

Pia sighed and remained silent. The whole afternoon had been like this, fraught with strained nerves and irritation as Sabatini waited for Vogel to telephone from Paris.

The situation had been aggravated by incessant calls from newspapers, television stations and magazines, each demanding an exclusive interview with the publisher. As soon as Pia arrived back in Rome, a little after one o'clock that afternoon, she instructed the operator to tell everyone that Sabatini was not available for further comment under any circumstances. She found it odd, though, that there had been not one word from the Vatican.

"All right then, let us go home," Sabatini said suddenly. "I have had enough of this madness!"

"When is Fransci coming over tomorrow?" Pia asked him.

"Sometime around midmorning, I expect. I couldn't put him off any longer. This time the request came through official channels."

"Then let's hope Vogel telephones tonight. I gave him your home number, even though he said he had it. His confirmation of the Collection's authenticity would help you explain to Fransci why you haven't yet produced the papers."

"Fransci will understand," Sabatini said. "If he is insistent on seeing proof, there is always the copy."

It was not a coincidence that the Black Prince was walking down the Via Mortebella at the same time as Sabatini and Pia Monti came out of the Unita building. Jacopo Lorenzo Borghese was on his way to evening mass, and he had chosen this roundabout route to his church because he wanted to look at Sabatini's bastion one more time.

Neither the publisher nor his secretary or bodyguard saw Borghese standing across the street. The Black Prince was watching them with the mild interest of one examining a butterfly under glass. It would be the last time he would see Sabatini alive, and it was a curious feeling to watch one's victim go his way in a state of blissful ignorance.

The council of war which had been held in Borghese's

home earlier in the day had decided that Sabatini should die. From the network of strategically placed SAM agents within Rome, a detailed report of Sabatini's movements over the next few days came into Borghese's hands. Sabatini had left very little to chance, Borghese thought. His bodyguard was with the publisher constantly; he had special alarm systems both at the Unita building and in his private flat. Sabatini had even hired private protection for his mistress. But all this was worthless, as the final page of the report bore out.

The *matrona* was a devout Catholic woman, a true Italian mother. Sabatini had hired her more out of pity than because of her qualifications. The *matrona*'s husband had died very suddenly, leaving her with an unmanageable family of twelve. What Sabatini did not know was that her eldest son belonged body and soul to Borghese's SAM. Since the son contributed most to the family coffers and brought home unexpected "gifts" of food or clothing, the *matrona* hid nothing from him. When he called her that afternoon and casually asked her how things were on the job, he first heard her usual diatribe about Sabatini's living in sin and then the minor gossip. The *matrona* did not notice that her son asked her twice about Sabatini's decision to meet with Saghi on Thursday. She did not catch the excitement in his voice when he demanded whether she was certain Sabatini would not cancel his appointment. She repeated three times over that Sabatini had had the car's repairs postponed because of the lunch. The *matrona* was only displeased that her son should have hung up so abruptly. She could usually count on him to hear her out.

* * *

At six o'clock on the afternoon of September 18, Eberhardt Krieg had moved into his room at the Hotel Excelsior. Here, in close proximity to Cavaliere Siboda, he would stay until the hunt for the Tetramachus Collection was finished.

Shortly after his meeting with Siboda, Krieg telephoned Zurich and spoke with the head of Eurotek's internal-security control, a sallow-faced death's-head of a man called Günter Fischer. Before moving to Eurotek, Fischer had served on the homicide squads of three city police forces, including the notorious Squad One in Munich. His rank of detective sergeant had given Fischer access to files on the best safecrackers, alarm systems men and hired guns in Europe, a knowledge that served Eurotek very well. Krieg had taken Fischer's advice on the most delicate thefts the company had engaged in. He had been prepared to take his word now, although admittedly, Krieg was surprised by Fischer's choice of an operative.

She was twenty-seven, perhaps twenty-eight. It was difficult to tell exactly since small women always appear younger than they actually are. Her golden hair had a touch of glitter to it, indicating coloring. When she chose, she could shift her green eyes and shy smile into an unmistakable invitation. But the eyes were also shrewd, suggesting an ability to evaluate men and circumstances quickly and effectively. They also hinted at treason.

Krieg thought her a beautiful, desirable woman who could have been any one of a number of things; whether housewife or attorney, it mattered not at all. But no one would have guessed that Heidi Seppes was one of Europe's top free-lance killers. Her name had been first on the list Krieg had looked at in Zurich.

"It is a pleasure to meet you, Herr Krieg," Heidi Seppes said, taking a proffered cigarette and settling back on the divan.

"The pleasure is mine, I assure you," Krieg replied with a slight bow. "May I offer you a cocktail?"

"No, thank you. When Herr Fischer spoke with me earlier, he indicated that your problem is an urgent one. I suggest we discuss it. Business is rather brisk these days. I am expected elsewhere within the week."

"Exactly what did Fischer tell you?" asked Krieg, taking a chair opposite her.

"Your firm is interested in securing certain papers from the publisher Sabatini. This may or may not necessitate killing him. There is also a priest as the second target who is not to live."

"That is very succinct," Krieg observed calmly. "And accurate."

"The theft of this collection will cost ten thousand marks, excluding expenses." Heidi Seppes continued. "If Sabatini is eliminated in the process, there will be an additional twenty-five thousand marks paid. The same for the priest, twenty-five."

"Agreed."

"Have you any information for me concerning Sabatini?"

Krieg reached for a file of papers and drawings Siboda had supplied him with after lunch.

"Here you have the blueprints for the Unita building, a special design of Sabatini's office, a list of employees and the hours they keep and finally the security arrangements. This is Sabatini's home address, an analysis of his daily movements and so on. I'm afraid there is nothing on the priest so far that would be of any value. But I have no doubt we will locate him before too long.''

Heidi Seppes glanced through the papers and nodded approvingly.

''This appears to be in order. Is the Tetramachus Collection in the safe?''

''We expect so,'' Krieg said. ''According to the manager of his bank, Sabatini hasn't been to his safety-deposit box or to the bank vault. If we eliminate those two locations, it appears logical the papers should be in his office.''

''Possibly,'' Heidi Seppes murmured. ''It would make matters easier if they were.''

She stood up and smoothed her skirt.

''Please try to find the whereabouts of the priest as quickly as possible,'' Heidi Seppes said. ''If the papers are not in Sabatini's office, I will have to try his apartment and one or two other places as well, considering he has a mistress. This will take time, and it would be better for all concerned if we didn't have to ferret out the priest too.''

''We will do our best to oblige you,'' Krieg answered.

''And now you may take me out for a light dinner.'' Heidi Seppes smiled. ''I haven't been to a true Roman supper for months.''

CHAPTER EIGHT

The Black Prince's attack team arrived in a light-gray gas van, the blue dome light flashing. The night porter had the door open as two men ran up and explained that the company had detected a leak in the main servicing this building. The crew had been sent to check the connecting valves for traces of escaping gas.

The porter carefully examined the credentials of the two. He should also have called the gas superintendent of the district to verify that there was an emergency in this area. But the men were in a great hurry. They said it would take at least ten minutes to go over the building's central pipes. If there was, in fact, a leakage, every minute was precious in evacuating the tenants. The night porter hesitated. He did not want to bear responsibility for an explosion, but he knew he should countercheck the crew's identity. The building's tenants paid extra for such special security. But he was afraid and agreed to open the doors to the underground garage at once.

The driver drove down to the second level and parked his vehicle lengthwise across the trunk of Sabatini's Bentley. The panel door slid back, and the bomb man jumped out, case in hand. The driver went over to the door of the utility room, opened it and switched the light on. He doubted the night porter would come down to look at the crew's work. If he should, he would see the light and presume they were busy. The driver hoped the porter's curiosity would not get the better of him. Borghese's orders had been precise: There was to be no violence. No one in the building was to think that anything was amiss, since the ultimate success of the operation depended on Sabatini's believing his security had not been infringed upon. There wasn't to be the slightest hint of what was going to happen.

The bomb man opened his tool box and set to work. The device he had chosen was an American-made limpet mine, eight inches in diameter, designed to blow a hole some twelve feet across in the side of an unarmored vessel. It was a weapon favored by commandos who made a specialty of raiding harbors. The bomb man had handled such an explosive many times during his career as underwater demolition expert for the Italian navy.

Priming the mine, he adjusted the timer and slid it under the trunk of the Bentley, wriggling toward the gas tank. The Bentley's suspension gave the car such a smooth ride that there was no chance of the limpet falling off. The magnetic plate on the mine would hold it, secure and flat, against the tank, making it invisible to anyone looking across at the car. The timer was one of the most reliable pieces on the market, a German Exacta unit. It would detonate the charge exactly to the second, almost twelve hours from now when Sabatini would be leaving the Unita offices for his customary drive to lunch. The publisher might have a minute and half to live after the car began moving.

The bomb man's low whistle alerted the driver that the work was complete. Turning out the lights, he locked up the utility room and ran back to the van. The bomb man slid his tool box along the truck's metal floor and jumped inside. The panel door closed, and the van began moving up the grade toward the exit, which opened automatically.

The driver braked before the main entrance, assured the porter the pipes were secure and returned to the truck. With the blue light whirling silently, the gas van disappeared into the darkness of the early morning, Thursday, September 19.

Heidi Seppes kept her working weight at once hundred and one pounds. Dexterity coupled with speed enabled her to make her way up the fire escape in less than a minute, carrying twenty pounds of equipment strapped to her back. She swung herself onto the roof and in a crouching run made for the heavy fireproof door that connected the air-conditioning unit with the uppermost level of the interior emergency staircase. She had no difficulty in picking the lock.

Heidi had studied the Unita blueprints until she had memorized the internal design of the building. Moving in total darkness, she needed only another minute to reach the floor where Sabatini had his offices. Although the hallway was lit, there was no guard to be seen. The absence did not surprise her since a publishing house does not ordinarily require extensive security measures.

The door to the whole of Sabatini's suite, which included Pia Monti's office, was open. Heidi moved past Pia's desk and stopped abruptly at the entrance to Sabatini's private quarters. Again the door was open, almost too inviting. Yet there was no electronic alarm cutting across the frames or any sign of sophisticated infrared cameras on the far walls. She looked up at the corners of the ceiling, searching for the telltale glint of lenses. There was nothing, and she stepped in.

The safe, a small Chubb with the usual tumbler combination, was one she was familiar with. It was located in the most unimaginative place, behind and to the right of the massive draftsman's desk. Heidi Seppes exchanged her nylon gloves for a pair commonly used by surgeons and curled her fingers around the safe's handle to test it. The man who had taught her the art of safecracking told her always to try the door first before running a combination. It was a chance in a million that the door would be unlocked, but sometimes people were careless. They might close the door while speaking to someone or, simply out of forgetfulness, never lock it. Such good fortune had never befallen Heidi before tonight.

She was tempted to laugh. The vault was completely empty. Sabatini had not forgotten to lock it. There simply hadn't been any need.

The same was true for Sabatini's desk. Every drawer, although it had a lock, was open. The bookcase was a picture of innocence. The publisher had been expecting uninvited company and had simply neutralized the efforts of whoever would be coming. After a quick check of the bookcase, Heidi Seppes left the office.

Thus far Sabatini had the upper hand. With foresight, he had chosen to remove the Collection from the office rather than surround it with expensive warning systems. Heidi was certain she would not find the Collection anywhere in the Unita building, but that did not necessarily mean her trip was valueless. Sabatini might have neglected to take the same preparations with his secretary's desk.

Pia Monti's day calendar lay open on the blotter. There was no better way to check what the publisher had done in the last few days, to discover who had called on him and the calls he himself made, than by checking his secretary's appointment schedule. Using a microfilm Minox with infrared film, Heidi photographed each day sheet beginning with September 16.

Two minutes later she was ready to go into the last phase of her operation. From her pack she brought out a long-range microphone, seven by four centimeters. It was, for its use, a bulky instrument, one she did not particularly like. But the transmission unit could send out signals for over a mile, and since she could not monitor the publisher's conversations from within the building, the Bellart Transistor System was her only option. After returning to Sabatini's office, she unscrewed the grille to the ventilating shaft and taped the microphone to the inside. Not even a conscientious cleaning woman would find it there.

Heidi Seppes took a full five minutes to make certain there were no traces of her intrusion. It was mandatory that Sabatini not even suspect that his office had been entered. For the microphone to have any value the publisher would have to continue to work normally, placing calls and holding discussions under the assumption that his territory was as private as he thought it was.

Within seven minutes Heidi Seppes was making her way down the fire escape. A half hour later she arrived at the small hotel where she had taken a room and began to develop the Minox film.

The Cloiserie de Lilas is situated at the corner of the Boulevard St.-Michel and Montparnasse. The large café had become respectable since the Hemingway era of sawdust on the floor. Now everything is spit and polish, the oysters served on gleaming silver platters instead of on chipped metal trays. But if the oysters are as good as they were then, the clientèle of artsy matrons, young hacks, gossip journalists and gallery operators leaves much to be desired.

Eli Mandel loved oysters. Since they were outrageously expensive in Tel Aviv, he ate them abroad as often as he could no matter the hour of day or night. He had also thought of the Cloiserie because it was a stone's throw from Vogel's flat on the rue de Rennes.

Eli Mandel was a short, unassuming man, very strong, with the physique of a swimmer. A graying fifty, he had worked for both the Hagannah and Simon Wiesenthal's Vienna Documentation Center before going into the Mossad. Mandel was not a survivor in the true sense. He had been with U.S. Army intelligence liaison to the Canadian troops that had cleaned up Buchenwald. It was Mandel who had ordered the bulldozers to bury the stinking corpses of the 13,000 inmates the Germans had hastily gassed but had been unable to cremate. Mandel noticed one of the ovens had even been cleaned in preparation and the pipes refitted. He went to the nearby village, rounded up the quaking citizenry and forced them to look inside the chamber so that they might see what it had been like.

Although his methods earned him reprimands from his superiors, Mandel stayed on with G-2 when the POW interrogations began. He was handed most of the captured SS men of the district and broke them one by one because he was a Jew who did not hesitate to use his fists or boots. When one camp guard, who had taken great pleasure in preparing female prisoners for sterilization, made an unfortunate reference to Mandel's genitals, Mandel threw him out the fourth-floor window and calmly reported the incident as suicide.

So it had gone in the years since. Skillfully, methodically, without emotion the tracking, the killing, the revenge on the tormentors of his race. A professional hunter, Mandel had come to be feared even by his neighbors in the Tel Aviv suburb where he made his adopted home. On quiet afternoons, he might be seen casually whipping a long flat-bladed knife into a lemon tree at twenty paces.

Eli Mandel delicately crushed a quarter of a lemon over an oyster, watching the delicacy curl up at the edges before scooping it into his mouth. Across the white tablecloth, Aaron Vogel stared mutely at his cooling café crème. Mandel thought he looked as bad today as he had sounded yesterday. His face was drawn and, for the first time in five years, unshaved.

"You should have had oysters," Mandel said.

Vogel started and smiled wanly. "Doctor will not permit it. Too acidic."

"Not for you."

Vogel looked up at the impassive nut brown eyes that were carefully surveying his every movement. He, too, was afraid of Mandel.

"I don't want this!" he said suddenly, pushing his cup to one side.

Mandel reached over and covered Vogel's gnarled hand with his own.

"All right, Aaron, I'm here. You wanted to talk, let's talk. Get it out of you."

"What is Israel receiving from the Vatican?" Vogel asked quietly.

The question startled Mandel, but he recovered quickly.

"What should Israel be getting from the Vatican except attempts to convert us all and slaps on the wrist for our raids into Lebanon?"

"I mean reparations, money for our blood that was spilled while the Holy See looked on."

"We get no money from the Vatican," Mandel said. "Oh, there is a little bit, but that has to do with Jerusalem. Nothing like the Germans send us."

"Why not?"

"Why should the Roman Pope pay the sons of Abraham? He owes us nothing."

"He owes us everything," Vogel insisted stubbornly, "because he did nothing!"

"Aaron, lower your voice," Mandel ordered calmly. From the corner of his eye, the Israeli had noticed heads turning in their direction.

"Why hasn't the Vatican paid?" Vogel repeated.

"Again I ask you: for what?"

"For the fifty kilograms of gold the Jews of Rome rendered up for their lives on September 28, 1943," Vogel whispered. "Lives that were later lost anyway. Let us begin with that!"

Mandel knew he was no match for Vogel's memory. Every incident, no matter how small, that related to the Holocaust was etched on the scholar's mind. Letting Vogel lead him on was useless, so Mandel struck at the heart.

"What information do you have, and who passed it on to you?"

Vogel blinked rapidly and tugged at his ears.

"What will Israel do? Can she get money?"

"That depends on how trustworthy your information is and what it pertains to."

"Operation Spring Wind," Vogel said woodenly. "You have heard of it?"

"I have," Mandel said.

"Sea Spray?"

"That also."

"I have evidence that the Vatican knew of these and other operations before the time of their execution. Knew and did nothing! Is *that* enough for Israel?"

Mandel remained silent. Vogel's vehemence was completely unexpected. Something he had read or heard, someone he had seen in the street, had removed the clamp from his bitterness. It mattered not at all how long or how well the charade of a respectable existence had been played. Bitterness never disappeared from the hearts of a survivor. It allowed him to exist, to work out a new life, perhaps even to dream, if the capacity to dream had also endured. But out of bitterness there would eventually come the moment of revenge, a split second in which the survivor beheld an opportunity to punish his old oppressors, not merely to reflect on and remember them. That moment had to be seized before the guilty escaped once more. Mandel had seen the syndrome many times. It was moving and pitiful, and usually the evidence that had brought it to life could not be substantiated or acted on because the proof was tenuous.

"I don't make Israeli policy on war crimes, Aaron. I promise you nothing until you tell me more. Then I will speak to Tel Aviv."

"But can it be done?" Vogel insisted. "Can Israel demand payment?"

"Israel can demand," Mandel said softly. "She has every right."

Vogel exhaled and sat back, limp, tired and very old. "You know about this *affaire* Sabatini?"

Mandel nodded.

"I have the papers. Sabatini sent them to me for verification. I have read them. They are true and real and contain cablegrams and letters on both Sea Spray and Spring Wind."

The old man paused and stared at Mandel's amazed expression.

"I knew," Vogel said through tears. "For thirty years I sensed this evidence in my heart, but no one called on me to testify about what I knew in my heart. The guilty went unpunished because no one would believe me. . . .

"Anna, Esther, Mordecai—my wife and children whose graves I have never found. This Collection will be their monument. Remind Tel Aviv, remind them of how Vogel has helped them before. And *tell* them that if they do not want to settle accounts with the Vatican by using the Collection, I shall!"

Mandel took Vogel by the arm and helped him to his feet. Together they walked slowly back to the apartment house, and Mandel asked if he might see the papers. The historian shook his head.

"You can read it after you have spoken with your superiors in the Mossad. Before the Collection leaves my hands, I must know what is intended for it. I will not let you take it away from me!"

"Then you might also pack a bag," Mandel advised him. "We may have to move quickly."

But Eli Mandel did not return to the Israeli embassy immediately. Instead, he went to the Bourse, where most natives and virtually all foreigners placed overseas telephone calls. Mandel trusted neither his embassy's cryptocode, which had been broken three times in the past year, nor the special embassy lines constantly monitored by the DST, French internal security. The safest way to call Tel Aviv was from the center of Paris.

The connection crackled with static from the scrambler device on the other end. Mandel waited until the deputy chief of the service, Colonel Joachim Lanthem, came on the line, and began speaking rapidly.

"You are certain it is the same set of papers all the uproar is about?" Lanthem asked him.

"One and the same," Mandel answered. "But before I see them, I have to tell him what we propose to do."

"What does he want?"

"Revenge."

Even a thousand miles of bad connection could not erase Lanthem's sigh of impatience.

"Be more specific, Eli!"

"He's thinking of blackmail actually," Mandel said lightly. "He wants Israel to demand some kind of reparations from the Vatican, in exchange for the papers."

"And what does he want us to say?" Lanthem snapped. "Fine, the floor price is a million pounds? Two? Why not fifty?"

"Joachim," Mandel said, his voice dangerously smooth. "Vogel lost his entire family in Catholic France. This is his own very good reason for asking that something be done. The days of retribution are *not* over, no matter how soft your ass gets back there. So listen to me, Joachim, a man who has helped us before, financially and in terms of raw intelligence, wants us to help him, us and himself. I don't think you're giving him the attention he merits."

There was a moment's pause on the line.

"Believe me, Eli," Lanthem said at last. "If I could get you back here to talk to Rabin himself, you might understand what you're asking for. Do you seriously believe the government would consider holding the Vatican to ransom? Aren't the implications of antagonizing the Catholic world clear enough? It may not love us, but some Catholic countries do sell us arms and support our existence. What do you think the PM would say when I offer to bring him material which may or may not relate to war crimes, which *was* stolen from the Vatican and which one man demands to be used for blackmail!"

"Where is Rabin now?"

"In the Knesset, listening to the opposition explain why we must take our settlements off the Golan Heights."

"Then I tell you what, Joachim. Why don't you spare the prime minister the agony of that debate and give him a really tough situation to ponder about? Tell him the man is Aaron Vogel. Tell him what Vogel has and what he wants. Who knows? What Rabin says may surprise you.

"But if I do not hear from you within a few hours, Vogel and I will be on the evening flight to Tel Aviv."

"I promise you nothing," Lanthem said. "Just try to remember, Eli, you do not dictate what the service can and cannot do."

"I told that to Vogel, and he all but spat in my face." Mandel laughed. "You know something, he should have spat. He made me remember what you have forgotten—what it is to be Jew with a memory. I'll be waiting, Joachim."

And he hung up.

Eli Mandel was not happy with Lanthem's reaction to his call, and because he was unhappy, he decided to go ahead with a plan of his own, one that at least would protect Vogel and the Collection.

In other circumstances of a similar nature, Mandel

would have had no qualms about burglarizing the location where the information he wanted was stored. But he would not do this to Vogel. The historian did not deserve such treatment. So Mandel settled on the next best solution. He called up two of his men at the embassy and dispatched them to Vogel's apartment. One agent would patrol the hallway leading to Vogel's apartment, the other would station himself opposite the building. Communication would be maintained by two-way radio. If anyone tried to break into the apartment, Mandel was to be notified at once. The agents were armed, but the Israeli resident cautioned them on the use of their weapons. They were to use their hands first, revolver last.

After he was satisfied he had done what was possible, Mandel returned to the embassy to await the call from Tel Aviv.

At precisely five minutes after nine o'clock on the morning of September 19, Dottore Emilio Frenza rose from his place at the end of the conference table and addressed the prelates sitting around him.

"Your Eminences, a little over an hour ago, His Holiness, Urban the Eleventh, suffered a cardiac arrest which has left him completely unconscious. His condition has deteriorated to the point where, barring a miracle, His Holiness is not expected to recover. A respirator unit has been installed in the papal bedchamber should it be needed, and other equipment, including an electrocardiograph and life-support system, has been called for.

"It would be understating the fact to say that His Holiness' condition is critical. I considered proposing to you that he be moved to a hospital. However, it is my opinion, supported by my colleagues, Dottori Stoppani and Di

Veroli, both of whom are with the Pope now, that all that can be done is being done. At this time, it would be dangerous to move His Holiness, and the facilities we are arranging here are equal to the best in any hospital."

Frenza paused and looked at the eyes fixed on his face.

"I cannot say, even guess, at how much time is left to Urban the Eleventh. Perhaps only a few hours if the hemorrhaging should start again, perhaps weeks if the condition stabilizes. It is medically impossible to predict how much strength the body has or how great the will to live is. But I feel I must reiterate what I said to the press yesterday: it is extremely doubtful that Urban the Eleventh will ever regain consciousness. Even if he should, under no circumstances will he be able to speak since I do not believe he will be aware of his surroundings. I beg of you, prelates of the Church, to understand and accept my words: nothing more can be expected from this man."

Frenza remained standing, waiting for questions. There was only one.

"Dottore, are you in effect saying that the Pontiff is no longer capable of governing the Holy See?" Meyerczuk asked him.

"Yes, Your Eminence," Frenza answered. "That is it exactly."

"Thank you, Dottore."

The council waited in silence for the physician to gather up his papers and leave the room.

"So there we have it," Volpe said, his great black brows forming a deep ridge over his eyes. He thrust his glance at the others.

The council had been called by Volpe and Meyerczuk. It included only Da Silva and the two other cardinals who knew of the theft—the Frenchman Foucault and the doctrinist Settembrini. Both Meyerczuk and Volpe had agreed not to include the sixth prelate who was aware of the robbery, Claudio Cardinal Marrenzo. As far as they were concerned, Marrenzo was a simple historian who had received permission from John XXIII to study the contents of the Secret Archives from a strictly historical viewpoint. Marrenzo was considered one of the most apolitical prelates of the Church, and neither Meyerczuk nor Volpe felt he would have anything to add to the council's discussion.

For the time being, the secretary of state and the Polish prelate did not wish to consult the rest of the senior papal advisers. Both cardinals felt that if a consensus could be reached among the five men present about how the Holy See was to reply to Sabatini, then this group could form a united front in the face of possibly opposing views from the rest of the Curia.

"Our duty is to inform the whole of the Vatican of the dottore's opinion," Foucault said, twisting the thin gold chain of his crucifix. "The Sacred College itself has already expressed its impatience if what I hear in the corridors is correct."

"The summonses for an election have gone out," Meyerczuk answered. "The secretary of state is looking after the details, and I suggest we turn our attention to the main concern, which is Sabatini."

"We have no power to excommunicate him," Settembrini muttered savagely. "We have even less authority to negotiate with him, assuming he is a rational being, which I severely doubt."

"Did His Holiness make no mention of a possible way of dealing with the publisher?" Da Silva asked.

Only last night had the prefect of the Secret Archives

learned that the cablegram to Father Domingo Martínez had never been sent. Meyerczuk had refused to discuss other possible courses of action with Da Silva.

"Nothing to my knowledge," Meyerczuk said.

"Nor to mine," Volpe added.

"So we have not even retained civil counsel to meet his challenge of a libel suit!" Foucault finished grimly.

"What good would a suit do?" Volpe demanded. "You are all familiar with the contents of the Tetramachus Collection. We might be able to receive an injunction to stop Sabatini from publishing, but then he would simply bring the documents into court. The press would doubtlessly print the most sensational parts of the material, and Sabatini will have achieved as much as, if not more than, he would have by publishing a book."

"What about the priest, Belobraditz?" Settembrini asked at once. "Has anything been heard of him?"

"Not a word," Meyerczuk said.

"I believe we have nothing to lose by asking Guarducci to send his Jesuits to search him out," Foucault remarked.

"Belobraditz has probably left Rome by this time," Da Silva murmured. "In any event, he would be of little use to us now."

"I agree with Foucault," Settembrini shot back. "Perhaps Belobraditz seems unimportant, but I for one would still like to question him. It was he who chose Sabatini as the instrument of his revenge or whatever. The priest might be able to deal with Sabatini better than we can. I am certain that if we were to find him, he could be persuaded to rectify his error."

"Is it agreed, then, that we ask Guarducci to send his Jesuits through the city, beginning at Father Martin's former parish?" Meyerczuk asked.

"Yes, I agree to that," Settembrini said immediately.

"I also." Foucault nodded.

"And you, Antonio?" Meyerczuk asked, turning toward Da Silva.

"Of course, I have no objections," the prefect replied.

"Now there is the problem of Sabatini," Volpe said heavily.

"I have given this considerable thought," Meyerczuk said. "Before it is decided whether or not to retain counsel, I believe the Church should speak with this man, provided he is willing. Truthfully, I do not know what can be expected from such dialogue, but I believe we must try this approach before we adopt any other course. If his reaction is what we expect, truculent and noncooperative, then we have this fact to present before the courts and the faithful. If he fails to deal with us in good faith, so much the worse for him."

"What will you ask for, Rozdentsy?" Volpe demanded.

"To begin with, an honest discussion as to what he feels can be gained by publishing the Collection and whether or not his goals can be achieved in another manner. Secondly, a plea that he understand the position of the Church at this time, that we are without a leader and incapable of a settlement which would not be subject to the approval of the new Pontiff. Finally, no matter what the climate of our discussion, I will ask for the return of the Tetramachus Collection."

"An exercise in futility, I say," Settembrini announced bluntly. "But I can see the ground you are preparing."

"Is there no way pressure might be applied to Sabatini?" Foucault mused.

"We might use the influence of the Christian Democrats to lobby for us in Parliament,'' Volpe said. ''It is possible to organize a blacklist of Unita books abroad. But to what end? The papers, only the papers are important. The minute we move against Sabatini overtly, he will unveil the Collection and attempt to discredit our actions by showing the Holy See to be a supposed accomplice in crimes against humanity!''

''If Rozdentsy's meeting with Sabatini does not get the Collection back, we will have no option but to fight him in the open and accept the consequences,'' Da Silva observed.

''There will be few consequences for the Holy See to accept,'' Meyerczuk interrupted coldly. ''If Sabatini does not reason with me, the Roman Church will mount one of the biggest offensives in its history. We will bring to the weight of world Catholic opinion upon his head. He thinks the Church is evil. Very well, there is more than sufficient evidence, both in our archives and in world libraries, to attest to its valor and charity, not only in the last war but throughout history. That evidence can be used by both the *Osservatore Romano* and Radio Vatican and whatever public newspapers, radio stations and magazines side with us. I say that if Sabatini does not choose to withdraw his challenge, I will bury him along with the communism that supports him and his kind!''

The spirit of Meyerczuk's words drew commendations from his audience, and Settembrini, feeling a fight in the offing, shook off his gloom.

''Let us call together the remainder of the Curia,'' he said, ''and present them with these proposals. The greater the number of men involved, the more power we can put into our defense.''

''I suggest that I call Sabatini at once,'' Meyerczuk

said. "If he does not wish to speak with me, there is more evidence that no half measures will suffice and that the Church must begin to rally Catholic opinion around her."

"Done," Volpe said. "In the meantime we can inform the Curia of Dottore Frenza's latest report, which, if worded correctly, will be enough to bring forth the indignation and outrage that Sabatini's actions against the Vatican deserve. I will ask Sandri of the *Osservatore Romano* to publish the report in today's edition."

"A small point," Da Silva broke in. "Are we to inform the other members of the Curia of the contents of the Tetramachus Collection, specifically where members are mentioned by name or implication?"

"I believe each one of us in the Church understands how he acted and why during the period covered by the collection," Meyerczuk answered. "Certainly if someone has forgotten things said or done and asks for clarification, it will be impossible to oblige since the papers are not with us and we, who have read the Collection, cannot rely completely on the accuracy of our memories. I doubt, therefore, that there will be any need for going into details, Prefect."

The Polish prelate was looking directly at Da Silva when he said this, and he did not miss the prefect's minute shrug of resignation. As far as Da Silva was concerned, if Meyerczuk wished to place himself as de facto leader of the Church during this crisis, all the while understanding that the Tetramachus Collection could in the end destroy him, then that was his business. Da Silva had no designs on the papacy, but if Cavaliere Massimo Siboda were to retrieve the Collection and return it to the archives, the prefect would remind the Polish prelate of who it was that truly made him Pope. Then Da Silva would make his claim.

The room had become unbearably warm during the night. Alexander Players awoke with his sinuses blocked and a dull persistent ringing in his ears. He stumbled out of bed, glancing at the alarm clock. It was half past eight in the morning. He made for the shower and stood under the cold jet of spray until his flesh ached. Gradually his vision sharpened, and his breathing came more easily. He turned on the hot water and scrubbed himself vigorously.

Returning to the front room of the suite, he threw open the french windows and, still naked, looked over the city.

Although by nature a traveler, Players, like an animal entering a foreign preserve, was suspicious of a change of territory until he had sniffed the streets and viewed the contours of the landscape and the peculiarities of its inhabitants. He preferred to arrive at his destination a day or two before a mission was to commence and use that time to acclimatize himself to the surroundings.

On this occasion, there had been no time to accustom himself to Rome, a city he had not worked in for four years. A bad night's sleep only aggravated his feelings of suspicion and caution.

The Paganini Terrace was not really a terrace at all. Tucked away in one corner of the hotel, with no signs to indicate its presence, it was almost empty at the height of the breakfast hour. An aging maître d' leaned toward Players and slowly led him to a table by the windows.

Giulio Musco had been reading his menu carefully, looking down at the lists of fruits, meats, eggs, juices and coffees. He took breakfast at the terrace three or four times a week and invariably ordered Eggs Benedict, but it was his ritual to study the menu each time in the hope that a new choice might leap from the large velvet-bound carte. It never happened.

"One day, I shall fool them, Alex," Musco said as Players raised his eyebrows at Musco's plate. "They will bring me eggs, and I will insist on melon instead."

Players smiled and reached for the orange juice resting in a bowl of crushed ice.

Giulio Musco was one of the few intelligence people Players not only respected for his ability but also liked as an individual. A man several years older than Players, with a classically sculptured Latin face and dress that bordered on the foppish, Giulio Musco had spent almost a decade in the counterespionage branch of the SID, the Italian Secret Service. For five of those ten years, Musco had been working for ISIS while also performing his duties as chief lieutenant to Domenico Pereira, head of the SID unit.

In 1970 Musco, who had been in charge of domestic counterintelligence, recruited Torquato Niccola, a professed fascist whom Musco turned into a double agent. Musco had been surprised at the ease with which Niccola had given himself over and wondered if the fascist organizer wasn't in fact an *agent provocateur.* One month later, early in November, 1970, Niccola proved he was genuine. He provided Musco with precise details of a coup organized by the Black Prince, the Squadra Azione Mussolini, and armed by none other than Major General Giunio Micelli, chief of the entire Italian espionage apparatus.

Code-named Operation Tora-Tora after Japan's December 7 Pearl Harbor raid and set for the same date, the plan included the assassinations of Italy's top moderate, left-wing and labor leaders, among them the present prime minister, Giannino Fransci. Communications centers in Rome were to be destroyed or taken over by SAM commandos to isolate the city, and guerrilla operations, designed to create panic to bring about the intervention of the army, were to be undertaken. The plan also called for the poisoning of Rome's water supply by radioactive waste, procured by Micelli, who was also to lead the armed forces over to the fascist side.

When Musco read this report, he was relieved that Niccola had been recruited without anyone's else's knowledge. Pereira, head of the counterespionage unit, was not yet privy to the defector's information and, Musco thought, might never be. Pereira's name was on the list of those who were to take part in the coup, although Niccola was not certain what his position was vis-à-vis Micelli or the SAM. The double knew only that Pereira had been mentioned in conversations between the chief of the SID and the Black Prince. That in itself was enough to warrant suspicion.

By December 1, six days before the coup was scheduled to take place, Musco still had no plan. Having checked Micelli's movements over the last fortnight and matched them with the dates and places Niccola had provided on the general, Musco had no doubt Micelli was involved. But he could not go to his own chief, Pereira, since he too was under suspicion. Nor was the President of the republic, Giuseppe Saragat, of any value since he relied too heavily on Micelli for political and intelligence information. Going to the Americans was also out of the question. The CIA's contacts at the highest levels of the SID included too many of the plotters. But unless the agency was backing the coup, which Musco doubted after the CIA debacle in Greece, it had no knowledge of what was to happen.

On December 2, Musco elected to follow the only course he thought was both viable and effective. He telephoned Stephen Waters, director of administration for ISIS, in Geneva. Waters, who had worked with Musco through NATO intelligence and Interpol, arrived in Rome that night. Twelve hours later Rokossovsky was speaking to the head of the CIA, and on the morning of December 5, Roman citizens were startled to see formations of F-4 Phantoms from the U.S. Mediterranean fleet winging overhead.

Musco's information had been verified in Geneva and passed on to the CIA by Rokossovsky. The agency in turn alerted the State Department and the President. With the adverse publicity concerning U.S. support of the Greek junta still fresh in his mind, the President did not want more trouble in the Mediterranean. He ordered a low-level yellow alert for American military forces in the area, thereby obliging his NATO partners, including Italy, to mobilize their troops. As soon as the Italian generals assumed command of their army, the American ambassador called on the president of the republic and presented Musco's information without mentioning Musco by name. With troops already on a yellow alert, Micelli's plan to use Italian soldiers to help oust the government was undercut. The final blow fell in the early hours of December 6.

Shortly before midnight some fifty fascist commandos infiltrated the headquarters of the SID at the Viminale Palace. They expected no resistance and encountered none. Taking a hundred and eighty submachine guns from the armory, the commandos waited until another unit, using the unlikely guise of forest rangers, had taken over the state radio-television center. The would-be forest rangers never reached their objective. As the lead group moved in on the communications center, it saw two tanks parked before the building's gates, with a patrol of crack airborne units, machine guns unslung. The fascist contingent, which, like everyone else, had puzzled over the flight of the Phantoms, now understood: The Americans had somehow got wind of Operation Tora-Tora. And what they knew, the Italian government also knew. The commandos took one last look and melted away into the darkness.

For Micelli, chief of the SID, it was all over. The ease with which the first unit penetrated the Viminale Palace was proof of his complicity. At the general's trial, the procurator-general also accused Micelli of having developed a personal intelligence network within the SID and among the junior officers of the Italian armed forces. There also came to light an organization called Rosa dei Venti, Points of the Compass, an underground group of right-wing industrialists whose financial contributions had helped finance Micelli's men. But the procurator-general did not elaborate on the activities of this group. The evidence against Micelli was overwhelming enough.

Thus, the coup of 1970 never materialized, although the political atmosphere of the country remained charged well into the new year. Pereira, Musco's superior, was cleared by a subsequent government inquiry, although he was never told how the Americans were warned. There was good reason for the Americans to keep their silence. Giulio Musco had by that time been recruited by Waters. He was to become ISIS' central agent in Italy, responsible for, among other things, the tap ISIS had placed on the papal telephone. One of the Points of the Compass seemed to include the Vatican.

"You have no appetite, Alex," Musco observed as Players pushed away his plate of rolls, asking only for more coffee.

"It's been a rotten night. I'm tired."

The Italian regarded him thoughtfully and at last said, "There is more to it than that."

"What do we have so far?" Players asked, lighting his first cigarette of the day.

"Nothing as far as the priest is concerned," Musco said. "I have checked a few of the more likely places myself—Belobraditz's parish, for example. A few of my men are doing the rounds. Officially, of course, we are not supposed to be involved, but Pereira is a man after my own heart. Curious."

"The Vatican hasn't touched the SID?"

"Not a murmur. They are playing this one very close to the chest."

"And Sabatini?"

"I had his line tapped yesterday," Musco said leisurely. "Only one thing of interest: a number of calls to one Aaron Vogel, twenty-four rue de Rennes, Paris."

"The Jewish historian?"

"The same." Musco smiled. "So what does that lead you to believe?"

"That Sabatini wants confirmation on the authenticity of the Collection. He wants it from an unimpeachable source. It could also mean that Vogel already has the Collection."

"Highly doubtful," Musco countered. "I say this because the prime minister is meeting with Sabatini in"—he glanced at his watch—"an hour from now, at eleven."

"You think that Sabatini will show Fransci the Collection."

"Precisely," Musco answered happily.

"What about the Squadra Azione Mussolini?"

"Now that is interesting," Musco murmured, signaling the waiter for the check. "Naturally we have increased our surveillance of the leading members, such as Borghese and his lieutenants. But there has been no unusual activity at all. I myself walked behind Borghese on his way to church last night. He is a deeply religious man, you know."

"This lack of activity worries you, doesn't it?"

"My men were in the street within two hours of Sabatini's press conference," Musco said softly. "For two days they have not seen a single known fascist—not one! Yet my nose tells me the Black Prince has not been idle. There is something in the wind, Alex, something very bad. When Fransci goes to see Sabatini, he may not notice, but his guard will have been doubled."

"I assume Fransci does not know you have tapped Sabatini's line," Players said. "Why not go one step further and take the Collection from him?"

"That thought had crossed my mind," Musco admitted. "Particularly when Rokossovsky called to tell me you were coming. But I cannot do it. One, I have no clear directive from Pereira to retrieve the Collection, in which case I would easily be able to send a copy to Geneva. Two, if I went ahead with a burglary and was caught, not only would Fransci be embarrassed—how could he explain to Sabatini, his friend and political ally, such a base action! —but I would be cashiered and of no further value to Geneva."

"I didn't think I could get out of this operation so easily," Players said only half-jokingly. "Tell me, why do you think the Vatican has made no public move either toward or against Sabatini?"

"The official reason, not stated but implied by the good Dottore Frenza, is that His Holiness already has one foot in the grave. In these circumstances, the Church cannot deal with an issue such as theft of Vatican property without the leadership of a pontiff. Therefore, they have an excuse to say nothing."

"And the unofficial reason?"

"Frenza has bought the Holy See time to group together and decide who, in fact, will speak for the Church and what he will say. My guess is that either Meyerczuk or Volpe, the secretary of state, will emerge as spokesman. I would not be at all surprised if the silence were broken very soon."

"Are the police interested in the priest, Father Martin?"

"Indeed," Musco said. "But since the Church has not officially lodged a complaint, there is little Criminal Investigations can do."

"What can you do?"

"Try to get to Father Martin before anyone else so that we might have a chat. ISIS is very keen on him."

"So I was told," Players said dryly.

Musco signed the chit and replaced his American Express card in his wallet.

"And what do you propose to do, Alex?"

"Well, I can't very well intrude on Signor Sabatini while he's chatting with the prime minister, can I? But if Fransci should offer to treat his friend to lunch then I might have a look at Sabatini's office. By the way, how close is he to his secretary?"

"Like this," Musco said, crossing two fingers.

Players nodded and said nothing.

Alfredo Sabatini set the receiver down very carefully and rubbed his forehead.

"Where is Giuseppe?" he demanded.

"Outside," Pia answered.

"Ask him to take the next flight to Paris. Vogel is not answering. I want to know why."

Pia Monti was about to object but thought better of it. Sabatini's patience had run out. For almost a day he had been trying to reach Vogel. Each time he put the phone down his nerves grew sharper, a little more raw. There was nothing Pia could do which would distract him, and after a while she had given up trying. Sabatini would not rest until he had heard the French historian's voice, and in a way she could not blame him. There should have been word from Paris long before now. Perhaps some of Sabatini's concern had rubbed off on Pia, for she too was worried.

"What time is it?" Sabatini asked absently.

"Ten minutes before eleven."

God, he looked terrible! The face was pale and drawn, without the slightest trace of its energy or vigor. His appearance, in spite of his well-cut suit, was rumpled; he had shaved carelessly, and his hair was uncombed. She thought he had lost weight. He was smoking incessantly and eating next to nothing.

"What do you want Giuseppe to do?"

"Get to Vogel, either at his apartment or the university,

and call me at once. After that, we shall see. But I must know what has happened to the Collection!"

"I will make the necessary arrangements," Pia murmured.

When she left, Alfredo Sabatini folded his arms across the desk and let his head collapse on top of them. His eyes were burning terribly. He coughed, bringing up thick yellow mucus, which seared his throat. Raising his head, he spat the phlegm into a dirty handkerchief. Working with three, at most four hours of sleep over the last forty-eight hours had dulled his mind. He had looked at no correspondence, done no other work. He thought only about the Tetramachus Collection and the cardinal error he had committed, a mistake so obvious he had not seen it or, if he had, had dismissed without a second thought as an impossibility. He should never have allowed the original collection out of his hands. Vogel could have been asked to come to Rome, where Sabatini might watch him read it. Yes, he had made an error in forgetting that Vogel was not only a historian but a Jew and a survivor as well. He had not remembered this even when reading the cabelgrams referring to Spring Wind, the operation that had sent Vogel's family to its death. When he realized his mistake, Sabatini stopped cursing Vogel every time the phone rang and it was not Paris. It was he, not Vogel, who was ultimately responsible for the silence. Still, Sabatini had hoped the historian would not betray his trust, although the publisher could wait no longer and had to send someone to find out what was going on in Paris.

"He's come!"

The voice on the intercom broke into his reverie, and Sabatini rose, going over to his private bathroom to splash water on his face.

Players was in the foyer of the building when the Mercedes limousine drew up. As Musco had said, the prime minister had extra protection. Instead of the usual three security guards, there were five, all tall, obviously competent men who formed a wedge on the sidewalk before the rear car doors.

Giannino Fransci emerged alone, a slight figure but one who carried himself smartly, without arrogance, and who paid as much attention to the passersby as did his bodyguards. A quiet, intense man whose family had emigrated to Spanish Sardinia at the time of the Moors, Fransci had been leader of the Socialist Party since the end of the war. Architect of the historic "compromise" between the left wing and the Christian Democrats, ideological leaders of polycentrism, which saw the Italian left break away from the Soviet model, Fransci had built his reputation and success on his beliefs in the power of the Italian working class and the uniqueness of the socialist experiment in Italy. He understood the nature of the great economic in balance of the country, the industrial strength and wealth of the north versus the poverty and backwardness of the south. He realized that the success of socialism in Italy depended not on pitting the south against the north, as some orthodox Marxists claimed, but on working through the great labor unions of the northern cities to establish a power base which would in turn attract and finance support in the south, a part of Italy in which the Church was still very influential. Fransci counted his party's successes in Naples, Taranto and Reggio di Calabria as a result of the promises the PSI had delivered in the north after a sweep of the cities there. He had offered the south only what he could actually achieve: a social progress based on increased prosperity for all. Forty-five years ago it had been the fascist dictator Mussolini who had made the trains run on time. Fransci could boast that and much more.

Players watched as the diminutive politician entered the elevator with three of his security escorts while two remained in the lobby. The car rode directly to the third floor where Sabatini had his offices.

"Pia, my dear!"

Fransci reached out and embraced her three times in the traditional fashion. "How have you been?"

"Very well, Mr. Prime Minister," Pia replied, blushing deeply.

"And where is that old taskmaster of yours?"

"He's expecting you, sir. This way, please."

She turned around and walked smartly past the receptionist's desk into her own office and knocked on Sabatini's door.

"Alfredo!"

In the reflection in the windows, Sabatini watched Fransci enter, his hand outstretched. He turned around and met the firm grip, throwing one arm around Fransci's shoulder.

"It is good to see you, Giannino."

The prime minister stepped back and appraised his friend.

"You look terrible," Fransci pronounced. "I have not seen you like this in God knows how many years."

"The wages of sin," Sabatini answered wryly.

Fransci snorted and seated himself on the sofa by the far wall.

"Can I offer you anything, Giannino?"

"Yes, an explanation," the prime minister said crisply.

"Down to business, eh?"

"Alfredo, you knew that I wanted to speak with you unofficially. You returned none of my calls over the last three days. I am sorry indeed that I was obliged to make an official request for your time, but there was no other way."

"Has the Vatican begun to flex its muscles among the Christian Democrats? Or perhaps Urban has called you up himself?"

"If that were the case, you would have been in my office ten minutes later. No, as far as I know, there has been no report of any theft lodged with the municipal police, the Criminal Investigation Division or even the chief of security for the Vatican. And the Christian Democrats have remained like little mice, squeaking but saying nothing. Obviously, the Vatican has not touched them either."

Fransci paused. "You wouldn't know where the priest is, in case it becomes necessary to question him?"

"Our arrangement calls for him to come to me," Sabatini replied. "And really, Giannino, I do not see the problem since the Vatican has not leveled any charges."

"There was a full Cabinet meeting this morning," Fransci said. "The subject of discussion was your speech and the Tetramachus Collection. Our decision was to ask you to now make these documents public."

"You are trying to steal my thunder." Sabatini laughed.

"On the contrary," Fransci said. "We, the government, are prepared to put our collective neck alongside yours on this matter. You see, Alfredo, you have, in fact, done the PSI a disservice," Fransci continued, his tone level, without inflection. "You knew we were staking the party's past successes, everything we have built over the last thirty-five years, on this abortion referendum. We believed, and still do, that the time was ripe to break the challenge and morale of the conservative forces in the country. And what did you do for us? You withdrew your planned appearance at the conference of the sixteenth. That hurt, in terms of moral support, but we managed. Then, without even asking me, either as a friend or as prime minister, you went out the next evening and played Samson to the Vatican's temple!"

Fransci smacked his hand against his thigh and stood up.

"I know what you will say. You did not want to involve the party in something that could be handled strictly as a commercial matter, just as the publication of the Pentagon Papers were the responsibility of the New York *Times* and no one else. But you overlooked one element, Alfredo. You are a committed man, not only privately but publicly as well. Because of your association with the PSI, this attack on the Church was bound to reflect on us. And it did. You don't know how many calls I have been receiving from local party offices across the country demanding that I say *something* about your speech. People are thinking that the abortion referendum was only a smoke screen, to hide the true nature of our policy, which is now thought to be an out-and-out attempt *to break Vatican power in Italy and cripple it around the world!*"

"And what have you told your local secretaries?" Sabatini asked quietly.

"What could I tell them but the truth! But do you think they believed me? Most of them were very put out because they thought I was hiding the full extent of the party's involvement with the papers."

"We could remedy this feeling very easily," Sabatini

said. "I am quite willing to go on national television, with or without you, and *reiterate,* not say for the first time but repeat, what I stated at the press conference: neither you nor the party was in any way involved in my obtaining the documents, nor was there any influence from any quarter to prompt me to bring the collection to public attention. Will that satisfy you?"

"If it could, Alfredo, I would not be here," Fransci said quietly. "Yes, you absolved me and my government of any complicity, but who believed you? Do you think people will listen now? I don't have to tell you how cynical the electorate is. No, my friend, the time for denials is past."

"Then I ask you, what is it you want?"

"The Cabinet also discussed the possibility of disowning you," Fransci said. "Several ministers, whom I shall leave unnamed, felt that the party would be well advised to demand your resignation. They believed such a drastic measure, keeping in mind your political record, would be the only one truly to absolve the PSI of any association with your actions."

"How charming!" Sabatini said, his voice cool. "I thought the Church might have considered excommunicating me, but never, *never,* my own people."

"The ministers' suggestion died a quick and natural death," Fransci said. "Instead it was agreed that I speak to you, examine the evidence you have and then, if the Collection is as damning as you say, go before the party membership to secure a general vote of confidence in order that the PSI throw its full weight behind you."

"So if you like what you read, the PSI will be committed to defend me before the Church and, probably, the civil courts."

"Exactly."

Sabatini stretched his arms and placed his hands behind his neck, pacing, always pacing.

"You feel the party has either got to be with me or against me, that it cannot remain neutral and let me act as a citizen and publisher."

"It is impossible for reasons already explained," Fransci said.

Sabatini stopped and pivoted, his arms falling by his side. He pressed the intercom button and asked Pia to have the Bentley brought around to the front of the building.

"We can go either to my apartment or wherever else you think is suitably private."

"The apartment is fine—"

The red light on the telephone came on. Sabatini had asked Pia to hold all calls except two: from Vogel or the priest, Father Martin Belobraditz.

"Who is it, Pia?" Sabatini asked softly.

"The Vatican. Rozdentsy Cardinal Meyerczuk."

Her voice was barely audible. Sabatini cupped his hand over the mouthpiece and said to Fransci. "The Vatican is biting. I'll put it over the intercom."

There was a slight pause as the call was transferred and a calm, dignified voice began to speak.

"Signor Sabatini?"

"Yes."

"This is Cardinal Meyerczuk. I am calling in regard to some documents you profess to have in your possession."

"The Tetramachus Collection."

"The same. Will it be convenient for you to meet with me at the Government Palace at two o'clock this afternoon?"

"It would."

"May I ask you to bring the Collection with you?"

"You may, but I must decline to do so."

"Very well. At two o'clock then, in my offices."

The line went dead.

"I seem to be in great demand today," Sabatini said blithely. "What do you think, Giannino?"

"No idea," Fransci replied. "All I can wish is that good fortune may follow you."

The two men left the office together, and the microphone under the ventilator grille picked up nothing but the whisper of the air conditioning and the distinct ticking of the desk clock.

Three blocks away Heidi Seppes began packing up the electronic receiving unit with which she had been monitoring Sabatini's conversations since he had stepped into the office that morning. She left her room at the *pension* and went into the corridor to use the communal telephone. An Alitalia ticket office informed her that the next flight for Paris was leaving at half past one. Only first-class seats were still available.

At five minutes to noon when Sabatini stopped by Pia's desk and asked her to call Vogel one more time, most of the staff had already departed for lunch. In the elevator the three bodyguards formed a rough triangle around the prime minister and his friend. On the ground floor the other two memebers of the security team joined them, and the small group made its way through the lobby toward the tall glass doors of the Unita building.

Across the street Alexander Players stood watching. He had seen the staff's luncheon exodus and was waiting for the prime minister and Sabatini to make their appearance. He thought he had as much as a half hour to examine the publisher's office.

The Bentley had drawn up some five feet behind Fransci's Mercedes. Both cars had their engines running; both were attracting the attention of passersby. The security team formed a corridor through which Fransci reached the rear door of his car, held open by the driver. Sabatini was saying something to him. Then the publisher walked quickly to the Bentley, opened the door himself and got in beside the chauffeur. Through the glass doors, Players saw Pia step out of the elevator, walking briskly as she noticed Fransci's limousine moving off.

The force of the explosion hurled him backward against a newsstand. Players fought for breath, bringing his head between his arms, sucking dirty air into his lungs. Someone fell over him, landing heavily on his back.

Mortebella was in flames. When he staggered to his feet, Players saw that nothing remained of the Bentley. The force of the explosion had completely ripped the car apart, scattering burning metal and rubber into the crowds on the sidewalk. Between spits of flame, all he could hear were the groans and screams of the wounded.

Had Fransci's driver not already pulled into traffic it is doubtful that the prime minister would have survived the explosion. The rear doors of the Mercedes lurched open, and the dazed security men stumbled out, revolvers drawn. Fransci was also struggling to get out, but one of the guards unceremoniously shoved him back in the seat and shouted at the driver. The limousine began to move but stopped after a few yards. The street was impassable, clogged with shattered cars and crowds of people, some lying unconscious in the middle of Mortebella. Fransci emerged from the car, staring stupidly at the shattered rear window and twisted trunk. He called for the driver to hand him the mobile telephone.

Players didn't pause. Zigzagging between bodies and autos, he ran to the other side of the street. He didn't even look at what remained of the Bentley but made for the blown-out doors of the Unita building. He found Pia Monti leaning against a pink and cream marble pillar, stunned, her face covered in blood from the effects of the blast.

Players swung an arm under her shoulders and half carried, half dragged her into the street. Separating the Unita building from its neighbor was the alley in which he had parked his rented Fiat. Opening the door, he helped her inside, then got in himself and gunned the engine to life.

CHAPTER NINE

The first army unit to arrive on the scene of the carnage was the elite Second Airborne Regiment under the command of General Mario Rocca. After cordoning off a one-block area around the explosion, the unit began pushing cars off the road so that ambulances and military vehicles could get in. But the wounded and dying numbered so many that Fransci asked the general to bring in helicopters to speed up the evacuation operation.

While three members of his security corps began to sift through what remained of Sabatini's Bentley, Fransci himself never looked back at the wreckage. The air was filled with the bittersweet odor of flesh consumed by oil and fire. Beside the official limousine, soldiers were laying out the bodies of the dead, a dozen thus far. From every direction there came the cries of the wounded, punctuated by a shrill scream whenever a victim was recognized. Fransci looked about him and wondered if at some time in his life Dante had not witnessed a similar scene. Surely this was hell brought to earth.

Fransci raised his eyes to the sky as the first helicopter appeared and felt tears slide across his face.

"Priority, Prime Minister. The Squadra Azione Mussolini is broadcasting: 100.7 megacycles. The radio station received a taped message a few minutes ago."

Fransci turned around to find General Rocca standing beside him along with the regiment's radio operator.

"Let us go to the car," Fransci said. "Have you found anything yet . . . by the car?"

"The explosive unit will be here shortly," Rocca answered, his voice tight. "God knows what they will turn up. The force of the explosion probably obliterated the bomb completely."

"Keep the area closed for as long as you think necessary," Fransci told him. "Call for any help you need. I want to know who did this, how and why!"

The radio operator adjusted his set on the limousine's hood. The broadcast was already under way.

". . . we repeat! Traitor Fransci, you have betrayed those countrymen who belong to the right wing. Remove yourself from power before it is too late, for if you do not leave, we will force you out. Remember, the Squadra Azione Mussolini is the iron fist of the nation, the true patriots who have not forgotten the glory of our nation. The arms are in our hands. . . .

"Traitor Fransci, you and your miserable cohorts have tried to undermine the very foundations of our national state. Our country is already in the throes of crisis brought upon it by your socialist policies, policies which have no place in Italy. If that were not enough, you have attempted to challenge the sovereignty of the Roman Catholic Church, the bastion of our civilization and culture. We, the true patriots, cannot let this challenge go unanswered. Our voice has been heard today. It will ring out again and again until the people rise up and overwhelm you.

"Death to all traitors who dare to spit upon the sanctity of the Holy Roman Church! Long live fascism!"

"You swine!" Fransci whispered. "You murdering swine!"

He wanted to smash the radio in his fury so as to silence forever that nasal voice which had spoken to him. But all the dry choking sobs caught in his throat. There was no time to mourn yet, not yet.

"General Rocca, you will please arrange for a helicopter to fly me to the Quirinal Palace. Within the hour, after I have met with the Cabinet, a state of emergency will be deemed to exist in Italy. My authority to invoke martial law is found in Article One Hundred." Article 100 permitted the government to act without Parliament's sanction if there was evidence of a possible armed insurrection. "You will have all armed forces units within and around Rome on full alert. Condition Blue for the rest of the country. Is that clear, General?"

"It is, Prime Minister. Only one question, sir."

Rocca paused. "Sir, why did the SAM claim responsibility for this terrorism? Surely they must have known that the government would respond quickly and effectively. It's as though the SAM is begging to be rounded up."

"I do not think the SAM leaders expected Article One Hundred to be invoked," Fransci said. "I am certain the squadra's leaders are presently chatting with their lawyers, waiting for the arrival of the police. They expect a mild interrogation and subsequent release because their alibis are doubtlessly flawless. If such is the case, then they are sadly mistaken. Habeas corpus is repealed under Article One Hundred.

"The SAM and possibly other right-wing groups have openly challenged my government. Would they have done this if their paramilitary units were not prepared for further destruction? *That* is the question, General, and part of my answer is to make Rome a closed city! I will not have any repetition of Tora-Tora!"

* * *

''Here, clean yourself up a little,'' Players said, passing her a handkerchief. She took it and, wetting a corner with her lips, mechanically began to wipe her forehead.

The blood around her face had congealed, plastering strands of hair against her skin. He had expected her to start screaming for him to take her back to where Sabatini lay, but she had not uttered a word. Pia Monti kept running her fingers over her face, picking at the blood. Twice he thought he heard her mutter the name Alfredo, but when he turned to her, her features were immobile.

Players took her through the side entrance of his hotel, avoiding the front desk. He caught an elevator just as the doors were about to close, and a minute later they were in his room.

''Sit down there,'' he said, pointing to a stuffed chair in the front room. She stared at him mutely as he cupped her face in his hands, his fingers tracing over the wounds of her forehead.

''There won't be any scars,'' he said softly. He disappeared into the bathroom, and she heard the sound of running water. When Players returned, he was carrying a hot wet towel with which he gently washed away the remainder of the blood.

''Who are you?''

Pia felt as though the words had not come from her mouth but somewhere very far away. They echoed and reechoed in her ears.

''It would accomplish nothing to tell you,'' Players said. ''The less you know, the better, since the police will interrogate you and I do not want you to tell them anything about me. Officially I am not supposed to be in Italy.''

"Who are you?" Pia repeated, a little more firmly this time.

"Interpol." Players brought out the false identification and held it before her. "You were his secretary."

"Yes." Pia winced at the use of the past tense.

"In the last few days, since the theft of the Collection, did he have any special visitors, any calls that could have indicated this was going to happen?"

"None. He was nervous and upset because—" She caught herself and stopped short, looking away from him.

"Why was he upset?"

"It's finished," she said dully. "He's dead. Oh, God, I wish the Collection had never touched him."

"There are other people who wish the same thing," Players said. "One of them had Sabatini killed."

Suddenly she felt very tired, and her face ached terribly, as though it had been exposed to a glacial wind. All she could remember was the sound of glass breaking and the force of the explosion that had pinned her to the pillar.

"I come to you tonight to speak of justice. . . ."

The fool, the stupid stupid fool! Murderers did not care for words as he did. They hit out from the darkness, and the result was enough, for terrorists were not men but rats, and like rats, they struck only when they could run. So they had murdered him and he was dead. . . .

Pia Monti did not notice she had started to cry or how long Players had been sitting before her, watching. He lit a cigarette for her.

"I will be back in a minute."

He went into the bedroom, closing the door behind him. As he reached for the telephone, it rang.

"Do you have the girl?" Musco asked.

"Yes. Where are you?"

"At the slaughterhouse on Mortebella. Fransci has declared a state of emergency."

"Any details on the blast?"

"The army bomb unit is turning over the wreck now. We won't know anything for at least a few hours. You had better get away from the girl," Musco added. "The police are rounding up the Unita staff for questioning. Pia Monti has priority on their list."

"I have to speak to her first. Could you arrange to have a plane standing by for me at Ostia?"

"Certainly. Where is it you intend to go?"

"That depends on what Monti tells me."

"Go to the Aero Club in Ostia. There will be a Lear Executive Jet ready for you."

"I think you should pick up the girl yourself," Players said. "She's badly shaken, and I do not want her talking out of turn about me."

"I will be there in about thirty minutes. Good luck, Alex," Musco said and hung up.

When he returned to the front room, the girl was butting her cigarette, having smoked it down to the filter.

"Where is the Collection?" Players asked her.

She looked up at him, her eyes glazed, and shook her head.

"I have to leave in a few minutes. There is no time for long discussions to decide whether you can trust me or not. I did not reach Sabatini in time for him to tell me. That cost him his life."

"Do you think he would have told you?"

"In time, yes," Players said quietly. "I think Sabatini realized he was out of his depth, that the Collection was far more dangerous than it had first appeared."

"I want you to promise me something," Pia Monti said

slowly. "I want you to promise me that you will find whoever did this to him. I, too, was a fool. I had the papers and didn't read them. Perhaps I could have saved him had I known what they spoke of. So promise me you will find his murderers."

"I can promise you that."

His voice was flat and emotionless and Pia knew his word would be kept.

"Professor Aaron Vogel, Twenty-four rue de Rennes, Paris. I delivered the collection to him on the morning of the eighteenth. He was supposed to have called the same day. But we haven't heard from him at all. That is why Alfredo was so upset."

"What was the arrangement with Vogel?"

"He was to verify the authenticity of the Collection."

"But wasn't Sabatini certain the papers were genuine?"

"He was a careful man. When the Vatican's rebuttal came, he wanted to have the best authority in Europe behind him. That was Vogel."

"What about the priest?"

"Alfredo did not know where to reach him. Father Martin was to contact him, not the other way around."

"Did Sabatini make any copies of the Collection?"

"One was made before I left for Paris. Alfredo hid it in the Bentley. He thought that would be the last place anyone would look."

"He was right," Players said softly. "When the police come, you needn't bother telling them about this conversation," he continued. "You will hear from me again. We have made a bargain."

"Find who killed him," Pia said softly. "Find them

and destroy them. That is the only thing I want now. Nothing else is important."

At half past three in the afternoon of September 19, the prime minister, with unanimous Cabinet approval, decreed a state of emergency to exist in Italy. As of that hour, civil rights were suspended, the police were given powers to detain and arrest any person without warrant or cause, bail was canceled in all but the most exceptional cases, and the judicial machinery, normally slow and inept, ground to a halt. The Rome military garrison, under the command of General Rocca, was already on patrol throughout the city, prepared to keep public order by bayonet and bullet if necessary. At the Viminale Palace, the first SID squads were leaving the building, their destinations, the homes and offices of prominent facists.

The government expected public outcry and rage in Parliament. Rightist extremists could still provoke an incident as an excuse to take to the streets after government forces. Ambassadors would be calling hour after hour, as would financial controllers, demanding to know whether Fransci's party was still capable of running the country. Even after repeated assurances some would not believe it.

But Fransci had resolved to turn a deaf ear on his detractors. Invocation of the State Security Act, Article 100 of the Government Procedure Code, had also freed him to deal with the Vatican in a direct fashion. The Church-State Concordat of 1929 established the Vatican as a law unto itself within the Italian state. The Holy See retained its own diplomatic representatives, minted its own currency and operated an independent post office. However, Article 100, drafted to cover circumstances which affected the very existence of the Italian nation, erased this sovereignty and brought the Vatican under the jurisdiction of the civil authority.

On a sheet of stiff official paper with red and gold seals at the bottom, Fransci placed his signature over that of the minister of the interior. This was a copy of the state order which proclaimed Article 100 to be in effect and one the prime minister was about to forward to Cardinal Volpe at the Vatican's Secretariat of State. For the first time in seventy years the Church authority would be obliged to bear cross-examination from a lay government. The first questions Fransci had for the secretary were quite simple. Why had the Squadra Azione Mussolini taken it upon itself to defend the Church by murder, and what had Cardinal Meyerczuk wished to discuss with Alfredo Sabatini earlier in the afternoon?

Eli Mandel had committed very few professional mistakes during his long career with the Mossad. But in dealing with Vogel's circumstances, he had already made one. Mandel had gone against his instinct, which had told him to move both Vogel and the papers out of Paris immediately. Instead, he had chosen to wait until Tel Aviv had approved such a course of action. At noon, September 19, the seemingly insignificant error was compounded by a second.

At the same time as Alfredo Sabatini was stepping onto the Via Mortebella and walking toward his Bentley, the Israeli ambassador to France, David Fainzilberg, was gently chiding Eli Mandel for having forgotten their appointment with French defense officials. Mandel had not even remembered the subject they were to discuss over lunch: a possible secret sale of the much-vaunted AMX tank to Israel. Fainzilberg had specifically included Mandel's name on the invitation list because the Mossad *rezident* knew exactly how many surplus tanks the French had, their leasing agreements with NATO countries and the production schedule. If Gallic defense officials began lying, the ambassador would use Mandel to undercut them before the luncheon degenerated into a charade.

Mandel had no choice but to accompany the ambassador. Fainzilberg was not privy to the surveillance Mandel had put on Vogel, and had he known, Fainzilberg would have been incensed. Israeli diplomacy in France was on very frail ground. Even a minor scandal could serve to sever relations between the two countries, and the coverage of a French national by armed Mossad agents, if revealed, would be scarcely a small affair. Mandel left the number of the restaurant where the meeting would take place with the embassy switchboard. The operator had clear instructions to telephone him at once if either "Cain" or "Abel," his two lookout men, called in. The same directive applied to a message expected from Tel Aviv. What Mandel did not specify, for security reasons, was that he was interested in anything which had to do with the theft of the Tetramachus Collection.

His second mistake was to be virtually incommunicado, away from general sources of news such as radio, television or embassy bulletins during the initial stages of a clandestine operation. Ten minutes after the explosion had razed the Via Mortebella, Mandel was taking his seat in a private dining room at Maxim's. As soon as all dignitaries had been seated, French security sealed the room. The Israeli embassy received a report on the Rome blast within a half hour of its occurrence, but the cipher clerk, through no fault of his own, merely filed the original and sent up a copy to Mandel's empty office. Even if Mandel had been walking along the street, he would have heard of Sabatini's death within the hour. There were constant news bulletins, and by the middle of the afternoon Paris was talking of little else.

Mandel's ignorance of what had happened in Rome left Dr. Aaron Vogel without adequate protection at a critical time. "Cain" and "Abel" were under instructions to watch him but not necessarily to interfere with anyone calling on the professor. Doubtless those orders would have been changed to seizing Vogel and the Collection and transporting both to the safety of the Israeli embassy had Mandel known that terrorists had already struck once.

Heidi Seppes' Alitalia flight arrived a little ahead of schedule, at two forty-five in the afternoon. Leaving her luggage at Paris' center terminal, at the Gare Montparnasse, she looked up Vogel's address in the city directory and arrived at the rue de Rennes shortly after three thirty. She spotted "Abel" at once, a husky, burly man with an ill-cut jacket that presumably owed some of its lack of tailoring to the fact that it covered a revolver. Heidi Seppes did not think "Abel" was French, but he appeared to be opposition, and she had not been told to expect it. Passing him by, she was conscious of his gaze on her back as she stepped inside number 24.

She searched for Vogel's apartment number among the letter boxes and rode the lift to the third floor. The professor's door was straight ahead of the elevator, at the end of the corridor. Although she could not see him, Heidi was certain there was another man on this floor. She pressed the buzzer to Apartment 38 and held it.

It was obvious Aaron Vogel had been expecting someone. He was dressed in a full three-piece suit with a blue silk tie. A coat was draped over a suitcase standing by the door.

"Yes, what do you want?" The historian's eyes darted across her face, seeking some kind of recognition.

"Good afternoon, Dr. Vogel," Heidi Seppes said brightly. "I am from the *Berliner Zeitung.* My editor scheduled an interview with you for this afternoon. I had been told to meet you at the university, but when you didn't appear. . . ."

"There must be some mistake," Vogel stammered. "I don't remember anything about an interview—"

"My press identification," Heidi Seppes said coolly, bringing out a bona fide press card stolen a year ago. "I'm sorry I left my letter of introduction at the hotel, but I didn't think it necessary to bring it."

Vogel squinted at the card without taking it.

"Please, call my office tomorrow. I am ill, too ill to see anyone today. . . . Forgive me."

The door clicked shut before she could say another word.

For the benefit of the suspected observing party, Heidi Seppes glared at the door in an outraged fashion and marched back in the direction of the elevator. The good doctor was afraid, which fitted her impression that the ill-at-ease "Frenchman" outside the building was not French at all. If anything . . . Israeli . . . the suitcase. So the Tetramachus Collection would soon be on its way to Tel Aviv. Of course.

Heidi turned the corner at the rue de Rennes and Montparnasse and entered the first café she saw. Fifty francs persuaded the proprietor to let her place a long-distance call.

The third error on the Israelis' part occurred now. "Cain" contacted "Abel" on the radio to inform him of what had taken place at Vogel's doorstep. "Abel" raised the question of whether or not Mandel should be informed. The matter was briefly considered, and both agents agreed not to bother Mandel with something that looked like an obvious oversight on the part of a worried, probably absentminded academic. The girl had not tried to force her way in. Nothing was said that even remotely referred to the collection. "Cain" suggested sleeping dogs should be allowed to lie.

The reluctance of the Israeli surveillance team to contact their chief allowed Heidi Seppes to get in touch with Eberhardt Krieg in Rome and, subsequently, for Krieg to set in motion a plan which would end in the death of Aaron Vogel.

At forty-three, Philippe Sléton de Bercy was the youngest minister in the French Cabinet. A Jew by birth, he had legally added the "de Bercy" to his surname in an attempt to remove himself and his career from his family's petit bourgeois origins. A man of medium height, watery gray eyes and a complexion that resembled kneaded dough, Philippe Sléton assiduously cultivated the manner of a dispossessed seigneur. Arrogant toward subordinates and meticulous in his dealings with superiors, Sléton had risen quickly and seemingly painlessly through the ranks of the French civil service. Although a staunch Gaullist, he had never been able to penetrate the "old boy" network, the senior ranks of the government presided over and permeated with De Gaulle's own handpicked men. Sléton's time came with the death of *le grand Charles.*

The inheritor of the Fifth Republic, Georges Pompidou, plucked Sléton from the service and appointed him to the unenviable post of deputy minister for internal security, a position considered a dead end as far as political ambitions were concerned. In this capacity Sléton would be the one to bear the brunt of student and worker rage over the breaking up of demonstrations, yet the May, 1971, riots proved the reverse. While the press vilified him, and his chief, the minister of the interior, virtually disowned him for his brutal use of the paramilitary CRS police, Pompidou and the majority of the government were impressed. Two years later, during a major Cabinet shuffle, Sléton was quietly handed the Interior Ministry and commended by the president for his excellent work.

Looking out the checkered windows onto a blazing Paris twilight, the minister was relaxing in a worn leather chair. At the far end of the courtyard, beyond the wrought-iron gates decorated with the twin emblems of the Republic, he could see the first streams of rush hour traffic thundering down the Faubourg St.-Honoré. In a half hour, after he had put the finishing touches on a report to the president, he would be driven down the faubourg to a small gemshop, where a beautiful tiara was waiting for him. An hour later it would adorn the lovely nude body of his mistress, Natalia Kasyk. The prospects for the remainder of the evening were promising.

The minister had only another ten minutes of work left when a voice on the intercom interrupted his concentration. He jabbed at the button impatiently.

"Priority call, Minister. Line one."

Without bothering to reply, Sléton reached for the gray phone.

"Sléton speaking," he said curtly.

"This is Krieg of Eurotek. There is an urgent matter I must discuss with you. Is it safe?"

"It is."

Sléton was lying. As a matter of course, he tapped the lines of not only his juniors but those in his own office. The minister was a prudent man. One never knew what information might become valuable in the future.

Philippe Sléton had not heard from Krieg for more than a year, and he had hoped never to have that dubious privilege again. Krieg was one of the very few men Sléton was afraid of.

"I am sorry there is no time for pleasantries," Krieg said, speaking in a quick, clipped tone. "There are some papers in Paris which my company needs—badly. I am asking you to intervene and procure them for me."

"What papers?" Sléton asked softly, feeling his mouth go dry.

"The Tetramachus Collection stolen from the Vatican Secret Archives on the sixteenth of this month, formerly in the hands of the publisher Sabatini, now held by Professor Aaron Vogel." Krieg rattled off a brief description of the documents.

"When did the papers come here?" Sléton asked stupidly, trying to absorb the data Krieg was throwing at him.

"I do not see what difference that makes," Krieg answered irritably. "The point is this: I have an agent in Paris. She tracked the papers down to Vogel's flat at the rue de Rennes but was unable to get at them. The reason for that, Philippe, was the presence of two Israeli operatives hanging about the apartment house. My agent believes Vogel is about to leave with the collection You can guess his destination. I am asking you to stop him."

"On what grounds?" Sléton retorted. "No crime has been committed."

"I beg your pardon," Krieg said icily. "The papers are stolen property. Secondly, they may be material evidence in a murder charge against whoever killed Sabatini. Finally, you have in Paris at least two foreign operatives who may or may not be accredited to the Israeli embassy. Those are three reasons why you can act. You can think of a half dozen more, I'm certain!"

"It may take some time," Sléton began feebly.

"Not too long, Philippe," Krieg said. "We expect the Ministry of the Interior to be placing fresh orders for riot equipment, vehicles and communications apparatus within the next three months. Just as in previous negotiations, Eurotek is prepared to undercut all other competitors and pay you your share of the sales profit for making certain that our bid is accepted. But we could not do this if you were to turn your back on us now. There might even come to light certain evidence pertaining to your past arrangements with us, which would indicate that you have added to your fortune by accepting—what do the Americans call them?—kickbacks. . . . The same evidence would show that the French government paid more in the end for our equipment than it would have for that of any other supplier and that you were aware of this but did nothing. I do not believe such revelations would do much to preserve your career, would they?"

"There is no need for further discussion," Sléton said, his voice losing its customary hauteur. "Give me the name of your courier."

"You will call me in Rome at this number when you have the Collection," Krieg answered. "We will make arrangements then. I trust I will hear from you within a few hours. Good night, Phillipe."

Like any coward, Sléton made up for his polished brilliance by a brutish fear that set in when he himself was threatened. As minister of the interior he had provided Eurotek with lucrative contracts, and the firm had rewarded him with a well-filled Swiss bank account. If Krieg made such information public, certainly Eurotek would suffer some bad publicity. Sléton's career, on the other hand, would be destroyed. It was permitted to lie and cheat in politics so long as no one found you out.

Sléton picked up the telephone which linked his office with that of the DST, the French counterespionage unit, Direction de la Surveillance du Territoire. The second-in-command, Charles Deutz, answered.

"Yes, Minister."

"Charles, we have a rather delicate matter on our hands. I want you to act immediately."

"I am at your service, Minister."

Deutz punched two buttons under his desk. Downstairs in the garage, heavily armed men dropped their dice games and raced for their cars.

"I have been informed by the best sources that a certain manuscript of immense political value has been smuggled into France. We must get it without delay. The address is Twenty-four rue de Rennes, Apartment Thirty-eight. The occupant is Professor Aaron Vogel."

"Minister, you wish us to use a defensive operation against a person such as Vogel?" Deutz asked incredulously.

"You will be looking for a folio volume titled the Tetramachus Collection," Sléton continued, ignoring Deutz's comment. "The Collection is the reason behind the killing of the Italian publisher Sabatini. I am also told that there is illegal activity on the part of Israeli agents around Vogel. It is possible that this Collection is to be taken to Israel very shortly."

Deutz permitted himself a low whistle. "That makes a great difference," he said. "You shall hear from me within the hour, Minister."

"I expect to."

Sléton dropped the phone onto the hook and went into the bathroom. Methodically he began to scrub his hands. His face had gone the color of ash; the lower lip was trembling visibly. No matter how hard he tried he had never been able to rid himself of that tic, and it irked him, for he considered it a sign of weakness.

There may come a point in the course of a security operation when the various factions involved emerge from the hidden depths where they normally work and break through to the surface, into the everyday life of people who know very little or nothing about intelligence work. Sometimes, as happened in Italy in 1970, when tanks suddenly appeared in Rome streets "to handle Sunday traffic," the whole of a country is affected. At other times only one or two men, whose paths accidentally cross those of a government service or private operators, are touched. But the reaction, personal or public, is always the same: bewilderment and confusion tinged with a fear that turns to horror.

Aaron Vogel, waiting patiently for the arrival of Eli Mandel, did not know he had become the matrix for three lines that were inexorably closing in on him. Had he been listening to a radio broadcast and had heard of Sabatini's death, perhaps he would have got in touch with Mandel himself. But the historian did not know what had taken place in Rome.

From the Quai d'Orsay two Citroën DS 21s pulled away with a sharp squeal of tires, the claxons screaming. Charles Deutz drove the first, threading his way through the early-evening traffic along the Boulevard Anatole France, then shooting through a red light onto the Boulevard Raspail. In the backseat, two DST operatives drew out their nine-millimeter Mausers and flicked off the safety catches.

At the Isaaeli embassy at 143 Wagram, Eli Mandel opened the door to his office and picked up the dispatches that had been placed on his desk. The Mossad operative was tired and in ill humor after the long so-called lunch. Fainzilberg's meeting with French defense officials had gone on and on until Mandel was visibly squirming in his seat. He leafed through the cables. The bottom one told him of Sabatini's death. Mandel grabbed his jacket and ran downstairs to a Renault parked inside the embassy compound.

The taxi carrying Alexander Players crossed the far boundary of the Boulevard Montparnasse and swung down a small side street to avoid an accident. At the corner of Montparnasse and rue de Rennes Players paid off the driver and began walking along the side opposite the even numbers. He was at 36 when the Citroëns hurtled past him and swung around lengthwise in front of Vogel's building.

Since Deutz had silenced the claxons well before reaching the target, Aaron Vogel heard no commotion in the street. Nor did he notice the pounding footsteps in the hall. Only when Deutz slammed on the door with an open palm did Vogel emerge from his study.

He opened the door cautiously, keeping the chain on.

When he saw the hard eyes staring back at him and a mustache stained yellow by tobacco, the truth exploded in his memory.

"La Sûreté de la République! Ouvrez la porte!"

Aaron Vogel uttered a low guttural moan and started to close the door. The blow that tore the chain off the wall carried the door into his face, knocking off his glasses. Vogel staggered back, tripping over a chair.

He picked himself up and began running into the study. Deutz managed to catch him by one arm, but Vogel flung himself around in a roundhouse punch that caught the security chief squarely in the face.

"Sale juif!"

The gun in the hand of another man barked once, the bullet tearing into the desk. Orders had been given to shoot low if one had to shoot at all, and the DST didn't train for that.

What happened in the seconds to follow is unclear. According to the official report presented to the minister two days later, Vogel had been yelling something about a spring wind and hurling Nazi insults at the men coming after him. He then flung himself through the french windows, his body teetering insanely on the balcony before plunging four stories onto the hood of one of the Citroëns.

An eyewitness account, never reported to the police, differed in all essentials. According to Madame Dubrac, whose apartment faced that of Vogel's across the street, the professor was picked up bodily by one of the men and thrown through the window. Madame Dubrac told her version to her husband, Dr. Dubrac, a well-known gynecologist and "white door" abortionist. The doctor made it clear he did not want his wife to go further with her account, pointing out that any investigation of his wife would uncover his extracurricular activities. There were not many doctors of Dubrac's competence and conscience, who risked their licenses and prison terms by performing abortions for women who needed them but who had little money. Madame knew that one doctor's arrest meant ten others would stop giving service and acquiesced.

Charles Deutz swore softly under his labored breathing as he stared at the broken glass. He was pressing a hand to his badly bleeding nose.

"Stay away from that window," he snapped at one of his men. "Gaston, send a couple men to look after the son of a bitch! Call for an ambulance, then get back to headquarters. You"—he turned to the other two in the room—"you go to the morgue with him. Seal the place on your way out!

"Son of a bitch!" Deutz repeated softly, walking over to the desk and picking up a red leather volume from the blotter. He glanced through it, verified the title and removed it from the apartment.

By the time the security chief was downstairs the police had their hands full, controlling a sizable crowd that had gathered around the cars. Deutz asked a senior constable to file a copy of his report with the Quai d'Orsay. Meantime the case was under the jurisdiction of internal security, so one needn't ask any questions.

Deutz did not notice two men standing by the side of one of the cars, watching him silently. If he had, he would have seen the undisguised hatred in the eyes of Eli Mandel, whose gaze was riveted on the grotesquely twisted, bleeding form of Vogel. Mandel had arrived five minutes too late. Running down the rue de Rennes, he had seen Vogel hurtling backward through the balcony doors.

There was no doubt in Mandel's mind what had happened in that apartment a few seconds earlier. Deutz's tight grip on the red leather volume was all the evidence he needed.

Alexander Players recognized not only Deutz but also what he was carrying and had a fair idea of where the collection was going now. He tapped Mandel on the shoulder and said, "Was he one of yours, Eli?"

Mandel shook his head without turning around.

"Let's get the hell out of here!" he said tightly and, with a toss of his head in the direction of his two shaken operatives, began to elbow his way through the crowd.

"It's been a long time, Alexander. Where have you been hiding?"

"Off the Continent."

"Back in the Soviet Union?"

"Wrong direction."

"The Americans? Well, well. But I suppose they have to be more careful these days, what with Watergate and all that. *Lechayim*!"

"*Lechayim*!"

Mandel threw back his double whiskey and signaled the bartender for another.

"What's your interest in Vogel, Alexander?"

"Same as yours, no doubt. The papers he was carrying."

"What do you know?"

"Only that the Vatican wants them back."

"I never thought the Church would stoop so low." Mandel laughed harshly. "Is that whom you're working for?"

Players did not answer him.

"Why is Israel in on it?"

''We're an interested party, like yourself.''

''More than interested, Eli. Much more when you provide Vogel with a double cover. Lanthem will be very disappointed when you call him.''

''Screw Lanthem!'' Mandel said savagely. ''But yours won't be any happier!''

''Why Israel, Eli? For money?''

''We need every scrap we can get our hands on. With three billion going on arms this year we can't afford to be generous. But there was something more than that, at least for me.''

''And you think the Vatican would have dipped into its real estate holdings to help you out a little.''

This time it was Mandel who kept silent.

''Are you interested in settling your account with us, Alexander?'' Mandel asked reflectively.

''I wasn't aware I owed you anything.''

''Teitelbaum, the bacteriologist.''

''Not my work.''

''Yes, yours, Alexander. It had your trademark, right down to the escape route. Of course, we are not certain, and that is why there had been no revenge. But if we ever make the connection, you might well be dead within forty-eight hours.''

''Unless. . . .''

''Unless you offer your assistance in this matter.''

''Forget it, Eli.''

''No, Alexander, listen to me. I know how important those papers are to the Vatican. Your presence in Paris is proof of that. So I'm going to tail you now. I'll pull every man in France into this city to make certain you don't move without me. And when you get the papers, we will talk again.

"Remember, Alexander, Aaron was a friend. His family had been handed over to the Gestapo by scum like Sléton. Unfortunately, I can't get at Sléton, nor do I know why he wanted the Collection. But only one man could have put that kind of firepower on Vogel, and he's the man. And you will be in a position to tell me why because you will get to him. Again, I don't know how you intend to do this, but I have never known you to fail a contract.

"So we shall talk again, my friend. Consider it carefully."

"No, Eli," Players said quietly. "You have just lost it for both of us. I won't go for the papers now."

"I think you're lying to me, Alexander," Mandel said gently.

"I work only for money, remember? You said Vogel meant something to you. Well, he didn't to me. I will be paid whether the papers are delivered or not, whether Vogel's alive or dead. But I won't go after them now, not with you on my back. You spoke too soon, Eli. *Shalom!*"

Mandel stood there looking after him as Players walked quickly out of the bar.

Alexander Players registered at the Hôtel Lancaster in the rue de Berri under his Canadian passport, asked the concierge to call a certain operator in Geneva and followed an elderly valet up to his suite.

Rokossovsky was less than pleased with the latest turn of events.

"In less than six hours, two men who had the collection are dead. Suddenly the minister of the interior is very concerned about the papers. If that wasn't enough, Mandel has to appear. What began as a simple retrieval operation has become a bloodbath!"

"I want another chance at the papers," Players said. "Could you send me Sléton's file, everything we have on him? I will also need a few things from Jan Kasyk's safety-deposit box, the letters to his sister. Pass them along as well."

"You will not get the Collection if the French government is officially involved," Rokossovsky said. "Letters or no letters."

The director knew Natalia Kasyk was Sléton's mistress and that her brother, a former ISIS agent, had been very close to her. If Players had to pressure someone who knew Sléton, in order to get near the papers, Natalia was the obvious choice. The letters might be enough to convince her exactly how Jan met his end. On the other hand, if the French Cabinet had sanctioned the raid on Vogel, the papers would be placed beyond the reach of anyone.

"Do we know for certain the French were involved?"

"No."

There was a distinct pause on the other end, and Players sensed Rokossovsky was puzzled by the DST's intervention. If the operation against Vogel had been sanctioned by the Cabinet, Sléton would have had to have excellent sources telling him where the documents were. The Cabinet would never commit itself without good reason. Who or what were these sources? According to Pia Monti, only she and Sabatini knew that the original documents were in Paris. But it would not have made any sense for the publisher's secretary to tip off the French since the government would probably hand the Tetramachus Collection back to the Vatican. The other possible source was the Church itself. Yet in that case, surely Marrenzo or Cliotia would have notified ISIS that its services were no longer needed. If the Church had called on the French, it would have worked out a satisfactory arrangement with Sléton beforehand, thus giving him another good excuse to use the force he had. Players' instinct told him there was a third and as yet unidentifiable party that had somehow ferreted out the location of the papers. That party had contacted Sléton, and for some reason he had acted at once.

"There are too many question marks," Players said. "If Sléton acted officially, the government will be obliged to issue a statement to that effect. Vogel was too reputable a man for his death to go unnoticed—unless, of course, Sléton will use the old national security argument to muzzle the press."

"He might do that," Rokossovsky agreed. "If the French Cabinet issues no statement, we have some basis to assume Sléton was acting privately. But I do not want you to go after him yet. I will send you his particulars, but I repeat, do nothing until we are certain who had the DST break in on Vogel."

"What about the priest?"

"Musco is still looking."

"Call me as soon as he is found."

Players rang off and went over to the small cabinet bar to pour himself some vodka. The image of Vogel's twisted body kept appearing as he tried to push his mind away from the events of the day. He had not seen death so close for too long. Vogel's face, the eyes stark and wild, reminded him of some of the men he himself had killed. Two feelings rose in Players at the same instant. The first was a primeval sense of danger that automatically put him on the offensive. Alerted, he felt a certain exhilaration at the possibility of conflict. This was where he was at his best, watching, stalking, finally striking.

But the second emotion almost paralyzed him. By staring down at Vogel, he had suddenly become aware of his own mortality. In operational work he had accepted death as his constant companion, but he never believed, while working, that it would claim him. A man knows instinctively when the bell tolls for him, and for Players that bell had remained silent until today. Today he had felt afraid. It was as though he had glimpsed behind the veil of destiny and for the first time discovered death as an opponent, not a fellow journeyman.

CHAPTER TEN

The secretary of state of the Holy See replaced the telephone receiver on its hook and turned to Rozdentsy Cardinal Meyerczuk, who was standing by the windows.

"The prime minister is sending his car," Volpe said. "He has asked to meet with me at once. The government has invoked Article One Hundred."

Meyerczuk's lips pressed together in a bitter smile of disdain.

"Who could have believed it?" he mused softly. "Who would have conceived that here, in the ancestral home of the Church, the Holy See would come under siege by lay authority?"

He ran his finger over the warm dusty pane, looking out at the mosaic factory to the east of the Government Palace.

"I saw the Church broken under communism, mutilated and disgraced. But to see the same thing happen here, God help me, I do not understand!"

"I do not wish to see Fransci," Volpe said abruptly. "If I do, I shall undoubtedly lose my temper with him, and that would be tragic. We cannot antagonize a wounded beast."

"Still, we *must* meet with him," Meyerczuk said. "The Socialists and Communists are already claiming that it was the Church who incited the Squadra Azione Mussoline to kill Sabatini."

"I know," Volpe answered testily. "Listening to them, you would come to believe Sabatini was a saint!

That fool, Borghese! What did he think he was doing?"

"It was an act of desperation," Meyerczuk commented, "ill conceived and barbarous, but it demonstrates how close Italy is drifting to outright civil war."

"There will be no war!" Volpe snorted. "The army has been mobilized. Fransci has acted resolutely. By Article One Hundred he has not only neutralized whatever attack plans the right might have had, but has also achieved the means of forcing the Church to deal with him."

"I was willing to speak with Sabatini. I am equally willing to see Fransci," Meyerczuk said. "He made no mention of the Collection?"

"Not a word."

"Then I do not understand why he wants this conference," Meyerczuk said.

"He may have the papers," Volpe said. "In any case, you will find out soon enough. Meantime, I will ask the Curia to close the Vatican to tourists and visitors. I do not want any sabotage from the leftists."

"The Curia may ask why the Holy See does not issue a statement denying any complicity with the actions of the SAM," Meyerczuk added. "Certainly Fransci will not forget to ask me that."

"Sede vacente," Volpe said bluntly. "That is our excuse for the moment. For all intents and purposes the chair of Peter is vacant. As individual prelates, you and I can say that the Church had nothing to do with the SAM. But for the Church, Urban's condition speaks best. How could a dying man, who has been unconscious for two days, have had any role in this murder?"

"Your reasoning is sound," Meyerczuk agreed. "And I believe we should put it forth before the general public exactly as you expressed it. But I do not think that at this moment there are many beyond our walls who would be prepared to listen to it. Even the faithful may begin to nurture doubts if Fransci has the Collection. . . ."

When he turned again to the window, the Polish prelate saw the government limousine curve around the drive. He crossed himself and walked out of Volpe's office. He thought it ironic that his career as a man of the Church might end in the highest seat of a civil government.

Sabatini's death had thrown sand into the machinery the Church had been preparing to use after Meyerczuk's call to the publisher.

Following the council meeting that morning, Meyerczuk had met with Sandri, editor of the *Osservatore Romano,* and had him go through the Vatican newspaper's files for material pertaining to the Church's charity and good works during the war. Sandri was also instructed to use private libraries, notably those of old aristocratic families, who had had intimate contact with the Holy See during 1939-45. The first line of defense was to unearth and promote evidence of Roman Catholic beneficence and heroism in the war years.

What the second phase would be depended on how Sabatini received the Vatican envoy. Meyerczuk believed that little, if anything, would come of the meeting and that the Church would be forced to issue a public appeal for the publisher to return the Tetramachus Collection. Both the *Osservatore Romano* and Radio Vatican would play heavily on Sabatini's refusal to render up what was indisputably Church property and attack his collaboration with a renegade priest who was, by Sabatini's own admission, a thief.

The third move could come as early as Friday. If Sabatini were not to return the collection, the Curia would be asked to vote for criminal proceedings against him.

''Now,'' Meyerczuk reflected, ''there is no one to move against.''

The Polish prelate leaned forward in his seat and peered out the limousine window. In spite of Article 100 the first leftist demonstators were already massing along the Via della Conciliazione. It was not for nothing that Fransci had sent an escort of eight motorcyclists, each with a man in the sidecar. The protesters, men and women of all ages, were standing along the sidewalks, staring at the limousine as it swept by. Had they been chanting abuses at him, Meyerczuk would have felt relieved, for he knew how to deal with that. But the people were orderly, lest they provoke police retaliation, and they watched in a stony silence that unnerved him.

''Indeed, they have already decided who it was that murdered Sabatini,'' Meyerczuk thought somberly. ''Quiet, they are dangerously quiet!''

The car crossed the Tiber and headed for the Corso Vittorio Emanuele II. At the Piazza Venezia, Meyerczuk saw an army unit slowly patrolling its perimeters, their automatic weapons unslung. A little farther on, armored personnel carriers were rolling along the Corso Umberto, backed up by tanks.

''We have waited too long,'' Meyerczuk muttered softly. ''If the Church had answered Sabatini immediately, the people would not now see our silence as sinister. As it is, we have allowed the SAM to speak for us, and deny their actions as we may, the populace will still not believe us!''

The prelate shook himself out of his reverie as his

cortege turned into the compound of the Quirinal Palace. He could not afford the luxury of ruminating over past errors. God willed it that the Church should suffer but that it endure also. It was his sacred duty to preserve the Holy See to which he was heir.

Giannino Fransci was standing by the open door to his office watching the cleric's approach. Although he had not met with a Church officer for more than six months, Fransci had had his intelligence units submit biweekly reports on the state of the Vatican politics. Therefore, while Fransci had heard much about Meyerczuk, he had not expected the Polish prelate to replace Volpe at such a critical hour. The old secretary of state was famous for the blunt fashion in which he dealt with civil authority. But neither was there any mistaking the attitude behind Meyerczuk's bitter expression, the almost savage look in his eyes. He had come to fight.

"Your Eminence. . . ."

Meyerczuk barely glanced down at him as he brushed by Fransci, stopping abruptly before the desk and turning around.

"You will forgive me if this must be a brief meeting," Meyerczuk said. "As you are undoubtedly aware, His Holiness is very ill. There are many matters requiring my immediate attention."

"I have heard Dottore Frenza's statement, Eminence," Fransci replied quietly. "The illness, is it still of a serious nature?"

Meyerczuk clasped his hands together and nodded silently.

"Mr. Prime Minister," he began slowly, "my relationship with you has always been cordial. Sometimes I believed it was even more, for you are not a man without spirit, without reflection or consideration. Perhaps that is why I do not understand this betrayal. I do not understand what was in your heart when you decreed this so-called state of emergency. I do know you have succeeded in bringing the wrath of the Catholic world on yourself and your government. You have acted in the same fashion as those Communists you supposedly condemned a few months ago, who would violate the sanctity of the Church and defile its sanctuary."

The attack caught Fransci completely off guard. Meyerczuk recognized he had gained the upper hand and pressed on.

"I realize what you will say to this. Article One Hundred is designed to protect the Italian state against insurrections, the kind of violence which has already claimed a number of lives, including that of Alfredo Sabatini. Yes, Mr. Prime Minister, I am well aware of the pressures that must have been upon you, but I ask you: Why did you, within an hour of Article One Hundred becoming law, command the Church to send a representative to you? What is such a unilateral action if not a blatant example of what Article One Hundred is really intended for—the subjugation of the Church?

"Therefore, while it was you who wished to speak with me, I must make the first demand. I want your assurance, Mr. Prime Minister, that no drastic action against the Church will be taken by your government even though the state now supposes to hold power over the Holy See."

"Not supposes, Eminence," Fransci interrupted quietly. "My government *has* the power to subjugate, as you put it, the Vatican. But I feel you have outlined the situation in a rather one-sided manner," Fransci continued. "For the sake of brevity, I pass that by. Let me say this: If the matter of the Tetramachus Colleciton can be disposed of between us, then there will be no need for the government to use the powers of Article One Hundred. I trust that you, as *pro tempore* spokesman for the Church, can discuss such matters with me."

"I fail to see, Mr. Prime Minister, why a property of the Church should be of such great interest to you," Meyerczuk said, changing the subject.

"It is possible that property has already cost seventeen lives," Fransci said tonelessly.

"I sympathize with you, but you will forgive me if I say that Sabatini might have avoided his tragic death by returning what did not belong to him."

Fransci's cheeks turned white with anger, but he dropped the temptation to retort.

"What is the Tetramachus Collection, Eminence?" he asked coldly.

"A gathering of ecclesiastical papers and personal journals describing the occupation of Rome during the last war. It also includes several state papers and diaries of prelates who worked in occupied Europe. Nothing, I assure you, as damning as Sabatini believed or wanted to believe."

"Would these papers lead one to think, for any reason, that the Church had engaged in treasonable activities now or in the near past?"

"Absolutely not!"

"Then why did the Holy See not issue a rebuttal to Sabatini's statements? Why has this loss not been reported to the police? Finally, if the manuscript is as benign as you say, why did the SAM state it was *protecting* the Church from a man who ostensibly wished to destroy it?"

"I shall answer you point for point," Meyerczuk said

with a hint of contempt. "To begin, a rebuttal would have given Sabatini exactly what he wanted—a sparring partner. The Church was not prepared to descend to that level. His Holiness instructed all concerned to keep the silence while his own investigations were being carried out. There was no debate on the issue since it was felt that an answer would be forthcoming in due course.

"Secondly, His Holiness determined that the matter could not be entrusted to the police. He was confident the Tetramachus Collection could be secured by other means. Unfortunately, His Holiness did not elaborate on his plans, and now it is impossible for him to do so. For two days, Mr. Prime Minister, Urban the Eleventh has been completely incapacitated. I ask you then, do you honestly believe that the Pontiff in his condition would have conspired with the SAM to murder Sabatini? Where was there time to concoct such a scheme, and what purposes would it have served? If you are seeking a categorical denial that the Church had any involvement in the act of the SAM, you have it now, Prime Minister. Only those in the squadra, the perpetrators, know why Sabatini had to die. It was their act."

"And there was no one else within the Church who formulated other plans for the retrieval of the collection, plans which His Holiness might not have been privy to?" Fransci asked.

"I cannot even entertain such a notion," Meyerczuk answered. "On a matter as delicate as the collection, only the Holy Father could rule."

"Are there any plans to move His Holiness to a hospital?" Fransci inquired.

"Dottore Frenza has discarded that possibility. According to him, all that can be done is being done."

"How much time is left to Urban the Eleventh?"

"That is impossible to say."

"Stalemate," Fransci thought. He would have to move very carefully from now on. It would be so easy for Meyerczuk to say the government was moving in on the Vatican literally over someone's dead body.

"Have you heard from Father Martin Belobraditz?" Fransci asked softly.

The question was meant to catch Meyerczuk off guard, but the prelate was not to be had.

"No."

"Nor do you know where to find him."

"That is correct."

"Then I propose we look for the thief together," Fransci said.

"I am afraid that is impossible," Meyerczuk answered sharply. "Only His Holiness could conclude such an agreement."

"You said yourself these are extraordinary circumstances," Fransci reminded him.

"And I tell you I do not have authority to permit you to subject a member of the holy orders to the interrogations of a civil police without a clear directive from the head of the Church! Father Martin answers to two beings: God and the Church. We shall find him with our own resources."

"I doubt that very much, Eminence," Fransci said, shaking his head. "I think Father Martin has already answered for himself. Besides, the police consider him a material witness in the investigation of Sabatini's death."

"Surely you do not think Father Martin was involved in the murder."

"I am quite certain he had nothing whatsoever to do with it, considering that it was he who brought Sabatini the papers. Yet he is responsible for the events leading to that murder. I must ask you, Eminence, to cooperate by disclosing everything you know about Father Martin. Through him we may eventually locate the Tetramachus Collection."

"And I must refuse," Meyerczuk said stolidly.

"Unequivocally?"

"Only if both Father Martin and the collection are returned to the Vatican before you either question him or read private Vatican papers."

"That would constitute my agreement for Church interference in a criminal, possibly treasonable investigation," Fransci said, letting the irony melt in his words. "I'm sorry, no."

"Then I presume our discussion is finished!"

"And the Tetramachus Collection?"

"Please do not insult me by asking such a question," Meyerczuk said icily. "I have said I expect you to return the Collection should you find it. Uncopied and unread. But I know there will be the temptation to use the Collection to conduct an official inquiry into the workings of the Church. The cry for that is already in the air!"

"Is that what you would have asked of Sabatini in the meeting arranged for two o'clock this afternoon?" Fransci asked softly. "I was in his office when your call came in."

"Even though the Curia had, by canonical law, no right to approach Sabatini, it was decided that the matter of the Tetramachus Collection was serious enough to merit an unusual course of action. I was elected to speak to Sabatini on behalf of the Church to persuade him to return the papers to us. But I had no powers to negotiate. His answer had to be either affirmative or negative."

"And if he had refused?"

"Then there would have been no recourse but to take the issue to civil courts and seek an order for the return of the papers."

"You needn't bother about that now," Fransci said. "The police have opened the vault in Sabatini's office and gone through his safety-deposit boxes. The Collection has not been found. Our interrogation of the Unita staff is continuing, but thus far no one knows what Sabatini did with the documents.

"My government," Fransci continued, "is conducting a number of other, concurrent operations. We are looking for the papers because their theft, reported or not, constitutes a felony. We are also examining the possible motives of the SAM for the bombing while keeping civil order through Article One Hundred. Finally, the Criminal Investigation Division is seeking Father Martin Belobraditz as the possible present holder of the papers. It may be that after ascertaining their authenticity, Sabatini considered the possibility that some move might be made against him to retrieve the Collection and so passed it back to Father Martin for safekeeping. Therefore, I must ask you to bring me Father Martin's personal file. It is to be here by noon tomorrow. If the Holy See does not comply or should the file have been altered in a way as to render it inaccurate or misleading, I shall impound the personnel records of the Church, as well as those of the Court of Belvedere, and focus the investigations on the substance of Sabatini's accusations."

Meyerczuk's expression of disbelief would have stopped the devil in his tracks.

"May God have mercy on your soul," he uttered.

"I wish so too, Eminence," Fransci said coldly. "If the SAM had not murdered Sabatini and were he not my friend, the government would have looked much more closely at his allegations. As it is, I am willing, for the time being, to leave the Secret Archives intact. My prime objective is to find Sabatini's killers, mass murderers, and keep peace in the country. If you wish to aid me, I accept your help. If you do not, and hinder me, I shall not hesitate to pick up where Sabatini left off, and with Article One Hundred, I think I could find a dozen Tetramachus Collections in the Court of the Belvedere!"

"You will never bring the Church to kneel before you," Meyerczuk whispered. "Sabatini could not have done so, nor will you. But I see now that you have no intention of returning the Collection to the Holy See. Your government will use it as Sabatini had intended. I warn you, Prime Minister, do not be so foolhardy!"

"I assume that was not intended as a threat," Fransci said in the same glacial tone. "Do not prejudge the future, Eminence, and do not try my patience either!"

Secretary of State Volpe had called the other prelates who constituted the council of five even before Meyerczuk left to answer the prime minister. Now they were all assembled, waiting. The Polish prelate surveyed them with his usual humorless expression, then smiled faintly.

"We have time," he announced. "Not very much, but enough for us to act."

The relief, if not audible, was marked.

"How much?" Settembrini spoke up quickly.

"Fransci is to have Belobraditz's file by noon tomorrow. If he is satisfied, he will not ask for more—at the moment."

"I don't understand," Da Silva said uneasily. "What does he want the file for?"

"That is his concern, not ours!" Volpe laughed harshly. "He is forming an investigation of the priest and needs information. Fransci is methodical. He likes to begin at the beginning. So let him!"

"Since Fransci will undoubtedly publicize Belobraditz's name in an effort to find him, we have acted correctly by putting our resources to work," Meyerczuk said. "Guarducci's Jesuits have access to places the police could never enter."

"I agree," Volpe said, nodding his great head. "We have done well, especially considering what Frenza told me while you were absent. The end of the Pontiff's struggle is in sight. He will not be with us much longer."

"Then it is clear we must gather the Sacred College and discuss with them what to do under the present circumstances," Meyerczuk said.

"Some of them have already been informed of the extent of His Holiness' illness," Volpe told him. "I am instructing the master of the bedchamber to expect the first cardinals from abroad in a day's time."

"Then the *Osservatore Romano* may as well print news of Urban's condition along with our condemnation of Article One Hundred," Da Silva said. "It is time to take the battle into the enemy's camp."

"Perhaps the same release could be carried over Radio Vatican," Foucault spoke up.

"Agreed." Meyerczuk nodded. "Which leaves us with the delicate question of the confessional record in Belobraditz's file."

"Rozdentsy, I have a firm opinion on this," Volpe said, raising his eyes toward the group. "I think it essential we delete nothing from the file."

"What a man says to the keeper of his conscience

cannot be permitted to come before lay authority,'' Da Silva reminded them. ''Even among ourselves there are rules governing those who might see such a record.''

''My dear Antonio, according to canon law, you are perfectly correct.'' Volpe smiled wickedly. ''But if we show Fransci that we are holding back nothing, not even something as private as a confessional record, do we not stand a better chance of guarding those papers which are truly sacred?''

''The suggestion is tempting,'' Da Silva murmured. ''But it might have the opposite effect. Fransci could demand further documents on the grounds that if we are willing to give him so much, a little more will not matter.''

Volpe was about to return the argument when Meyerczuk raised his hand and turned to Settembrini.

''What do you say?''

''I no longer consider Belobraditz a priest but a common thief. If there is any chance that the giving over of his file will dissuade Fransci from further demands, I say let us go ahead. Belobradtiz owes the Church at least that much.''

''Your words are harsh, brother,'' Foucault said heavily. ''But I must concur: Belobraditz brought this down on his head.''

''I really do not think we have a choice,'' Meyerczuk said tonelessly. ''I am not prepared to have Fransci's clerks loose in the Court of the Belvedere! The file shall be handed over to the prime minister. I myself shall deliver it.''

As the meeting drew to a close, a thin crack of a smile appeared on Volpe's lips. He had not chosen incorrectly. Meyerczuk was indeed a man with the makings of a pope.

* * *

Charles Deutz was standing in one corner of the minister's office. A few yards away, the minister of the interior was leafing through the red leather volume handed to him a quarter hour before.

"Where did you find this?" Sléton asked.

"It was on his desk. He had been reading it when we arrived."

"Did you look any place else?"

"No. . . ."

"Why did Vogel throw himself out of the window?"

"He was crazy, completely crazy! Not one of my men touched him."

"No one is suggesting the contrary," Sléton said coldly, catching a defensive note in Deutz's voice. "However, the fact is that this"—he tapped on the leather cover—"is *not* what I sent you to get."

Deutz choked on the cigarette smoke.

"I do not understand, Minister," he said hoarsely.

"I can see why you made the error," Sléton continued smoothly. "The description of the volume in question fits this book. The material pertains to ecclesiastical matters, but Vogel was reading something which belonged to him. I repeat: This is not what I sent you to get."

Deutz was at a loss for words.

"Perhaps Vogel gave the papers to someone else, the Israeli agents for example, or even destroyed them," Sléton suggested. "Perhaps you would like to check his apartment once more, carefully this time."

"And what if the Collection is not in the apartment, Minister?"

"There is not much we can do, is there? Vogel is dead. No one else will tell us where the Collection is. The operation is closed. I will see that there is no inquiry."

"There will be no inquiry. . . ." Deutz did not miss the implications behind these words. The red leather folio was exactly what the minister had wanted. But now he was denying it. So the whole operation had been nothing more than a robbery using official thieves.

"Add to that an official murder," Deutz thought, suddenly sickened by the whole affair.

Yet Deutz knew there was nothing he could do. If he chose to go over Sléton's head, the minister, who would now make certain the Collection did disappear, would challenge his story. Without the Collection, it was Deutz's word against Sléton's, and there was no doubt whose carried more weight. No one, not even the newspapers, would listen to him without evidence.

All right, let the son of a bitch do what he wanted!

"I offer my apologies, Minister, for having made such an error," Deutz said in his best official voice.

"It was an understandable one," Sléton said, matching his tone. "After you search Vogel's flat once more, I will expect an official report. It will undoubtedly include a mention concerning the presence of Israeli agents in the area." That was a statement, not a question.

"Of course, Minister," Deutz answered. "I recognized one myself—Eli Mandel, the *rezident* control of the Mossad."

"Then that will be all for the moment, Colonel. My commendations for acting with such dispatch, although not with success."

The minister of the interior picked up the folio volume and, without so much as a glance in Deutz's direction, went back to his private offices.

"What an excellent performance, Philippe! You

twisted that poor little man right around your finger. But won't people want to know why Vogel killed himself?"

He whirled about, afraid and startled by the cold, accusing voice. But he smiled when he saw the reclining form on the settee. She was as cold as ice, hard to the touch and vulgar in bed—and she excited him as no other woman ever had. She could mock him, as she often did, then play on his vanity and flatter him. But when he commanded, she would kneel and did so greedily.

"My dear Natalia, how very nice of you to come here instead of waiting for me. But how on earth did you manage to get in?"

There was a sting to the question, for Sléton enjoyed the trappings of his position which included the bodyguards who screened all his visitors.

"You're stupid, Philippe," she said softly. "Whom do you think we're fooling after all this time? Your own men escorted me in."

"There will be no fuss over one Jew, I assure you," he said smoothly, changing the topic. "And you should not make a habit of listening through keyholes, darling. It can be a dangerous pastime."

She laughed lightly, shaking her long red hair.

"Vogel wasn't just one Jew."

"It was a security operation. No one could have foreseen this tragic ending."

"Even more tragic when you don't wish to produce the evidence that made it supposedly necessary."

"Vogel's death helps me tremendously," Sléton said. "He knew he was at fault and did himself in to avoid investigation and scandal."

"So there might be a semblance of an inquiry, his papers will be examined, you will tell a few lies about

Israeli agents, and in three days, Paris will have forgotten Vogel ever existed."

"Precisely."

"Con!" she said gently. "You are a true *con*!"

"And that's why you love me, no?" he whispered, squeezing her wrist until he knew he was hurting.

She wrenched her hand free and pushed herself away from him.

"Go and wait in the front office," Sléton said sharply. "I will be a few more minutes, and then we are going out to dinner."

"I don't want it to be a late night," Natalia said, tossing the words over her shoulder. "We are invited to lunch with Meursault tomorrow."

"I remember!"

Sléton stared coldly after her and abruptly sat down at his desk. He opened the volume and began to read. Within fifteen minutes he understood why the Church would be very concerned about the papers, but he could not make the connection to Eurotek. Even when he read the financial dossiers attached to the end of the Collection, he did not understand how the money transfers between Hulais and Siboda affected Eurotek. But like any man faced by an object others considered powerful, Sléton was tempted to keep the Collection, keep it for that day when he might use it against Eurotek, the Church, anyone the papers could touch. Unfortunately, he did not have the slightest idea how he might do this. If he did not call Krieg, who would hear of Vogel's death over the next newscast, Eurotek would move against him. For all the attraction of keeping the papers, a risk using the DST to procure the documents, and the gamble had paid off. Now Eurotek was indebted to him, and as ambitious as Sléton was, he did not feel he should push his luck. A more immediate concern was to ascertain that there would be no outcry over Vogel's death.

In the United Kingdom, a D notice is an official request on the part of the home secretary to newspapers editors asking that a certain story not be published on the ground of security. The secretary's big stick behind the gentlemanly words is the Official Secrets Act, which empowers the government to prosecute media people refusing to heed the warning.

In France there is a similar procedure, although it carries no official status. One hour after the papers had come into his possession Philippe Sléton telephoned individual editors of each of the five big Parisian dailies, explained the delicacy of the Vogel affair as far as the government was concerned and, in return for future considerations referred to in the trade as "informed sources," was promised that the death of Aaron Vogel would be given no more than three lines at the bottom of the obituary notices. The reporters who had been sent to 24 rue de Rennes handed over their tearsheets with a Gallic shrug of resignation and forgot the matter.

Finally, the minister placed a call to Rome and spoke with Eberhardt Krieg. The German was more than pleased with the fortuitous turn of events in Paris and asked when it would be convenient for Sléton to transfer the collection to Eurotek's courier. Because of Sléton's heavy schedule, it was agreed that Heidi Seppes would come by the minister's apartment at seven o'clock the following evening.

The minister picked up the Collection and went over to the safe. He placed the papers on the bottom shelf, closed the door and set the time lock. No one would be able to open the vault until the next morning. At that time he would remove the collection and, before going to Meursault's luncheon, transfer the papers to his apartment safe. As a final precaution he would have one of his bodyguards remain in the apartment until he had returned home. By tomorrow evening the *affaire* Vogel would be over.

The man from Geneva arrived at the Hôtel Lancaster at one o'clock on the morning of September 20, a little earlier than Players had expected. Nor had he thought the man would be Pelikan, director of ISIS operations.

"May I come in, Alexander?"

"By all means, do."

Philip Pelikan was slender, with sharp brown eyes and swept-back hair. Stepping into the suite, he appraised it and looked inquiringly at Players.

"It's safe," Players said. "I have gone over it for microphones."

Pelikan took his coat off and seated himself before the coffee table in the front room.

"I take it there has been no special news of Vogel's death," he said.

"None. The government must have pressured the media to keep the affair quiet."

"That is not the government's doing," Pelikan said. "It is the work of one minister—Sléton. Had the French been involved, word of the Collection's recovery would have reached either Fransci or the Vatican authority, depending on who told Sléton the collection was in Paris. But Musco informed us that there has been no communication between the Elysée Palace and the Quirinal. Nor has Sléton been in touch with either Volpe or Meyerczuk, the two prelates who appear to have taken the reins of the Church into their hands. This we know from Pio Cliotia, who has been keeping us informed, as best as possible, on what the Curia has been doing.

"The Board has therefore concluded that Sléton was acting on his own initiative. He was told, by parties as yet unknown, that the papers were in Paris. Obviously, they must have held great importance for him to risk using the DST to retrieve them. The question before us is what will Sléton do with the Collection."

"Destroy it?"

"That is a possibility, if his instructions were not explicit about returning the Collection to whoever ordered him on Vogel," Pelikan admitted. Clearly this option did not hold much favor with the director of operations.

"On the other hand," Pelikan suggested, "Sléton may be holding onto them, waiting for a transfer."

"In which case I am to stay close to Sléton to see what happens in, say, the next twenty-four hours."

"We doubt he will hold onto the Collection for much longer," Pelikan said. "I have asked the Mole to watch the minister's apartment for the evening. He will continue surveillance until noon. But I doubt very much that Sléton carried the papers home with him. Being a security-minded man, he no doubt left them in the ministry safe."

"Does Sléton actually believe he can cover up Vogel's murder so easily?" Players asked him.

"Murder? I believed it was either an accident or suicide," Pelikan remarked.

"I was there," Players said. "It was murder."

"And Eli Mandel was there with you, wasn't he?" Pelikan added. "If you know Mandel was present, so does Sléton. Having a Mossad agent in the operational area is all the excuse Sléton needs to justify bringing in the DST."

"Have you any idea of what Sléton will be doing tomorrow?"

"Here we are lucky," Pelikan said, offering one of his rare smiles. "He has a luncheon date at the Ritz, the event being Meursault's birthday. It will doubtlessly be an ostentatious affair, as befits Meursault's character, with many guests. Just the sort of occasion Sléton would use to exchange briefcases with someone and complete the transfer."

Pelikan reached for his jacket pocket and brought out an engraved note of heavy vellum paper.

"An invitation we have provided you with."

Players left the card on the table.

"I assume I have complete freedom to deal with Sléton as I see fit."

"You still hate him, after all this time," Pelikan said thoughtfully.

"Sléton was responsible for Jan's arrest," Players answered quietly. "Jan was one of our best agents. I never understood why Rokossovsky accepted his virtual death without retribution."

"Rokossovsky considered pulling you off this assignment because of sentiments like that," Pelikan said. "I assured him there was no need for concern. You will execute this operation in the manner *we* think is best, not on the basis of your personal antipathy toward Sléton.

"ISIS has been commissioned to return the Tetramachus Collection to the Vatican, specifically, to Claudio Cardinal Marrenzo," Pelikan continued. "Since other parties have become involved in the hunt, it may be neccessary for you to use operational action to prevent their interference. But I want you to understand, Alexander, that only under the most extraordinary circumstances may you use such action against Sléton. Both Sabatini and Vogel were private citizens. The investigations on the cause of their deaths may vary in depth, Fransci's will be very thorough, but neither will create the furor that accompanies the death of a Cabinet minister. You operate freely in France. The police have absolutely no interest in you. Let it stay that way."

"It will be very difficult," Players said. "By sending Deutz after Vogel, Sléton killed him as surely as if he had squeezed the trigger. Should he try the same with me, I shall have him pay for it."

Pelikan did not bother to answer him. From his briefcase he removed a slender file and handed it to Players.

"These are Sléton's particulars. Jan's letters to his sister are appended," Pelikan said tonelessly. "If you need to reach Sléton, you might consider using her. Obviously, she has no idea that Jan will never see her again."

CHAPTER ELEVEN

The sun rose majestically over the ancient city, touching first St. Peter's Basilica, then spreading its slow golden warmth from street to street. The morning of September 20 dawned clear and perfect, a promise that the good weather would continue. But Rome was a muted city. Although today's traffic was no less than usual, there was little noise in the piazzas. Drivers eschewed the use of their horns and began obeying signal lights, while pedestrians went about their business with a quiet, almost grim resolve. The laughter and bustle of the city had evaporated, and the sparkling temper which characterized its citizens was replaced by a tension visible in the darting looks thrown at soldiers.

The soldiers. They were to be seen every second block, standing about in groups of two and threes, talking or pacing, their guns resting easily on their shoulders. A few of the younger ones would wink at girls or call out affectionate invitations. These were country boys with no combat experience for whom the emergency had become an adventure. They wore their fresh uniforms with an obvious pride and hid their nervousness under a light banter. They wanted to believe they were rendering a great service to their nation, although the exact nature of what they were doing was not clear. Very few of these soldiers thought they might be called on to fire on their own people.

But there were others, the NATO-trained and -equipped paratroop units stationed at the city's strategic points—the electric generating stations, waterworks, oil depots and government quarters. These men did not talk to each other or to people passing by. They walked together in groups of five, each unit with a radioman so it could keep in touch with the central command at the Quirinal Palace.

There was no ambiguity as to what their orders were: In case of attack upon themselves or the installations they were defending, firepower was not to be used sparingly.

At ten o'clock in the morning of September 20, Rozdentsy Cardinal Meyerczuk was driven to the seat of government in one of the Vatican's Fiats. His meeting with Prime Minister Fransci lasted only a few minutes, the time it took to exchange courtesies and for the prelate to pass over the Church's record on Father Martin Belobraditz.

There was little for the two men to say to each other. The morning edition of the *Osservatore Romano* had carried an editorial whose message was blunt and to the point. Written by Sandri, the editor, and approved by Meyerczuk himself, the piece stated that the Holy Roman Church was grieved that the government had reacted so strongly to an incident which, although tragic, did not warrant a suspension of democratic rule in Italy. The perpetrators of Sabatini's death could not be excused, yet the editorial reasoned that the publisher had been the first to wield the sword by attacking the Church in a gross and sinful manner. He who lives by the sword often dies by the sword. The fathers of the Church prayed that all those arrested under Article 100 would have recourse to due process, and the Holy See called upon the Prime Minister to ensure that all prisoners would be treated humanely. The editorial ended by stating that only the true enemies of the Church would continue to believe the Vatican had been in any way involved in Sabatini's demise. There was no mention of the Tetramachus Collection, not a word about whether Sabatini's accusations were based on any kind of fact.

Fransci had thought the Church's statement mild enough. The gloves would come off if and when the Tetramachus Collection was safely behind the locked doors of the Court of the Belvedere or should the government go ahead and impound other Vatican papers, either the personnel records or a part of the Secret Archives. But Fransci did not want to move against the Church at this moment. His main objective was to keep order in the country, which, save for a few towns in the south where the fascists had held demonstrations, was reasonably quiet. Secondly, he wanted Sabatini's killers. The round-up of known SAM members and other splinter groups on the extreme right had gone well. There had been outrage and protest but no casualties. SID counterintelligence estimated that the SAM had been effectively neutralized, with some forty percent of the ranks now sitting in Santas Prison. What did worry Pereira was the lack of arms his men had picked up. There were three stockpiles of weapons that the SID knew of, but when the agents arrived at the depots, they found only empty crates and hastily abandoned loading gear. The Black Prince had managed to save his arsenal, if not himself.

As Radio Vatican continued to broadcast its hourly reports on the declining condition of Urban XI and churches opened their doors for special masses to be given for his salvation, the prime minister sat down with his Cabinet and chief security officers to go through the file of Father Martin Belobraditz.

This dichotomy between the secular and sacred states

was reflected in the streets of the city. Some Romans heeded the Church's call and gave up their lunch hour to offer a prayer for Christ's Vicar. Others, including some whose blood still stained the Via Mortebella or who had lost a son, father or loved one before the now-disfigured Unita building, joined Alfredo Sabatini's long funeral cortege which was winding its way along the banks of the Tiber toward the cemetery on the Viale delle Milizie. The coffin the bearers were carrying contained a few charred bones and clumps of flesh, nothing which resembled a man. The mortal remains of the publisher were to be interred in the place chosen for them by Pia Monti, on a grassy knoll at the end of the cemetery, where the trees shelter the earth and flowers grow until late in the fall. Here, a stone's throw from the Vatican walls, she would bury the man she had loved, and she would do this without the help of a single priest, committing him herself with the tears and silence of those three thousand mourners who were quietly walking behind her.

Alexander Players had stayed up until four o'clock that morning, reading the material Pelikan had brought him, forming a plan as to how he would deal with Sléton later in the day. After he was through with the report, he burned it in a wastepaper basket, turned out the light and closed his eyes. Yet as tired as he was, sleep eluded him. He returned to the front room, carrying cigarettes and a bottle of mineral water.

The Paris dawn was hot and airless, the odor of exhaust-laden asphalt and dead flowers drifting up from the streets and through the half-open windows. In the darkness Players felt gooseflesh crawl along his arms and his fingers turn ice cold. Nerves, nothing more than nerves, telling him he was finished. Death was his opponent, not his companion now. It rode after him, not alongside. When he asked himself why this should be, he remembered a few lines from Bulgakov's masterpiece *The Master and Margarita.* The devil says, "I am speaking of compassion. Sometimes it creeps in through the narrowest cracks. That is why I suggested using rags to block them up. . . ."

He had fallen in love with a new land and then with a woman, and the cracks had appeared in his work, for he had found a part of himself he did not know existed, a part he began to hold precious. When he started to care for something and someone, he became vulnerable, growing wary of risks easily taken in the past, watching for danger in places where danger had been taken as given. Before, he had thought it enough to make his tiny contribution to the political history of his time and enjoy the fruits of his labor, the freedom from routine and boredom which fettered so many. He had touched other men in a rare spirit of comradeship, and he had loved some women as long as interest and circumstance permitted. He had not sought more or wanted more. But when the cracks appeared, he had discovered that a man might truly need more, however much he thought he was satisfied.

There was still a chance to stuff rags under the door. The lure of familiar work and past experiences was strong. But he also understood he would be returning with a memory of a place and time that was equally strong and becoming familiar. The past and the present could not live side by side but demanded he choose between them. So long as the choice remained before him, his work on this operation would suffer. He could become careless, and with carelessness came an early death.

Alexander Players had been told of intelligence men

who had had to choose between two lives, that of their work and the one that had been formed outside the profession, by a chance meeting with a woman, a conversation with a trusted friend, a sudden and violent death of a relative. Those who hadn't the courage or will to make that choice or who tried to pretend it needn't be made became dying fish, slowly spiraling away into the blackness of a sea, consumed by nerves, drink and torn desires. He had heard such stories but never saw these men around him. The failures, the suicides and the wrecks were carefully kept away from the healthy so as not to infect them with the poison of doubt. Now Players had wished he had known such a failure so that he might understand a little more about himself.

As he watched dawn creep into the rue de Berri, Players wondered what kind of man this priest was, Father Martin Belobraditz. He asked himself if the priest had been faced with decisions too overwhelming to ignore, which slowly ate away at one if left unattended. The image of a man who suddenly wrenched himself away from all that he had lived for and served found favor in Players' reflections.

The one thing Paul-Emile Meursault cherished as much as his lovely planes was his reputation as an eccentric.

When the tall, lithesome Petroushka was all the rage of the fashion world, Meursault wooed her with gifts and surprises until she succumbed. Then he installed her in his Bois mansion, where he kept her a virtual prisoner, allowing her to go out only for modeling engagements. Even so, a bodyguard accompanied her to watch over his master's interests.

At a party given by a well-known Parisian hostess, Salvador Dali appeared with a leopard in tow. Meursault arrived pushing a little red wheelbarrow in which was nestled a pair of furry wombats, compliments of the Australian high commissioner in London. Fortunately Dali displayed a sense of humor and did not sulk at having been so upstaged.

Paris society found Meursault charming, witty, and pleasantly unusual. North American Rockwell and General Dynamics, Meursault's major competitors in the tactical fighter field, thought him sly, devious and a liar. Meursault had cultivated a talent for business no one in the armament trade could question. His rise, beginning shortly after the war, had been swift. A fervent patriot, he had caught De Gaulle's ear at a critical time and from the early fifties on had never ceased to play on the late general's vanity and nationalism. His influence had become so strong that even under Georges Pompidou the French air force had standing orders to buy nothing but Meursault aircraft.

Meursault entertained a meager three times a year. These were normally subdued affairs since he preferred guests he knew well, of a common background and interest. The subsidiary *invités,* who would add color to the party, were left to Meursault's secretary, who usually relied on Opus Dei members to fill out the list. The secretary knew his master regarded trendy people with distaste, held most entertainers in contempt because of their liberal politics and gave the arts a wide berth. But since Meursault was, next to the president of the Republic, the most prominent figure in the Opus Dei in France and took an active interest in that organization, any member was likely to prove acceptable at his table.

When Players arrived at the Salon Bleu of the Hôtel Ritz in the Place Vendôme and presented his invitation along with an Opus Dei identification, the secretary thanked him profusely for attending. Twenty minutes later Players saw the minister of the interior step into the foyer, where Meursault greeted him. The two men exchanged a few words before Sléton presented Natalia. Meursault raised her hand to his lips and with a courtly flourish led them around for introductions.

Players nodded to a servant wishing to refill his drink but kept his eyes on the three people making their way around the salon. Since the cloakroom was just behind the entrance to the salon, Players had seen the minister help Natalia with her coat, deposit his own and walk immediately to the reception line. Sléton had not been carrying anything, not even a paper bag. Players' attention turned to the girl.

The minister of the interior had not planned to stay long, but for some reason Meursault refused to part with him and took him from associate to best friend until Sléton found himself the center of interest and serious questioning. For an hour he completely forgot about Natalia, who had finally slipped out of the charmed circle and gone to the buffet set on the terrace. No one except Players paid any attention to her departure.

"Good afternoon, mademoiselle. I see you are not enjoying M. Meursault's hospitality in the least."

She whirled about, her eyes growing large, her pink mouth half open in surprise.

"On the contrary, monsieur, I consider M. Meursault a perfect host," she replied coldly.

"You lie poorly, mademoiselle," Players said. "Forgive me, but I know. Michael told me. Michael Bellamy, whose real name is Jan Kasyk, just as yours is Natalia Kasyk, brother and sister."

A faint cry escaped her lips and her first instinct was to run.

"If you go, Natalia, you will never know the truth," Players spoke softly. "He will keep you forever by a promise that is not real. When was the last time you heard from Jan? Why has Sléton never talked about him since your last birthday, July twenty-sixth? Stay, Natalia, and I will tell you."

A group of people materialized on the terrace, moving toward the buffet. Players took her arm and guided her to a deserted bar, where he picked up two champagne cocktails. They moved beyond the diners into a portico.

"How do you know Jan?" she asked in a hard, flat voice.

"Did he ever speak to you about an organization called ISIS?" Players asked her.

"He told me he was working for that group—in Prague. But he never told me what it was all about."

"I am from ISIS, Natalia."

"Then Jan must have sent you," she said quickly, her eyes lighting up. "But how did you find me? How did you know I would be here today?"

"For obvious reasons we cannot talk now," Players interrupted her gently. "The minister has already been deprived of your presence long enough to notice. Can you meet me later in the afternoon, after the reception?"

"I have a fitting at Dior's at three."

"Good. I shall meet you at the front entrance, Avenue Montaigne."

"Why can't you tell me anything now?" she asked. "Philippe will be talking for hours now that he's started."

"Time and this." He gestured at the terrace. "I want to

see you alone. Please do not mention our meeting to Sléton or anyone else."

"I don't even know your name," she said, puzzled.

"It doesn't matter. I will be waiting for you, Natalia."

When Alexander Players returned to the Lancaster, he went over his room for signs of intrusion. In twenty minutes he found two microphones, the obvious one in the telephone, another in the studs in the headboard of the bed. There were others, but he didn't bother about them. Mandel wouldn't get anything that way and probably realized it, but like an experienced operator, the Israeli hadn't overlooked the obvious.

Players went downstairs to report a dead phone. After profuse apologies the clerk showed him into the manager's office to allow the guest to place his call. Rokossovsky came on the line as soon as the scrambler unit had been activated in Geneva.

"I need an exit plan for tonight, to be held open until I call in," Players said.

"Do you have the Collection?"

"I am very close. Sléton brought nothing to Meursault's party. The Mole did not contact me. I think the papers are still in the ministry. I will be meeting with Natalia Kasyk shortly. Perhaps I will know more after that."

"Very well. Use Mole when you are ready to come out."

"I shall call you as soon as I have determined that the Collection may be retrieved without operational action against Sléton."

"One moment, Players. I have something else to tell

you. We have found the priest, Father Martin Belobraditz."

That Paris continued to be blessed by excellent weather made Eli Mandel's task much easier. Fog-laden skies and light drizzle may set an excellent atmosphere for espionage cinema, but it makes life miserable for surveillance men. Under such conditions the quarry always has the upper hand, moving in semidarkness, usually along deserted streets whose emptiness makes it easy to spot a shadow.

Dressed in the blue uniform of a French telegram boy and driving a yellow Duex Chevaux stolen the evening before, a burly Israeli sabra braked the car to a halt before a café opposite Dior's and came in for a Vichy. He didn't bother to glance at the man sitting behind him. The agent's arrival was all the signal Eli Mandel needed to know that Players had come to Dior's as well.

Mandel would never underestimate a man like Players. He knew Players had lied to him when he said he wouldn't go any further in his search for the Vatican papers. Only under direct interrogation is it difficult to tell when a professional isn't lying. But Mandel had made one move Players had not suspected. He himself had begun to follow the girl, Natalia, leaving the ISIS operative to one of his agents. Mandel had gambled thinking that Players would not be able to go for the documents through Sléton himself. He would need a pressure point and a conduit. The girl locking up her Alfa Romeo was both. Mandel wondered what Players had tempted or frightened her with that she should cooperate with him.

Alexander Players entered Dior's through the Avenue Montaigne doors and intercepted Natalia as she was coming down the stairs from the second floor. He greeted her warmly, like an old acquaintance, but the smile and friendly words were only a mask for his tight, chopped words.

"The Meurice Bar, twenty minutes."

He had chosen the Hôtel Meurice for two reasons. If someone were tailing Natalia, he would have to cross the open space of the Place Vendôme. Secondly, there was only one entrance to the bar, through a corridor of mirrors which permitted one to see almost to the front doors. Choosing the right seat, Players would remain unnoticed while at the same time able to observe anyone coming in.

Alexander Players arrived at the Place Vendôme in thirteen minutes. The Alfa Romeo passed Cartier's four minutes later. The open square was relatively free of people—some lingering tourists, bank messengers, *flics,* and the occasional well-preserved woman arriving for tea at the Carillion. Players gave Natalia one minute and followed her inside. He did not pay any attention to the chauffeur in the black Citroën parked across the square, nor was he aware that the car moved toward the hotel doors as soon as he had turned his back.

When he reached the bar, he gathered from Natalia's expression that she was annoyed. Nonetheless, he nodded his head in the direction of another table, forcing her to sit where he could watch the mirrors.

"Was all this necessary?"

The bartender overheard her. His eyes met Players' and an understanding expression came over his face. Since the regulars wouldn't be arriving for another hour, he left them a bottle of champagne, pocketed the hundred-franc tip and withdrew into the service room to look up yesterday's racing results and to phone in a large bet.

"It was quite necessary," Players said, raising his glass.

"May I at least know the name of the man who buys me champagne in the middle of the afternoon?"

"Alexander Players."

"*A votre santé,* Mr. Players."

They drank a glass together, and Natalia brought out her cigarettes. Her eyes, deep sparkling green ringed with brown, were anticipating his words.

"When was the last time you heard from Jan?" Players asked quietly.

"About three months ago."

"From Stanislas Prison in Prague?"

"Yes."

She took a cigarette and lit it brusquely.

"Nothing since then?"

"Nothing."

"Do you know why your brother was in prison?"

"For smuggling heroin. From what Philippe told me, there was a route from Turkey through Prague to London."

"And Sléton has been trying to secure Jan's release."

"He has."

"Is that why you stay with him?"

He was expecting anger but was given the truth.

"It wasn't always like that," she said with a ghost of a smile. "When Jan first introduced me to Philippe, I did like him. At one point I liked him very much."

"Now?"

She did not avoid his eyes, and the eyes bore the remains of a shattered dignity. "Now it is quite different. I am a kept woman, in the true sense of the word."

"Does Sléton still believe he will get Jan out of prison?"

"Yes, he does."

"Natalia, did you know Jan was working for the SDECE, French intelligence?"

"I knew he had worked for the French."

"He was working for both the SDECE and ISIS. The Ankara-Prague-London pipeline did exist. It was designed to circumvent the usual heroin route, Turkey to Marseilles, because too much heroin had been picked up by Interpol along that passage. The British and Americans tried everything to close down the Prague connection and failed. Finally, the French were convinced to lend a hand, and Jan was sent in to have a look at the Czech end of the operation. After a few months he began to suspect that someone very high in the French government had an interest in *not* closing the route. Jan couldn't go to the SDECE and tell them this because the man in question was very well connected. This minister could easily have got rid of him before any kind of investigation was formed. So Jan contacted the Americans, who in turn put him in touch with ISIS. Since Jan was officially working for the French government, the Americans did not want to take the risk of running him through one of their CIA field offices. They gave him to a faceless third party, ISIS.

"A year ago, the French lost two SDECE men to the Soviets. Through the defectors, word got back to Prague that a French agent was meddling in the pipeline and was coming to know a little too much about the operation. Prague passed the word back to Paris, to the minister involved. That person revealed Jan's identity to the STB, Czech intelligence, to save himself and the pipeline.

"Only four people knew what Jan was doing in Prague. Two of those are in Geneva, one in Washington, and the man who first sent Jan into Prague."

"You are suggesting Jan was betrayed," she said slowly.

"Jan's arrest was no accident or stroke of fortune on the part of the STB, and Sléton will never get Jan out of Prague, Natalia. He was the one who betrayed him. Jan has been dead for two months. Sléton sent Jan in, and when the SDECE defectors mentioned someone was getting too close to the source of the pipeline in Prague, Sléton knew who that man was. He had Jan killed."

The silence was broken only by the sharp fizz of the wine as he poured out more. Natalia did not touch her glass.

"Philippe was working to set Jan free," she said woodenly.

"Then why haven't you heard anything for so long? Before, the letters came regularly, on the seventeenth of each month."

Her head jerked up, the eyes narrowing in pair.

"You know. . . ."

"Jan had an account at Banque Nationale Suisse. The number is 483966. There you will find his last letters to you, not the ones he was forced to write but the ones ISIS managed to smuggle out of Stanislas Prison."

"Why did not Jan die before, when they caught him?"

"Because Sléton's hold over you was not strong enough. Sléton benefitted in two ways from Jan's exposure. He was rid of a man who would certainly become dangerous to him in the future. Secondly, Sléton was not above telling you that without his intervention as minister, Jan would never see the West again. What better way to ensure that your relationship with him continued and developed than by setting himself up as your brother's only possible savior?"

"What did Philippe have to do with the heroin?"

"French police concentrate on breaking the big factories in the south, specifically around Marseilles. They tend to forget about the rest of the country. Knowing this, Sléton chose Strasbourg as an entry point for the already-processed drug. Czech cargo jets touch down regularly at Strasbourg airport. Along with Bohemian crystal and excellent hunting rifles, there also arrive a few crates of heroin, which is then forwarded to London and Paris."

"Why would he get involved in something like that?" Natalia asked, unbelieving. "He doesn't need the money!"

"Philippe Sléton is a greedy man. He does need money. I do not know who it was that first involved him in this, but it was very easy for Sléton, as minister of the interior, to make certain that the customs facilities at Strasbourg remained understaffed, that all the new drug-detecting equipment was sent off to Marseilles and Nice, where it was supposedly needed more urgently, and that reports mentioning Strasbourg as a possible entry point were conveniently dismissed as nonsense."

"And he had Jan killed because . . . he felt he owned me by now?"

"Either that, or the Czechs went ahead and executed Jan on their own initiative."

This was a slight deviation from the truth. Jan Kasyk had been kept alive for seven months only to be tortured. The STB was desperate about his information on the pipeline. Prague did not need a drug scandal on its hands, considering how sympathetic France and the West had been during the 1968 Soviet invasion.

It was also a lie that Jan was dead, although he might as well have been. He was alive somewhere in Czechoslovakia, living out the few years left to him as a useless vegetable.

No feeling remained in her anymore. She looked around her absently, her fingers grinding and poking the cigarette ashes into a fine dust. Empty, used and dirty, she had been robbed of the last hopes that had made her life bearable.

"Why did you tell me this?" she asked, like a child puzzled by a reprimand.

"Because I need your help. Sléton has something I want."

"You think I believe you?"

"Yes, I think you do. I have had Jan's letters sent from Zurich. They are at my hotel. You can wait until you've read them if you want proof of what I have said before you decide whether or not you should help me."

"Could you not have saved him?" Natalia asked suddenly. "Surely you could have when your organization managed to smuggle out the letters."

"We lost three men trying," Players said quietly. "It was too late then."

"But it was too early to tell me!" She turned on him. "You had no use for me then!"

Players said nothing. There had been no use for her before. ISIS seldom notified the next of kin of a dead agent unless the board felt that the group could in some way benefit from the family's knowing.

"What is it you want of me?" she demanded harshly.

"Yesterday Sléton received some papers. A red leather volume called the Tetramachus Collection."

"I know. I was there when it was delivered. A man was killed for that," she added bitterly.

"I was standing in the street when Aaron Vogel was thrown over the balcony. He dropped five feet away from me. Sléton had him murdered."

Players took one ice cold hand and squeezed it hard. "Sometimes it is always too late," he said. "Too late to save a man's life, too late even to say you're sorry. I am not trying to play on your feelings. I am saying I saw what Sléton did—because the papers are that important."

She pulled her hand away and brought it under the table, where he wouldn't see it trembling.

"The papers are still with Philippe. For some reason he doesn't want anyone to know he has them."

"Is it possible for me to get at them? If I knew where they were, I could have them out in fifteen minutes."

"You needn't bother yourself," Natalia said quietly. "I can get them out for you. Philippe brought home a red leather volume from the office this morning. I recognized it from the night before, when a security man appeared with it. The volume is now in Philippe's safe. He left it there before we went to Meursault's party. One of the bodyguards stayed behind in the apartment, but I doubt he will be there when I return."

"I haven't asked you to become involved in this way."

"You might as well have," she said softly. "Or did you think that telling me about Jan was worth only a little information?"

"Can you get them tonight?"

"I think so. Meet me at the Bratislava Restaurant, rue

des Pauvres Clarisses, around seven. It will be closed to the public because of the owner's birthday party. I told Philippe I would be going for a little while."

"Are you certain you can get the papers alone?" he asked, his voice carrying an unexpected urgency. "If Sléton is carrying them, it might be better for me. . . ."

"He is a man, and I know what I must do to please him." She shook her head. "I don't need you."

"And afterward? You will not be able to return to him, you know that?"

"Let us leave that until later. We have talked enough."

She stood up, very smart in her cream-colored skirt and dark blouse set off by a jade scarf. But a dull whiteness was setting in on her cheeks, and her large eyes were torn between hatred and sorrow.

"You will understand, Mr. Players, if I do not say it was a pleasure to meet you."

With that she turned and walked out.

Natalia Kasyk moved along the Faubourg St.-Honoré, her step quick and firm. She stopped twice at a café for coffee but each time barely managed to drink her cup without being sick. Some women would have sought to bury their grief in the oblivion of pills, others in a bottle or the arms of a lover. Natalia walked, terrified to stop lest grief overwhelm her, knowing where she was going, knowing what she would do, afraid, alone and dying with each step.

She crossed over to the Champs-Elysées, across the Pont Alexandre III, along the Left Bank before the French Academy to the Pont Neuf, across to what was left of Les Halles, then down past the Théâtre Durac and the monument to Parisian Jews killed at Bergen-Belsen. Standing beside this obelisk, she could see the green peace of the Île de la Cité and I St.-Louis.

She had wanted to believe Players was lying, using her for his own ends as Philippe had used her for his. But Jan had told her about ISIS. . . . Jan. . . . She could still see his smiling, cocky face, so alive, happy. He had always been there to cup her face and lift her over and through her nightmares. She remembered asking him if he ever had nightmares.

"No. I see them every day in the street, in people's faces. I don't need any more."

Jan had gone to Prague because he hated those who dealt in human misery, the purveyors of nightmares.

"I would kill a pusher," he had told her. "I would kill him more quickly than I would a spider. At least a spider has a meaningful role to play in nature. Pushers are subhuman. They are parasites feeding off misery."

She found herself before 17 rue Querbes on the Île de la Cité, facing the quiet green Seine. It was half past five. Philippe's red Mercedes was parked in front of the baker's shop. She hesitated for a moment, then climbed the two flights of stairs, suddenly realizing how hot and tired her feet were.

"Natalia, where have you been! I had called four times. Did shopping at Dior's take up your entire afternoon?"

"And you are home early," she answered with a languid smile.

"Because I have to go out in a little while," he said, striding into the living room fresh from a shower, his face paler than usual, the stomach pulled in but still revealing the growing flab. His skin was stark white, unhealthy, against the black Chinese print robe. "I had wanted to spend *some* time with you but. . . ."

Now he would sulk and try to deny himself only to call for coddling and attention. Natalia almost laughed.

"But what, darling? I'm here with you."

Standing behind him, she pressed his head to her breasts, her fingers wet from his hair.

"Nice?"

He grunted and closed his eyes.

"If we are going out tonight, darling, I want my tiara. Did you put it back in the safe?"

"I thought you said you were expected at the Bratislava?"

"Only to make an appearance."

"I told you I have business tonight," he said lazily. "And when I come back, I want you here, for the rest of the evening."

He mistook her pained expression for something else.

"My, my, aren't we becoming possessive." He laughed. "Yes, your tiara is in the safe. Take a look if you wish. You know the combination."

Shaking his head, he disappeared into the bathroom, and she heard the high-pitched whine of the hair dryer.

Natalia went over to a landscape painting and removed it from the wall.

The hair dryer continued to moan unabated. Quickly she spun the dial and viciously jerked the handle. There was enough light coming through the window for her to see the red volume immediately. The tiara and her other jewels were neatly piled on top of it in black velvet cases.

"Take out the ledger!" he called suddenly.

"Which one?"

"How many are there?" he snapped impatiently, stepping out of the bathroom into the kitchen.

She heard the sound of ice dropping into tumblers and

squeezed her eyes shut. Philippe had been responsible for Jan's death, and Vogel's. That was all she had to remember.

THE TETRAMACHUS COLLECTION
VOLUME FIVE
THE ACTIVITIES OF THE HOLY SEE DURING THE SECOND WORLD WAR
REFERENCE FLX/40-48
KEEP FOREVER WITHIN THE SECRET ARCHIVES

When the minister came back into the room, Natalia was standing before him dressed only in her panties. The red leather volume lay on the sofa where it appeared she had carelessly thrown it. She came to him and slid her fingers over his cheeks.

"You can't go out like that," she murmured. "Sit down and let me shave you."

"Don't you think we might spend this time in another fashion?" he suggested.

"Your hands are too cold. Always use tongs for ice. Now come here and sit. Take off your robe."

She led him over to one of the dining-room chairs and pressed down on his shoulders. From the bottom shelf of an armoire, Natalia gathered up a large fresh sheet, around his chest and secured it at the back of his neck. Suddenly he began to laugh.

"You are crazy!" he said. "What on earth has got into you?"

Without bothering to reply, Natalia ran into the bathroom, bringing out his hot lather machine and a straight-edged razor.

"Would you like a towel around your neck?"

"No, this is all right. I just hope you do as good a job as Enrico."

"Much better, Philippe. After all, can Enrico give you tender loving care?"

He was beginning to relax under the sweet scent of the cream and the smell of her body. She applied the lather generously, rubbing it in gently around his chin and under his jaw. His heart jumped when the cold edge of the razor touched his cheek.

She began shaving him with luxurious slowness, guiding the Wilkinson steel over his face, scraping away a very small area at a time. All the while she would lift some of the cool cream away and replace it with fresh foam.

"Philippe, why haven't I heard anything from Jan?"

"Jan? What made you think of him? I told you last time—the Czechs wanted to make a deal. One of theirs for Jan. I tried, but the president's security adviser vetoed the idea."

"I worry about Jan, Philippe."

"Don't. As long as I am looking after the affair, he will not be mistreated, and there is a good chance for him. An excellent chance, in fact. It is simply a matter of timing, timing and patience."

"I was thinking of Jan today, while I was walking. It was such a lovely day. I walked until my legs ached. And then I realized I never told you about Jan, what he means to me and why. How could I have done that after all the effort you made to try to free him!"

The minister muttered something unintelligible, and his eyes strayed to the clock on the mantlepiece. She rinsed the blade in warm water, watching the tiny whiskers swirl away and tilted her head forward. For the briefest instant,

Sléton saw the cold bright flicker of the razor's tip swing past his eye.

"When I thought of Jan, I remembered my parents. It always happens like this, one thought leading to another. . . . Did you know that my father was with the Czech commando team that killed Reinhard Heydrich, the chief of the Gestapo?" she asked matter-of-factly. "He was, Jan told me.

"Five days after Heydrich was shot, the Gestapo arrived in Lidice, a small town about seven kilometers from the farm where Mama, Jan and I were living. One of the commandos had been caught, and he betrayed the names of the others. But the only other man the Germans caught was my father. Before they killed him, they made him watch as the entire town of Lidice was systematically looted and every citizen, I mean every person, including day-old infants, slaughtered.

"The last one they killed was my mother. They bayoneted her a few feet from where my father was standing. Then they turned their machine guns on him and emptied their magazines.

"Mother had been the only one at home when the Gestapo arrived. Jan and I were out hunting. When we returned to find her gone and the house destroyed, Jan led us around the hills overlooking Lidice. He carried very powerful field glasses and could see what was going on from a hundred and fifty meters. When the shooting began, Jan pushed my face into the ground and kept it there for a long time. I began crying, but he pushed it only that much harder.

"He later said, with that sad smile of his, how he had watched an entire town die. He couldn't let go of the glasses even when our parents were led into the square. Then he told me how stupid the killing of Heydrich had been. The orders had come from London, but it was Lidice and its people who paid for such senselessness. They suffered the retribution, and the Gestapo continued to work without Heydrich. . . ."

Another cheek was done, pink and smooth. The heavily tempered blade tapped against the basin, Natalia applied fresh lather to her lover's neck.

"Natalia, why are you going on about this?"

"It means something to me, Phillipe. It tells you why Jan is so important to me. You see, Philippe," she continued softly. "The pain Jan felt, the loss and hatred at that slaughter all poured out of him, and from that came his love for me. I was the only person in the world he could call his own. No one has loved me as he did, and I was the only person who could bring a smile to his eyes. My brother was a very weary man, Philippe, for he had seen too much ugliness in the world. He still felt that way, thirty years after Lidice. When he left for Prague, he told me he was going to burn out a nest of vipers. He was going to stop the heroin operation."

The razor was moving slowly around his Adam's apple, stopping abruptly at a forty-degree angle, the far end of the blade set on the jugular, the tip pushing against the bone in his throat.

"I don't know what you mean by an operation," Sléton began, but she let him go no further.

"Why did you kill him, Philippe?"

The question came from her words like a caress, her breath brushing the back of his neck. His first instinct was to move, and he did until the tip of the Wilkinson sword bit into his throat.

"Natalia, what are you doing?" he whispered hoarsely. "Let me out of this chair."

"Why did you kill him, Philippe?"

"Natalia, put that razor down!" he barked suddenly.

She didn't answer him. Her fingers pressed the ivory handle, and the lather on either side of the blade grew pink.

"Natalia, please!"

"Why, Philippe?"

He was staring up at her, his mouth flung open in a dry scream, the eyes straining in their sockets. But she wasn't looking at him. Standing directly behind the chair, she was like a statue with a blind gaze fixed on some invisible point in space.

"I had no choice!" he groaned in a strangled whisper. "No choice. . . . Jan knew too much. He could have destroyed me. . . ."

"The pipeline?"

"Yes, yes, the pipeline!"

Involuntarily Natalia's grip on the handle tightened, and a quarter inch of steel sank into Sléton's neck, cutting muscle. The cream was running red onto the white sheet that covered him.

"Why didn't you tell me, Philippe? If not the truth, no, I would not have expected that. But at least a lie, that you could never get Jan out. Why, why did you force me to live at your feet like some dog?"

"You would have left me. . . . I was afraid, Natalia. I was afraid you would leave. . . ."

The last words were horribly spat up as blood spurted from beneath the razor's edge. Natalia dragged the tip, embedded a full inch, halfway around Sléton's neck, severing every artery on the way. Only when his back was covered in blood and the razor embedded against the top of his spinal column did she stop.

At that moment the distant chimes of Notre Dame rang a solemn seven o'clock.

CHAPTER TWELVE

The Bratislava Restaurant is hidden in one of the score of tiny side streets between the Boulevard St.-Germain, the Place Odéon, and the Seine. A gathering place for Paris' tiny colony of Czechs, it boasts one of the finest Rhine wine cellars in the city.

The evening of September 20 was a special occasion, the birthday of the proprietor Ivan Rabka. The low-beamed ceiling was hung heavy with garlands, the bar thrown open for friends and old customers. Outside, the doorman had posted a sign CLOSED BECAUSE OF ILLNESS. Players was sitting at the bar, nursing his Slivovitz, and watching a parade of cold cut platters pass before him to the already-laden tables. He had managed to get in only because he had mentioned the name of Natalia Kaysk to the doorman, who in turn had called Rabka. Upon hearing Natalia's name, Rabka made it clear Players was his friend for life.

At seven fifteen the barmaid answered the phone, spoke into it through the din and passed Players the receiver.

"I have it. I am coming down now."

Even before Natalia hung up, Players knew something had gone wrong.

Players swung off the bar and elbowed his way through the throng to the door. Once outside, he looked up and down the street, searching for some vantage point. He didn't know how she had obtained the papers, whether

Sléton knew and was after her. If Players had to fire, he wanted a clean shot.

Standing about forty paces down from the Bratislava, across the street, was a Volkswagen bus, dilapidated, dirty, with British plates. It was parked with its side doors facing the street. Provided no one was inside, it would be perfect.

The doors had been left unlocked since there wasn't much one would want to steal. The air inside was heavy with the smell of old mattresses and unwashed bodies. Players closed the doors behind him and after stepping over the blankets, crouched down next to a plastic bag of garbage. He left the panel door open just enough to accommodate the barrel of the Hanyatti. The range was clear, but since he was only a few feet off the ground, Players hoped he wouldn't have to shoot. A level shot carried the danger of someone innocent stepping in the way.

Natalia Kasyk arrived at the Bratislava five minutes later. Her white Alfa Romeo shot past the Volkswagen and screeched to a halt as she spotted a parking space. Down the street a Renault taxi also stopped, and a woman got out. By the time Natalia passed the Volks bus the barrel of the revolver was even with the side door, trailing a little ahead of her, watching.

The woman crossing the street toward Natalia was young, blond and dressed in a light wool suit. She brushed by the group of men coming out of a bistro and stepped onto the sidewalk, quickening her pace. At first Players thought it might be another arrival for Rabka's party, but the woman said something, and Natalia backed off, almost losing her balance on the curb. Natalia began running for the steps of the Bratislava.

The other woman took two steps to follow her and suddenly stopped, reaching for something inside her purse. Players heard her call out. At the same time he caught sight of a fat heavy silencer on the end of a small-caliber pistol.

His finger curled around the trigger. The bullet crashed through the barrel, and in the next instant passed through Heidi Seppes' back, ripping her stomach and burying itself in the trunk of a car.

He flung back the door and was running as Natalia began to scream. When she saw him, she clumsily threw her handbag at him and disappeared into the restaurant. As he came up to the curb, Players saw the red leather volume in the handbag. He scooped it up just as the shouting began. The time had finally come for him to run and there was only one place to go, to the Mole.

Heidi Seppes was to wait for the minister outside his apartment on the rue Querbes, the meeting having been scheduled for seven o'clock. When Sléton failed to appear, she made her way up immediately. The girl stepping into the elevator on the third floor was pale and trembling, carelessly dressed, wearing no stockings or makeup. Heidi Seppes had been told about Natalia, and she recognized Sléton's mistress at once. She also noticed a red folio volume that stuck out over the top of the bag Natalia was clutching.

The door to Number 39 was unlocked. Heidi Seppes pushed the door open cautiously. Ten seconds later she found the body of the usually punctual minister and his reason for having missed their meeting.

She ran downstairs in time to see the white Alfa Romeo slide away from the curb. Up the street she spotted a taxi and began waving frantically at the Alfa, knowing its driver wouldn't stop, but that the taxi would catch the entire scene. He did. The Renault drew up and, without being told, went after the white car.

Checking her watch, Heidi Seppes realized Eberhardt Krieg would call her hotel in less than forty minutes. If there was no answer, Krieg would ring again every quarter hour for one hour to make certain his agent had collected the papers from Sléton. She hoped Natalia wasn't going too far.

The taxi barreled through a red light, the driver leaning hard over the wheel. The white Alfa turned off the Boulevard St.-Germain onto Pauvres Clarisses and slowed. Natalia was searching for a parking space. Heidi Seppes fished in her change purse for two ten-franc notes and dropped them beside the driver. Before getting out, she also made certain that the butt of her revolver lay just underneath the zipper to her bag. Normally Heide Seppes would not have considered using a gun. She knew enough about martial arts to drop a black belt judoist. But whoever had delicately bled Sléton merited extra caution, even if she appeared to be nothing more than a frightened running girl.

When she caught up to Natalia, Heidi called to her once. The girl stared wildly at her and backed away. Not wanting to take any chances, Heidi Seppes had gone for her gun. At that moment, the steel-jacketed bullet from Players' Hanyatti slammed into and through her. She died instantly, with no last thoughts, no final memories.

The Mole was not an appropriate cryptonym for the man who ran the ISIS safe house in Paris. The Mole was short, wiry, with brown curly hair and a slouching, lazy walk. He also managed a popular crêperie on the Boulevard St.-Michel, opposite the Luxembourg Gardens.

The Mole recognized Players as soon as he stepped inside the tiny restaurant, crammed to bursting with customers. He took him by the arm and, through the sweet odor of butter pancakes, led him out the back way, into an open square between the four apartment blocks.

"Up the staircase, all the way up to the seventh floor. It's a small room with a girlie poster on it."

"Is there a telephone?"

"Certainly."

"Safe?"

The Mole shrugged. "It's the number they have in Geneva. Weren't you told?"

The Mole handed him the key with a thin smile. "Did you have to kill Sléton?" he asked. Noting Players' glacial stare, he tossed his head in the direction of a blaring radio. "Don't feel so bad. A lot of people will sleep better now—at least until another prick is put into the ministry. Sléton was a first-class son of a bitch!"

Players took the old-fashioned key and without a word started up the stairs. The Mole returned to his pub, whistling at the thought of an extra three thousand francs which would nicely fatten his personal account in Zurich.

The room had once been part of the servants' quarters. A third of it was partitioned off to make a tiny kitchen, complete with two electric rings and a refrigerator. But there was no hot water or a toilet. The front of the room, with its slanted window opening up on St.-Michel, was comfortable enough with a tiny fireplace, a threadbare rug and a battered sofa that doubled as a bed. The only drawback, as far as Players was concerned, was that there was no exit save the back stairs. But he had no choice.

Players had intended to wait until the crêperie had closed for the night, then go with the Mole to whatever exit route had been arranged by Geneva. Players doubted that ISIS had meant him to read the collection.

Aaron Vogel, Sabatini and the innocents butchered by the explosion, Sléton and now some girl he had never set eyes on—they were all dead because this red leather volume had in one way or another touched them. Players wanted to know what it was that was so important about these pages that they cost such a price.

Two hours later he understood.

"This is Players, I have the papers."

"Very good, Alexander. I assume you are at the safe house?"

"I am."

"The Mole has instructions to get you out. We shall be expecting you around four o'clock tomorrow morning. Is Mandel still with you?"

"I expect so."

"Should there be any difficulties, tell the Mole to use Code Three, Inter-Air Europe, Le Bourget. We shall notify them to stand by. Avoid encountering Mandel if at all possible. I do not want any more blood in Paris than has already been spilled."

"I was not responsible for Sléton."

"Be that as it may, you will have a harder time convincing the French police of that than me. No more complications. Sléton is dead. Jan Kasyk has been accounted for. You have your eye for an eye."

"What about the priest?"

"He is with us under the best possible protection in Rome. All hell has broken loose down there as well."

"I can imagine," Players said softly, and rang off.

It was twenty minutes to eleven. Players slid the red leather volume into a Samaritain shopping bag he found in the closet and left the room, moving quickly and silently to the fifth floor. There he tested the back door of an apartment which would have access to the elevator at the front of the building. It rattled but gave, and he found himself in a small kitchen. For one minute Players stood motionless, letting his eyes accustom themselves to the darkness. From another room, to the right, he heard the grunts of a man, broken by the protests of a bed.

The elevator took him to the ground floor, and he stepped past the concierge's door into a damp drive leading to an open square. He didn't bother to check if anyone was waiting for him around the back. Someone was, and Players recognized the pungent smell of coarse Israeli tobacco. Mandel would never have approved of his men smoking on the job. Still, he thought, it had been clever of Mandel to follow Natalia as well as himself.

Players opened the trap cut into the two large garage doors and slipped out onto the sidewalk of Boulevard St.-Michel, one hand delicately holding the butt of his revolver. He spotted the stakeout immediately, leaning against the blue post car, wearing the uniform of a telegram boy. He never heard Players walk up to him.

"Shalom!"

The man whirled around. The grin on his lips disappeared as soon as he recognized the speaker. Players caught the hand going for the gun and smashed the wrist against the side of the car. The bone snapped like dry sticks.

"Where is Mandel?"

The Israeli screamed and flung his other arm in the direction of the crêperie. Although there was still plenty of time to do business on a Friday night, the grille had been drawn across the front door and the interior light dimmed, leaving only the kitchen lamps blazing. Players imagined what the Mole was going through in there at the hands of Eli Mandel, as the Mossad agent encouraged him to tell where Players was hiding.

"Appelez la police," he barked at a passerby.

"Comment?"

"La police! Il y a des voleurs là dedans!"

The bespeckled Frenchman blinked uncomprehendingly and ran off to the next café.

"Tell Mandel never to interfere with me again," he hissed into the Israeli's ear. "Never again! Understand?"

Players' fingers groped for the nerve just under the ear, found it, and the agent sank to the ground.

By the time the police arrived Players' taxi had already reached the Périferique, the highway leading out to Le Bourget airfield.

Natalia had reached the steps of the Bratislava when she heard the shot that killed Heidi Seppes. She closed her eyes, waiting for the indescribable and inevitable pain to flood over her. But her body was still moving, and she was behind the door now. There was the familiar eagle emblem and the cloakroom stuffed with raincoats. She was alive and could not believe it until two beefy arms circled her waist in the dark alcove.

"Natalia! My beloved Natalia!"

Rabka swung her off the floor in a crazy spin that made

her legs fly out. She felt the heel of her shoe collide with someone's back.

"Ah, Natalia, I thought you were never going to come!"

"Happy birthday, sweet."

She put both hands around his gleaming fleshy cheeks and kissed him hard.

"And now," Rabka roared. "I am not letting you go!"

"Please, Ivan, I can't breathe!"

Some young gallant finally broke Rabka's iron grip, but the huge Czech slapped his arm when he tried to lead Natalia away.

"Mine! Tonight she is my guest!" he bellowed.

And everyone cheered at Natalia's obvious embarrassment.

"Slivovitz!"

A glass was slapped down before her, and she was lost in a whirlwind of cheers, laughter and toasts. The clear liquid burned her throat, choking her and bringing tears to her eyes.

"Ivan—the bathroom! Before I really celebrate."

The gentle giant rose and, shouting over his shoulder, escorted Natalia to the back. She slammed the door behind her, locked it and sat down on the toilet fully dressed. The odor of disinfectant assailed her nostrils, but that was better than that unbearable cigarette smoke outside. Here it was cool and safe. . . .

"Natalia! Natalia, wait! Give it to me!"

Her eyes opened with a start. The girl had called to her, Natalia had never seen her before. She looked back, and the girl was bringing out a gun. Then the shot . . . and Players was running at her. Natalia shivered in the cold cubicle.

"Get up!" she told herself fiercely. "Get up *now!* Flush the toilet so they can hear it. Look at yourself in the mirror. Use a towelet to wipe your face, around the cheeks. Open the door. There is Ivan standing by the bar. Don't let him see you. Go into the kitchen."

"Yes, mademoiselle?"

"I need some fresh air," Natalia said unsteadily. "Ivan told me to go out the back way."

The kitchen boy pointed in the direction of the gray metal door.

"It's open."

Then she was outside, staring at the garbage bins and a loose mixture of cans, paper, rotting food at her feet. At the blind end of the alley she could see a blue light flicker off the ancient brick. Undistinguishable voices were calling to each other. Natalia Kasyk began running in the opposite direction.

Every person is capable of murder. A single passion—hatred, despair, fear or revenge—can build up within a human being until he or she will strike down the object that nourishes that passion and so be free of it. But the driving force behind murder evaporates as soon as the act is performed and a person is faced with nothing but the silent evidence, the victim of his act. At the precise instant of beholding one's deed a person realizes it was not enough to commit murder but that one must now *accept* it also.

Natalia Kasyk understood she had killed Philippe Sléton out of vengeance. A woman with a phobia about knives, she had not thought of her fear but taken a razor and buried it in her lover's neck. Subsequently, she had picked up the Tetramachus Collection, walked from the apartment, closed the door and driven in her car to the Bratislava. Only when the second killing, that of Heidi

Seppes, took place before her eyes, had her resolve failed, and she had fled to the restaurant in panic.

The second murder forced her to see what she had done only a few minutes earlier and destroyed her ability to push her act from her thoughts. Natalia was suddenly faced with the necessity of accepting her murder. But once the passion was spent, she could not do this. The vicious circle was forming: nonacceptance, yet no desire to repent and, therefore, a growing feeling of helplessness, of not understanding the exact nature of the forces that were playing on her.

This circle whirled around and around as she walked down a maze of streets toward the bright neon glitter of the Place Odéon. Wanting to cry out, she stared at the frozen anonymous faces passing her by. Whom would she cry out to? Who would stop and take her into his arms to comfort her and whisper reassurance, that all would be well, that she could now rest? She wanted someone to care for her, if only for a little while.

At the rue des Colons Natalia saw a bakery stand and a taxi driver leaning against his car, delicately picking sesame seeds from a bun.

"Gare du Nord," she said, thrusting a fifty-franc note into his hand.

The driver opened the back door for her.

Why Gare du Nord? Because that was her first memory of Paris, of a day the train had finally pulled in from Vienna, a rainy autumn afternoon in 1950. In a third-class compartment, a little girl was gently roused from her sleep by her brother. They were both orphans, alone except for each other.

"It is such an ugly structure," Natalia thought as the taxi rounded the corner.

She got out, and a familiar scent overcame her. Sweet, sweet diesel oil and the pungent aroma of warm rock beds hid the sour odor of travelers. She walked quickly through the station, looking at the faded Dubonnet and Cinzano advertisements and posters showing gleaming SNCF electric trains that served the suburbs. She thought she too might like to go somewhere. But where, and to whom? A panhandler accosted her with a stare that suggested more than money. Natalia drew back, her lips forming an ugly snarl, and walked around him.

The girl at the cigarette counter, anemic, with black, oily hair plastered across her scalp, slapped down her movie magazine impatiently and moved out from behind the cash register.

"Mademoiselle?" Her tone was bored and the smile mocking. Natalia looked into the mirror on the counter, dirty from a thousand fingerprints, and her mouth fell open. Her face had gone completely white, the lips blue as though she had been swimming in ice-cold water.

"Razors—Wilkinson."

"Seven francs."

Moving quickly around the grime-encrusted girders, she made her way through a colony of pinball machines into the back, to the washrooms. A wizened woman passed her a token in exchange for thirty centimes and went back to reading her *France-Soir*. On the woman's table a transistor radio was broadcasting the news. Mercifully the end toilet was free.

Natalia looked up into the full force of the naked light bulb surrounded by wire mesh. She ripped open the cellophane and eased the fresh blade from its tissue paper. It was ironic, she laughed to herself, and before another thought crossed her mind, her hand flashed by the left wrist.

There was almost no pain, but the blade became slippery from the warm blood. The left hand moved a little more slowly, but the cut was hard and deep.

Natalia sat down on the toilet, her arms hanging from her sides, the blood flowing quickly and silently from her body. She saw a picture of Jan, laughing, and then she started to pray as the blackness melted across her eyes.

CHAPTER THIRTEEN

Although the evening of September 20 was pleasantly warm, with a light breeze shifting through the trees in the gardens, Rozdentsy Cardinal Meyerczuk met no one along his walk from the papal apartments by the Court of St. Damaso. He thought he might see some of the earlier arrivals among the cardinals gathering for the papal election, but there wasn't a soul in the vicinity of St. Peter's. The prelate guessed that the cardinals were busy installing themselves and their entourages in quarters provided for the occasion or else were preparing for the council with himself and Volpe later this evening. Meyerczuk expected foreign prelates to divide their concern between the condition of Urban XI and the crisis that was wracking the Church. He would have no difficulty in summing up Dottore Frenza's latest report, which showed the Pontiff inexorably slipping beyond the bounds of medical help. But answers concerning the Tetramachus Collection, its theft and the implications thereof, including the government's use of Article 100, would be more difficult to come by.

The problem did not lie in how much the cardinals from abroad could be told. Meyerczuk had already decided that a straightforward account of the facts, including his own actions for the defense of the Holy See, would best serve the Sacred College. The cardinals would doubtlessly come to see that the Church was not as helpless as many of them thought it to be. The Polish prelate's concern was for himself. After he had spoken with Frenza, Meyerczuk had knelt in prayer before Urban XI's altar. He appealed to the Lord to have mercy on his soul and to grant him the strength with which to carry on his work.

Now, walking across St. Peter's Square, the Iron Cardinal begged that the Tetramachus Collection never be found. He had defended the Church, all the while knowing that if the papers came to light, he would be lost. He had confronted Fransci and had been spared the humiliation of the prime minister presenting him with the collection, evidence of his sin. He had spoken with Fransci only three hours ago, and again no mention had been made of the papers. Fransci had thanked Meyerczuk for bringing Father Martin's file and had asked for nothing more. Yet the longer exposure was held over the Polish prelate's head, the heavier his burden became. Every time he signed his name to a Church statement or met in conference with Volpe and the Curia he felt his pen tremble and his mouth taste of ashes. He was afraid that the careful path he was laying toward the papacy might suddenly open beneath him. If the Tetramachus Collection were found and exposed, Volpe, Da Silva, the Curia, the Sacred College, the whole of the Roman Catholic world would turn on him, would despise him. He would be seen as a liar, a man who condemned others for that which he himself was guilty of. And they would shun him until his shame became so great he would have to abandon the Holy Church, which was his only refuge.

That is why he had prayed for himself, for he understood that no matter how generous a man's intentions, if his actions were based on deceit he would be denied forgiveness.

Claudio Cardinal Marrenzo, walking with his secretary, Pio Cliotia, passed the Palace of the Holy Office and entered St. Peter's Square from the west side. Both clerics noticed Meyerczuk at once.

"His Eminence appears to be meditating over some matter," Cliotia observed.

"There is a great deal for him to think about," Marrenzo murmured. "He has been carrying a great burden."

Cliotia wondered if the irony was intentional, whether Marrenzo was referring to Meyerczuk's defense of the Church or his fear of the collection.

"Will you tell him now?"

"I do not see any point as yet," Marrenzo replied.

The clerics came within earshot of the Polish prelate, and their conversation ceased.

"Good evening, Claudio," Meyerczuk said.

"We are on our way to inquire about His Holiness' condition," Marrenzo said.

"I have just come from the papal suite. His Holiness is unconscious. Dottore Frenza is not permitting any visitors."

"How much longer will His Holiness suffer?" Marrenzo asked, bowing his head.

"Not very long," Meyerczuk intoned. "The end will be merciful."

"And in the midst of all that is happening in this city, we must now prepare for an election," Marrenzo said softly. "I should congratulate you, Rozdentsy, for the hours and effort you have devoted to the Church over these last days. It is indebted to you."

"These are difficult times," Meyerczuk said. "But with the grace of God we shall see them through."

"Has Fransci's government demanded anything of the Church, under the powers of the State Security Act?"

"Nothing," Meyerczuk answered. "I spoke with Fransci today. The government is more interested in whoever it was that murdered Sabatini than in making trouble for the Church."

"I see," Marrenzo murmured. "Well, we shall be on our way. If there is anything at all I may contribute to your efforts, Rozdentsy, please call on me."

"Thank you, Claudio."

The two clerics crossed the piazza in silence. When they were approaching the papal quarters, Cliotia turned to Marrenzo.

"I am certain there has been more activity than His Eminence cared to divulge."

"Of course," Marrenzo said. "But we have never been invited into the sacred council of Meyerczuk, Volpe and God knows who else. Rozdentsy is handling matters as he sees fit."

"With one eye on succession."

"Undoubtedly. But I feel sorry for Rozdentsy," Marrenzo said. "He lied about his dealings with Fransci, and he lied poorly. He is coming to the end of his tether."

"Perhaps he is thinking the papal election will occur quickly," Cliotia said, "and he will be able to wield the full authority of the Church against his detractors. It would be difficult to dislodge him as an incumbent pope, even with the revelations of the Collection."

"Indeed it would," Marrenzo said with a tiny smile. "But we shall not leave matters for as long as all that."

Across the Tiber from the Vatican, off the intersection of the Viale Trastevere and Corso Umberto, is the ancient fortress of the Villa Medici. In the adjacent park, once the preserve of the estate, stand five cottages, modern in design, a careful mixture of stone, wood and iron grilles. Four of these belong to prosperous doctors and lawyers. The fifth had been provided for Giulio Musco at the expense of the voting public. It was both Musco's home and a clandestine operational headquarters, an ISIS safe house.

Inter-Air's Hawker Executive Craft whined into Leonardo da Vinci Airport and came to a half before the last row of custom huts. The pilot cut his engines and turned to the passenger in the copilot's seat.

"Now what?"

"I have no idea. You will be paid as always. Probably a bit more for my having taken you outside your destination."

The pilot, a young American, said nothing. His income was handsomely supplemented by the occasional service call from Geneva. He had been told and so accepted that some of the flights might be dangerous. He was paid because he was willing to take that risk and not ask questions. Still it had not been easy to fly from Paris to Rome with a gun ten inches from his ribs.

"Can I call Geneva?" he asked at last.

"I imagine you must," Players said. "But no one is going to blame you. You might tell Pelikan that your passenger is on his way to the house. They will understand."

The pilot nodded. He waited until Players had disappeared into the customs shack before opening his radio circuits. By the time Pelikan picked up the signal on the prearranged frequency, Players was leaving the airport. Pelikan ordered an immediate alert, and had the ISIS Boeing readied for takeoff. He also put a call through to the ISIS safe house in Rome, but Musco wasn't there.

Pelikan had the switchboard keep the line open so that the phone would be ringing if Musco came in. Musco was to be told that Players had broken with orders and gone to Rome. His destination was almost certainly the safe house. Musco was to handle him with caution, but under no circumstances was Players to disappear before Pelikan arrived.

From the time of Pelikan's initial telephone call to the moment Musco inserted his key into the door, forty-two minutes had passed. The telephone was ringing. Musco cursed, flicked the light switch on and grabbed the receiver. Even before the message had been completed, he was patting the small of his back, making certain his revolver was within instant reach. By the time he had the full message the gun was in his hand.

"Put it away, Giulio. You don't need it."

Players had all but closed the door and was standing behind him, jacket open, the butt of the Hanyatti exposed.

"Good evening, Alex—or rather, good morning." Musco gave him a cheery brilliant smile, but his eyes never moved from Players' hand. Even though his own gun was out, Musco knew Players would have fired his shot before Musco had had time to aim his weapon. "Been shopping in Paris?"

Players smiled wanly.

"You have managed to cause quite a commotion, my friend," Musco said.

"Please put the gun down, Giulio," Players repeated.

Musco shrugged and threw the revolver on the sofa. "Shall we go into the library?" Musco suggested. "You look as though you could do with a drink."

"Did I pull you away from anything interesting?" Players asked him, stepping back to let Musco pass.

"Nothing more interesting than that." Musco gestured at the Samaritain bag. "The Tetramachus Collection?"

"The Collection."

"Why did you not go to Geneva, Alex?" Musco asked quietly. "Oh, and I should tell you. Pelikan will be here in a few hours."

"I know. It doesn't matter anymore. I only want to speak to the priest."

"There is more news, I'm afraid," Musco said sadly. "Natalia Kasyk killed herself in Paris, slashed her wrists in a bathroom at the Gare du Nord."

Players took the vodka Musco held out and drank half of the glass. He shivered as the liquor passed down his throat. There would be no need now to concern himself with that helpless, tortured woman. She was beyond all help. He had used her and broken her, capitalized on her shame. She had aided him without asking for anything in return. No, Natalia had no need of him, and he had no coin with which to pay her back.

"Did she kill Sléton?" Players asked woodenly.

"The police found dried blood on her dress, not very much but enough for identification. It looks that way. The only puzzle is the identity of the other woman, whom you shot."

"Who was she, Giulio?"

"We know her as Heidi Seppes, a free-lance killer. Very good. But we haven't found out whom she was working for.

"Why did you not go to Geneva, Alex?" Musco repeated softly.

Players looked up at him and abruptly held out the Collection.

"This is yours now," he said. "I do not intend to go

anywhere with it. I wouldn't know whom to give it to."

"You have read it?"

"I have. That is why I came here. Rokossovsky told me the priest had been found. I want to speak with him." Players paused for a moment as though not really wanting to ask the question. "How *did* you find him, Giulio?"

"Rokossovsky sent me down a communications team as soon as the operation was under way. We still had that tap on the Vatican switchboard, the one installed during Micelli's abortive Tora-Tora coup. It was an easy matter to activate the microphones on the papal circuits, those of Volpe, Meyerczuk and others. When Father Martin tried to call His Holiness yesterday, he stayed on the line long enough for us to get a fix on his location. We picked him up twenty minutes later."

"Very simply, very effective," Players murmured, almost in admiration. "Is Father Martin downstairs?"

"Stop it, Alex! Stop it now!" Musco said, suddenly angry. "Pelikan is furious because you didn't follow orders, but you can patch that up. You have found the Collection. The operation is finished!"

"Downstairs?"

For a moment it appeared as though Musco would lose control of himself and reach for Players. But he stopped himself, and one fist smashed into an open palm, a gesture of disgust. But he stopped himself.

"My orders are not to allow you to leave the house," he said tightly. "Nothing was said about not letting you talk to the priest." He beckoned Players to follow him and led the way to the basement staircase.

"I will have you both on video," Musco said. "If you attempt to destroy the Collection, I will use the machine gun. You understand?"

"I only want to speak to him, Giulio," Players said softly. "I want him to see the Collection. After that it is yours."

"He hasn't really slept since coming here," Musco added curtly. "You might try to make it brief."

"Thank you."

"For what?" Musco retorted. "Helping you dig your own grave?"

The room was sparsely appointed. The bed was a continental, neatly made. There was the right amount of dust on the cheap furniture and the rather damp odor of a place that had been empty for a long time. Players stepped inside and closed the door behind him. The crippled priest, Father Martin Belobraditz, rose to greet him. He was dressed as Players thought he would be, in a simple, slightly soiled cassock, with a worn metal crucifix around his neck. When he saw the Collection, Father Martin's expression changed from one of mild serenity to pain.

"Good evening, Father."

Belobraditz moved toward him, his body swaying grotesquely as he dragged his useless foot behind him. "What is your name?" he called out softly.

Father Martin's face was a mask of shining sweat, the mouth drawn in fear, the black hair oily and greasy. He ran his hand over the red leather volume, leaving a trail of perspiration. He looked at Players, who had seated himself opposite the bed, then hobbled toward the wall and leaned against it.

"I have been waiting for you, signor," he said in a light, boyish tone. "The others have been kind. They wanted to know if I required special medicines. They did not threaten or brutalize me. But I knew they were waiting, for you, the man who would bring the Collection. I was waiting, too."

"I am not here to interrogate you, Father," Players said. "I came for myself."

"I do not understand what you mean. But you can do whatever you wish. I don't care what happens to me. I am empty. It is clear I have failed in my mission. I have not only failed to bring forward some truth about the Church, but I also caused men to be destroyed. I have spent hours in atonement for those deaths.

"They were worried at first"—he smiled—"those who watch me through their cameras. I was too quiet. I think they forgot that suicide is a sin in the eyes of the Church."

"Father Martin, why did you steal the Collection?" The question came softly and quickly from his lips as though he were ashamed for having had to ask it. The priest was not offended.

"What do you know of your employer, signor, the man who has taken great personal risks in sending you after me? I am speaking of His Eminence Meyerczuk."

The name seared through Players' mind, but the only sign he gave that anything was amiss was a narrowing of the eyes. Belobraditz did not know that it had been Claudio Cardinal Marrenzo who had hired ISIS for the retrieval.

"I know of the accord with Bronitz," Players said.

"You have read the Collection," Father Martin observed. "You might know too, from Meyerczuk's record and the rest of the Collection, why I stole it. But it shall be given back to the Church, no matter what I say, no matter what your conscience may tell you. But there is one final element which you do not know, although you may have guessed it."

Belobraditz looked deeply into the green, expressionless eyes staring back at him. He thought them hungry, perhaps even desperate, and he did not understand what it was this man wanted.

"His Eminence is an ambitious man. He has suffered much for his Church, but he has suffered even more himself. The pact with Bronitz has been his cross, his pact with Satan. Every day of his life he has paid for it. He has paid doubly because the world has placed its laurels at his feet. It trumpeted his bravery, courage and spirit until he could scarcely bear it. But still he was an ambitious man. He had sold his conscience for the Church, and now he wanted payment from that Church. He wanted its throne.

"His Eminence wanted the chair of Peter," Father Martin repeated softly, "as much as I desired justice for the Church. But I was a very small man, unversed in the ways of the world. I believed an instrument of power is sufficient to bring change, no matter how weak the hands of the man holding it. I was wrong. The strength of the hands is even more important than that of the instrument. I say this because even though I robbed His Eminence of the records of his past and so held a weapon over him, it was he, not I, who prevailed.

"You may smile at my naïveté, and I could not blame you. I wished only to do good, and that proved impossible without resorting to some kind of evil. I stole, and so I initiated the evil."

Father Martin paused.

"Had His Eminence no desire to succeed Urban the Eleventh, I doubt I ever would have seen the Collection. But because Cardinal Meyerczuk sought the throne and knew his past actions could deny him Peter's chair, he brought the documents from the crypt. I was his secretary. I saw the Collection in his office, and I began to read it. A little at a time, until I had finished it. No one suspected anything, no one, for I gave nothing away. There was no reason to. . . . I had no plan. I had no plan, even though it had been Meyerczuk's accord with Bronitz that had meant the death of the Polish Communist resistance movement. My father and mother were part of that group. My brothers as well."

Father Martin paused as he watched Players come to his feet.

"Meyerczuk's past!" Players whispered. "And he never knew who you were, what he had done to your family!"

"Never." Father Martin shook his head. "My family was murdered because Meyerczuk believed their lives, which did not belong to the Church, should be sacrificed for the Church. Perhaps it was not difficult for him to make such a decision. He had hated Communists all his life. He could not believe that the son of Communists could ever become a priest. . . .

"So it was the Church, my last sanctuary, that murdered my family," Father Martin repeated softly. "And still I had no plan. I felt as alone as it is possible for a man to feel, and I cried out in pity for myself, begging God to give me guidance or, if that was not His wish, to destroy me."

These last words came softly from his mouth. They were born of all the rage, bitterness, helplessness and goodness that he had lived with to that day. Players understood why he had sought this man out. He saw himself as a pale reflection of this priest who had found the strength to break the rock upon which his life was founded and which had given it meaning. Father Martin had discovered that no matter how desperate a man might be for shelter, how cold and lonely he would be without it, he could not accept a sanctuary which cared nothing for justice.

"Did you want vengeance on Meyerczuk?" Players asked.

"A desire for vengeance is a pitiful emotion," Father Martin answered. "It reduces a man to the level of a beast. But, yes, I did want vengeance. Even so, I could not bring myself to act on that desire. Had I been able to, the Collection would have been taken long before the sixteenth of September."

"Why then?"

"I chanced to overhear Cardinal Meyerczuk speaking on the telephone with the prefect of the Secret Archives. His Eminence stated that he had at last resolved the 'problem' of the papers, as he put it. He told the prefect he would send me down to the Court of the Belvedere the following morning and that the Collection would never be available again to anyone. When I heard this, I knew the Collection was going to be destroyed and, with it, the fragment of one man's history . . . the histories of countless dead people, who would, from that moment, never have a chance to be heard again."

"But surely Meyerczuk could have destroyed the Collection long before that," Players interrupted softly. "He had the means and countless opportunities."

"That would appear to be so, signor. But I believe you overlook the essence of the matter. His Eminence spent a long time thinking about his action. The proof of that is the hours and hours he kept the Collection on his desk, looking at it day after day, experiencing the most exquisite anguish a man can endure. I venture to say it was very much like that terror he felt when he handed his countrymen over to the Gestapo. Then he had suffered for his Church; now he was suffering for himself, suffering because he did not know how much more his conscience could bear—even an action meant to save him.

"No doubt, His Eminence feels I stole the papers to compromise him personally," Father Martin continued, "since he was the one who would lose the most, the succession to the papacy. Yet this is not true. Many prelates and clerics would have had to come forward and admit that in the course of the war they had not always acted in keeping with the message of Christ, that they had been afraid, corrupt or weak. But the first step toward asking for forgiveness is always the most difficult. For a man such as Meyerczuk this would have been impossible. Since he could not bring himself to admit to wrongdoing, he will always believe that I wanted vengeance on him. He will not see that sometimes the line between vengeance and justice is very fine indeed."

Father Martin lapsed into silence. He kept staring at the red leather volume as though at any moment he expected it to disappear.

"You have suffered enough," Players said quietly. "God knows I am not the man to tell you this, but I feel you have."

"I have prayed for the Lord's mercy," Father Martin said, hobbling over to where Players sat. "I would like to pray for you as well."

Players looked up at him, his face drawn.

"Pray for me, Father," he whispered. "Please offer me that. I would do the same for you if I could."

"There is a story I was once told by a Spaniard of the

Hebraic faith,'' Father Martin said. ''It seems that in the village he lived there was a highly respected rabbi, a wise devout man but stricken with a terrible temper. One day he screamed at his housekeeper for some trivial thing she had dropped, 'Better that you should have been broken!' That night the housekeeper was run down by a team of horses. Every bone in her body was broken. When the rabbi learned of this he was horrified and went away to consult his elder. The elder listened to his account and decreed that the rabbi should never again speak a single word as long as he lived but that he must pray to God for forgiveness. So the sinful rabbi went to the elder's house, and there, in a small room by a window, he began to pray. Food was brought to him twice a day, but he never again uttered another word to any human being.

''Now I shall become like that rabbi,'' Father Martin said. ''I too must pray for God to cleanse my sins. Whether I do this in a prison cell, a monastery or some shabby little room does not matter. I must atone and I shall never omit you from my prayers, signor. I feel you should not have come here, but you did and so acted in accordance with your conscience. That is the most noble path for a man.''

When he heard this last sentence, Giulio Musco pursed his lips and shook his head. He switched off the tape recorder, wondering if there was anything left in Players that might be salvaged.

Alexander Players made his way up the basement stairs and into the hallway of the safe house. Waiting for him in the front room, the curtains drawn, was Musco, standing over a pot of tea and a silver dish of lemon wedges.

''Sit down, Alexander,'' Musco said.

Players did so, placing the red leather volume across his knees.

"Rokossovsky called from Geneva. He sends his congratulations. Sugar?"

"One cube."

"And lemon?"

"Yes."

He passed the cup over to Players, who set it aside.

"What will happen to him, Giulio?"

"He will be returned to the Vatican." Musco shrugged. "Meyerczuk and other members of the Curia will interrogate him, caution Father Martin to say nothing of the contents of the Collection to civil authority and then escort him to Criminal Investigations."

"Wouldn't Meyerczuk be concerned that Father Martin might tell CI everything?"

"I do not think the Iron Cardinal would permit the police to see his secretary unless it was in his presence and then only after he, Meyerczuk, was convinced the priest would talk of nothing that was unrelated to Sabatini's killing. From what I overheard of your conversation, Alex, Father Martin is finished with the Collection. He did not sound at all interested in pursuing its exposure."

"And after?"

"The Vatican has its own courts. I assume he will be tried and punished accordingly."

"No, he will not be punished," Players said. "I will see to it that no harm comes to him."

"Stay out of it!" Musco turned on him. "The assignment is finished, Alex! It's over. Let it go!"

"Where are the papers to be delivered?"

"Pelikan did not tell me."

Players regarded him thoughtfully, knowing Musco was lying.

"When I was downstairs, Giulio, you could have taken your revolver and been waiting for me when I came up. You didn't do that. I want to deliver the papers now. I want to finish this operation."

"You know Rokossovsky wants a copy of the Collection."

"Very well. Get your Ex-ma. We can photograph the entire volume in less than an hour."

"Pelikan will be here in two."

"I don't think there is any need to wait for him," Players said. "I will finish what I began."

Musco looked at him, and a broad smile came over his face. He saw no use in fighting Players anymore.

"If you are determined to tempt Pelikan's wrath, so be it. I can always say I obeyed under duress." And he laughed.

CHAPTER FOURTEEN

The secretary to Cardinal Marrenzo, Pio Cliotia, answered the telephone on its second ring. It was half past three in the morning of September 21. The secretary had been asleep for all of twenty minutes.

The voice on the other end asked for his name but did not identify itself.

"Tell the cardinal the package has arrived. It will be delivered immediately. Instruct the guards at the Vatican railroad station gates to pass through a taxi. One rider. Is that clear?"

"It is."

Cliotia replaced the receiver in its cradle. He rose to go into the cardinal's bedroom, but Marrenzo was already by the door.

"I listened on the other phone," Marrenzo said. "Call the guard; then fetch Meyerczuk and bring him here. But put him in the study. I want him to hear what is said when the transfer takes place but not to see the man bringing the papers. I will meet the car myself."

The taxi crossed the Piazza del Risorgimento and cut up the Viale Vaticano toward the railway station. In the rearview mirror Players could see the glint of Musco's black BMW sports sedan trailing a half block behind them.

The guard at the station flagged down the taxi and walked over to the driver's window, the barrel of the gun parallel to the ground.

"Cardinal Marrenzo's party," Players said in formal Italian.

The sentry peered at him and called out to another man. Players watched as a figure emerged from the darkness, escorted by soldiers. The rear door opened, and the gentle historian of the Church, Claudio Cardinal Marrenzo, got in. The circle had come complete.

Marrenzo turned to Players and murmured. "Let our discussion wait until there is privacy."

"Take His Eminence and his guest to the Borgia apartments," the soldier told the driver. "You will wait for your passenger and come out the same entrance."

The cab turned past the mosaic factory, went around the back of St. Peter's and drove slowly down to the Borgia apartments. Players followed Marrenzo up the staircase and into a vast hall of honey-colored marble. The prelate's quarters were on the second floor.

"Would you pass me that, signor?" Marrenzo said when they were alone in his office. "Yes, the Collection. Thank you."

Placing the Collection on a marble table, Marrenzo leafed through it, nodding his head as though performing a distasteful but necessary task.

"Your Organization has lived up to my expectations and its own reputation," he said. "On behalf of the Holy Father and the Church, I thank you."

He looked across at Players, waiting for him to make the next move. As far as Marrenzo was concerned, there was nothing more to be said.

Players remembered the words of his first political instructor at the training headquarters on Sadovaya Street: "You have been chosen because of your physical and mental abilities. Other professionals, like yourselves, will recognize you at once—by your stance, your carriage, the movements of your eyes. But there is a kind of agent, a kind of personality, who will fool all of you at one point in your careers, we hope, not a fatal one. He is the fat man, the harmless jovial buffoon, the small, timid man who looks like a clerk too afraid to ask for a just raise, the fawning but boastful lout who speaks too loudly. These men are the most dangerous of all. They are those deceptive trees which appear too old, frail or innocuous. You are the strong young trees who should weather a storm, but believe me, it will be they, not yourselves, who are left standing when the storm passes."

That was the kind of man Marrenzo was. Amid such giants as Meyerczuk and Urban XI, he counted for nothing. But when the storm had passed, only he would remain standing.

"Signor?"

"You have the Collection. Soon you will have Father Martin. What do you propose to do?"

Marrenzo laughed softly and took off his glasses.

"I trust you will understand if I do not answer that."

"I am afraid you are obliged to answer," Players said softly.

"Why is that?"

"Because I want to know what will happen to Father Martin after you ascend to the papacy."

Marrenzo regarded him with mild surprise but said nothing.

"You, not Meyerczuk, will become the next Peter," Players continued. "You, not Meyerczuk, commissioned ISIS to find the Collection, and you, no one else, will profit thereby. Once the papers are in your possession you will force Meyerczuk to step down as contender, possibly even encourage him to support your candidacy in the Sacred College. You shall be the savior of the Church and the college will have no difficulty in rewarding you. Somewhere inside you there is an ambition, a craving, which makes Meyerczuk's appetites seem normal by comparison. This was your chance; you saw it; you acted upon it. What would never have become yours by the normal course of events is already in your hands. Now you shall rule the Vatican, and ISIS, because they helped you, will always have your ear when they need it. Your secretary's trip to Geneva is on their tapes; his bank transfers are all duly recorded. You knew, when you decided to use ISIS, that the relationship between yourselves would continue even after the papers had been returned. The price you have paid for the Collection, for the papacy, was one of compromising the Church before a civil organization. And you paid this price gladly!"

There was no reaction in the old man's puffed face. It remained impassive and inscrutable, as though it did not care for what Players was saying or had expected it and so was bored.

"That is what you have done," Players said. "But I wish to warn you: Should anything happen to Father Martin, if there is the slightest attempt to punish him in any way, I will see you suffer for that."

"I presume that is a valid threat, signor," Marrenzo asked with a note of mockery in his voice.

"The distance between the gallery where the Pope makes his Sunday appearance and the nearest building of equivalent height is about one hundred and seventy meters. I do not miss an immobile target at that range. Nor do I have any compunction about carrying out such a mission."

"As revenge?"

"As revenge."

"I do not understand your reasons for bringing up such unpleasantness." Marrenzo sighed. "I feel very sorry for you, signor. People in your profession should not engage in introspective analysis to determine the good or evil of those who employ you. You carry too much on your backs to be able to do that. I feel you haven't much time left in your particular endeavors.

"But I do not underestimate you. You are a brutal man, a killer to whom holy vestments mean nothing. Belobraditz is of no value to anyone any longer. The Vatican will be obliged to try him for his theft, but I shall intercede on his behalf with a plea for mercy. As you doubtless know, signor, I was the one who first spoke for mercy in the presence of Urban. Belobraditz will be free to do penance and return to the Church, but I doubt he shall choose that course. It depends on his conscience. But I repeat: He shall not suffer, for there is no need for him to do so. He has endured enough, don't you think?

"As for the papacy, you are entirely correct. My hat will be in the ring, so to speak. I expect His Eminence Meyerczuk will adhere to my suggestion to step down. I shall also expect Da Silva's resignation as prefect of the Secret Archives."

Marrenzo looked up at Players with expectation.

"I trust this satisfies you? Is there anything more?"

"No, nothing more." Players stopped at the door and turned back. "Except nineteen people lost their lives because of the collection. The Church might offer them mass."

* * *

The door behind Claudio Cardinal Marrenzo opened. Pio Cliotia stepped out and held it open for Meyerczuk.

"He looks very old now," Marrenzo thought. "His eyes are shot through with blood, and veins are bursting on his cheeks. The past has ravaged him. By day he can hide the scars, but at night he is a feeble old man."

Meyerczuk walked over to where the Collection lay and picked up the volume, his large ancient hands caressing the red leather.

"Who was he, Claudio?" he asked. But there was no authority behind the words. They trembled under the weight of relief the prelate felt now that the Tetramachus Collection was in his hands once more.

"It doesn't matter, does it?"

Meyerczuk glanced up at him, not knowing whether to object.

"I believe you should tell me, Claudio," he said at last. "This man also mentioned Father Martin will be returned to us. When?"

"I suspect tomorrow," Marrenzo answered quietly.

Meyerczuk shook his head. "I find this whole matter very puzzling. Why did you say you were going to ask for the prefect's resignation? Was that part of some charade, just as the business of your becoming the next pope? There are too many questions, Claudio."

The Church historian offered him a trepid smile.

"I called you here tonight," he began formally, "because I wanted you to witness the return of the Tetramachus Collection. The conversation you heard, Rozdentsy, between myself and the agent, was *not* a charade. Somehow he guessed my intentions, but that too does not matter."

Marrenzo cleared his throat and continued.

"I have been watching you these past few days, Rozdentsy. I have heard by way of rumors and gossip how you had taken upon yourself to lead the Church through its crisis. There was mention that Volpe was supporting you, clearing your way through the Sacred College. Foucault and Settembrini were also involved because they knew of the Collection's contents. I watched and waited, Rozdentsy, but you never came to me. You never asked for my counsel, although I too was privy to the story the collection told. You and Volpe thought me worthless, a mere historian, an academic who would be lost in the heady air of your precious politics.

"Did you not think I understood the Collection would bury your hopes for the papacy? Urban himself said to me you would never survive its contents. And when he instructed me to secure the return of the papers, it was because I, among so many, was untainted by it. Under a directive from His Holiness I sought out men who could find not only the Collection but Father Martin as well. What were you doing in the meantime but plotting for the throne and praying that the documents, if not returned to you, would somehow be destroyed. God only knows how much you must have suffered in these last days, living with the possibility that Fransci would announce that he had, in fact, found the Collection. But now your wait is over, Rozdentsy. You need not concern yourself any longer."

"What are you asking of me, Claudio?" Meyerczuk demanded, his voice rising.

"Remove yourself as contender for the papacy," Marrenzo said tonelessly. "You are not fit, Rozdentsy, to lead the Holy See."

"And if I should refuse?"

"I shall be obliged to bring the Collection to the attention of the Sacred College. If you do not accept my verdict, you will have no choice but to abide by theirs. In spite of Volpe's efforts, Rozdentsy, and your personal popularity, you will not win the election."

The Iron Cardinal looked at Marrenzo and reached for the crucifix he had carried around his neck since the days of Poland. He held it before him and brought it to his lips.

"Sic transit gloria mundi," he whispered. "Thus passes away the glory of the world."

These were the words a pontiff would speak on the way to his coronation. But Cardinal Meyerczuk added to them: "How sordid has that glory become!"

EPILOGUE

Alexander Players returned to Geneva on the morning of September 21. That afternoon, after Pelikan had spoken with Rokossovsky, he submitted his resignation.

"Are you certain this is the way you want matters?" Rokossovsky asked.

"It is."

Rokossovsky said nothing and dismissed him with a wave of his hand.

The following morning in the presence of the entire board, Players undertook his debriefing, beginning with Operation IKONEN. For the duration of this process he was held in effective quarantine, free to move about headquarters and its grounds, but not beyond, not to the low-terraced flats where operatives lived before and after missions. He occasionally met a few of his colleagues, but no one stopped to speak with him. A deferential nod, a lingering look of curiosity, sympathy, sometimes disapproval, was all they would pass on to him. He was no longer one of them, not to be trusted, a suspect alien.

On the twenty-fifth the board was informed of Urban's death. As expected, Rozdentsy Cardinal Meyerczuk presided over the funeral and afterward announced his retirement. The move brought on a wave of popular sympathy for the Polish prelate and puzzled commentaries from Catholic journals. But Meyerczuk avoided controversy and quickly melted away into silence of the Alban Hills, to Volpe's farm estate, where no newspaper or television camera could reach him. His last words to the world were ones directed to his choice of a successor, a choice that stunned the Catholic community.

The same day saw the unexpected resignation of Cardinal da Silva, prefect of the Secret Archives. Da Silva, who was to have held the post for the term of his natural life, pleaded failing health. He informed the Curia he would remain in his appointment until a successor to Urban XI had been chosen and closed his address by supporting Meyerczuk's selection.

Two days later, on September 27, Rome saw white smoke pouring from the chimney in the Sistine Chapel, a signal that a majority vote had been reached. The Sacred College of Cardinals elected a new Pontiff, Claudius III, formerly Claudio Cardinal Marrenzo, historian of the Holy See. Not very much was known about the new Pope, but people remembered that John XXIII had also risen from obscurity. A new Pope meant new hopes and new goals.

Among the first pronouncements given by Claudius III was one regarding his determination to finish Urban XI's last and dearest project, the beatification of the wartime Pope, Pius XII. The only change in these plans was that the Church would now begin the process of beatification for Urban as well.

His Holiness also announced his desire to construct new peace between Church and state, to put an end to the animosity between the lay and religious, the spiritual and secular. It was a noble speech, and it moved the average heart. Giannino Fransci had learned of the return of the Tetramachus Collection from Pio Cliotia, the papal secretary, one hour before the Pontiff's televised broadcast. The prime minister had also been told that Father Martin had returned to the Vatican on the eve of Claudius' coronation and was prepared to speak with the police concerning Sabatini's death. Fransci thanked Cliotia, ending their conversation with a remark that perhaps Article 100 had served its purpose and could be repealed shortly.

On September 28, Rokossovksy interrupted a debriefing to show Players a cablegram from Musco. It stated that Father Martin had been interrogated by Criminal Investigations of the Rome police, freed and returned to the Vatican. A tiny article in the *Osservatore Romano* mentioned that one Father Martin Belobraditz would be traveling to Africa within the week to work with Cardinal Léger of Montreal in a leper colony.

The other piece of news Musco had concerned the Black Prince Borghese. His supporters had managed to free him from custody and spirit him out of the country. Spanish intelligence had reported Borghese in Barcelona, residing at 17 La Lucila.

That was the only information that interested Players during all the time he passed in Geneva. They were silent, lonely days, in which he did nothing but talk into tape recorders and answer questions. He spoke of agents he had run on three continents, networks he had set up or operated in, controls he had been loyal to or betrayed, analyses he had drawn up and judgments he had passed.

Players knew that only time could make a man like himself safe, with no secrets to trade. Operations he was privy to would end, agent cryptonyms would be replaced or dropped altogether. But still he was obliged to sign an agreement not to reenter the world behind the Looking Glass unless he had spoken with ISIS first. Rokossovsky didn't bother to tell him, since Players knew anyway, that ISIS would know if he transgressed and that the penalty for transgression was death.

On October 2 Alexander Players packed a few personal belongings into a leather tote bag and stopped by Rokossovsky's office for the last time. There was one more thing to be done before he returned to Canada. Rokossovsky was surprised at the request but after some consideration agreed that no harm could come of it.

The last view Players had of Rokossovsky was a man sitting erect in his tall leather chair, surrounded by sweet-smelling rubber plants, his eyes on the papers before him, his strong thick fingers toying lightly with a slim gold pen. Their good-bye was a gentle click of the door, and he left, for all intents and purposes, a free man, stepping out into the crisp autumn coolness of a Swiss morning.

Four days later European papers carried the story of the Black Prince's murder. Borghese had been shot outside his home in Barcelona by a man or men unknown. The police were still investigating.

When Pia Monti read this announcement, she thought back to the man who had led her away from the Unita building after the explosion. In the end, he had kept his word to her.